Farewell to a Friend

Steven Turner-Bone

Published by Amazon Createspace.

This book is a work of fiction. Names, characters, places, and incidents either are products of the author's imagination or are used fictitiously. Any resemblance to actual persons, living or dead, events or locales is entirely coincidental.

Also by Steven Turner-Bone

Friends and Enemies
The Enemy Within
Farewell to a friend

EBook ISBN: 9780993548772

Acknowledgements

To the ones I owe much and, without whom I could not have written this book.

My wife Sue: for her help, patience and understanding while I created this work. Thanks go to Diana Backhouse for her proofreading and editing, as well as her words of encouragement.

The Fairfax Battalia of The English Civil War Society

De Bergsche Battery, Geertruidenberg

And to the many readers of my previous novels, who have asked me repeatedly, 'when will the next book be coming out?'

Dedicated to

Annabelle, Craig and Laura Southcoat

Author's Note’s

This story is part three of the trilogy about Surgeon Mathew Fletcher and is set at the beginning of the English Civil Wars. The background to this story really happened. Many of the characters are based on real people, though Mathew Fletcher and his family did not exist.

One thing has become very apparent in the telling of this story, and that is, history repeats itself. The English Civil Wars came about because a King lost touch with his people and Parliament, and brought about a set of civil wars that changed this country’s politics forever. Today, it’s the Parliament that has lost touch with its people and the country is divided once again. Once again it will be the person in the street who suffers the most, just as they did nearly four hundred years ago.

The medicines and surgical procedures I describe in the book are taken from original 17c medical and apothecary books which I have collected. Under no circumstances do I recommend the use of these procedures today or attempt to make any of the medicines, most are very toxic and very dangerous.

I have tried to preserve the historical accuracy of the events as they happened, but I have had to adjust events and timings to fit the flow of the plot line.

About the Author

Steven Turner-Bone was born and raised in Kingston-upon Hull. He fell in love with adventure stories at school which led to an interest in history. After leaving school, Steven went to Hull College of Technology to train as a chef. After a year at the Savoy in London and a year and a half at a motel in North Ferriby, Steven changed careers and moved to AIM, in Hull to become a Computer Operator. Later, when he joined a historical re-enactment group, he began to learn about historical medicine, from which has sprung the Mathew Fletcher series of books. Writing historical novels now occupies Steven as a full-time career, with three books in print and more in the pipeline Steve has many more years ahead of him as a writer.

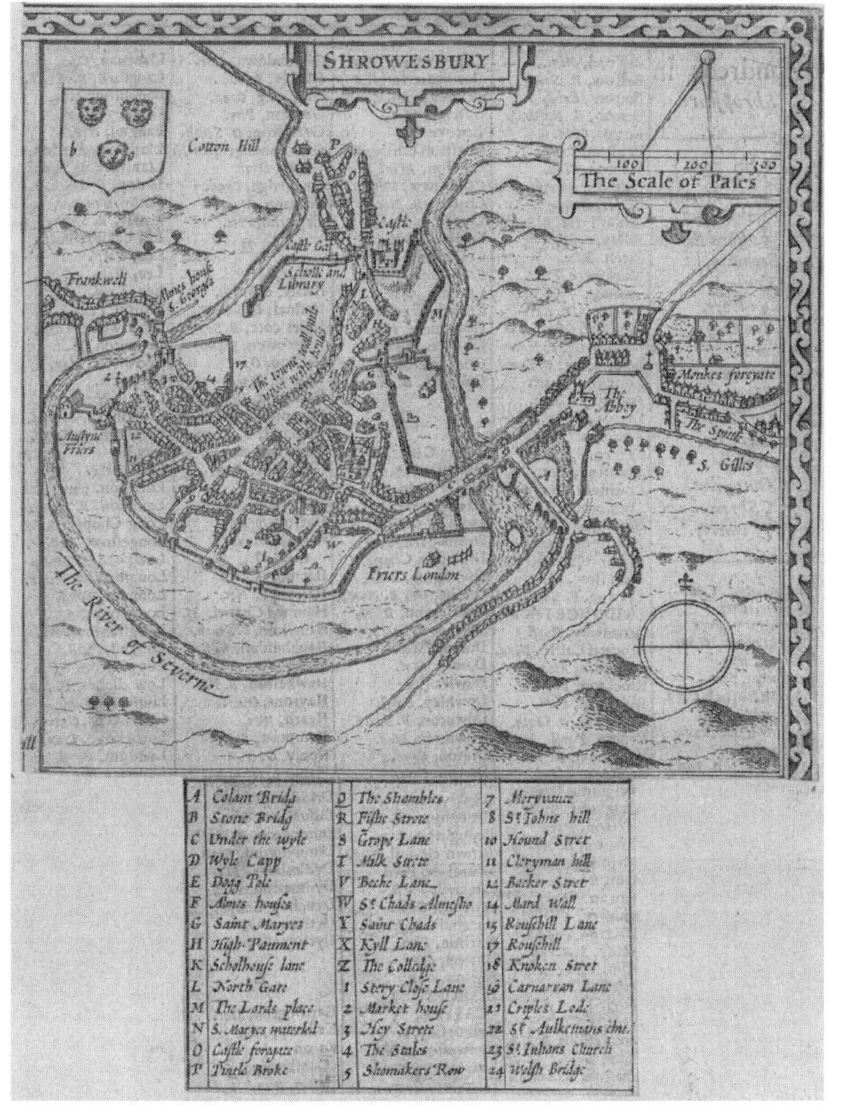
SHROWESBURY
Cotton Hill
The Scale of Pases
100
200
300
Frankwell
Castle
Friers London
The Abby
Monkes foregate
S. Giles
The River of Severne
A Colam Bridg
B Stone Bridg
C Under the wyle
D Wyle Capp
E Dogg Pole
F Almes houses
G Saint Maryes
H High Pavment
K Scholhouse lane
L North Gate
M The Lards place
N S. Maryes waterlod
O Castle foregate
P Pinels Broke
Q The Shambles
R Fishe Strete
S Grope Lane
T Milk Strete
V Beche Lane
W St Chads Almesho
Y Saint Chads
X Kyll Lane
Z The Colledge
1 Stery Close Lane
2 Market house
3 Hey Strete
4 The Stales
5 Shomakers Rew
7 Meryvance
8 St Johns hill
10 Hound Stret
11 Cleryman hill
12 Backer Stret
14 Mard Wall
15 Rouschill Lane
17 Rouschill
18 Knoken Stret
19 Carnarvan Lane
21 Criples Lode
22 St Aulkemins chu.
23 St Iulians Church
24 Welsh Bridge

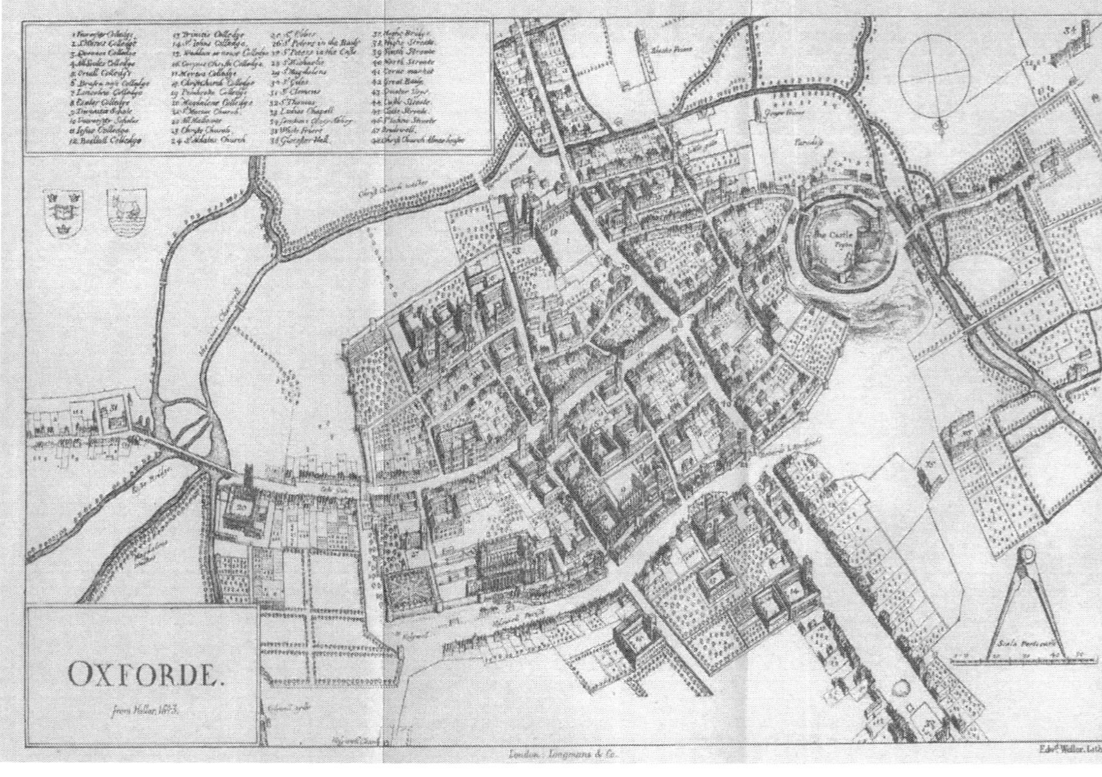
OXFORDE.
London: Longmans & Co.
Edw. Weller, Lith.

Chapter One

In Holland, on the back streets of Den Hague, Waltherus ducked to the right as his opponent's blade sliced through the shoulder fabric of his doublet. He continued the manoeuvre, turning it into a shoulder roll, coming to his feet again on the left side of his adversary, slicing neatly through the man's shirt sleeve. He smiled to himself as he saw the look of shock on his attacker's face.
'Fair is fair' said Waltherus.

The man spun to face his target, but Waltherus had stepped back out of range of the wild slash of his attacker's blade. His opponent was a lesser swordsman than he had hoped for; *no, he wouldn't kill this one, the man didn't deserve it*, but before had Waltherus finished with him, he would play with the fool a little longer. Waltherus stepped forward and waited for the back slice he knew the man would make and parried it easily. It was time to annoy his opponent a little more. Waltherus entered into a Cadence with his inexperienced adversary, enjoying the exchange of easy swordplay, lulling his opponent into a false sense of security as he stepped back under his opponent's thrusts. The man took the bait and lunged at his unguarded side which Waltherus had deliberately left open for him. With a circular parry, Waltherus deflected his opponent's sword up and away; he stepped into the unprotected side of the swordsman and, with the merest flick of his wrist, his sword tip brought a bright red line across his opponent's cheek. He jumped back as the man raised his left hand to the wound while his right brought his blade back under control and into the on guard position.

'I am growing weary, Sir, apologise and we can call it honour served,' said Waltherus.

'I will never apologise to a braggart youth who needs teaching a lesson,' said the man.

Waltherus shrugged his shoulders.

'But, I only inferred your good lady had a face like a horse's arse, Sir, I didn't say *it was* a horse's arse, or maybe I did, I can't quite remember.' Waltherus tucked his blade under his arm and feigned an impression of thinking the matter through.

His opponent came forward fast and hard, Waltherus skipped back with the skill of a dancer, dropped to one knee and, with an upwards thrust, pushed his blade through his opponent's arm from below. The man screamed in pain, releasing his own sword instantly.

'I did give you the opportunity to apologise,' said Waltherus matter of factly.

Waltherus wiped the blood from the tip of his sword and returned it to its hanger.

'Why do you play these games?' Sjaak asked Waltherus as the two men hurried away from the scene outside the tavern, leaving the loser of the duel screaming in pain, even though he had suffered no more than a flesh wound.

'Because, when I practise with you, I know you won't try to kill me, so I don't fight at my best. It's only when I fight with someone I don't know, and I can provoke into wanting to kill me, that I find I am truly tested.'

'One day you'll come unstuck playing games like that,' said Sjaak.

'When I meet someone better than me, I will know it and make friends with him.' Waltherus laughed. 'Come on, the countess is waiting for us.'

Aboard the Dutch ship, Westfriesland, the Countess Ineke van Gils along with her maid, Betje, and trusted friends and guardians, Sjaak and Waltherus, had set sail from Den Hague, out into the German Sea, heading for Hull in the East of England. In two days time, if the wind held true, they would be disembarking to continue their journey to visit with the baron Belasyse at Newburgh Priory, near Thirsk in North Yorkshire.

The captain of the chartered ship had reluctantly put his cabin at the disposal of the countess. Passengers usually slept with the cargo but, as he was being paid triple his regular fee, and in gold, for transporting this vital cargo of passengers, he was prepared to put up with the inconvenience for a couple of days. The countess settled into the small cabin without fuss and was even looking forward to the sea crossing. She had been to England many times, but this would be the first time to the north of the country. As the countess looked out of the rear windows of the captain's cabin, she watched as Den Hague seemed to drift away. She marvelled once again at how small and compact the city looked the further away the observer viewed. Countess Ineke watched ships entering and leaving the harbour wondering what they were carrying, and wondered where they were going to or coming from. She turned away from the vista to watch her maid neatly laying out the clothes she would need for the journey. 'I would like you to brush my hair please, Betje.

Betje retrieved the ivory-handled brushes from a casket and joined her mistress. She released the countess Ineke's hair from the pins that held it in place, suddenly taking a quick step sideways as the ship rolled, at the same time Betje inhaled deeply, holding her breath while grabbing onto her mistress's chair back. Betje was determined not to be seasick. The ship rolled to larboard each time it was struck by a wave, causing the maid to brace her left foot against a wooden chest to stay upright. She put down the hairbrush and used both hands to steady herself, taking another deep breath before she felt stable enough to continue brushing the countess's hair.

'The wind has made a nasty mess of your hair, My Lady, would you like me to get a cap for you?'

'Thank you, Betje, no, there is no need to fuss so while we are on board this ship, there is no one of importance here. When we get to England, if it is still windy, I will do as you suggest but, for now, it is invigorating to feel the wind and smell the clean sea air. Just brush out the tangles, then finish laying out the things I will need for tonight.' Betje tutted disapprovingly and carried on brushing the Countess's hair.

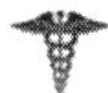

Up above, Sjaak and Waltherus watched the sailors going about their business high in the rigging. 'Why are we on this mission?' ask Waltherus, 'What is so important in England?'

'The countess is taking news from the English Queen, Henrietta Maria, to Lord Belasyse about the weapons she has bought and that will soon be shipped to England for the king, her Husband,' said Sjaak.

'I hear tell the English Queen has sold all her jewels to finance arms for the king,' said Waltherus.

'Not all of them. The Queen wishes to raise loans against the state jewels, but the nobles of Holland don't trust the English King to pay back the loans or hand over the jewels if he loses this war with his parliament,' said Sjaak.

Waltherus watched as a sailor walked out onto a spar and released the ropes holding a sail. The loose fabric fluttered in the wind for a moment then filled with air, billowing like a trapped cloud.

'But why was The Countess chosen for this mission,' Waltherus persisted.

'The Countess is a close friend of Prince Frederick and his wife, who now reside in Den Hague. Prince Rupert, their son, and nephew to the English King is already in England helping King Charles bring the English Parliament back under the king's control,' said Sjaak. Waltherus gave the matter some thought for a moment or two, then asked, 'Will we be in danger when we land in England?'

It was Sjaak's turn to ponder the question, 'No. We will not be meeting with the king; we will be meeting one of his allies in the north of the country. Our job is to keep the countess safe from unwanted surprises as we travel. That is why you are here. You are one of the best swordsmen in the Dutch Republic, My Friend, and I am here to see you don't go sticking your sword in the wrong people.' Sjaak laughed loudly at his own joke. Waltherus backhanded Sjaak across his upper arm playfully.

'I know how to control my blade,' he rebuked the older man in mock protestation. 'The Countess has nothing to fear while I'm at her side.'

'Pass me my sewing, would you, Betje. The problem with travelling by sea is that there is so little to see and do once we have left the coast behind us,' the countess yawned lazily.

'I don't know why you bother with it, My Lady. You have been working on that bit of sewing for as long as I can remember and it doesn't seem to get any closer to being finished.'

'I may not be as good or as fast at sewing as you, Betje, but I do enjoy it from time to time. It also allows me the time to think, especially when men are about. When they see a woman sewing, it lulls them into a false sense of security. They don't believe that women have minds of their own or have an intelligence that can exceed their own, so they talk without thinking in our presence. A woman can learn a lot if she keeps her ears open and her mouth shut from time to time. I am grateful to my father for allowing me an education. It allows me to follow the conversations of men and outwit them when the need arises.'

'Well I'm not sure, My Lady, whenever I try to think things through I get a headache, maybe my brain's not as big as yours,' said Betje. Countess Ineke laughed at her maid,

'Very well, Betje, you had better let me do the thinking for you, and I will ensure you have no more headaches.'

There was a knock on the cabin door, Betje went to open it. Outside were two sailors. 'Begging your pardon Ma'am, we've brought you some food,' said the first sailor defensively. He stepped through the doorway followed by his compatriot, both carrying trays containing covered plates, a cup and a jug. Leaving the trays on what had once been the captain's table, the lead sailor bowed to the countess, 'Will there be anything else Ma'am?' he asked as politely as he knew how and licking his lips as he eyed the countess lasciviously.

'That will be plenty for now,' Betje said indignantly, as she ushered the sailors from the cabin, closing the door firmly.

'They smell a bit, don't they, My Lady? I couldn't imagine having to be on a ship like this for more than a couple of days, who knows what might happen, just us and all those men.' Betje went to investigate the two trays. She lifted the lids on the dishes and found boiled lobster, a fruit pie, roasted quail with eggs, spiced sausage, two kinds of cheese, one dark the other light in colour, bread and a jug of wine.

'The captain has at least tried to arrange a decent meal for us,' confessed Betje.

'Would you like me to set the table, My Lady?' asked Betje as she sniffed at the lobster to ensure it was fresh.

'No, no, Betje, thank you; just place some food on a plate for me, I think we will just have to make do for the next couple of days,' instructed the countess. Betje tutted, unhappy her mistress wasn't receiving the kind of food or service she was used to.

'My Lady, will we be safe in England?' Betje asked sheepishly. Countess Ineke laughed warmly,

'Yes Betje, we will be safe, we have Sjaak and Waltherus to guard us. I also have this; Countess Ineke opened her jewel box and removed a large diamond and gold ring. This ring was given to Queen Henrietta Maria by her husband, Charles, the king of England.

Look here,' the countess encouraged her maid. Betje looked carefully at the gold ring with its square-cut diamond, her eyes widened in awe as it sparkled in the candlelight.

'It has a pattern scratched in the surface My Lady,' the maid exclaimed in wonder. 'Yes Betje, that pattern is the crest of England, and when I show this ring to the right people, it will open many doors for us.'

'What happens if you show it the wrong person, will they steal it?' Betje asked naively.

'They may try,' said the countess with a smile. 'Then I suspect the only door that will be opened for us will be the one to our cell in the Tower of London.' Betje looked alarmed.

'Maybe you should put the ring back in the box and not show it to anyone, My Lady.' 'Don't worry, Betje; I plan on keeping this ring safely hidden until it is needed,' Countess Ineke said genially.

After two days sailing, the Westfriesland entered the Humber estuary on the final leg of its journey. The rising tide and an Easterly wind quickly carried the Dutch ship up the River Humber to Hull.

It was late in the evening when the ship pulled in at the quayside, too late to go in search of lodgings for the evening. The ship's crew unloaded Countess Ineke's coach and horses while the passengers of the Westfriesland did their best to get what sleep they could, but the noise of the quayside labourers working through the night disturbed their slumber. Early next morning with an overcast sky, and to the screech of seagulls searching for an opportune breakfast amongst the herring boats, the countess was helped into her travelling clothes by Betje.

'I shall be glad to be off this ship, My Lady. I don't think I will ever want to get on a ship again. I haven't slept properly at all. The food tastes mouldy, the water tastes salty, and I like the ground to stay in one place, so my feet know where to find it,' Betje complained to her mistress as she laced the countess into her dress.

'You mean you wish to stay in England forever once I have conducted my business here?' asked the countess, dryly.

'Oh no, My Lady, I wouldn't want to stay in England. My duty is to care for you, Miss. If I stayed in England you would have to find someone else to look after you, and I wouldn't want that,' Betje sounded confused at why her mistress thought she would want to stay in England.

Countess Ineke smiled, 'Betje, if you do not want to travel by ship again, how will you get home?'

Betje thought about what she had said earlier, 'Oh yes, I see what you mean, but you know what I meant,' Betje laughed a little, embarrassed by her mistake.

'And you are correct, Betje, I wouldn't want anyone else to care for me. No one does that quite as well as you do,' continued the countess. Betje finished dressing Countess Ineke and helped her on with a cloak.

'I'll just go see if Sjaak and Waltherus are ready for us to go ashore, My Lady.' Betje left the countess alone in the cabin.

On the quayside, Sjaak and Waltherus stood next to Countess Ineke's coach which was waiting for her arrival. Betje appeared at the head of the gangplank and waved to them, they waved back indicating all was ready. Betje scurried back to her mistress.

'You'd better get aboard,' Sjaak instructed Waltherus, 'the countess will want to get away as quickly as possible once the last of her personal baggage is loaded on top of the coach.'

Waltherus was about to climb up into the driving seat when both men heard a scream from onboard the ship. Leaving the coach, they ran up the gangplank, swords in hand heading towards Countess Ineke's cabin. Two sailors barred their way, one with a cutlass the other with a belaying pin. Waltherus lunged at the sailor with the cutlass, but he parried the long lighter blade easily with his thicker curved sword, and Waltherus had to jump back quickly as the seaman's cutlass slashed again towards his face.

The large sailor with the belaying pin blocked the gangway leading to the interior of the ship. There was another scream that came from the countess's cabin. Sjaak lunged forward with his sword. The belaying pin crashed against Sjaak's wrist forcing him to drop his sword, as the sailor dodged to avoid the clumsy sword thrust.

Waltherus stepped back a couple of paces drawing his opponent away from his friend giving Sjaak more space to manoeuvre. The sailor with the cutlass followed him confidently, his heavy blade slashing back and forth. More of the ship's crew stopped work to watch the entertainment unfold on the deck, one or two shouted words of encouragement to their shipmates embroiled in the contest playing out before them.

Waltherus diverted each swipe of his antagonist's blows cleanly to one side or the other as he kept a careful eye of Sjaak grappling with the sailor in the doorway.

Sjaak grasped the belaying pin with his left hand as it had pinned his right wrist to the doorframe. The two men were now locked in a struggle over control of the wooden weapon. Sjaak may have been some ten years older and a few inches shorter than his opponent, but he'd kept himself fit. He twisted the belaying pin to the right, raising his left elbow to strike across the sailor's nose. At the same time, he brought his right knee up into the sailor's groin, both limbs impacting at the same time. The sailor let out a high pitched scream, releasing the belaying pin as he crumpled to the deck. With a bone-cracking blow from Sjaak with the wooden club, the sailor hit the deck and moved no more. Sjaak took a moment to catch his breath and to scan the deck for more attackers.

Waltherus took his cue from the scene at the doorway. On the next swipe of the cutlass, Waltherus pulled back his sword, then brought it down on top of his aggressor's blade slamming it down into a hatch cover, forcing the heavy sword to slice deep into the wood and stick fast. With lightning speed, Waltherus slid his own sword up the back of the cutlass and across the sailor's throat. The sailor stood frozen to the spot for a moment as a wide red smile opened up in his throat. Waltherus watched as the life-giving blood of the sailor gushed forth across the deck. The sailor fell forward, one hand still grasping the hand grip of the cutlass wedged in the hatch cover.

Sjaak pulled his dagger from his belt and stepping over the sailor at his feet entered the interior of the ship. In front of him was the door to the captain's cabin. Betje lay on the deck just inside the open doorway, blood dribbling from the corner of her mouth, tears in her eyes. The captain, with a pistol in hand, stood a few feet beyond. On hearing Sjaak in the doorway, he turned to face the sound and fired his pistol, the bullet splintering the door frame close to Sjaak's head. But, as the captain had been levelling his pistol, Betje had kicked him in the shins upsetting the captain's aim. He swung the pistol back, pointing his now useless gun at the maid. There was a flash of steel and another scream from Betje as the captain fell back into the cabin, the hilt of a dagger protruding from his chest. Betje shuffled away as the captain staggered, then fell to the deck. Seconds later, Waltherus appeared behind Sjaak in the doorway.

'Are you hurt, My Lady?' asked Sjaak.

'No, just a little shocked, I'll be fine. We had better go before all the crew come to their wits and turn on us,' instructed the countess.

Sjaak snatched two pistols from the wall of the captain's cabin; with guns in hand, and Betje close behind, they made their way outside heading for the gangplank. A few of the sailors had congregated at the ships exit, their curiosity aroused by the sound of the fight on deck, the screams and the gunshot. Sjaak gestured with the point of his pistol for them to stand aside and clear their passage to the gangplank. Betje led the countess to the dockside and the coach. Once the countess and Betje were onboard the coach, Waltherus and Sjaak made their departure from the ship, keeping their pistols trained on the crew as they backed down the gangplank and across the quayside. Waltherus climbed into the driving seat of the coach as Sjaak got inside with the two women. He snapped the reins, and the horses set off over the cobbles and away from the quayside. They rushed along Herring Lane and onto High Street, before slowing down in the busy streets of Hull. Minutes later they were through Beverley Gate and on the first leg of their journey to Newburg Priory to meet Baron John Belasyse.

'Thank goodness you arrived when you did,' said the countess praising Sjaak. 'The captain was demanding more gold, or he wasn't going to release me. Poor little Betje was like a she-wolf and threw herself at him, but he knocked her aside, then you arrived.'

Betje sat next to her mistress nursing a split lip, 'My Dear Betje, what would I do without you,' confessed the countess. Betje flushed a little, but enjoyed the attention and praises she was receiving.

'We were lucky, My Lady, It was only the Captain and a couple of his crew that were in on the plan to hold you for more money. Had the whole crew been involved, things would have turned out very differently,' said Sjaak.

'You are right. I suspect the captain only involved his trusted crew members in his plans and promised them a share of the gold he was demanding from me,' said the countess.

After a further three days of uneventful travel with overnight stops at Market Weighton and York, Countess Ineke's coach arrived at Newburgh Priory.

As the coach pulled up in front of the house, it was met by a stable hand who ran forward to hold the horses. Fisher, the steward to Lord Belasyse, the owner of Newburgh Priory, waited at the house door for the occupants of the coach to disembark. Lord Belasyse was the king's Head of Intelligence gathering in the north of England. Fisher opened the door to the house as Waltherus and Sjaak descended from the coach's driving seat. Sjaak opened the door to the coach and received a small box from the countess. Taking the box to Fisher, Sjaak told him to take it to Baron Belasyse immediately. Fisher looked at the plain little box and then back at Sjaak, thought better of opening it in front of the stranger, and went to do as he had been told.

Sjaak returned to the coach and, holding out his hand he helped the countess step down from the coach. Gracefully she descended the two steps of the coach to the gravel of the drive, momentarily surprised that the baron was not there to greet her. But by the time Betje had joined her, Baron Belasyse was through the front door of the house wishing his guest a warm welcome.

'My Lady van Gils, I must apologise, had I known of your imminent arrival I would have been here to greet you myself. I have sent Fisher to prepare rooms for you all. Do please come in and make yourselves comfortable.' The countess was led to a tastefully decorated room fashioned in the latest style and with an ornate marble fireplace in the back wall. A fire blazed fiercely in the hearth warming the room against the north of England cold and wind. The table, which dominated the centre of the room, was set on a patterned Persian carpet with an intricate hand-knotted design. The countess made her way over to the bowed window, one of a pair located in rooms that fronted the house and looked across the lawn to the formal garden which, during the height of summer, would have looked magnificent.

Sir John Belasyse's ancestors had bought the derelict abbey and lands for a song about a hundred years earlier rebuilding and converting the destroyed monastery into one of the grandest homes in North Yorkshire. Sir John worked tirelessly for the king, sending out an army of spies and informers to all the major towns and noble houses in the north of England.

Their job was to gather every scrap of information or indiscretion that anyone should carelessly let slip and bring it back to him, so he could use the information against those that might show sympathy to the parliamentary cause.

The countess took a seat on a couch set in the bay of the window. As the baron poured a glass of sweet red wine for his honoured guest, Sjaak, stood at her side, watching the English lord intently. Betje fussed around the countess, ensuring her clothes were neat and she was comfortable. The nobleman looked at Sjaak and Betje uncomfortably, 'should we be speaking in front of your servants?' asked the baron. 'Have no fear My Lord Belasyse, Sjaak and Betje do not understand your language or what we are about to discuss,' Countess Ineke lied. Sjaak spoke perfect English.

'How is the Queen, quite well I hope?' enquired the baron.

'Her Majesty is very well, thank you. She sends her regards to you and your family,' said the countess.

'To business if I may, Countess. How successful has her Majesty been in raising funds for the king?' enquired the baron.

'Not as well as she would have liked. No one wishes to lend money against the value of the crown jewels, they believe it to be too much of a risk should the king lose his war with his parliament. They believe their loans would not be repaid. As for the sale of the crown jewels, potential buyers are few and far between for such expensive jewellery and those that can afford them wonder if the king would actually allow them to be transferred to Holland,' the countess informed the baron. 'But, the raising of loans against the value of her own jewels is another matter, so long as she is prepared to leave them in Holland as collateral.' The countess went on to explain. 'Her Majesty is also trying to raise loans for King Charles by promising favours at the English court. In this matter, the members of the Dutch court are more willing to speculate. They would want to see the restrictions on trade through the English Channel lifted, that alone is potentially worth more to them than any English bauble. On a more positive note, I can inform you that the first shipment of guns and other necessities the king requires are being bought and stockpiled ready to be loaded aboard three ships. The ships are scheduled to arrive in Bridlington early in the New Year,' she continued.

'Good, good,' said the baron, trying to sound confident. But the inability to sell England's Crown Jewels would be a serious blow to the king's financial coffers.

'On my part,' said the baron. 'I have arranged for every wagon and cart I can buy, or borrow to be repaired and made ready for when the ships arrive, so the weapons can be unloaded quickly and the cargo escorted to York as soon as possible for safe keeping until the king requires them.'

The countess stifled a yawn. 'Forgive me, Countess. You must be tired after your long journey; you would do me a great honour if you will be my guest at Newburgh Priory to rest awhile. Fisher is preparing chambers for you right now. Have you plans to return to Holland soon or have you another mission while you're in England?' enquired the baron.

'My first mission was to meet you, Baron, and apprise you of the queen's progress in raising financial support for the king. The second is to deliver personal letters from the queen to His Majesty, the king. So I would be grateful if we could take advantage of your hospitality until I have had time to deliver them. I would also like to stay until the king's new supply of weaponry arrives from Rotterdam. Three ships will arrive at Bridlington in the spring after which I plan to return to Den Hague. I would like to stay until the king's new supply of weaponry arrives at Bridlington in the spring. I will naturally return to the queen any messages you wish to entrust to me,' said the countess affably.'

'I would be greatly honoured to have you stay at Newburgh Priory, Countess. And, as soon as I have confirmation of the king's new headquarters, I will let you know.'

'Do you know the whereabouts of the king, Baron?

'I do indeed, Countess. From the latest report I have received from my son, who is with the king, they have recently left Nottingham and are on their way to Shrewsbury, where they plan to build a great army.'

Chapter Two

Snapping the reins, Mathew encouraged the horses to take the strain and pull his wagon out of the mud where it had settled overnight. He was tired, wet, miserable and cold after another night with little sleep, and knowing he faced the prospect of many more to come. But right now, his job was to follow the rest of the baggage-train as it rolled out of camp onto the narrow lane which would take them around the outskirts of Derby. Their destination, at the end of another rain-soaked day, would be another muddy field somewhere Mathew had never seen before or would ever want to again. His goal, his mission, his obsession was to the kill the last man involved in the murder of his beloved Elizabeth. As Mathew sat with rain dripping from the brim of his broad-brimmed felt hat he could feel and smell the salve he'd applied to his buttocks in order to ease the sores which had started to erupt from sitting on a hard wooden seat in damp woollen breeches for days on end. Mathew's wagon, along with all those behind him, had been ordered across the country to their next destination somewhere between Derby and Stafford.

To add to his woes, his thoughts about what had happened to him and his friends troubled him; nothing was working out as he had hoped it would. Mathew's once-humble ambition to help save life had been corrupted by the man he was searching for and on whom he planned to take his revenge. One of the many problems that concerned him was Mary, his sister-in-law. She was travelling in the wagon behind his. Mary wasn't talking to him, or it seemed anyone else for that matter because no one had been able to find out why she had become so withdrawn. Mind you, with things as they were, even Mathew didn't feel much like talking to anyone right now, and he guessed from their silence the passengers travelling with him must have felt the same way too, for they were just as downcast. He looked up at the sky and cursed the black weather which was making everyone irritable and downhearted.

They were leaving their overnight camp on the edge of Derby after previously spending three weeks camped outside Nottingham. Their final destination, they had now learnt, was to be Shrewsbury where King Charles was planning on raising more troops before he marched on London to oust an English Parliament which refused to do his bidding. Mathew had never been to Shrewsbury, let alone London, but he had vowed revenge on the murderers of his beloved Elizabeth, no matter where he had to go. But now, after weeks of travelling, Mathew hoped and prayed that Shrewsbury would be as far as they would have to go before he was able to complete his quest. What

Mathew had expected to have managed in a few days had turned into months. Back home in Beverley, when he had made the decision to track down Elizabeth's murderers, he had given little thought to the difficulties he would face. He had explained what he planned to do to his father, who had tried to stop him from leaving on the foolhardy chase. They had fought, but his father relented, reluctantly, fearing the loss of another son after Mathew's brother had been killed. Mary had listened in to their conversations and insisted on travelling with him as his apothecary and assistant, but unknown to the family, she had secrets that she was running away from.

From the start of their journey together Mary would sit next to him on the wagon seat, but after the death of Hazel a few weeks earlier at Nottingham, she had become melancholic and had chosen to ride with Ethan Goodman on his wagon, the one that was following behind Mathew's. Mathew could only put Mary's dark mood down to the loss of Hazel, a young woman Mary had found injured on a farm after it had been ransacked by soldiers. Mary had stopped to use the farm's latrine as the baggage-train passed by on its journey from Beverley down into the English Midlands. She had found and taken pity on the woman, insisting that they deliver Hazel to her sister's home in Coventry. The woman's injuries and the death of her husband at the hands of royalist soldiers meant she was incapable of fending for herself, so Mathew had agreed that she could travel with them. Over the course of their journey, with Mathew's help and Mary's care, Hazel made a rapid recovery. But, on delivery to her sister in

Coventry, Hazel hadn't wanted to stay with her, and returned to her rescuers, only to mysteriously die a few weeks later while the baggage-train was encamped outside Nottingham.

Mary was taking the death very badly even though there had been times when the two women had seemed more like enemies than friends. Mathew had asked himself many times since that day, if he should have forced Hazel to stay with her sister and even if he should have left her on the farm to fend for herself, either way, she would probably be still alive now. The question he never thought he would ask himself came to him next, should *he* have stayed at home, instead of rushing off in a fit of foolishness and ill thought out revenge?

The image of Elizabeth wearing the blue dress he liked so much came to mind. She was standing in her father's apothecary shop, as she always did on a Saturday morning, waiting for him to arrive and place an order for more ingredients from which Mathew's employer could make medicines. He remembered the fleeting glances he exchanged with her, never really knowing if she liked him or not. That is, until that Saturday when he plucked up the courage to ask her father if he could court Elizabeth. How elated they both had been when he agreed. Then the image changed all too soon to the one of her broken body lying in a pool of blood, his feelings of helplessness at not being able to save her as she bled to death from the sword wound in her side. He felt his anger rising inside him as he thought about the life he had planned with her and how it had been brutally torn away from him.

Snapping the reins once more, he urged the horses on as if they could rush him to the last man he had to find to end his deadly quest. But the wagon in front of him blocked his path, and the horses slowed once again to the melodic clip-clop as they plodded along the narrow lane. Mathew's anger eased as he forced the image of Elizabeth's dead body from his mind. He brushed the rain from his face wishing he could wipe away his memory of her just as quickly but, like the rain, the memories of her would return to torment him. A quick glance at his passengers told him they hadn't noticed or even cared about his failed attempt to speed up their journey, their blank faces fixed and staring somewhere in the distance.

Mathew thought about his family home in Beverley and how he had reluctantly agreed for Mary to accompany him on his quest to find the murderers of Elizabeth. Mary had proven her worth by helping him with the king's wounded soldiers when they were still in Beverley, so he had given in and agreed to her coming. Now he had to ask himself, had he done the right thing by allowing her to go on this journey? His sister-in-law had been forced to put up with a lot during their travels; the discomfort, cold, tiredness, lack of privacy, but Mary had proven herself worthy time and again as his assistant, but it looked like the strain was beginning to get too much for her. She had become melancholic, her dark mood making her short and argumentative one minute, then leaving her in floods of tears the next and for no apparent reason that anyone could fathom. It bothered him that Mary chose to ride with Ethan instead of himself, after all was said and done, it was Mathew's responsibility to keep her safe and to care for her, not someone else's. There had been a time when she had been so very close to him, even pledged her love for him, so what was it that had now come between them? Yes, he had turned her down, because Mary was family, she had been his brother's wife, and Mathew still grieved for the love he had lost. As her brother-in-law and as a surgeon, it was logical that she should be with him so he could help her through this challenging period, but she would have none of it. He kept asking himself the same questions, what had he done to cause the sudden change; what had he done that had brought about melancholic despair in her? The problem nagged at him persistently; somehow he would have to get to the bottom it.

Everything had changed so much for Mathew over the past few months. Now he was a surgeon in the Royalist Army of King Charles. He had come to the notice of the Earl of Newcastle when he'd saved the lives of many of the king's soldiers billeted in Beverley. In Newbury, Mathew had saved the life of James Stuart, Duke of York, the second son of King Charles. Mathew's star was in the ascendancy, which put him at odds with his self-set, all-consuming, obsessive quest to find the murderers of his beloved Elizabeth.

But on that fateful day in July when Elizabeth had been killed and, the overwhelming desire for revenge had changed his destiny. Mathew had dedicated his life to bringing justice down on the murderers, not the law; it had to be his justice.

He had found Elizabeth close to death, alongside her father in the apothecary shop which her father owned, only for her to die in his arms. He had been unable to save her young life even though he was a surgeon. He later learned from a parliamentarian officer that the pair had been murdered by three escaping royalist spies, two of whom had hidden in the apothecary shop while escaping the soldiers chasing them. The spies had not only killed parliamentarian soldiers in Hull when caught trying to gather intelligence about the town's garrison, but they had also murdered Elizabeth and her father while hiding in their shop, to stop them raising the alarm. By a strange twist of fate, Mathew had later found out that the same men had killed his brother, Charles, on Beverley Westwood Common, as he and his wife Mary were out walking. Mary had escaped and run home to raise the alarm. Now doubly stricken, Mathew had made a promise to himself and his father to avenge the deaths and kill the three royalists. So he had joined the royalist army in an attempt to track them down. Over the past months, two of the killers had been found and killed, but not at Mathew's hand; circumstance had brought about their deaths at the hands of others. The last man on his list was John Franks, the ringleader of the murderers. He was determined that this time it would be him who would take revenge on the last murderer, after which, he would be free to decide his own fate and if he would return home or stay with the army?

At the start, it had all seemed so simple, or so he had thought: take revenge on the men responsible for

Elizabeth's death then rebuild his life as best he could. But it was turning out to be far from straightforward. For Mathew, a man who had taken an oath to preserve life, life had become very complicated. He was beginning to enjoy the notoriety that his abilities as a surgeon were bringing him. His name was linked to the king and his court after curing the king and his son when their own physicians had failed to do so. He was no longer anonymous; army officers offered him begrudging respect and the men he cared for thought him a marvel.

If he stayed, he would be able to develop his skills as a surgeon under the tutelage of Doctor William Harvey and get drawn deeper into the court of the king. But also, if he stayed in the army, Major Robert Overton would demand that he continues to spy for Parliament. The world around him was changing fast; he was no longer the naive young man that had left Hull and Beverley only months earlier. Mathew had taken the lives of three soldiers in a battle on Anlaby Common saving the life of his friend. Mathew had also saved the lives of countless royalist soldiers when disease struck Beverley. The irony was not lost on him; he had taken the lives of allies and saved the lives of his foes. To make matters worse, his sister-in-law, Mary, had fallen in love with him, though Mathew had told her he only looked upon her as his sister. She hadn't taken the news well, even though he had tried to explain to her that he wasn't ready to start another relationship and that all he wanted to do was concentrate on continuing his search for the murderer John Franks.

Mathew had been given an aide to help him with his spying duties. Charles Mortimer had been loaned to him by Robert Overton after Mortimer fell out of favour with the major. Mathew now had a circle of companions travelling with him, some had joined him out of friendship, others through circumstance; Mortimer was one of those who had been thrust upon him. Mortimer had failed his former employer, Major Robert Overton, and had asked for a chance to redeem himself by working for Mathew. Major Overton had agreed and also given Charles Mortimer the extra task of bodyguard to Mathew now that he had access to the king. The major was a parliamentarian officer who Mathew had met in Hull, and he acted as the collector of any intelligence that Mathew and Mortimer discovered. Others had joined Mathew out of friendship, but all of them were now tied into Mathew's quest one way or another. After weeks of travelling together, the friendships and bonds which had developed between Mathew Fletcher, Mary Fletcher, Charles Mortimer and Ethan Goodman had grown ever stronger. Only, now, they had a new member of the group, Thomas Potter.

Potter was a thief, swindler, cheat and conman who had been working for Captain Legge. Captain Legge was the royalist officer in charge of the three spies who killed Elizabeth, who was betrothed to Mathew Fletcher. After Potter had been left for dead, when he was shot in the streets of Coventry during a botched attempted to capture the town by Sir Spencer Compton, he had decided to become a turncoat and had gone into an uneasy partnership with Mathew

Fletcher. Potter had also been the man Captain Legge had sent to find a parliamentarian spy who Potter now knew to be Mathew. But after Mathew had saved Potter's life, they had formed an uneasy alliance. It was Thomas Potter who now shared Mathew's wagon along with Charles Mortimer.

Ethan Goodman was the cook to the royalist officers of the king's army. When Mathew, Mortimer and Mary first joined the royalist camp at Beverley in East Yorkshire during the siege of Hull, it was the friendly cook who had taken them under his wing, so to speak, to help them settle into army life. Ethan had become their wise sage, confidante and father figure.

Of the two murderers who had been killed so far, fate had determined that the first one of them to die would be at the hands of Ethan Goodman, though that had been more by accident than design. The second of the killers, Geoffrey Wilkes, had been shot by troopers under the command of Major Robert Overton. Geoffrey Wilkes had been making his escape from the house where he was being held captive and was shot in the back while trying to ride away. So now there was only the one murderer left, John Franks, the leader of the three murderers and the most dangerous. Franks, as far as Mathew knew, was somewhere up ahead of the baggage-train, riding with Captain William Legge who had escaped from Hull along with the three mercenary murderers. As far as Mathew knew, Captain Legge had not been directly involved in the murders of his family and had not ordered the deaths of Elizabeth and her father, so he was not on Mathew's list of marked men. But Mathew had decided that if Captain Legge got in his way, he would suffer the same fate as Franks and the others.

Mathew found himself in a dilemma, as a surgeon, he had proved to be a valuable asset to the royalist army, and after saving the life of the Duke of York in Newark, Mathew's reputation had risen to a point where the king had appointed him Surgeon-in-Ordinary to the royalist court. So should he be putting his own life at risk by trying to take revenge on Franks?

It was as all these thoughts distracted Mathew from the monotony of the drive and the rain while he drove away from Derby that his attention was suddenly brought back to the present by two riders coming down the column towards his wagon from the head of the baggage-train. The first rider was well dressed, probably one of the officers. The second was a lean, mean looking character, dressed mostly in black and wearing a large burn scar on the left-hand side of his face. Without explanation, Potter scrambled from his seat and jumped down to the road on the opposite side of the wagon to the riders, the partially healed wound in his side making him give a sharp cry of pain as his feet hit the road and he tumbled into the grass verge. At first Potter's sudden departure had made Mathew take his eyes off the riders, but as Potter hid, he turned back to look at the two horsemen as they rode past. Mathew recognised the second rider's face; the man's disfigurement marked him as John Franks. The riders swept past his wagon, they had passed Ethan's wagon before Franks pulled up his mount and returned to Ethan's wagon. Mathew spun around in his seat wanting to know why Franks had stopped to talk to Mary. He could not hear what was being said, but Mary was speaking to Franks, though she did look shocked and surprised by the sight of him. Mathew watched her as she edged closer to Ethan on the wagon seat. Mathew put Mary's initial look of shock down to her melancholy and the hideous disfigurement on the rider's face. But Mathew was curious to know where Mary would have got to know such a rough looking character and why he had stopped so abruptly to speak to her. Had Mary met him before where and why? Why was he talking to his sister-in-law if he had been involved in the murder of Mary's husband?

****

Charles Mortimer was sat proudly next to Mathew; at last, he had been told that he had regained Major Overton's trust after all the help he had given Mathew. At the time, he had been so pleased to have been offered the trustworthy job of bodyguard to Mathew that he had given little thought to the dangers it might entail in protecting the young surgeon. None the less, he was back in favour with the major after letting him down when he had been his servant.

Mortimer had been forced to spy on Major Overton by the Mayor of Hull who was also the employer of Mortimer's family back in East Yorkshire. His family worked on the Hotham estate at Scorborough, near Beverley. John Hotham, the Mayor, had blackmailed Mortimer into spying on Major Overton. Mortimer's treachery had been found out, and it was only after he had thrown himself on the mercy of the major, explaining why it had happened, that he had been given a second chance. Now his efforts had been rewarded, the major had rescued his family from the Mayor's country estate. In return, Mortimer had been given the critical job of ensuring Mathew's safety. '*At some point, I'm going to have to get myself a sword or a pistol. I need more than just a dagger if I'm going to protect Mathew,*' thought Mortimer while making plans for the future. He looked at Mathew sat beside him, but Mathew's attention was focused on the rider talking to Mary in the wagon behind. Then he looked down at Potter, who had jumped off the wagon seat as though it was on fire and was now kneeling in the grass, trying to hide below a hedge. Charles Mortimer was confused, *why had Potter jumped from the wagon and why was Mathew so engrossed in what was happening behind them? Were Mary and Ethan in danger?* Mortimer wondered what to do as the horses continued along the lane, leaving Potter behind. Mortimer wasn't sure if he should take the reins, pull up and wait for Potter, of if Mathew would go back to speak to Mary and the rider, or should he wait and see what would happen next. His dilemma was soon answered when the rider resumed his travels to the rear of the baggage-train. Potter, clutching at his side, staggered back to the wagon. Mortimer stopped the horses a moment to allow him to climb aboard.

****

Mary didn't want to talk as she sat next to Ethan; it was the terrible guilt she felt after the death of Hazel that was draining her. She had deliberately killed her rival for the affections of Mathew, even knowing

Mathew looked upon her as his sister. Back in Beverley when Mathew had returned to the family home, Mary had become captivated by him, even though she was married to his brother. So one day, while her husband followed her to a secret meeting with an injured man, he had been murdered. She had done nothing to prevent it, but had gone home and lied about how it had happened, all because of her infatuation with Mathew. Now when she closed her eyes, the image of her husband dead in the doorway of the cottage on Beverley Westwood Common filled her thoughts along with Hazel's last words '*Mary, help me.*'

'*I didn't kill Charles,*' she told herself, '*someone else had done that, it wasn't my fault he went there and got himself killed. He shouldn't have hit me.*' If it wasn't the image of her husband, that haunted her, it was the one of Hazel lying on the ground, her eyes staring blankly up at the sky, her blue lips open as she gasped for breath. The memories of Hazel raised the pulse in her temple making it throb and her head hurt. *'If only Mathew had returned my affections I wouldn't have had to get rid of Hazel, she should have stayed with her sister in Coventry, as she said she would. But no, she had to come back. And Mathew, the fool, had allowed her to do so. Hazel, Hazel, Hazel, why had I stopped to help that girl in the first place? If I'd minded my own business and ignored those whimpering cries, she would still be alive, and I would have Mathew. No, it wasn't my fault. Hazel had brought it upon herself. I had tried to warn her off Mathew, but she wouldn't listen. Hazel wasn't good enough for Mathew. I am Mathew's assistant, I am the one who makes the specific medicines that he prefers; I am the one who he asked to accompany him on this journey. Yes... deep down, Mathew knows I'm the right one for him; he just needs time to get over Elizabeth. Time to heal; I just need to give him a little more time.'*

It came as a shock to hear her name called and an even greater one when she looked up and saw the face of the scarred rider smiling at her.

****

Ethan tried to draw Mary into a conversation, but after only receiving monosyllabic answers or none at all, he'd given up. He suspected that Mary needed time to get over the death of Hazel and, that for now, she needed the consolation of her own thoughts to grieve for her friend. So Ethan concentrated on driving the wagon. Ethan had known that the friendship between the two women had not been a harmonious one over the few weeks in which Hazel had been travelling with them, but just before the end, they had seemed very close. Ethan remembered how his own wife had grieved at the death of their last child and had become sullen and inward thinking for weeks, and so, just as with his own wife, Mary needed time to get over the shock of the girl's death. '*I expect she'll break down in floods of tears very soon and need my shoulder to cry on,*' he thought to himself, '*I'll be ready to listen to anything she has to say, but only when she feels the time is right to unburden herself. Umm, when we stop for the night if I make them all a sweet milk-pudding for supper, it may cheer everyone up.*' For Ethan, food was a cure-all for many an emotional problem. The sight of the dark clad man surprised him as the rough looking rider pulled his horse up alongside the wagon and began talking to Mary.

****

'Geoffrey Wilkes is missing, Captain,' John Franks informed his commander, Captain William Legge.

'Are you sure? When did you last see him?' Legge quizzed Franks, annoyed at the inconvenience of losing the man.

'I haven't seen him since he was sent to Strelley to bring in new recruits, Sir. None of the men that went with him has returned either. It's not like Wilkes to wander off like that, Sir, not unless he's drunk or there's gold involved,' said Franks trying to make light of Wilkes' absence. The captain merely gave his subordinate a derogatory stare.

'We'll take a ride back along the baggage-train line and see if he's bringing up the rear with a gaggle of country miss-fits,' Captain Legge informed Franks. They turned their horses around and trotted back towards the rear of the baggage-train. It wasn't long before Franks caught sight of Mary sat aboard Ethan's wagon.

'Excuse me, Sir; I spotted someone who may just be able to help. I'll catch up with you in a moment,' Franks informed his captain.

'Good day to you nurse,' said Franks as he greeted Mary, pulling his horse into step alongside Ethan's wagon. As Mary caught sight of his face, she couldn't help but jerk back, unable to hide the shock and fear that gripped her.

'I'm sorry, Mary, I didn't mean to startle you, please forgive me,' said Franks, reminded of his appearance to women. Mary mumbled incoherently back at Franks before regaining her composure.

'Ah, Mr Franks, I, er, didn't expect to see you here. You startled me. I must have been daydreaming, forgive me,' Mary blustered. Franks tried to smile back at her, but it looked more like a snarl due to his deformed face.

'I'm looking for Geoffrey Wilkes; he hasn't come to you feeling ill by any chance?'

Mary cleared her throat which had suddenly become very dry. 'No, er, no, I haven't seen him since Bev..., er, for a long time,' stuttered Mary. She was aware that Ethan was listening to all that she was saying to this dangerous looking man and hoped that she had not given away the secret that she was more familiar to him than she rightly should be.

'What about Peter Martins. He should have caught up with us by now?' Franks queried.

'No, I haven't seen him amongst the baggage-train either,' said Mary.

'If those lazy buggers do turn up, tell them they've got to answer to me.' Franks touched the brim of his hat with his figures, 'I'd better go catch up with the captain; I don't want to lose him as well.' Franks chuckled at his own joke, heeled his horse, and sped off in search of Captain Legge.

Ethan looked at Mary questioningly, before asking, 'Where did you get to know someone like that?'

'Oh, he's just someone I treated when we were in camp. You must have missed him, it was nothing serious. That scar on his face is very old: I didn't treat him for that. He got that fighting in Europe a couple of years ago. He's quite a nice man really; it's just the scar that makes him look fierce.' Mary stopped talking, realising she was rambling and in danger of giving too much away about a man she wasn't supposed to know.

'Well I don't like the look of him,' Ethan informed her, 'You'd be better off staying away from men like that. Wasn't he something to do with that Peter Martins villain?' asked Ethan. 'I'm sure he just mentioned his name to you.'

'Did he, I was only half listening to him,' Mary lied. Ethan started to ask another question, but Mary cut him short, saying she had a headache and would like to close her eyes and rest for a little while. Ethan gave her a long questioning look as Mary hid her face in her hands and leaned back on the wagon seat, resting her back on a box stowed behind her. As troubled thoughts raced through her mind, she could feel herself trembling with fear, *'Ethan is sure to tell Mathew about Franks. Then he'll ask why the man dressed in black stopped to speak to me. Why me and not Mathew? If he keeps asking questions he might even find out how his brother Charles really died and then he'd also suspect me of Hazel's death. He will hate me, reject me. Maybe even report me to a magistrate.'* Tears ran through her fingers. *'Oh... but he can't... I know Mathew's secrets. He can't tell anyone about me, or I will have to tell them what Mathew is really doing in the king's Army along with his little friend Charles Mortimer. I know them for what they really are. But, I couldn't do that to him. I love him. How could I think I would do anything to hurt him?'* Mary's struggled with the conflict raging within her, *'If only there were someone who could understand how I feel.'*

****

'Did you see who just went past? He stopped to talk to Mary?' Mathew exclaimed to his two passengers. Charles Mortimer shrugged his shoulders as Mathew and Potter stared at each other.

'Are either of you two going to tell me what is going on?' asked Mortimer indignantly. Mathew watched Mary and John Franks conversing, but was unable to hear what was said over the creaking and rattling sound of the wagons as they made their way along the lane.

'That man is the last of the murderers I'm looking for,' Mathew told Mortimer.

'But why has he stopped to talk to Mary?' asked Mortimer.

'*I* don't know,' said Mathew.

'Perhaps it's because she's a pretty girl, but I guess you haven't noticed,' Mortimer jibed, giving Mathew a gentle shove.

'*I* know she's a pretty girl,' Mathew responded, 'but she also happens to be my sister-in-law, and that makes a difference.'

'Then I suggest you ask her about what he wanted with her when we stop for the night, she may be able to take you to him. All you will do is get yourself killed, no sorry, the both of us killed. Don't forget he's a mercenary soldier with plenty of experience in killing people. I am not, and I'm supposed to protect you from him. Please, remind me what your job is, ah, yes, you are a surgeon, and what is it you are good at, let me see, oh yes, I remember, *you save people's lives. You are not a heartless, trained killer like he is,*' Mortimer said sarcastically.

'All right, all right, so I couldn't better him in a fight. I know I'm going to need some kind of a plan to get him, but when I've worked one out, *I will* have my revenge on that man,' Mathew insisted.

Mortimer turned his questions on Potter next, 'How do you know that man?' he quizzed the little clerk who was nursing his sore side.

'I worked for his commanding officer, Captain Legge. We rode south together, with Wilkes, but you tell me Wilkes is now dead. It's therefore probable, it is he who they are looking for,' explained Potter. Mortimer sat thoughtfully, digesting what he had been told; he could now put a face to the captain who Mathew and Potter had talked about, and feared.

Chapter Three

By the time the baggage-train reached Foston Hall for the night, it had only travelled twelve miles, and Mathew felt more tired than he had ever been in his life. He turned the horses, as directed by a trooper on horseback, into a waterlogged field.

'How the hell are we supposed to make an overnight camp on that,' he exclaimed to Mortimer.

As Mathew looked around the sodden field for somewhere to camp, the good times he'd spent in Hull with Surgeon Adams and Elizabeth, and the reunion with his own family in Beverley, felt like they belonged to someone else. As he scanned the field, he noticed the ground rose slightly in one corner, so he headed for that, hoping it would offer a drier patch for their campsite. Climbing down from the wagon, the pain in Mathew's shoulders and neck from being hunched against the rain and the cold, felt like his body had been gripped in the jaws of a giant beast biting into his muscles and joints.

Potter stayed on the wagon seat, 'I would help you if I could, but the pain in my side makes it impossible for me to move. I think you need to look at my wound, it hurts real bad,' he pleaded, trying to sound pitiful and hurt. Mathew was too tired to care.

Mortimer and Ethan joined Mathew, 'the sooner we get a shelter built, the sooner we get out of the rain,' said Mathew.

Mortimer looked up at Potter, unable to keep the loathing for the little clerk from his face; all he wanted was an excuse to throttle the man. He'd long since made up his mind that Potter was a lazy bastard, feigning the pain of his wound, and that the crook was going to be more trouble than he was worth. Mathew looked across to Mary as she sat on Ethan's wagon. Lost in her thoughts, she didn't seem to care about how wet and cold she was becoming. Ethan noticed him staring at Mary.

'Isn't there anything you can do for the girl?' Ethan asked.

Mathew took a wooden stake and hammered it into the ground. 'I don't know. I'm also getting more and more concerned about Mary's black mood. If she carries on like this, she will very likely fall ill. Look at her, is that normal for anyone, any woman, to just sit in the rain.'

'She needs rest,' said Ethan.

'We all need rest,' said Mathew.

By the time they had finished pegging down the corners of the waxed sheet they were to use as a shelter, the rain had begun to ease a little. Mathew studied the sky, 'It's sure to rain again during the night.' He looked at Mary.

'I'm a surgeon, not a physician,' he said to Ethan and Mortimer. 'I only know a little about the demons of the mind. What little I do know is not good; the female mind is weaker than that of a man, and the death of someone close, like a friend or loved one, can weigh most heavily on a woman.'

Ethan looked over at Mary. 'She needs to be away from here, and very probably in the company of another woman, so they can talk. Talking always seems to be good therapy for women, but I can't see her getting either while we are following the king from town to town like we are.'

'Maybe you're right. In the meantime, what do we do with Mary?' asked Mathew. 'Let me have another peg for this canvas, I don't want to lose this shelter if the wind picks up.' He thought about what Ethan had told him, then added, 'if you could make a good meal for her tonight it may help lighten her mood a little.'

'I was going to make a sweet pudding, but everything is too wet, said Ethan.

'Somehow, I have to get her to tell me how she got to know John Franks so well. Has Mary said anything to you about Franks?' Mathew asked Ethan.

'No, not a word, I heard the man ask if she had seen Wilkes, but she denied it. Then Franks rode off. I don't want to tell you your job, Mathew, but I find that given enough time a person usually works a problem out for themselves, without others interfering. Leave her be, and let her have some time to herself.'

'Maybe so,' Mathew conceded, 'it's just that I didn't think Mary was that friendly with Hazel. So I can't understand why she is so upset by her death. In the last few days that Hazel was alive, Mary and Hazel could barely look at each other in a civil manner. It was only when Mary had to ask for Hazel's help after she cut her hand that they started speaking to each other again.

'Yes, I noticed that as well,' confessed Ethan.

'If Hazel had been a relative, a daughter, sister or mother, Mary's melancholy would make more sense, but for their feelings towards each other to change from one of loathing to one of friendship so suddenly seems very strange.' Mathew hammered another stake into the ground so Ethan could tie a rope around it.

'If you notice a change in her mood, try and encourage her to speak to me, or better still, suggest to her that she ride with me on my wagon. It will give me a chance to talk to her. Potter and Mortimer can spend a day or two riding with you,' suggested Mathew.

'Aye Mathew, I'll try, but at the moment she doesn't say anything to me either. She just sits there all day long muttering to herself, or else sitting in silence lost in thought. Sometimes she just stares across the fields, sometimes she weeps. I've tried speaking to her, but it's as though she cannot hear me,' Ethan informed his friend. As rain threatened once again, both men fell silent as they carried on working to erect a shelter.

Mortimer managed to get a feeble fire lit under the canvas shelter using dry wood he'd stored in the wagon. 'There's not much dry wood left,' he told Ethan.

'It will have to do for now. The best I can do tonight is to make a thick soup for supper with the last of the vegetables. The bread is going mouldy in this damp weather, so we better finish that off as well,' said Ethan. 'Oh, what I'd give for a warm kitchen and a ready supply of fresh ingredients.'

They sat huddled around the smoky fire extracting what little warmth they could from the feeble flames and Ethan's soup. The rain eased off again and, after rinsing out their dishes, Ethan produced a bottle of brandy-wine. 'To help keep the chill off,' he chuckled.

Mary only ate half her soup and showed little interest in the brandy-wine, her deepening melancholy now beginning to affect them all. Mathew tried to distract her by examining Potter's wound and asking for her assistance, but though it brought her to life momentarily, Potter really needed little help, so returning to her place, her face took on the blank expression they were all becoming familiar with as she slipped back into thoughtfulness once again.

There was little else they could do that night as they shivered around the smoky fire in damp clothes, so they began making preparations for bedding down. It soon became apparent that there was going to be little chance of sleep again that night; the sodden ground was rutted with wagon tracks which filled with water. In the end, they chose to lean against each other and, using the side of the wagon for extra support, fell asleep as best they could, sat up. Those that stayed awake fed the feeble fire and talked quietly amongst themselves.

'I can't keep this up,' complained Mathew. 'Tomorrow you will have to drive,' indicating to Mortimer. 'Before we set off tomorrow morning I'm going to make a space in the back of the wagon to lie down and rest. We will take it in turns to rest in the back while the other one drives.'

'What about me?' interrupted Potter.

'When you take a turn at driving the wagon, you'll get your turn in the back to rest and sleep,' sneered Mortimer.

The following morning dawned cold and cloudy, but dry. Mathew rearranged the boxes and bags in the back of his wagon then laid out a palliasse and blankets; while Mortimer and Potter, now keen to get involved, broke down the camp. Mary shivered and stretched, watching Mathew and the others work before she climbed aboard Ethan's wagon.

'Listen, My Dear, it's not that I don't wish for your company, but I'm tired, and I need someone to talk to me and keep me awake. Will you take a turn sitting with Mathew today and I'll get Potter to sit with me? Once I get him telling me his life story, he'll never shut up, and so long as it sounds interesting, I'll be able to stay awake.'

At first, Mary seemed a little taken aback by Ethan's request, but after a moment's hesitation, she climbed down from Ethan's wagon and went to join Mathew. She climbed up onto the seat without a word. Mathew, Potter and Mortimer looked from one to the other,' I'd better drive,' said Mathew as he ran his hands through his hair and down the side of his neck, 'no peace for the wicked,' he mumbled. 'Climb in the back, you may as well try and get some sleep' he instructed Mortimer. 'You can ride with Ethan,' he told Potter.

All that morning Mathew tried to get Mary into conversation with him, but she would have none of it. In the end, tired to the point of falling asleep as he drove along, he swapped places with Mortimer, and despite the jarring of the wagon as it rolled along the rutted road, Mathew was soon asleep, his dreams only disturbed by the most violent lurches of the wagon.

The king arrived in Shrewsbury with the Earl of Newcastle at his side and Prince Rupert with the Duke of York, close behind. Word had gone on ahead, and the people of Shrewsbury lined the bridge and streets of the town as Prince Rupert's cavalry escorted the king past Shrewsbury Abbey and over the span on the River Severn. As the king emerged from Stone Bridge Gate there to greet him was Lord Forth with twenty-nine other Scottish officers. The king raised his hat in salute to the elderly Scottish noble. Turning to Lord Newcastle, the king said 'you see My Lord, our Scottish allies have come to join us. Now we are truly a united kingdom against this traitorous parliament.'

'Truly so, Your Majesty, the Scottish nobles are a welcome sight, and with the promise of Welsh support, one would hope that the rebels will want to sue for a peaceful end to the dreadful and insulting ignominy they have inflicted upon Your Royal Person these past months,' said Lord Newcastle.

'We care not how the end comes about, my Lord Newcastle, only that we can return to our lawful and rightful place at the head of the government,' replied the king.

That night the baggage-train stopped outside of Uttoxeter, a small farming town in the Shropshire countryside. Mary had continually refused to be drawn into conversation all that day, but at least the weather had improved a little enabling them all to sleep and stay dry during the night. The next morning the baggage-train continued its westward trek towards Shrewsbury, and still, Mary's mood hadn't lifted. Day after day, Mary insisted on returning to ride with Ethan, though they never seemed to speak.

'I don't know what to do about Mary,' Mathew said to Mortimer as they ascended a hill. I've done my best to get her to talk, but nothing seems to work. She's been a big help to me at times, but I'm finding this sullenness too much to put up with.'

The ordinarily respectful Mortimer snapped back 'It's no good asking me, she's your family, and you brought her along. I agree, she's becoming a burden and a worry, but do you really think her being with us, crisscrossing the country like this, is the right place for her?'

'I know what you mean, but with no way of getting her home I'm stuck with her,' said Mathew irritably.

'Maybe when we get to Shrewsbury you'll get chance to talk to her, or maybe if we can stay there for more than a few days and with some rest, she'll just snap out of it,' said Mortimer trying to sound more respectful and helpful.

'Umm, you might be right,' said Mathew. The problem for Mathew was he knew if the turmoil in her mind became too great, it would break her and insanity would take over. He couldn't let that happen to Mary. He made up his mind, '*tonight; it will be tonight after we stop and make camp. I'll speak to her and demand to know what it is that is troubling her so much.*'

Mortimer interrupted his thoughts bringing him back to the present. 'Have you heard the rumour?' he asked.

'Which rumour would that be?' queried Mathew.

'I overheard some of the soldiers talking as they rode past. They were saying that the Earl of Essex's army has joined up with the army of Lord Brooke and that they are to the south of us, heading west just as we are. They must be hoping to cut us off before we reach Shrewsbury; attack us before we can reach safety,' recounted Mortimer urgently.

'I hope not,' said Mathew, 'How could the army defend us while the baggage-train is strung out along the road like this?' The three men looked around as though the baggage-train was in imminent danger of attack and wondered how they would defend themselves or, better still, get away. But, with no turning available to get off the road and with no royalist soldiers in sight to reassure them, their imaginations began to see danger lurking behind every tree. For the rest of the day, they spent more time scanning the horizon for enemy troopers than watching the road ahead of them. The baggage-train had been on the way to Shrewsbury for over a week. Apart from occasional breaks in the cloud, each day the weather had become worse than the one before, and now they had the threat of an attack to deal with.

As Mathew scanned the horizon for what seemed to be the thousandth time that day, his mind wandered. He imagined himself still tramping from town to town when winter arrived with its strong winds chilling them to the bone as they travelled the countryside continually being chased by enemy soldiers. He saw himself sat on his wagon wearing his soldier's cassock, his hat pulled down low, snow laying thick on his shoulders, his body aching as he faced the icy blasts and snow storms. The thought scared him; Mary would never survive a winter on the road. It was September now, and each night when they stopped to make camp, it was always a struggle to keep warm and dry, never mind when the snow started. No surely, he thought, they would find somewhere safe to spend the winter.

A bump in the road jolted his thoughts back to the present. He let out a long sigh; *'I'm going to have to get to the bottom of what's troubling Mary, it's beginning to affect the way I think, and there's still*

John Franks to deal with. I have to know why he was bothering Mary? I'll have to find a way to make her talk to me and tell me how she's got to know Franks. But that's easier said than done when I can never get her alone.' Mathew also toyed with the idea that Ethan was involved with Franks, '*he's been in the army since it started out from York, and now somehow he's involved Mary as well, after all, she has spent most of her time with him. No, he just imagined it, he was too tired to think straight, how could Ethan be involved with Mary and Franks, it was Ethan who had killed Peter Martins, though Mathew had to admit it, it had been an accident.'* Mathew's head began to hurt; '*am I going mad?'* he thought. He dismissed the idea.

Chapter Four

No attack was made on the baggage-train during the rest of their expedition westward. The wagoneers never once caught sight of any royalist soldiers on their journey. So, it came as a great relief, when a couple of days later, a trooper rode back along the length of the baggage-train telling everyone Shrewsbury was just up ahead. They were told that, when they reached the new campsite, they were to set up for a more permanent stay and await further orders. Even the weather seemed to be relieved the journey was nearly over; the clouds began to break-up as the baggage-train approached the town which was to be their new temporary home.

John Franks found Captain Legge eating breakfast in the Sextry Tavern on Candle Lane. The tavern had become a favourite meeting place for many of the royalist officers since the king's arrival in Shrewsbury. Without a word of greeting, Franks grabbed a chair from a nearby table, dragged it over and sat down opposite the captain.

He leaned forward across the table and in a low voice said 'I've left word in every place we've stopped since leaving Nottingham and still Wilkes hasn't shown up. No one has seen him for weeks. The thing is, I trusted Wilkes. He's not the kind of man to run off without letting me know why. Martins, on the other hand, is a mad bastard, I could believe him going off, distracted by a woman or easier picking's elsewhere, but not for both of them to go missing. It makes me feel uneasy, something's not right.'

'What do you want to do about it?' asked the captain.

'That woman Mary, the one travelling with the surgeon; we passed her a couple of days ago on the road. I want to find her and question her some more about Wilkes and Martins. Apart from you, as far as I know, she is the only other person who knew us all,' Franks advised the captain.

'Then you'd better go and find her: bring her to me, we'll question her together,' instructed Captain Legge.

The day dawned dry, sunny and warm. Mathew hoped that with this sudden break in the bad weather, it might be a good omen, as the baggage-train would reach Shrewsbury today. Feeling the warmth of the sun shining down on him after so much rain, almost made it feel like summer had returned. Mathew sighed, he knew it wouldn't last, September was drawing to a close, and he wondered if the baggage-train would get the chance to stay in Shrewsbury over the winter. As the baggage-train made its final leg of the journey along the old Roman road, they got their first glimpse of Shrewsbury Abbey ahead of them. Close by and on the same side of the river was the village of Colam. Between the village and the abbey was an expanse of grass which was to be their new campsite and temporary home. The old Roman road continued on and crossed the River Severn, becoming Abbey Foregate, leading travellers into the town. The baggage-train poured onto the field, with the most popular spots for the new arrivals, alongside the river. As Mathew drove his wagon to an unoccupied space, he could sense and hear the anticipation and excitement of the travellers as they unloaded their wagons and began to set up their camps. Very soon people were drying clothes and laying out sodden goods hoping they would dry in the sunshine. With Ethan's wagon pulling in behind his, Mathew jumped down and began to stake his claim to what was going to be their patch of the field. The others joined him enthusiastically, all except Mary. She tried to help Mathew and the others, but found the exertion too great an ordeal and had to stop. Traders from Shrewsbury began to wend their way through the newcomers, selling their wares to replenish the dwindling supplies of the travellers. Their camp was soon made ready, and Ethan set about preparing a good hearty meal to celebrate their arrival while everyone else took the opportunity to stretch out and rest in the sun with the knowledge they wouldn't have to repack their wagons the following morning.

That night, despite Ethan's best efforts, Mary only picked at her food even though Ethan had bought oysters in an attempt to make her favourite stew.

'When you're ready,' Mathew suggested to Mortimer, Potter and Ethan, 'you should go for a walk or go visit the town; it will give me the chance to be alone with Mary so we can talk privately.'

'Aye, I understand,' said Mortimer.

Mortimer quickly finished off his meal and hustled Potter and Ethan away, talking about a well-recommended beer that they all needed to try in town. Had Mary not been so inwardly focused she would have spotted the contrived gestures of Mortimer immediately, but it was Mathew who startled her when he sat down beside her. She looked up at him briefly before returning her gaze to the dish in her hand, in which she aimlessly stirred the now cold stew.

'How are you today?' Mathew asked. Mary merely shrugged her shoulders.

'We are all concerned about you.' Mary looked about her for the first time, noticing the others had left.

'Had I known you and Hazel were such good friends I would never have taken her to her sister's, but you never said anything. I got the impression you didn't like each other by the time we reached Coventry. I just didn't realise you had both become so close.' He paused, trying to think of what to say next. 'I'm sorry I wasn't there to save her: is it me you blame for her death?' Mary started to weep, large teardrops running down her nose and dripping into the dish. Slowly she looked up at Mathew, her eyes red, her shoulders trembling.

'You are so stupid, how I thought I could fall for someone like you I will never know, I should have let that tart, have you. I wish I'd never said I wanted to come on this ridiculous journey with you. All I want is to leave you, and get as far away from you and your precious Elizabeth obsession as I can. Do you understand? I hate you, I hate you all!' Mary dropped the dish of stew and buried her face in her hands, sobbing loudly. Mathew, temporarily taken aback by her outburst, sat bewildered, wondering if he should leave her or stay. He tentatively put his arm around her shoulder. She didn't resist him, she leaned against him and between sobs he heard her say, 'I'm sorry, I didn't mean it.'

It was a good while before Mary was able to lift her head from her hands and rest her head on Mathew's chest. 'I'm sorry,' she said without looking up at him. 'I don't know what came over me, I was just so angry with you, everyone, but I suppose mostly with me.' Looking up at him she wiped the tears from her eyes, 'I want to go home, Mathew. Can we go home – please? Mathew didn't know what to say. He wanted to say yes, but knew he couldn't and lying to Mary right now wouldn't be fair.

'We'll talk about it tomorrow,' hoping to avoid the subject. 'You will feel better after a good night's sleep. Go to bed, I've made a place for you in the surgery tent.' Mary got shakily to her feet and headed for the tent, and an early night with the privacy she longed for.

She flopped, fully clothed, onto the cot that Mathew had prepared for her, without the willpower to get up again and undress. Just being able to lie down in the privacy of the tent was heaven. She pulled the thick woollen blankets on top of her and closed her eyes to sleep, but visions of Hazel's dying face returned to torment her and prevented her from doing so. Mary was convinced that in those last moments as Hazel looked at her, that Hazel had understood what Mary had done to her. Mary sat up straight and looked around the tent; was Hazel haunting her? The tent was full of the memories of her. She lay back down with the blankets pulled up to her chin, her eyes wide open, waiting for her spectre to appear.

The next day started with the black star-lit sky turning grey on the horizon, slowly become pink and finally turning an orangey salmon colour as the sun rose above the horizon. The birds heralded the dawn with a chorus of joyous song as they fluffed up their feathers and shook off the early morning dew, preening their flight feathers before going in search of food. Not so the people of the baggage-train, they awoke with a cough, and to the sound of children crying as they reluctantly stirred from their beds. They split and chopped wood to rekindle dead or dying fires as, one after another, families sought to bring warmth to stiff and cold limbs. This was followed by the sound of pots and pans, as early morning food was prepared to break the fast of the long night, and fill empty bellies in preparation for the day's work ahead. The chatter of voices cut into the new day, and the cacophony of camp life settled into the familiar indecipherable background hubbub.

Mathew stretched out as he lay on his cot beneath his wagon and readjusted his blankets, thankful he wouldn't have to drive that bloody wagon along another mind-numbingly boring road today, or sit on its seat that had done its best to jar every bone in his body. As he lay there, he felt the chill morning air on his cheeks and yawned, now fully awake. A cold draft crept around the edge of his blankets and down his neck making him pull them higher up around his chin. He let out a sigh and looked across at his tent. He longed to stay where he was, but he would have to get up soon, his bladder wouldn't let him stay comfortable for too much longer. From beneath his wagon, it was light enough to be able to see other people starting their day. He waited just a few moments longer, listening to the camp come to life around him. His full and nagging bladder now told him it was time to brave the chill morning air and start his own day with a trip to the river.

By the time Mathew returned from the riverside, Ethan had a fire going. Mortimer joined them as they warmed their hands. No one spoke as, bleary-eyed, they stared into the flames, each lost in his own thoughts. It was Ethan who broke the silence, 'breakfast.' Mathew and Mortimer nodded in unison without uttering a word. They just continued their contemplative stare into the flames. Ethan returned from the back of his wagon with bread and three large cups of beer, 'that's all I've got, for now, I'll get some bacon when the merchants come around again.' After each had taken a mouthful of bread and a slurp of beer it seemed to break their trance induced state.

'What's the order of the day?' asked Mortimer.

'I don't know,' answered Mathew. 'Make ready for a long stay I hope. I expect someone will be along soon enough to tell us what we have to do.'

'I think we should all go into town,' said Ethan. 'We need fresh meat and vegetables. If we end up moving on again, I want to have a good supply of foodstuff to see us through to our next stop.'

'That's a good idea,' said Mathew. 'We'll take Mary with us; I'll buy us a hearty dinner and get Mary a new dress, that's sure to lift her spirits and take her mind off leaving us to go home.'

'Leaving us?' Mortimer and Potter said in unison, looking surprised at what he just told them. Potter joined the group around the fire. Only Ethan didn't respond to the news that Mary wanted to leave.

'Mary wants to go?' repeated Mortimer.

'Yes,' she's tired and unwell. With the death of Hazel, all this travelling, and the bad weather, it has all got too much for her,' said Mathew. 'I'd rather she stayed, but we can all see she is not well and getting worse.'

Mary appeared in the tent doorway as if she had known she was being talked about. Even after a few hours sleep, she still looked tired, and the worn clothing she was wearing didn't make her look any better. Mathew looked at his own worn out clothes.

‘I think we could all do to buy some new clothes,’ he informed the others.

They all nodded enthusiastically.

‘Who’s paying?’ asked Potter.

Everyone looked at Mathew. ‘Oh no, I don’t have enough money left to buy us all new clothes. I will buy Mary a new dress; she is my responsibility as is Mortimer, but I’m afraid you two will have to fend for yourselves. I need new breeches, and so does Mortimer.’ Potter tutted loudly and turned away. Ethan explained he had more clothes in his wagon, he just hadn’t bothered to wear them with the weather being so bad because he didn’t want to ruin them.’

Mary joined them by the fire and ate a little bread and drank a small cup of beer. Mathew explained what he had planned for them all. She smiled and nodded, looking down at her soiled dress.

‘Come on, let's go’, said Mathew. ‘Before someone comes along and tells us we can’t.’

For a short while Mary looked pleased with the idea of going into town, but slowly she slipped back into her old silent self as they walked into Shrewsbury. It was becoming evident to anyone who saw her that she had become very pale and was losing weight. The once confident young woman was now a shadow of her previous self, irritable, defensive, moody and unkempt. Mortimer tried taking her arm, but she shrugged him off, gradually slowing her pace to walk behind her companions.

At first Mathew, Mortimer and Ethan enthusiastically encouraged Mary to look at various shops selling clothes, but no matter where they indicated or how hard a trader tried to entice Mary into his shop, she refused to show any real interest in what was for sale. In one shop she found a dress of slate-blue coloured wool, trimmed with a pale grey piping around the hem, sleeves and collar. Mary handled the material and examined the lacing at the back; it was the only dress she'd shown any interest in, so Mathew and Ethan encouraged her to try it on. She stepped from around the screen at the back of the shop.

'You look like your old self in that dress,' said Mathew agreeably. Mortimer stood by his side nodding in agreement, affirming her choice. Mary looked down at her dress and gave her first genuine smile in weeks. She had to admit to herself that it did make her feel a bit better. The garment was of a simple design and cut but elegant and well sewn. She looked back at Mathew who encouraged her to buy it. The dress was a perfect fit, and she was in desperate need to be rid of the rags she had been wearing, so she accepted it.

'Our turn now' said Mathew. He chose a pair of russet coloured breeches and jacket to match, two pairs of woollen hoes and a new shirt. Mortimer, remembering his place, chose a pair of plain grey breeches matching the jacket, arguing he didn't need more than that as he was as good with a needle as any woman and that he would repair some of Mathew's old cast-offs and use those for spares. No matter how much Mathew protested, Mortimer wouldn't be budged on the issue. As they all left the shop, their spirits were high. Ethan took Mary by the arm; he nodded at her and smiled. She looked a little unsure at first but smiled back and then, as they walked the smile slipped from her face once again.

'Mathew, I think we all need to stop and have a drink,' suggested Ethan, leading Mary towards a tavern door. At first, Mathew and Mortimer were taken by surprise at the sudden need to stop, especially as it was still early in their visit to town, but they complied with Ethan's wish and followed Mary and him inside. The tavern was nearly empty at that time of the morning, but Ethan directed them to a table in the back corner of the taproom.

'I want us to sit here so we can talk privately,' said Ethan. 'A drink in our bellies will help with what I have to say.' He called for a bottle of brandy-wine and five cups.

'What news can be so terrible that we have to speak in here and need brandy-wine to give us courage?' asked Mathew.

Ethan waited until the landlord had left the drink on the table and departed before continuing.

'Mary and I have been talking. Yesterday, she told me that she wanted to go home.' Ethan paused and looked at Mary. 'I also have had enough of this baggage-train, the constant travelling and the fighting. I'm older than you four, and I don't want to spend my last day's perched on top of that bloody wagon or in a muddy field surrounded by ungrateful officers, with the prospect of death rushing through the camp after me. When I joined the army, it was with the understanding we were going to Hull, and I would cook for the officers once they'd captured the town, but ever since they buggered that up, it's been move on and stop, move on and stop all the way. Then we were told Coventry was where the king was going to make his new capital, and then that turned out to be another mess-up and we had to move on. We have constantly been moving from place to place and winter is not far away. I've had enough, I'm leaving, I want to go back to York and Mary wants to go with me.' Mary's face flushed bright red. Mathew and Mortimer sat mouths agape at the news, only Potter allowed himself a wry smile remembering what he had seen at Nottingham.

'Well, er, I don't know what to say,' said Mathew, 'are you sure you want to leave. I mean, we've become such good friends; it won't be the same without you. And Ethan, I didn't know you and Mary...'

'No it's nothing like that,' interrupted Ethan. 'After Mary told me she wanted to go home it kind of made-up my mind for me. I'm going home as well, and I have agreed to stop at Beverley on my way to leave Mary with your family.'

Mary kept her head down, not wanting to look at Mathew.

'Can you wait just a little longer?' asked Mathew.

Ethan held Mary's hand, 'I can't; we can't. There's no telling how long the baggage-train will stay here or where it will be going next. If we don't go soon, we may never get the chance to leave. I promise you, I will deliver Mary safely to Beverley.'

Silence fell over the group. No one knew what to say. Mathew hadn't wanted Mary to come with him to start with, but now she was leaving he felt guilty about her going.

'A toast then,' said Mortimer, breaking the gloom and silence that had descended upon them all, 'farewell to a friend, or should I say friends, and a safe journey to you both.' There was a bit of a pause as the realisation of what had been decided sank in and before everyone wished them a safe journey.

'We might as well finish the bottle them,' said Potter, placing his drained cup on the table. Mary looked at Mathew; she had her reasons for going home, meeting Franks had finally made-up her mind. She hoped that Mathew would assume it was all because of her rejected feelings for him, rather than the guilt she felt about other matters. She gave him a little smile.

'I'll let father and Henry know you are well and how important you have now become as surgeon to the king, or rather that you will be soon; they'll be very proud of you, said Mary. 'I'll also get to see my little Bess again; I've missed my little dog. I bet she's grown by the time I get back, I hope she remembers me.' A single tear rolled down Mary's cheek. She wiped it away quickly, turning her head away from Mathew. The awkward silence returned as they sipped at their second cup of brandy.

'When were you thinking of leaving?' asked Potter, placing his cup next to the bottle ready for another refill. Everyone glared at him for asking the question no one else wanted to ask.

'Tomorrow morning,' said Ethan.

'Tomorrow,' exclaimed Mathew, 'that's rather sudden isn't it?'

'Maybe it is, but there is no point in putting it off. I'm going to unload the wagon of most of its supplies and leave them for you before we go. If none of you makes a fuss about us leaving, everyone will think I'm going to fetch more supplies, especially if they see most of my stuff still in and around the camp, they'll think I'm stocking up for a long stay. If anyone asks about me, tell them I'm going for more flour and beans. By the time anyone realises we've gone for good, we'll be miles away. If they look for me, they'll be looking for a man on his own, not a father and daughter on their way home from the market. So with a bit of luck and no hold-ups, in a week or two we'll both be back home,' said Ethan.

'I'm going to miss you both,' said Mathew.

'Me too,' affirmed Mortimer. Potter said nothing: he just nodded in agreement and helped himself to another cup of brandy.

'Without you to help me settle in I doubt I would have made it this far. I owe you a lot in return for what you've taught me. You had to take a man's life to save Mary and me,' said Mathew. 'I'm sorry. I, we owe you so much.'

'That wasn't your fault, he ran into my knife. I wouldn't have had the courage to face him had I known what was happening, and anyway, it was you don't forget, that saved me from those soldiers when they attacked our camp. So you can say we saved each other and that all debts have been repaid. They all became thoughtful for a while until Ethan took the bottle of brandy-wine from Potter 'we'd better get our share of this before he drinks it all.' Now that Ethan had made the news of their departure public knowledge, and Mathew had taken it better than they had expected, Mary perked up a little. Mathew wondered what his father would say when Mary turned up without him.

As Mathew gave more thought to Mary's departure, it gave him a sense of relief, more so than he'd first thought it would. Somehow he felt as though a burden had been lifted from his shoulders. There would be no more women around to worry about; he could concentrate on getting even with John Franks. Women, he'd decided, were too much trouble and complicated matters when there were more important things to deal with.

Chapter Five

The following morning Ethan made breakfast for them all one last time, great thick slices of fried bacon, fresh bread and lots of butter, washed down with a large cup of beer, it had become everyone's favourite way to start the day. Then came the solemn task of unloading Ethan's wagon, everyone helped, including Potter; Mathew felt like he was being deserted. Mary though seemed brighter than she had done for a long time, but there were still tears from Mary when Ethan's wagon rolled out of camp. There were no shouted farewells; they couldn't afford to attract the attention of the rest of the baggage-train camp to what was happening. Mortimer had asked Ethan if he would be deemed a deserter, but Ethan explained that he wasn't deserting in the real sense of the word because he was a civilian employed by the army, but he should have asked for permission to leave first. Mary turned on her seat and gave one last wave as the wagon turned a final corner and was gone from sight.

The stores Ethan had left behind, that would all keep if kept dry, were placed in Mathew's wagon. All the pots, pans and anything Mathew, Mortimer and Potter couldn't find a use for, were collected up and taken across the field and dumped. Later that day when Mathew went to see if it was still there he was pleased to note that everything they had discarded had now disappeared, pilfered as they had hoped, by people from the baggage-train.

Later that morning, a corporal came looking for Mathew. He was letting all the surgeons in the camp know that they were to make ready. Tomorrow, the army was going to start recruiting, and the new men would need a medical inspection before being allowed to sign-up. Mathew informed Mortimer and Potter of the order.

'What if someone comes looking for Ethan?' asked Mortimer.

'We'll just say we got split up and haven't seen him. And as for Mary, we tell anyone who asks that she decided to stay in Nottingham.'

'What if Franks comes looking for her again?' asked Mortimer.

'I hope he does, then I will get my chance to deal with him,' said Mathew.

'No you won't,' Mortimer interrupted indignantly; 'WE will get to deal with him. Don't forget, keeping you safe is now my job.'

Potter looked from one to the other, 'you're both fools if you think even together, you are a match for a man like Franks. You're going to need brains not brawn to get the better of him.'

While the travellers made themselves at home in the field and Mathew and Potter unpacked all Mathew's surgical equipment at home in Shrewsbury, after a morning of teaching at the Shrewsbury Grammar School, Kenneth Clayton, schoolmaster, watched his sister Alice playing the guitar as he finished his meal. 'Is the day going well for you, My Dear?' asked Alice, laying aside her guitar.

'Tolerably well, Sister. I had to impress upon one of the boys that the failure of his parents to pay his school fees was not acceptable. After his punishment, he promised to write to his family and ask about their late payment of his school fees. I reminded him that this is not a charitable school. That this is the kind of school that teaches boys with parents who have the financial income, foresight and position in society, that enables them to give their sons an education which will lead them to future wealth and privilege, as well as being a credit to their family,' responded her brother.

'Quite correct, Brother of Mine: thankfully, the young ladies to whom I teach guitar do not have to sully their minds with thoughts of money; their fathers send a servant with my fee each lesson,' Alice said loftily.

'Your young ladies do not board at the school, Alice, and they require little in the way of education. Whereas the young men I teach must learn to become leaders of lesser men for whom they must set an example. Though I have to admit, the English are not as diligent in their studies as the Scottish boys I used to teach in Edinburgh.'

'Yes Brother, but you know why we had to leave Scotland; you became a little too fond of beating the boys. I hope you have learned from that mistake,' Alice's penetrating stare made Kenneth look away without responding.

After school had finished for the day, and when most folks were in their beds, a small lone figure emerged from the back door of the school and limped away into the darkness. Following the edge of the river east towards Shrewsbury Abbey, Watling Street and the way home, the slim figure made slow and painful progress through the school grounds. He stopped many times when the pain in his bottom became too intense to go further. At one pause in his escape, when the pain was at its worst, and his head was feeling fuzzy and dizziness making the world around him spin, he considered going back. But, as the new day began to defeat the darkness of night, he could see the smouldering campfires of the baggage-train campsite ahead of him. Passing over Colam footbridge, he stopped for a moment at a hedge that marked the edge of the camp field before stumbling on towards the encampment. Shrewsbury Abbey stood silhouetted against the lightening sky beyond the camp and in front of the abbey was the road to his salvation and home. He had avoided the main streets of Shrewsbury in case his absence had been spotted, and people were searching for him; the baggage-train camp was the only obstacle he hadn't expected.

Sweat ran down his pale face as he stumbled over every anthill, rut and bump that marred his path. As he passed between an array of wagons and tentage which barred his way, it was a deeply embedded tent-peg that brought him crashing to the ground in a scream of pain, just before he blacked out. Through the fog of pain and blackness which befuddled his mind, he could hear voices and felt himself being lifted up and carried. He cried out, but his voice was dry and hoarse, his words indiscernible. After an indeterminate amount of time and pain, mixed with unknown voices, he felt himself being laid on a hard surface and someone removing his breeches. James didn't care anymore; the pain that racked his body was more than he could bear; at least if he were going to die, he would be free of the pain.

****

Mathew, awakened by shouts drawing closer to his tent, rubbed his eyes. He could hear an urgent voice calling for Surgeon Fletcher. Within seconds he was wide awake and on his feet just as the first man burst through the flap door of his tent.

'We've found a badly beaten young lad at the edge of the camp,' yelled the intruder, 'the seat of his breeches is all soaked in blood!'

'Very well, I'm coming,' said Mathew as he followed the man outside. The sun was touching the horizon, and the dawn chorus was in full voice when Mathew emerged into the morning light. Two men and two women stood over a youth who was laid on the grass. Mortimer, also disturbed by the yelling, was coming over to see what all the fuss was about. Still half asleep, Mathew rolled the boy onto his back to study his face. 'There's not a mark to be seen,' he exclaimed.

'No!' said the first man, 'look at his backside.' Rolling the boy over again, he saw the dark, damp stain in the seat of the boy's breeches, the stain continued on down towards his knees. Mathew had mistaken the stain as a shadow in the low morning light; it was only when reminded, that he took a closer look at the boy's clothing.

'Bring him into the tent and place him on the table,' ordered Mathew.

Inside the surgeon's tent, Mathew cut away the boy's breeches with a large pair of scissors and lifted the boy's shirt which was also soaked in the boy's blood and urine. The black and red pulp of the lad's bottom brought a sharp intake of breath from all the onlookers.

'The poor lad,' exclaimed one of the women, 'does anyone recognise him: I'll fetch his mother.'

'Lad's not one of us lot,' responded one of the men, 'his clothes are too fine. This is a local lad, a runaway; probably been caught stealing and punished for it.'

'Whatever he's done, he didn't deserve a beating like this,' Mathew pronounced. 'Leave him with me, and I'll tend to his wounds. When he can talk, I will find out where he has come from.' As Mathew started work on the boy's injuries, Mortimer ushered the onlookers from the tent.

'Is there anything I can do?' he asked the surgeon.

'You can make up a bed for him in the corner, and then see if you can beg or buy a pair of breeches for the lad, though I guess it'll be a few days before he's ready to wear them,' said Mathew.'

While Mortimer busied himself with the second bed, Mathew treated the lacerations on the boy's rear with a balsam made from *Sheep-Suet, Gum of Elemi, Turpentine and Hogs-Fat*, smoothing the balm gently over the damaged skin, after which he covered the wounds with a sheet of linen soaked in *Rosewater*. When he was finished all Mathew could do now was leave the boy to sleep. Mathew had him placed on his own bed while Mortimer constructed a second cot in the corner for him to use. Hopefully, when the boy awoke, he would be able to talk and tell them what had happened to him. As the boy slept Mathew stood in the door of the tent surveying the camp; he wondered where the boy had come from and why he had been beaten so mercilessly. He looked towards the cold campfire with no Ethan busy cooking breakfast over the flames. There was no smell of frying pork or Ethan's happy smile as he went about his preparations for the day. Mathew looked over to the wagon; Potter still lay in his bed, untroubled by the commotion of the boy's arrival. Somehow the camp felt smaller and incomplete without Mary and Ethan, their absence making him feel like he had lost something important. Thinking about the missing cook made Mathew's thoughts stray back to Mortimer. When Mortimer had finished making up the cot for the boy there was another duty his friend was going to have to learn, he would have to take over the job as their cook.

It was around midday when the boy awoke, and Mathew heard him call out in pain. He rushed into the tent to find the boy on his hands and knees struggling to get up.

'And where do you think you are going?' asked Mathew sarcastically. Mathew knelt beside him, rested his hand on the boy's shoulder only for the boy to shy away from him.

'Don't worry, you're safe, no one here will harm you, you need to rest and some time to heal. Who did this to you? The boy stared at Mathew like a trapped, frightened animal.

'You're safe, no one will harm you here,' Mathew reassured the boy.

The boy inched himself back onto the low bed, all the while keeping an eye on Mathew, before letting out a long sigh, a tear pricking from the corner of his eye.

'Who did this to you?' Mathew asked again.

The boy turned his face away from Mathew and did not answer. Mathew poured a little *laudanum* into a cup and proffered it to the lad.

'This will ease the pain and help you sleep. If you're hungry, I can fetch you some food,' offered

Mathew. The boy turned to look at him, 'thank you, Sir.' He took the small cup and drank the contents, pulling a face as the taste of the bitter liquid filled his mouth.

'I'll be back in a few moments with some bread and cold meat,' Mathew gave the boy a smile and left. By the time he'd returned the boy was asleep again, so he left the plate of food and tankard of beer within easy reach of his patient.

The afternoon warmth was cooling fast when Mathew returned to the tent to find the boy still lying face down on the cot, but at least he was eating the bread and meat left for him.

'Feeling better lad?' asked Mathew.

'Yes, Sir, thank you, Sir,' the boy forced a smile. Drawing up a stool, he sat close to the boy.

'It will be a week or two before you'll try sitting down again, but there is no permanent damage, save to your pride. Are you willing to tell me who beat you like this and why?' Mortimer and Potter on hearing the two talking in the surgeon's tent entered to listen to boy's story.

'My name is James Copperhead, and I was a student at the Shrewsbury Grammar School until I ran away. It was my teacher, Mr Clayton, who beat me because my father is late paying my school fees.'

James Copperhead explained that his father is a merchant, importing spices and goods from the East Indies. His father had received news that one of his ships, which had been due to dock at Bristol one week ago, had been lost at sea off the coast of Spain. His father was now short of funds and unable to pay his investors, and that also meant he had not been able to pay his son's school fees. But Mr Copperhead had explained to the school's headmaster that, when a second ship docked in a month or so's time, he would gladly put right his debt with interest if necessary. Following instructions from the headmaster, Mr Clayton, James' schoolmaster, had been told that this was not good enough, there could be no exceptions to late payments of fees. The letter sent to Mr Copperhead in reply had stated that James would be beaten and given instructions to write to his father demanding immediate payment of the school fees. It went on to explain that James would receive a beating every Friday noon until the debt was repaid including interest owed and that, at the end of one month if the debt had not been paid, his son would be expelled.

Potter spat on the ground, 'the bastard needs teaching a lesson if you ask me.'

Mortimer looked sideways at him and smiled, 'Maybe he does, any ideas?'

'I might be able to come up with something.' Potter grinned at Mortimer, allowing it to turn into a wicked smile as he looked down at the boy.

'Now then you two, I don't want any trouble for the lad, he's suffered enough,' contested Mathew, but none too forcefully. Mortimer and Potter left the tent plotting their next move.

In the Clayton lodgings, at Shrewsbury School, Alice and Kenneth were enjoying their supper.

'You are quiet this evening, Brother. Did you have an unpleasant day's teaching?' enquired Alice. Kenneth thought carefully about how to answer his sister, knowing she would be angry with him if he told her the truth.

'It's one of the boys, he's, er, run away. I suspect he became homesick or something,' answered the teacher. Alice laid aside her spoon and glared at her brother in disbelief.

'It wouldn't be the boy you told me about yesterday, would it?' she asked accusingly. 'Er, yes, as it happens. It may simply be because his father couldn't pay this term's school fees and he is too embarrassed to face the other boys,' spluttered Kenneth unconvincingly.

'You fool!' exclaimed Alice, slapping her hand down on the table. 'I like it here. I have built up such a good reputation for my music teaching lessons, so much so that I have more young ladies waiting to join my classes. I was even thinking of an increase in my tuition fees. But when this boy arrives home and tells his father what you have done to him, his father will come to the school to complain, and you will lose your position here, or he'll have you arrested and carted away. Will you never learn to control yourself? Now I expect I will be forced to return to Scotland and explain to the family why you are in gaol. This is not your school; if a boy cannot pay, it is for the school commissioners to rectify, not you,' yelled Alice.

'The headmaster insisted all the teachers remind the boys their fathers should pay more promptly and this boy was brought to my attention. His father may not complain to the school, the scandal of his debt would become public knowledge and could ruin his business,' Kenneth liked his explanation and hoped it would appease his sister.

'And what happens if his father finds the means to settle his debts and takes the boy out of school because of what you have done to him?' Alice retaliated. 'If the boy's father is a man of influence he could make a great deal of trouble for the school, and you.' Her brother remembered the part in the letter from the boy's father, stating another ship was expected to arrive in England within the month and he would settle his debts with interest, a chilling shiver ran down his spine. 'But the headmaster said...'

'I don't care what the headmaster said,' interrupted Alice. You have a reputation to live down.'

The following morning work started early, all the surgeons who'd been travelling with the baggage-train were inundated with new recruits waiting to be inspected and their fitness to serve in the king's Army assessed, so Potter was left very much to his own devices. He had been given instructions to keep an eye on James while Mortimer helped Mathew with the new recruits. Potter sat talking with the lad a while, getting the measure of his school teacher. It seemed to Potter, as James told his story, that Mr Clayton liked to beat the boys for any indiscretion or failure in school lessons he chose, far more so it seemed than any of the other teachers, and because of this the boys feared and hated him. Potter thought back to his school days, he'd been expelled for gambling and cheating the other boys out of their allowances. Too fearful to return home, he had lived on the streets using his wits to survive ever since.

'Leave Mr Clayton to me lad. Tell me, if your teacher should happen to leave the school, would you be happy to return and continue your lessons?' asked Potter reassuringly.

'Well, er, yes Sir. It is a good school, and I have many friends there. But what will they say about me running away?

'Oh, I wouldn't worry about that, after I'm finished with them, I think they will welcome you back with open arms. In fact, from what you have told me about Mr Clayton, the other boys will hold you up as some kind of hero when they hear your teacher has had to find alternative employment.' James looked at Potter unconvinced by his reassurances and gave him a half-hearted smile.

'Now, I'm going to make some preparations; I won't be gone long, is there anything you need before I leave you?' asked Potter.

'No, thank you, Sir; the medicine that Surgeon Fetcher has given me makes me feel tired, so I think I'll sleep awhile if I may. You must have more important things to attend to, than talking to me.' James yawned as if Potter needed proof of what he was saying. Potter left the boy and went in search of paper, pen and ink. It was while Potter was fumbling around in the back of Mathew's wagon, looking for some paper on which to write to Mr Clayton, that he heard the sound of an approaching horse. It made him glance around the side of the wagon. To his horror he saw that it was Franks, coming through the camp: turning on his heel, Potter headed off in the opposite direction. Franks spotted Mathew and Mortimer checking over a new batch of recruits and turned his horse to go and speak to them.

'Hey, Surgeon, I need a word with you,' stepping down from his horse, he stood threateningly close and tall in front of Mathew. He was taller than Mathew had imagined and certainly in comparison to the local men Mathew was examining. Mathew's hand instinctively tightened around the whalebone tongue depressor in his hand as though it were a weapon. At first, intimidated by Franks, Mortimer stepped away from their tall, sinister adversary before regaining his nerve and stepping closer to Mathew, ready to defend his friend.

'That woman, Mary, she works for you: where is she?' demanded Franks.

At first, Mathew struggled to find his voice, having his enemy so close unnerved him.

'Well, what's the matter with you?' exclaimed Franks, unaware of the war of emotions that was taking place within the man he was speaking to.

'She left,' was the best that Mathew could come up with.

'What do you mean 'she left:' when, where to, why?' probed Franks.

'She's gone. A friend died, and she became melancholic and fearful, so she left; said she couldn't stay any longer,' said Mathew, struggling to get his thoughts in order. The mention of someone dying raised Franks' suspicions.

'Who died, how?' Franks' face hardened as he looked into Mathew's eyes.

'Hazel Farley,' interjected Mortimer. Franks relaxed a little at the sound of the unfamiliar female name and looked at Mortimer for the first time.

'She got very low spirited and was in danger of becoming ill, so she said she wanted to go home,' said Mathew.

'We took her into town, found a merchant going north and paid him to take her with him,' said Mortimer.

'I gave her enough money to last her till she got home' volunteered Mathew. Franks looked keenly at the two men in front of him, somehow knowing that they were holding something back.

'She knows two friends of mine, Peter Martins and Geoffrey Wilkes: do you know where they are?' asked Franks with a sharp edge to the tone of his voice. Mathew and Mortimer looked at each other.

'We haven't met anyone travelling with the baggage-train by those names,' Mortimer said dodging the question.

'If we see them, where should we send them to find you?' continued Mathew, quickly. 'As you can see we have a lot of work to do,' indicating to the queue of waiting men: 'as I have said, tell us where they can find you, and if we see them, we'll let them both know where you are.'

'The Sextry Tavern, off Candle Lane; know it?' said Franks bluntly. Mathew wasn't sure if he did or didn't, but he'd find it, so he just nodded. After one more piercing stare from Franks, he mounted his horse and rode off.

'Can we get on now,' said an inpatient voice from the queue of volunteers waiting to be assessed by Mathew.

'Good of him to let us know where we can find him,' said Mathew.

'Don't be stupid;' responded Mortimer, 'he'd kill the both of us without missing a heartbeat.' Mathew didn't answer but turned back to the task in hand.

A familiar voice from behind them made Mortimer turn around.

'Nice little chat with our Mr Franks?' Potter asked sarcastically.

'Piss off, we're busy' retorted Mortimer.

'Yes we did, he's quite a pleasant well-educated person,' said Mathew sarcastically, trying to deflect any animosity between the two men before it got started.

'*We are* talking about the same man?' retorted Potter.

Mathew gave a little laugh. 'Later, Thomas, we'll talk about him later. I must get on with my work, or we'll have officers asking what is holding us up.'

So Potter returned to their wagon and resumed his search for writing materials.

That evening, the three of them walked into town and found a table in the Pheasant Tavern. After a meal of poached salmon with parsley, thyme and rosemary, accompanied with spinach, peas and beans, Mathew, Mortimer and Potter pushed their plates away and drained the last of the beer from their tankards. 'Not as good as Ethan would have made for us,' confessed Mortimer.

'Let's have some bag pudding with cream,' suggested Potter.

'Umm, I could find space for some pudding,' agreed Mathew. A few minutes later with their stomachs full to bursting with pudding, they were ready for another drink.

'Ethan would have made a better one than that. He would have put more fruit and cinnamon in it,' confessed Mortimer.

'You're right, and we have to pay for it,' said Potter.

'Correction,' said Mathew indignantly, 'I paid for it.' Potter shrugged his shoulders.

Mathew signalled to the landlord who bought another round of drinks.

'What about the lad?' asked Potter.

'We'll get a pie to take back with us,' said Mathew.

'Do either of you have any suggestions on how I'm going to get the better of Franks?' asked Mathew in a low voice.

'Forget it,' said Potter, 'you don't stand a chance, not in a fair fight anyway.'

Mathew and Mortimer looked at Potter for further insight.

'It's no good looking at me for help. I don't know how to kill Franks,' Potter protested.

'He's right,' said Mortimer. 'Franks is a trained killer and enjoys it. Two of the three people you are after are dead, isn't that good enough?'

'No, I want Franks. The other two died at the hands of other people. I made an oath with God and over Elizabeth's body and I mean to see it through: if not now, then as soon as I can,' Mathew said firmly. Mortimer and Potter sipped their beer and fell silent, not wanting to upset Mathew further. It was Potter who broke the impasse.

'The way I see it,' said Potter 'if I were you, I would pay someone else to kill him.'

'Yes, they could lie in wait for him one night and shoot him in the back,' added Mortimer.

'I am not paying someone else to do it, and I don't think I could kill him in cold blood; I don't have it in me, I know that much. I am also fully aware that I'll never beat him in a fair fight,' confessed Mathew. 'But I have to see this through.'

'Can we get the major to help you?' asked Mortimer.

'No – he'll just tell me the same thing you two have,' said Mathew reluctantly. 'We'll have one more drink, and then we head back to camp. Maybe after some sleep, one of us might come up with an idea on how to get the better of him.'

By the time they reached Colam Bridge, they could hear music coming from the baggage-train camp. Instinctively everyone's step quickened. When they had passed through Colam village and reached the entrance to the camp, they could hear laughing, singing and loud voices. A glow from the centre of the field showed where a large fire blazed. As they drew closer to the merriment, they could see people dancing.

'What is the celebration?' Mathew asked a man watching and clapping.

'The young couple in the centre of the group got married today, and once word got around the camp about the wedding, people came to congratulate the bride and her husband and give them best wishes in their new life together,' said the man. 'Then someone turned up with a fiddle, another with a whistle and it just sort of started from there.'

'Is this allowed – the dancing and the music – where we come from the church frowns on this kind of frivolity?' said Mortimer.

'I take it you are town's folk. We country folk prefer the old customs. Besides, the bride won't have cause for much dancing after tonight, she's got a full belly,' said the man.

Mathew watched the young woman in the blue dress and floral garland headdress, for a moment. As she turned to speak to the woman next to her, the bulge in her dress showed her to be pregnant. The new husband stood a few feet away with a group of men laughing and drinking.

'I am going to enjoy myself,' said Potter as he headed off to the celebration. It was at this point that James arrived, walking uncomfortably and holding the seat of his new breeches away from his buttocks. Mathew gave him a concerned look.

'I'll be fine, thank you Sir; it's just the material pulling on one or two scabs, that's all. I'll rub on some of that salve you gave me later when I go to bed,' said James. The two of them watched the dancing while Mortimer went in search of the beer.

'I brought you a pie, I thought you might be hungry by now,' said Mathew.

As James demolished the meat and turnip pie, they watched Potter dancing with a young girl who was almost his own height, as her parents watched her from close by. Mortimer returned with three cups of beer.

'I brought this one for Potter, but as he's not here, you may as well have it, Lad.'

James emptied the large cup without stopping, gulping down the beer thirstily.

'Are we going to join in?' asked Mortimer. 'Give our blessing to the new husband and his wife?'

'No, not for me – you stay if you wish, I think I'll go to my bed, and I don't think young James here is ready for dancing just yet either,' said Mathew.

'But, couldn't I just stay and watch, Sir; I've never seen a celebration like this before?' pleaded James.

'Aye, if you wish,' Mathew finished his cup of beer and with one final glance at the festivities, turned and walked away.

'What's the matter with Mr Mathew?' asked James.

'Weddings make him sad, and you'd better not go pestering him to know more about why that is either, or you'll have me to answer to,' said Mortimer, 'Mathew's got troubles enough without being reminded of what might have been.'

Mathew removed his jacket and sat on a stool to remove his shoes and breeches while listening to the celebrations in the distance. Looking around his surgeon's tent, it felt empty, cold and lonely. On a low table next to his bed sat a single candle burning inside a horn lantern along with a book on surgery, his only companions for the evening ahead, he began to feel very alone. He was still only twenty-one years of age, and he was going to bed early to read a book on surgery and medicine. He longed for the days when he was back in Hull with Elizabeth, making plans for their future together. If all had gone to plan he would be newly married by now, in his own home, warm and dry with the woman he loved. He shivered as a chill breeze blew under the wall of the tent. He quickly finished undressing, grabbed his book and climbed into bed. He hadn't felt much like reading since he'd been on the road, so some time to himself now that they were to be staying at Shrewsbury for a while, would give him a chance to study again. If the king made good on his promise to have him brought to court as a surgeon to the royal household, he would have a lot more learning to do.

Potter was having a good time dancing with the young girl despite the pain in his side from the bullet wound. She may have been around half his age and not as pretty as he would have liked, but she was happy to be dancing with him, after having had no one else take notice of her, not even her father. The music came to an end, and he returned her to her family. She took a seat next to her mother smiling happily, her chest rising and falling rapidly as she caught her breath. The girl's father glared at Potter, 'you have a charming daughter, Sir. You must be very proud of her,' Potter quickly interjected.

The man eyed Potter suspiciously for a moment, 'She is my only daughter, and I plan to marry her to a respectable gentleman as soon as we find a permanent location from which to set up our new residence and business. I have a contract to supply victuals to the king's army. I'll not have my daughter marrying some pauper,' said the girl's father, judging Potter to be a ne'er-do-well.

'I totally agree with you, Sir. It is a father's duty to ensure his daughters marry well. I am but a humble clerk to the king's own surgeon and have no family of my own.' Potter bowed to the man and turned to walk away.

'Just a moment,' the girl's father called after him. 'I have a jug of good French wine; may I offer you a cup?'

Potter smiled, turning back slowly to face the girl's father, 'that is very gracious of you, Sir, thank you.'

The two men spoke for a while, Potter extolling Mathew's abilities as a surgeon and his connections to the king and his court. The girl and her mother listened to him intently. A pause in the conversation coincided with the start of another tune, so Potter took the opportunity to ask the girl for another dance. Potter's exaggerations seemed to have worked as the girl's mother almost thrust her daughter at him, 'Katherine would be delighted to dance with you,' she insisted.

Katherine and Potter joined the dance while her parents watched on attentively. The music was lively, and all the dancers danced enthusiastically. Potter and Katherine Crossed and Cast, Dipped and Dove, formed a Star with the other dancers and Stripped the Willow. Dance after dance they passed the time together until

Katherine was quite breathless and Potter holding a hand to his side, groaned as his wound complained about his exertions.

'Are you hurt, Thomas?' asked Katherine.

'No... not really... it is an old wound,' said Potter giving a little grimace.

'Should I fetch help? You seem in pain,' asked Katherine.

No, no, just a short rest will do fine. It has been a long time since I have enjoyed myself so much. It is my own fault for not stopping sooner, but you are such a delightful dancer I didn't have the heart to stop dancing while you were enjoying yourself so much,' Potter gave a weak cough. 'Shall we go for a stroll, it will ease the pain in my side, and we can talk a little?' suggested Potter.

Katherine looked back over at her parents. Her mother gave her a wave and a smile.

'Very well, Thomas, but not far, my father will worry,' said Katherine.

Potter took her hand and slowly led her away from the festivities into the surrounding darkness. They walked down to the river's edge and looked across at Shrewsbury. The lights twinkling from the windows of distant houses, some reflecting off the water in front of them as it slowly flowed passed. People carrying lanterns could be seen walking back and forth over the two bridges which linked the abbey and village to the town on the far bank of the River Severn. They stopped by a tree and Potter raised Katherine's hand to his lips gently kissing it. Katherine stepped a little closer and stroked his face, her touch, gentle and warm. His hands moved to her waist, pulling her closer still. She did not resist him. Their lips met, and he felt her body stiffen.

'POTTER!' the shout cut through the night air like a gunshot to the heart. Potter and Katherine jumped apart, their hearts thumping at the sudden intrusion into their intimacy. Not far away stood Mortimer and James holding a lantern aloft.

'We were watching you. I think it is time the young lady returned to her parents before something happens that complicates matters for you both and adds to the problems that Mathew could well do without.'

Katherine didn't wait to be escorted back. She took off like a startled rabbit.

'You bastard!' screamed Potter. 'What the hell has it got to do with you if I take a girl for a walk?

'That; is precisely the issue, she is little more than a girl and not ready for someone like you to take advantage of her. If you want a woman there are plenty to choose from in the taverns of Shrewsbury, they will be happy to slake your lust and separate you from your coin,' said Mortimer angrily.

Potter rushed at him, his fists raised ready to strike at the man who had ruined his evening. Mortimer stood his ground and when Potter came in range, knocked him down with one punch to the jaw. Potter fell backwards stunned for a moment, blood running from a split lip.

'I'll get you for this, Mortimer, mark my words I'll get you if it's the last thing I do?

Chapter Six

The schoolboy awoke early, not used to the sound of snoring coming from someone else close by. He raised himself up on one elbow and looked at Mathew asleep on the far side of the tent. Mathew was fast asleep, on his back, mouth open and snoring loud enough to wake the dead. James gave him a withering look and flopped back down onto his cot, but it was too late, he was wide awake now, and there was absolutely no prospect of him going back to sleep with that amount of noise coming from the body in the next bed. James looked around the tent from his cot, he was bored; so, deciding to try and stand, he gingerly got to his hands and knees. James winced as his shirt, which had stuck to some of the scabs on his bottom, pulled free flecking new spots of blood onto his shirt. Slowly and carefully he got to his feet, steadying himself with one hand on the surgeon's table. He tenderly rubbed more of the balm Mathew had given him into his buttocks. It offered some relief, but he was paying the price of being on his feet at the wedding last night, the bruises from his beating had spread down his thighs, and the scabs were itching. Now he was on his feet in the fresh morning air, the call of nature could not be ignored any longer, the urgent need for a pee was all-consuming; so he slipped on his jacket and took himself out and around the back of the tent to relieve his complaining bladder.

It was getting light on this chilled September morning, and the camp was slowly coming to life. Smoke rose from rekindled fires as the dawn chorus heralded the new day. His first call of nature satisfied, the second one made itself known to him with a loud rumble. As with most young lads, hunger was a constant companion, and it now gnawed at his belly. The campfire was cold, and there was no sign of any food left over from the night before. He made his way to the wagon and began to search amongst the boxes and bags, trying to be as quiet as possible, but his clumsiness awoke Mortimer and Potter sleeping beneath it.

'If you find anything edible in there you share it with me' said Potter rubbing the sleep from his eyes.

'Not before I've had my share,' responded Mortimer.

'Well, there's nothing here that wouldn't take some time to prepare or a long time to cook,' said James disappointedly.

'Then it's time to wake Master Fletcher and go in search of some breakfast. It's a pity Ethan didn't stay with us, we'd be eating bacon and fresh bread by now,' said Mortimer.

'With fresh butter and a large cup of beer,' interrupted Potter. 'I reckon Ethan took all the best grub with him.'

'That's because none of us knows a thing about cooking,' said Mortimer.

You'd better find some breeches and get your shoes on if you're coming with us, lad. The only place we'll get food is in town,' said Potter as he crawled out from beneath the wagon. As James made his way tentatively back to the surgeon's tent, Mortimer went ahead of him to wake Mathew and tell him everyone was hungry and in need of breakfast. James found his new breeches and stepped into them. They were an old pair Mortimer had bought for a penny and repaired, but if James wanted to eat, wearing them was a discomfort he was going to have to put up with.

Once Mathew was on his feet and fully awake he checked on James' wounds. Where the skin had been badly torn by the rod used on him, his young flesh had crusted over, and he would carry the scars for the rest of his life. The rest of the injuries were healing fast. He made James drink a small draft of *laudanum*, 'If you insist on being on your feet and coming with us, you will need this.'

The effects of the drug began to work very quickly on James' empty stomach: the sensation of pain in his backside was soon gone, and so was the feeling of hunger, but those sensations were replaced with another. He began to feel relaxed and at ease with all around him. Mr Clayton, the school, his parents didn't seem to matter anymore. Potter watched the lad as his eyes took on a glazed look, as he stared into some far off space; Potter sniggered and nudged Mathew, pointing at the lad.

'I may have given him too much *laudanum*, you'd better keep an eye on him,' said Mathew. So with guidance from Potter, James stumbled after Mathew and Mortimer. As they crossed the Colam Bridge heading into Shrewsbury, Potter made sure he kept a careful hold on the lad less he suddenly decide to go for a swim. The sun was up, the town was coming to life, and the whiff of cooking food wafted from the town, putting impetus in their step as they crossed the narrow stone footbridge. To the hungry men, the distinctive smell of cooking meat was almost unbearable as it grew stronger. They made their way along Under the Wyle Street to Wyle Cop following their noses. Then they noticed the enticing aroma of frying pork coming from a tavern entrance, with a quick look at each other and a nod of agreement, they chose this establishment from which to purchase their morning meal. Mathew ordered beer, bread and bacon for four. James tried to sit at the table with them but found it too painful; the *laudanum* had its limits, the sharp pain in his buttocks clearing his fuzzy head and bringing back his appetite. When the food arrived, to their dismay the bacon was too salty, fatty and chewy, unlike the bacon Ethan used to prepare for them, but their hunger was too strong to ignore. With hands full of fatty well-cooked pork, they devoured the meat, following it up with thick wedges of bread smothered in creamy butter, washing it all down with great slurps of beer, before greedily taking another piece of pork.

James dropped a thick piece of bacon rind on his plate, licked his fingers and let out a great burp which rumbled on for a few seconds before he wiped the grease from his chin. 'Thank you, Mr Mathew, I wish they'd fed us that well at school.' He sloshed down the last of his beer and slammed down his cup signalling a satisfying end to his breakfast.

Mathew smiled at the lad, 'Time we all got back. If today is anything like yesterday, we'll be rushed off our feet again. I don't understand it, men are coming from far and wide to join the army, I can only suppose, with winter coming, there is going to be little work in the fields for them, and they're short of money.'

'If it's agreeable with you,' said Potter, 'I'd like to stay in town with the boy. I fancy a visit to Mr Clayton. I have a letter that I've written, and I'd like to deliver it to him,' Potter checked inside his jacket to ensure the letter was still safe. At the mention of his teacher's name, James went pale and took a step away from the table, unsure if he wanted to be part of Potter's plan of fun and revenge with his teacher.

'Very well,' agreed Mathew. 'I want to know how he manages to justify beating the boy like he did. We are going back to camp; I expect there'll already be men waiting for us when we get there.'

James looked from Mathew to Potter; feeling a bit shaky at the prospect of returning to school. His stomach churned uneasily, and he now wished he hadn't eaten all that greasy meat. He watched as Mathew and Mortimer left the tavern and was tempted to call after them, asking them to wait for him to catch up.

'Do I have to go back to school, Mr Potter?' James asked with a tear stinging his eye.

'That's up to you lad, but I plan to have some fun with your teacher, and I thought you might like to see it. You heard Mathew; he wants to know what that bastard Clayton thinks he's doing beating you like he did. Don't worry lad, everything will be fine,' Potter smiled reassuringly at the boy. James managed to respond with a half smile.

'First, we call upon Mr Poole, your headmaster. I have to have his support before confronting your teacher, and he may not be willing to turn on one of his masters, so I am going to have to be very persuasive and convince him it will be better for him and the school to side with us.'

Mathew and Mortimer were soon busy sifting the fit men from those who were too old or too infirm to serve in the army. The last thing on Mathew's mind was his new status as surgeon to the king and his court. So it came as a surprise when an officer rode up and insisted that he follow him back to Shrewsbury Castle immediately.

'What has happened, who is ill,' queried Mathew.

'I have only been tasked with finding you and ensuring you return with me to the castle. Once we arrive you will be informed about what is required of you,' the officer insisted.

'What about my instruments, if I don't know who is in need of medical assistance and what is wrong with them how will I know what to take with me?'

The officer paused, giving the matter some thought, before crossing to another part of the camp and commandeering a horse and small cart.

'Load everything you think you will need on this, you can return it when you are finished at the castle.'

Mathew apologised to the owner of the horse and cart who had followed the officer across the camp, protesting vociferously at the theft of his possessions. Eventually, a deal was struck. The cart's owner was suffering from a particularly bad in-growing toenail, so Mathew agreed to treat him free of charge for the use of his horse and cart.

It was with a mixture of trepidation and curiosity that Mathew passed under the arched gateway into Shrewsbury Castle and crossed the courtyard. The castle wasn't as large or well fortified as Newark Castle; it was more like a large house with a defensive wall around it. The guards on the gate watched him as he followed the officer to the front of the Great Hall, the only building of note in this smaller castle.

'Leave all your things on the cart,' instructed the officer, you can send for them if you need them. Mathew was led into the hall; it was full of finely dressed people and military officers all talking at once, their voices ringing around the hall. The officer who had been sent to collect Mathew strode on ahead of him, parting the people in the hall like a ship parts the waves at sea. Mathew followed behind, wishing he'd at least had time to put on his new clothes, as all eyes in the hall followed his progress to a door at the rear of the chamber. Beyond the door were stairs leading to the upper private apartments. At the top of the stairs, two guards separated to let the officer and Mathew through and into a small anti-chamber.

'Wait here,' instructed the officer, before entering another chamber. Mathew looked around the small anti-chamber; it was devoid of furniture apart from a bench up against the back wall and a small table in the corner on which a jug and goblets sat. The guards at the top of the stair ignored him as he paced the floor. They stood resolute and silent, dressed in half-armour with helmets and holding Halberds. The officer returned, leaving the door behind him open, 'this way,' he instructed Mathew.

The grand chamber he entered was much more lavishly decorated. Officers milled about talking in a relaxed fashion, each with a large drinking vessel in his hand; they all looked like they had been drinking for some time. Lying on a couch in the centre of the chamber, with two beautiful ladies in attendance, was a man Mathew assumed to be just a little older than himself but, unlike Mathew, he wore his hair long, and his clothing was as beautiful as any Mathew had ever seen. He wore no jacket, his shirt hung loose and open around his neck, and Mathew could see he was clearly nursing one arm. With a glass of wine in hand, he greeted Mathew warmly but didn't stand.

'You must be the surgeon I've heard so much about.' His English was perfect but heavily accented. Mathew stepped closer and bowed. The two women looked him up and down and giggled.

'How may I help you Sir?' said Mathew.

'I am in a great deal of pain after falling from my horse this morning. I think my arm may be broken. I am unable to move it,' said the man on the couch.

'May I know your name, Sir?' enquired Mathew.

The man laughed,' I Sir, am Prince Rupert of the Rhine, nephew to your king and leader of the finest horse regiment in Europe, here to put your disrespectful parliament back in its box where it belongs.' The rest of the men in the chamber cheered loudly at Prince Rupert's declaration, raising their glasses in salute, before draining them of their contents.

Prince Rupert gave his empty glass to one of the women he shared the sofa with and forced himself into more of a sitting position with his right hand, wincing with pain as he did so.

'May I examine your arm Sir?' asked Mathew.

'That's what you're here for man. They say you work wonders. Doctor Harvey wanted to tend to it, but all I hear from the Duke of York is how you saved his life when he was ill with fever in Newark Castle, so I want to see how good you are for myself by letting you cure me of this damned useless arm.'

'How did this come about, Sir?'

'We were out hunting this morning. We had a stag on the run when my horse put its hoof in a hole; fell, and threw me. The horse broke its leg; he was a good horse, he'll be hard to replace, but I guess I won't be doing much riding until you cure me of this bloody painful limb.'

Mathew moved closer to the prince, 'with your permission, Sir,' Mathew indicated that he would like permission to sit beside him.

'I think our young surgeon would like you to move my dear Phoebe,' said Prince Rupert with a beaming smile. The woman reluctantly removed herself from the couch giving Mathew a withering look as she did so.

'If I may be so bold, Highness,' said Mathew lifting the prince's left hand. The prince winced at the slightest movement of his arm but said nothing. Mathew examined his patient's hand, then his forearm noting the grazes and scratches. Holding the elbow quite still he moved the forearm a little. The prince cringed but again did not complain. Mathew slowly worked his way up the prince's upper arm to his shoulder, examining it as he went. He'd already noted that the shoulder was dislocated, but he needed to reassure himself that the prince's arm was not broken, before starting on a course of treatment.

'Your Highness, your shoulder is dislocated. The upper arm has come out of its joint and is trapped above your shoulder. To put your arm back into its correct location I am going to need some help and some equipment.'

'Ah, ha, it's not broken then. I get to cheat the saw bones of my arm, the ladies will be pleased,' scoffed Rupert, before wincing and regretting his sudden animation. 'Inform Captain Belasyse of your requirements and he will ensure you have all you need.' The captain stepped forward at the mention of his name.

'Sir, I would like a high backed chair, a strong one, with a straight top to the back. I will also need blocks of wood to stand the chair upon. I need to raise the chair higher up off the floor so the Prince's arm can be draped over the back of it. I will also need the assistance of two of you gentlemen to help me when it is time to relocate Prince Rupert's shoulder.'

All was made ready in accordance with Mathew's wishes. 'Before we start, Your Highness, you will need to take a draft of *laudanum*,' said Mathew.

'I don't need *laudanum*, the sooner you get on with it, the sooner I can get back to entertaining Phoebe and Mariella,' said the Rupert flippantly.

'If you will indulge me a moment, Your Highness, I am not doubting Your Highness's ability to withstand the pain of manipulating your shoulder. It is more so the *laudanum* will relax Your Highnesses muscles, enabling me to more easily manoeuvre your shoulder joint back to its natural position,' said Mathew.

The Prince thought about it a moment, 'as you wish. I don't want it said I am unwilling to do what I can to assist you in your work.'

With the quantity of wine the Prince had drunk that morning to ease the pain, and the larger than usual draft of *laudanum* Mathew had given him, when the time came for the prince to stand he needed to be helped into the high backed chair by Captain Belasyse and Mathew.

'I will assist you in the manipulation of the Prince's arm,' said Captain Belasyse, 'so will I' said another officer, setting down his glass on a nearby table.

'Thank you, Sir's,' said Mathew. 'I am going to put the Prince's arm over the back of the chair in a moment. I would like you both to take hold of his wrist and draw it downwards in a slow, steady fashion. I would like you to increase the strength of your pull until I request you to stop. It is important that once you start to pull, that you do not release the pressure on the Prince's arm until I say, or the shoulder will not relocate itself correctly, and that may cause the Prince's shoulder joint more damage.'

Both men nodded, understanding their task, and took their places on the floor ready to draw down the patients arm. Mathew tied the Prince's right arm to his side to prevent him from flailing it about when the procedure started. Turning his patient sideways as he sat on the chair he positioned his patients left arm over the backrest. The onlookers gathered around and fell silent as they watched Mathew work.

Kneeling as best he could on the seat of the chair on which the Prince was sitting, Mathew placed his left arm around the Prince's neck and took hold of the Prince's upper shoulder with his own right hand.

'Very well, Gentlemen, commence pulling,' Mathew felt the arm extend as the upper arm joint was drawn outwards from its position above the shoulder joint. With the palm of his hand resting on the top of the royal shoulder, Mathew eased the dislocated joint back into the Glenoid Cavity. As the shoulder relocated, there was an audible click. Prince Rupert cried out briefly in pain. Mathew asked for the two officers to slowly release their pull. The pain of the procedure had reanimated the Prince who struggled to be released from the chair almost knocking Mathew backwards. Mathew struggled with his patient for a moment before Rupert regained enough of his senses to realise what he was doing and relaxed. The two officers released their grip on the Prince's wrist, once the shoulder was relocated. Once released Prince Rupert instinctively tried to recover his arm from over the back of the chair, but as he did so, the in pain in his shoulder and arm muscles rebelled at their immediate use after being stretched un-naturally out of place for most of the morning. Mathew released the prince and stepped away. The royal patient nursed his arm and shoulder, regaining his composure in front of his friends and officers.

'I can move my arm again,' the Prince exclaimed in welcome surprise.

'Yes, Sir, but I still need to bandage your arm to prevent you using it for a few days, the tendons need time to recover their strength, but within two weeks you should be using the arm freely,' said Mathew.

'Two weeks,' protested the Prince, 'I've never been an invalid for two weeks in all my life.'

Mathew didn't know how to respond to the Prince's outburst, but Captain Belasyse came to his rescue.

'Just think, My Prince, you will be at the mercy of Phoebe and Mariella, would that be so bad?' The chamber erupted into laughter.

The Royal patient smiled and eyed the ladies in question. 'Very well, Gentlemen, I will concede to your wishes, but only for one week or I may miss out on this rebellion that Parliament is making against our king. I can't let you have all the fun on your own.' Another round of raucous laughter broke out. Prince Rupert watched Mathew as he unfastened the bindings on his right arm. The prince flexed it, before using it to lift a glass to his lips and taking a drink. Raising his left arm slowly he felt a pain deep inside his shoulder and eased it back down. He gritted his teeth and continued, demonstrating to those around him that movement had been restored to his dislocated shoulder, before bringing his arm to rest on his lap in preparation for Mathew to put it in a sling and bind it to his side.

'I shall remember this good deed you have done me today,' said a grateful Prince Rupert, in a low voice, flexing his shoulder a little painfully one more time. 'Now bind me up so I can play the invalid to these two lovely ladies,' he said loud enough for all in the chamber to hear. Rowdy laughter and cheers rang around the chamber from the half-drunk officers. Mathew did as he was requested and, as soon as he had finished, the two women who had previously been at the prince's side when he arrived, returned and draped themselves over him, showering him in kisses, caresses and words of sympathy.

The officer who had fetched Mathew over from the camp took him aside.

'You may return to your work now, Surgeon Fletcher, we will take care of the Prince now.

Chapter Seven

Potter and James arrived at the door to Shrewsbury Grammar School. 'Take me to your headmaster; I want to talk to him first,' said Potter.

They arrived at the headmaster's chambers to find he wasn't there. Delighted at such an advantageous start to his plan, it didn't take Potter long to fiddle with the locked door to the headmaster's office and let them both inside.

'Stay by the door and listen for anyone coming, I want to have a look around for anything useful I can use to our advantage. One of Potter's previous jobs had been as a legal clerk before he discovered the illegal opportunities his trade opened to him, so it was to the headmaster's ledgers that he applied himself first. James kept his ear to the door listening out for uninvited guests.

'Where do you think the headmaster might be?' asked Potter over his shoulder while he rummaged through the ledgers.

'He may be teaching a class. There are only four schoolmasters and over two hundred boys, so from time to time he has to take a class. It may be he's not even in school, sometimes he has business to conclude in the town with the mayor,' answered James.

'Alright for some,' remarked Potter.

It was while searching through a draw in the headmaster's desk that Potter found a small book with no title. Flicking through the pages, he quickly noted that it was full of names and figures, spotting James' name. He called the boy over.

'How much are your school fees per term?' asked Potter.

'Five pounds,' said James.

'Well, it would seem that the headmaster is creaming off a percentage of the fees for himself. From what is noted here, it looks like a pound per pupil per term,' Potter indicated to the figures in the book. 'See here, each pupil's name and next to it the fee for the term, four pounds. He bills the parents for five pounds and puts four pounds through the books, pocketing a pound per pupil for himself each term. No wonder your headmaster applies pressure on the teachers to ensure pupil's parents pay up on time.'

Potter slipped the book inside his jacket and, with James in tow, they left the office in search of James' teacher, Mr Clayton. They found him just as he was coming out of a classroom after a lesson. James pointed him out to Potter as they walked down the corridor leading to the classrooms. James' hands began to shake, and his pace slowed as they closed on the teacher.

'Ah, Mr Clayton, just the man I am looking for,' Potter declared in his most officious voice. 'It is my duty to inform you, Sir, that I have been appointed by solicitors of Mr Copperhead, James' father, to issue you with this summons,' Potter produced the paper he'd written the night before. 'You are being summoned on the count of actual bodily harm on the person of Master James Copperhead here. In that, the punishment metered out was beyond that appropriate to the crime of debt owed by the boy's father and not by the boy. My employer deems the boy innocent in the matter of the debt owed to the school and therefore the punishment illegal.' Potter proffered the paper up to Mr Clayton who refused to accept it.

By now, a group of pupils had gathered around Mr Clayton and were listening to what Potter was saying. Sniggers were distinctly heard from the assembled boys, but Mr Clayton, transfixed with fear, his face a deathly white, didn't respond to the sneers, he was focused entirely on Potter and the document in his hand. The memory of how he had been hounded out of his last school in Scotland, playing over and over in his mind, reminding him of being publicly disgraced over his previous bout of over-enthusiasm in punishing a child.

James looked at Potter, astonished at the wanton lies he was spinning to his teacher. Clearly, his father knew nothing about what had happened to him. Mr Clayton stood with his mouth open trying to take in what Potter was saying. Snapping at the first idea that came into his head, he blurted out, 'We shall see what the headmaster has to say about your bit of paper.'

Potter smiled, 'Oh we shall, Mr Clayton, oh we shall.' Potter turned and pushed James ahead of him in the direction of the headmaster's office. Mr Clayton and his schoolboy entourage brought up the rear.

By the time they all reached the headmaster's office, the headmaster had returned and was seated in his chair behind his desk enjoying a pipe full of tobacco and a glass of Madeira. Potter didn't bother knocking before he entered the chamber, he just pushed the door open and marched in followed by James and Mr Clayton, the rest of the boys waited at the entrance.

'What's the meaning of this intrusion,' demanded the headmaster.

'I'm sorry, Sir, it's this man and James Copperhead,' blustered Mr Clayton. 'He says he is here to present me with a writ to stop me beating the boy and a summons to appear in court to answer for the crime of bodily harm on the boy.'

By now the headmaster was on his feet. 'Punishing a boy is no crime,' he declared confidently.

James Copperhead began to wonder if this had been as good an idea as Potter had claimed it would be, as the headmaster towered over the height-deficient Potter.

Potter stood his ground, 'I have a witness to the boy's injuries, one Master Surgeon, Mathew Fletcher, surgeon to the king who now resides in Shrewsbury

Castle. Surgeon Fletcher treated the boy for his wounds, and he is willing to testify in a court of law, that the wounds received by the boy were beyond any reasonable basic punishment and that they were gratuitous and unnecessary. Adding to this fact, the boy is innocent of any crime and that it is his father who is the defaulter and debtor of the monies owed to the school. Mr Clayton is thus guilty of the crime of wounding. It is my employer's opinion that the school may also have a case to answer in allowing such extreme punishments to take place to one in its care.' He turned to face Mr Clayton and asked, 'Do you plan to beat the boy's father in the same manner?' Clayton took a step backwards, thrown by the question.

'Don't be ridiculous,' protested the headmaster.

'On the contrary, Headmaster; it would seem that Mr Clayton was acting under your orders or at the very least with your consent,' continued Potter calmly.

'Get out, get out at once,' demanded the headmaster, 'and as for you boy, you are going to receive the thrashing of your life for bringing this idiot to the school.'

'You forget the writ and the summons,' Potter waved the papers in the air as though they would ward off his two adversaries. The headmaster paused in his raving.

'If you really are the representative of a solicitor, the court can have Mr Clayton,' countered the headmaster, suddenly taking a more conciliatory stance 'I knew nothing of this beating, if there were one and, I certainly didn't order one, and you cannot prove that I did.'

Potter let the headmaster's outburst hang in the air a few moments while he stroked his chin in thoughtful contemplation. 'Maybe we can come to a compromise,' said Potter. 'I'm sure my client, the school governors and the Mayor of Shrewsbury, could do without the scandal of a court hearing.'

'Now I know you are insane,' laughed the headmaster.

'Not so hasty headmaster. When did the school governors last inspect the school's finances?' Potter contemptuously smiled back at the headmaster.

'What have the school finances got to do with this matter?' demanded the headmaster. 'Get out, get out of my school.'

'That little book you *had* stashed away in your drawer, it made interesting reading.' Potter spoke the words as deftly as an assassin would wield a dagger. The headmaster shot round to the back of his desk and dragged open the bottom drawer, spilling its contents on the floor.

'Where is it?' He demanded.

'Safe...When I present it to the court and the governors, I wonder what they will make of it? Four hundred pounds is not an insubstantial amount to accrue over your years as headmaster,' purred Potter.

'What do you want?' demanded the headmaster.

'Ah, now we come to the matter in hand. Let me see now...You will dispense with the services of Mr Clayton immediately,' Potter seated himself in a chair near the headmaster's desk.

'Done,' said the headmaster, not even bothering to look at Mr Clayton.

'You will give each boy in the school a free term at school,' was Potter's second demand.

The headmaster hesitated, before answering, 'Done.'

'And lastly, this is for Mr Clayton. He will join the king's army. A man of his stature will make a fine pikeman.' Potter looked up at the schoolteacher, 'after all, once you've put it about, Headmaster, that you dismissed him for committing sodomy with the boys, I don't think anyone else will be interested in employing him.'

'Done,' said the headmaster instantly. 'When do I get my book back?'

'Ooh... you don't.... it will go to the boy's father, for safekeeping, with a letter of explanation from me. After all, we wouldn't want anything untoward to happen to young James here, would we? I think that concludes our business here, Gentlemen,' said Potter. 'Oh, by the way, James will return to school when he is ready, and Mr Clayton will report to the army camp in the morning.' Potter was about to leave the office when another thought occurred to him, 'I am sorry Headmaster, but I have one final request. I would like a map, a map of England: one showing lots of detail of towns and roads on it, please.' The headmaster looked puzzled, but went across to a bookshelf and removed a number of documents from one of them. He spent a moment or two examining them before handing one to Potter, 'will that suffice?' asked the headmaster. Potter unrolled the large scroll, 'Yes, excellent, thank you.' As Potter and James Copperhead passed Mr Clayton on the way out of the office, the schoolteacher, overcome by the enormity of the sudden change in his circumstances, could only lean against the wall of the chamber, looking very pale and ready to faint.

'Thank you, Mr Potter,' said James Copperhead once the two were back on the street.

'Think nothing of it lad, I enjoyed myself,' sniggered Potter. 'Come on, let's go celebrate with a cup or two of beer, and I'll teach you how to play cards.'

After a long day's tiring work, Mathew and Mortimer went into Shrewsbury for their evening meal. Potter and James hadn't returned from their school visit yet so Mathew and Mortimer would be able to talk in private for the first time in a long while.

'I've decided to find John Franks sooner rather than later and kill him,' said Mathew as they walked through the streets of Shrewsbury.

'What are you going to do when you find him?' asked Mortimer, 'ask him for a duel or sneak up on him and stab him in the back? He'd kill you in the blink of an eye. You can't murder him on the street.

You would cause a riot and be caught straight away. You can't do it, it's impossible.'

'I don't know, I haven't had a chance to think it through yet,' replied Mathew. 'I just want the matter over and done with.'

'Well, don't you think that's a rather important part of your plan?' interjected Mortimer. Mathew stopped and stared at him, his face reddened, his anger rising at the impertinence of the question. Mortimer took a step back.

'I'm sorry, forgive me, I didn't mean it to sound like that, I'm just frightened we do meet Franks and are totally unprepared for the occasion,' apologised Mortimer.

Mathew relaxed a little but continued to stare at Mortimer, annoyed by his friend's honesty, before turning and resuming their walk along the street. A few minutes passed before Mathew spoke, 'You are right,' he said tersely. 'I am not prepared. I know that I can't get the better of Franks in a fair fight so I won't give him the chance of a fair fight. He doesn't deserve one as far as I'm concerned, and you can bet he wouldn't give me one.' They both walked on in silence for a moment.

'I'm going to purchase a pistol for each of us; that will even the fight a bit. We've gone past a few shops selling weapons while we've been walking. The next shop we come to selling pistols, we will go in and buy what we need.' A couple of shops further along the street they found a gunsmith.

'This seems to be the place we're looking for,' said Mathew over his shoulder to Mortimer as he entered the shop. The interior of the shop, though brightly lit with lanterns, only had a small and narrow shop floor, the counter just a few feet from the door. The remainder of the interior was taken up as a workshop for the gunsmith. The shop smelled of oil, fresh wood shavings, metal and a faint smell of sulphur. A man working at a bench in the back looked up as Mathew and Mortimer entered, 'how may I help you, Gentlemen?'

Mathew and Mortimer looked at each other, not really knowing what to say.

'I would like to purchase two pistols, please?' requested Mathew nervously.

'What for?' asked the gunsmith. Mathew and Mortimer looked at each other again, seemingly confused by the question.

The gunsmith waited for an answer, then asked,' would they be for sporting purposes, self-defence or are you joining the army and want something better than the basic pistol they provide?'

'Self-defence,' blurted out Mathew, pleased that was all the gunsmith wanted to know. The gunsmith produced a number of boxes from beneath the counter, opening the lids, each box contained a pair of fine pistols with all the paraphernalia to load and clean them. Mathew viewed the pistols in awe, the intricate workmanship of the gunsmith's skill its own testimony to the quality of the weapons. 'I think we need something a little more affordable, we are not rich men,' confessed Mathew.

'If you've no money to speak of, why do you need pistols for protection?' queried the gunsmith.

'There's trouble brewing in the country, and we've already been waylaid once by a robber. With all the travelling we are doing we just wanted a pistol each in case someone tried to rob us again. All we need is something to frighten them off with, so to speak; make them think twice about pushing their luck.' Mathew smiled politely at the gunsmith. The gunsmith snapped shut the lids on the gun cases and returned them to their shelf below the counter. He retrieved a large box from the floor, giving his customers a disappointed look.

'These are my more affordable range of guns. They are a mixture of pistols I have repaired for customers who have not returned to claim them, and guns I have made from leftover materials after I made those finer weapons.' The gunsmith removed a few from the box placing them on the counter for Mathew and Mortimer to view. They both picked through the assortment trying to find one they liked, though they knew very little about firearms.

'I like this one,' said Mortimer, holding up a short, but wide barrelled gun, 'it looks very intimidating.'

'Um,' said the gunsmith thoughtfully, 'a good weapon indoors, or over short distances, in the street say: not very accurate though over longer distances: but it will seriously maim or kill anyone you hit, that's for sure.'

'This one is for me I think,' said Mathew, holding up a more slender pistol.

'A good choice, Sir, its plainness belies its quality. It doesn't have the artistic decoration of my finer pieces, but it's made from the same materials as those pistols I showed you first of all. It's a reliable and accurate weapon in most situations you will encounter.'

Happy with what they had found, Mathew purchased the accoutrements that went with each pistol.

'We'd better get something to eat before we go back', said Mathew, 'I don't want to have to walk back into Shrewsbury twice in one evening.' They found the nearest tavern and purchased a meal of pie and peas and after just one jug of beer they were ready to go back to camp.

As soon as they had returned, Mathew and Mortimer hid their new purchases and went to join Potter and James. Mathew and Mortimer had barely managed to sit down before Potter started to recount the day's events he and the boy had enjoyed. As he told them about his meeting with the teachers, James stood beside Potter encouraging him on. At the end of his tale, James showed Mathew the map that Potter had obtained. 'I thought you might find it useful,' said Potter proudly as he proffered it to Mathew. Mathew unrolled the map; it showed England and Wales, though the top showing Scotland was missing. The map had been partly coloured to define different counties and depict the major towns, cities and roads that traversed the country.

'It looks like you two have had a productive day,' said Mathew. 'The map may come in very useful. At least we'll be able to mark on it all the places we have visited. As they sat around the campfire, they examined the map, Potter taking great delight in talking about all the places he had visited on his travels.

Chapter Eight

There was a knock on the door; Kenneth Clayton looked at his sister, 'who could that be this early in the morning?' he asked her, not really expecting an answer. He adjusted his jacket and went to investigate who the caller could be.

'Mr Poole, I was planning on coming to see you this morning, please, do come in. Alice, fetch Mr Poole a glass of our best Madeira. Take a seat by the fire, Sir, warm yourself,' Kenneth Clayton fawned over his headmaster as Alice scurried away to find a glass and the best Madeira.

'I will not sit, and I do not want your Madeira,' said the headmaster firmly. 'Last night the school governors and I had a meeting, and it has been decided you are to leave Shrewsbury Grammar School immediately. You are ordered to be off the premises by the end of the day, the end of the day; do you understand?' demanded the headmaster. Not waiting for a response from his dismissed subordinate, the headmaster turned on his heel and was out of the door just as Alice returned with the Madeira. Kenneth Clayton stared, white-face and trembling with shock, at his sister, 'I'm sorry, Sister; we have been ordered to leave.'

Tears filled Alice's eyes and rolled down her cheeks, 'how will we live, where will we go?' she whined pitifully, before putting down the Madeira and her mood changing.

'It's your fault,' she raged, 'it's Always your fault; you were always a bully. That's why you became a teacher isn't it; so you could torment the boys, take out your revenge on those who could not fight back, just because *you* were bullied at school. I have had enough of you, Brother. Had our parents still been alive I would have been married by now, but I've had to rely on you instead, and all we have done is move from place to place because you couldn't keep your hands off the boys? Well. I'm not going to be homeless; I knew this day would come one day, so I've been saving money. I have enough put-by to take me back to Edinburgh and purchase a small house of my own. I will continue giving music lessons, without you to hinder me.' At the end of her tirade, Alice turned and fled to her bedchamber slamming the door behind her.

Kenneth Clayton flopped onto a chair cursing himself for being so stupid and self-indulgent. He looked around the room and tried to imagine life outside this privileged enclave. He had enough money to find himself lodgings for a short while, maybe he could find a job teaching privately. The thought of being homeless didn't appeal to him at all. '*If I'm careful with my money, I could travel south and find a teaching post in another town, somewhere small, where they wouldn't insist on references from a previous employer, anyway, I could always write my own.*'

Alice reappeared in the doorway with a cloak around her shoulders, 'I'm leaving you. As soon as I have lodgings arranged, I will be back to collect my things.' With another slam of the door, she was gone. The room was ominously quiet, just the occasional crack from wood burning in the fireplace. He couldn't believe what had happened to him; one day everything was rosy, a secure job, a nice home and now, because of one stupid, stupid lapse, it had been snatched away from him. He sat listening to the silence, disturbed every now and then by the sound of boys laughing or shouting in the distance. '*They would all know by now,*' thought Kenneth. *'They will be mocking me, making me a laughing stock: I will be the talk of the school.'* Another troubling thought occurred to him; '*how will I get out of school without being seen by the boys? I will wait until the morning lessons have started, cut across the school garden and into Shrewsbury that way. Then, I'll find somewhere to stay and send a man back to collect my possessions. If I take what money I have with me and sell some of my books, I could rent a house and start again. No, not here in Shrewsbury; word would soon get around about me; better to stick to my original plan and head south to find another school.'* Rejuvenated by his plan, he emptied the strong box of what little money he had, grabbed his cloak, checked the corridor was empty and was gone. '*Once I've got somewhere else to live they won't be able to make me join the army.'*

The streets were busy with shoppers, traders and soldiers. He pushed his way through the crowds as he made his way up one street and down the other, working his way south through the town and away from the school. Everywhere he tried to find lodgings he received the same answer, there were no houses or rooms to rent anywhere, even the inns and taverns were full, the king's officers and soldiers were occupying every available space, which only days before had been vacant for weeks. Disheartened, he went into the closest tavern for a drink and a pie. He found an empty stool at a table and joined the men already enjoying a drink and a talk. Kenneth couldn't help but listen in. They were talking about how they had enlisted in The King's Army and how they were going to make their fortunes when the king rewarded them for defeating the rebellious parliamentarian army. Some of the men spoke about how easy life would be in the army, as there would be no fighting when the two armies met because the king would command a force so vast, so superior to the Parliamentarians, that they would run and hide rather than fight. One man said the best thing of all was that they would be paid six pence per day for doing it. At first, Kenneth dismissed their babble as rubbish, then he remembered the bargain Potter had made with the headmaster; unless he joined the army, the headmaster was going to put it about that he sodomised boys at the school.

'Maybe, joining the army could be a temporary solution to my problems.'

'Pardon me, Gentlemen, I couldn't help overhearing what you were saying about joining the army. I have recently fallen on hard times, and I am in need of work, do you think the army would take me?' asked Kenneth.

The men around the table fell silent and eyed up the eavesdropper. 'Why not?' said the man sat closest to him.

The question stunned Kenneth into silence a moment wondering how he should answer it, but another man intervened saying, 'they took us.'

Kenneth looked from one to the other, 'how do you know what you've been told is true?' he asked.

'Because everyone is saying it and, if it's coming from the king's men, it's got to be true, ain't that right friends?' volunteered one of the drinkers.

'Look here, if you're not sure we are telling you the truth, come with me, my name is David Seale. I've joined up as a pikeman; that's the honourable and noble side of the army, for gentlemen like yourself. When I was at home my father wanted me to join the family business, I've had schooling, I can read and write, but I wanted to be more than just a clerk, so I joined up. I tell ya, a fine big fellow like you would make a formidable pikeman, and I bet you're educated to boot.'

'Er, yes I am as it happens,' confessed Kenneth.

‘Well then, come with us, we’ll take you down to the place where they are taking on volunteers, and we can all be pikeman friends together. What kind of work do you do then Mr er, er?’ asked David.

‘My name is Kenneth Clayton. I used to be a teacher...a private teacher in a private house, but the boy grew up and went to college, so only having girls left in the house, they had no further need of my services,’ lied Kenneth.

‘Too bad,’ commented David and the rest of his friends nodded enthusiastically in agreement.

‘Drink up, and finish your pie and we’ll be setting off,’ suggested David.

So Kenneth was hustled out of the door and down the street with his new friends around him, encouraging him all the way as they headed off towards the field where the baggage-train was camped. Just as they were about to cross the Colam Bridge, two of the group slipped away up an alley.

‘Where are they going?’ asked Kenneth. David looked around.

‘Got cold feet I suppose,’ volunteered one of the remaining men.

‘Aye, suspect so,’ agreed David.

It wasn’t long before Kenneth, and his hastily discovered new friends, found themselves waiting in a queue to be seen by a company surgeon.

‘Have you a couple of pennies to spare?’ David asked Kenneth, ‘we could be here for some time, and

I'm getting hungry enough to eat a scabby donkey. I'll go get us a couple of pies to eat while we are waiting for you to be seen by the surgeon.'

Kenneth wasn't sure about giving away his money to a man he'd only just met and, instinctively, his hand went straight to his purse only to find it gone. He looked down at the place where it had hung from his belt to see the two cut ends of leather straps where a purse had once been attached to his belt.

'I've been robbed!' screamed Kenneth.

'Must have been one of those little buggers that ran off,' tutted David Seale. 'We won't see them again, you can bet your life on that. Did you have much money in your purse, Kenneth?'

'All the money I had in the world,' confessed Kenneth finding it hard to comprehend how bad this day was turning out to be. 'Now I'm penniless with nowhere to stay,' he wailed in frustration.

'Don't worry about that. Once the surgeon has passed you fit we can get a sergeant to give us lodgings and food to eat,' said David, slapping Kenneth on the back. 'I told you, that's one of the advantages of being in the army; they look after us.' An hour later, Kenneth had been passed fit by the surgeon and signed his name in the regimental register. He had been signed up to Sir Edward Fitton's Regiment of Foot as a pikeman.

He, along with his new friends, had been ordered to report for training. Kenneth knew what a pike was, but he had never handled one before, let alone learnt how to fight with one. As the new recruits were passed fit, a sergeant assigned them to a company. Each company was made up of ninety-six soldiers, sixteen men wide (a rank) and six men deep (a file), plus four sergeants, two lieutenants and a captain in command. The heavy metal helmet on his head trapped and pinched his ears and made it difficult to hear what his sergeant was saying. Being a new pikeman, Kenneth had been placed close to the centre of the division (a unit of men within the company) with his pike lying on the ground with the butt closest to his right foot. The pike was sixteen feet long, and the thought of how he was expected to fight with such a weapon in so tight a formation of men baffled him.

'What do I do?' he whispered to his friend, David Seale, standing next to him.

'It's easy, listen to the sergeant, but watch me, do whatever I do, but follow the man in front of you, where ever he goes you go. You'll soon get the hang of it.

Kenneth soon learned that wielding the pike within the division was like a highly choreographed dance, every step precisely placed in coordination with everyone else's, his hands holding the pike so that he could keep it balanced and easy to manoeuvre. By the end of the day, he had mastered the basics of picking up his pike and marching with it without dropping it on the heads of the men around him. The back and breastplate armour he wore rubbed on his shoulders, making them sore and he found its tightness made it hard to breathe, as well as making him hot and sweaty. The metal tassets, which hung down from the bottom of the breastplate to protect his thighs, made it hard for him to bend down and pick up or lay down his pike. By the time he had finished for the day he was hungry, thirsty and more tired than he had ever felt in his life. He had never been a great lover of beer but, right now, he thought he could drink an entire barrel of the brew to himself.

The lodgings he had been given by the sergeant were, in fact, just a barn at the back of an inn. David assured him that this was only temporary and, once they settled somewhere permanent, he would have a proper roof over his head.

'Don't worry about where you're sleeping, it's warm and dry, and that's what counts. The best of it is we are only yards from our food and drink and, now that you are a proper soldier and a guest of this fine establishment, we have nothing to worry about. You see, it's the landlord's duty to feed and water you. Just give the note the sergeant gave you to the landlord, and you can eat and drink for free. The army will reimburse him for your food and lodgings, he'll make a stack of money on the back of that note, you mark my words, he won't go short.'

Kenneth didn't remember returning to the barn that night. He awoke at cock crow with a head feeling like it was being crushed, a mouth so dry he thought he would choke on his tongue, and his belly was so full of liquid he could feel it sloshing about. He tried to get up but only vomited harder than he had ever done before, so hard he pissed himself and, to make it worse, he vomited again. He felt as though someone was driving nails into his head and that he was helpless to stop the torture.

'Come on, Kenneth, my good friend, you'll feel better after some breakfast,' David Seale slapped him on the back before dragging him to his feet. 'It'll soon wear off when we are doing a bit of drill with the sergeant.' Kenneth couldn't believe anyone could feel this ill and live to tell the tale.

Chapter Nine

A line of men streamed into camp the following morning. Mathew and Mortimer watched as junior officers, sergeants and corporals shouted and jostled them into some sort of order. 'There seems to be plenty of keen volunteers in Shrewsbury,' said Mortimer, surprised at the seemingly never-ending supply of new blood wanting to join the army.

'Yes,' said Mathew, 'I think we are going to have another busy day checking this lot over. Start getting them lined up. If you spot anyone obviously too old or infirm, send him home.'

The day seemed to be going well, most of the men being reasonably fit and healthy until that is, Mathew spotted Mortimer passing a man fit after looking into his mouth and not turning him away for having too many rotten teeth. Mathew gave Mortimer a tap on the arm and suggested he look at the man. After checking in the man's mouth, Mathew gave the potential recruit the option of going home or having all his teeth removed if he still wanted to join up. The new recruit opted to stay, saying, 'I know they're all bad, but it won't cost me anything if you do it, and after you've finished, I'll have a job into the bargain.' Mathew smiled at the man's logic and told him to come back later in the day when he'd finished checking this batch of new recruits.

A few hours later the man dutifully returned looking undaunted at the prospect of having all his teeth removed. Mathew prepared an array of dental forceps, tweezers, pelicans, levers and an oral speculum, laying them out neatly on a small table in preparation for the work ahead.

'What is your name?' asked Mathew.

'Jacob Makepeace, Sir.'

'Very well, Jacob, I will need you to sit here,' Mathew indicated to a high backed chair. 'I want you to drink this, it'll help you relax and ease the pain.'

'Thank you, Sir, but I'm not afraid of the pain. My teeth have pained me for years; I'm looking forward to being rid of them.' Mathew smiled at Jacob as he made himself comfortable in the chair.

'You had better drink this anyway; you will find the procedure more painful than you think.' Mathew waited a few minutes for the *laudanum* to take effect before indicating to Mortimer it was time to tie Jacob's head to the back of the chair. Mathew started by inserting the Oral Speculum into Jacob's mouth to hold it open while he extracted the teeth. The device forced his jaw downwards until his jaw could not release its grip on the speculum. With Jacob's mouth held wide open, there was nothing to stop the stench of rotten teeth and infected gums rising up to greet Mathew. He took a step back for a moment, the powerful stink making his stomach heave. After catching his breath and steeling himself to the task, Mathew stepped forward and starting with the teeth at the back of Jacob's mouth set to work. Taking hold of a blackened molar with his forceps, Mathew pushed down hard on the tooth and rocked it from side to side, with a slight roll of the hand the lower left third molar came away from its socket.

'One down, thirty-one to go,' said Mathew confidently.

As Mathew worked he was surprised Jacobs' teeth hadn't fallen out on their own accord, they were coming away so quickly. Having removed the lower molars and premolars, he was about to start on the upper set of teeth when Jacob began to gag and panic, trying to remove the speculum from his mouth. Mathew shouted for Mortimer to hold him still while he loosened the screw on the device which was forcing Jacob's jaws apart. The speculum fell away; Jacob retched and coughed up a great goblet of semi-congealed blood.

'I'm sorry, Jacob I should have given you a chance to spit that out earlier, but your teeth were coming away so easily I got a bit carried away. Here, rinse your mouth with some brandy-wine.'

Mathew rinsed the blood from his instruments and his sticky hands in a bowl of water.

Jacob spat the last of the blood from his mouth and took a good swig of the brandy-wine while Mathew's back was turned.

'I am going to find Franks tonight,' Mathew whispered to Mortimer.

'You're going to what?' exclaimed Mortimer.

'I have to, for my own peace of mind. I can't make any plans for the future until I have settled this matter with Franks: no matter what the outcome might be, it must be finished tonight,' Mathew insisted.

'Then *we* will have to plan our attack very carefully because *you* are not going to last long in a fight with Franks.'

Before Mathew started work on Jacob again, Mortimer dutifully lent over the patient and wiped the blood off his chin. Jacob looked from Mortimer to Mathew, blood, dirt and tears covered the rest of his face. Jacob spat out another clot of blood and opened his mouth for the surgeon to start work again as though what was happening to him was an everyday occurrence.

Mathew finished drying his hands and forceps, exchanging the robust pliers he'd been using to pull Jacob's molars for a smaller set, ready to start on Jacob's incisors.

'Did I ever tell you the secret of removing a tooth?' said Mathew, not waiting for an answer. 'It is to grasp it well, push down hard, rock it from side to side, once, twice and then roll it over to the side, and it comes out as neat as a pea from a pod.' He held up the black and bloody remains of Jacob's left lower canine tooth.

'You tell me that every time you pull a tooth,' said Mortimer.

Jacob stared at the object in question with fascination.

'It doesn't look as bad as the others,' said Jacob. Mathew dropped the tooth in a bucket with the rest of them.

'Eleven left to go,' he informed Jacob. 'You are holding up far better than I ever thought you would. I expected you to feel more pain.'

'Pains not too bad, I expect it's 'cos they were all loose and close to dropping out anyway. One or two did hurt a little bit not so long back,' gurgled Jacob, 'I'm just glad I don't have to have that contraption in my mouth anymore.'

'Fetch that large box over will you, Thomas?' asked Mathew. Mortimer smiled; it always made him feel special when Mathew used his Christian name: it made him feel more like a friend than a servant.

'I want you to lean the back of Jacob's chair against it, so he's leaning backwards, it will make it easier for me to reach the teeth in the top of his mouth. Mathew continued to work until he came to the last tooth; it shattered under the pressure of the forceps while he was preparing to extract it. Jacob winced and spat the broken bits of tooth out. After he had finished rinsing his mouth with brandy-wine, he asked Mathew if he was finished.

'No, not yet, I'm afraid, the remains of that broken tooth still need to be removed. I want you to drink some more of this,' Mathew handed Jacob a small cup of *laudanum*. 'Drink it in one swallow', he ordered. While Jacob was distracted drinking the *laudanum*, Mathew indicated to Mortimer he needed to be ready to take a firm hold of Jacob. Once Mathew had Jacob in the correct position, Mortimer got a firm grip on the patients head. Mathew needed to dig out the roots of the broken tooth with a tooth elevator. It was the only time that Jacob cried out in pain during the whole procedure. Mathew worked as quickly as he could while his patient struggled and kicked, trying to fight his way free, but Mortimer held him fast. With the last of the broken tooth extracted, Jacob began to settle down. Mathew threw the remains of the rotten tooth in the slop bucket and wiped the blood from his hands. Jacob sat in the chair with his hands to his face moaning, blood seeping between his fingers. Mathew handed him a cup of Brandy Wine, 'don't drink it yet. Swill it around your mouth and spit it out. You don't want any puss left behind in the tooth sockets in case it causes an infection,' instructed Mathew.

Jacob did as he was told, then looked up at Mathew, 'hey, that one hurt a bit,' he said, before helping himself to another swallow of brandy.

'Sorry,' said Mathew. 'But if I'd left that bit of root in place it would have caused you pain for the rest of your life.'

After they had finished with Jacob, Mathew and Mortimer went into Shrewsbury to get something to eat and drink, look for the Sextry Tavern and search for John Franks.

'All I want to do this evening is watch him, see what he gets up to and who he associates with; hopefully, I'll find out where he's staying,' said Mathew as they crossed the River Severn.

'And what happens if he sees us watching him? He'll notice us as soon as we sit down. He's sure to get suspicious about what we are up to. He already knows who we are, so how the hell are we going to watch him without him spotting us? demanded Mortimer.

'It doesn't matter if he does see us,' conceded Mathew. 'All we have to do is search the inns and taverns until we find him. We let him see us when we enter: we don't try and hide, that way he'll just think it's a coincidence we are in the same place. It's only if we start acting as though we are trying to hide from him that he'll get suspicious. We will stay in the tavern with him until he leaves and then we will casually follow him. That's going to be the hard part, following him without him seeing us. Once we know where he is lodging, we can plan a trap for him,' said Mathew, beginning to feel confident as he explained his plan.

'I'm not sure it's going to be as easy as that,' said Mortimer.

'Trust me, I've thought it through,' Mathew lied.

The two began their search, looking in every inn, tavern, eatery and alehouse they could find. An hour must have passed while they searched and now they were both getting hungry, tired and irritable.

'Give it up, Mathew, we're not going to find him tonight,' said Mortimer.

'Not yet. I just want to finish searching this along here, then we'll stop and eat,' said Mathew as he doggedly marched on.

Just before they reached the end of the lane, they found the Sextry Tavern, and as soon as Mathew walked through the door he spotted John Franks sitting alone in the back corner. He was smoking a pipe with an empty plate on the table in front of him and a tankard of beer in his fist. Mathew hesitated in the doorway before a gentle shove from Mortimer made him step forward. It was the type of hesitation that drew John Franks' attention, and he watched the two men as they entered and took a table near the door. Mathew sat with his back towards the door, while Mortimer sat opposite him with his back to Franks. As Mathew looked around, he noted that the tavern was busy with royalist officers. It was a little cleaner and better furnished than all the other places they had seen in Shrewsbury, and the smell of food cooking from the kitchen reminded him of the food Ethan prepared for him.

Mathew summoned the landlord as Franks eyed them lazily from the far corner of the taproom. 'A jug of beer, two cups, and two plates of whatever is your best to eat this evening,' said Mathew at the same time trying not to stare at Franks.

'What's he doing?' asked Mortimer after the landlord had left.

'He's just sitting there watching us,' Mathew answered, giving a quick glance in the direction of the back corner.

'He must be doing something,' responded a frustrated and nervous Mortimer. 'Has he noticed us?'

'Yes,' answered Mathew, as he leaned across the table to hiss the words at his companion.

'Well, what do we do?' Mortimer snapped back.

'Nothing, I told you. We sit and have our meal. When Franks leaves, we'll follow him. Until then we stay here and enjoy a drink, the food and some conversation, just like everyone else is doing,' instructed Mathew.

There food and drink arrived, and the pair ate and drank in silence. 'I don't know what to talk about, 'said Mortimer after they'd finished their meal. 'If Potter were here he'd know what to say. There are times when the little bugger won't shut up.'

'You know he won't go anywhere near Franks because Franks thinks he's dead.' Mathew found it hard to resist the desire to keep looking in Franks' direction, he just wanted to stare at the man all the time.

Franks downed the last of his beer, placed his large black hat on his head and rose from his seat. He readjusted the position of his sword hanger and leisurely strode towards Mathew and Mortimer.

Mathew stiffened in his seat, finally staring straight at Franks as he came closer. 'What's happened?' said

Mortimer a little louder than he wanted to on seeing Mathew's expression.

'He's coming over,' said Mathew between clenched teeth. Before Mortimer could respond, Franks sat on the stool next to him and looked directly at Mathew. Mathew's knees began to shake beneath the table and the colour drained from his face. He now found it hard not to stare at the hideous scar on the face in front of him. Franks lent forward placing his elbows on the table, 'you're that surgeon that Mary works for, aren't you?' asked Franks in a deep voice that sounded like it came from a gravel pit.

Mathew swallowed hard, his throat suddenly parched. 'Yes,' he croaked, before clearing his throat.

'Where is she, I want to talk to her,' said Franks.

'We told you last time. Mary, er. She, er, left, decided she'd had enough of all the travelling and went home,' said Mathew, more nervously than he had liked.

'Yes,' said Mortimer. 'As we said, someone had died, at home, so she left.'

Franks lent back a bit. 'I'm looking for two friends of mine. Mary knows them, one with a bad arm wound and the other I've not seen since Nottingham. What did Mary tell you about them?'

'Nothing,' said Mathew.

Franks looked at Mortimer, 'she said nothing to me about them, either,' he said nervously.

'How did Mary get to know you all?' asked Mathew, curious to know why she had never mentioned them and beginning to get a grip on his fear of the man opposite.

Franks eyed him a moment, 'back in Beverley, she helped us. Treated my friend's arm and brought us food. You sure you've not seen them?'

'No,' said Mathew coldly, His mind trying to make sense of what he had just been told. 'But if they turn up, I'll tell them you're looking for them.' He looked Franks in the eye holding his stare. Franks pushed back from the table and stood up, paused a moment then nodded to Mortimer and Mathew before heading for the door.

'What the fuck was that all about?' blurted out Mortimer in great gasps, as though he'd been holding his breath in.

Mathew didn't respond; he was too busy thinking back to the first time Mary had told him about the three men, Beverley Westwood Common, and the death of his brother Charles. *It didn't add up. She had evidently known them for longer than she had at first admitted. Why had she been feeding them? Had they some hold over her? Why hadn't Mary told him about meeting Martins, Wilkes and Franks before? And, if she hadn't told the truth about knowing the three men she knew who had murdered Elizabeth and his brother, what other secrets was she keeping from him? Was she really ill when she left the baggage-train to go home or was that a lie as well? Was Ethan involved in the lies with her? No, no. If anything, she had spun Ethan a story to get him to help her. She is on her way home, how can I get word to them? I must warn them about Mary. Maybe, Major Overton can send word for me; he'll be able to get a letter back to my father.*

'Well; what are we going to do now?' demanded Mortimer, dragging Mathew's thoughts back to the here and now.

Mathew took a swallow of beer, 'we are going to follow Franks and see where he goes.' Mathew quickly got to his feet, keen to be after Franks before they lost him amongst the crowds in the lane. As Mathew and Mortimer emerged from the Sextry Tavern, they spotted the tall, dark figure of Franks further up Candle Lane. Mathew and Mortimer set off after him.

Franks continued walking up the lane, passed Market House then turned right onto the Stales and out of sight. Mathew and Mortimer ran to the top of Candle Lane and peered around the corner of the house, Franks was no more than twenty paces ahead of them. Franks paused, looked back over his shoulder and then carried on walking. Mathew and Mortimer pulled back out of sight, 'did he see us?' asked Mortimer.

'I don't think so,' panted Mathew. Mathew led his partner forward. Keeping their distance, they followed Franks to the corner of the High Street where he turned right again. The busy thoroughfare thronged with people, 'Well have to get closer or we will lose him,' Mathew insisted.

Franks paused again to glance over his shoulder before moving down the street. At St Julian's Church, he turned left on to Fish Street. 'Where the hell is he going?' asked Mortimer.

'He could be going to a secret rendezvous with other royalist spies,' replied Mathew.

Just before he reached St Aulkeman's Church, Franks turned in to a narrow lane. 'That's where the secret meeting must be,' puffed Mathew as they raced along the street to catch up with Franks.

'Wait, it could be a trap. What if he's seen us following him and, he's now waiting down there for us?'

Mathew looked down the short lane. At the end it broadened onto the open ground between the two churches which sat either side of it. In the dim light that escaped from the windows of the buildings that lined the lane, he just caught sight of Franks going around the corner towards St Aulkeman's Church.

'Come on, or we'll lose him,' declared Mathew.

They both dashed down the lane in pursuit, not wanting to let Franks get too far ahead of them.

In the darkness afforded him by Yew trees at the edge of the churchyard, Franks silently drew his sword as he listened to the feet of his pursuers come down the lane after him. As Mathew and Mortimer rounded the last corner, Franks stepped forward.

'Why are you two following me?' he demanded. Mathew and Mortimer staggered back out of reach of his sword. Still panting, both men stared at the sword, transfixed by its deadly spell they were unable to speak. The point of the sword flicked from side to side threateningly as though it was the head of a snake about to strike. 'Well,' demanded Franks. Mathew, his eyes fixed on Franks, knew either he or Franks was going to die in the next few moments. He cleared his throat and took a deep breath.

'Do you remember Elizabeth Moor?' Mathew asked cryptically.

'I've met plenty of women, why should I remember that name?'

'She was the apothecary's daughter you and your friends murdered along with her father in Hull.' Mathew paused, waiting for Franks to think back.

'She was my betrothed,' Mathew continued. 'I have been looking for you ever since. Major Overton, remember him, you or your men killed two of his soldiers outside the block houses in Hull. It was the major who helped me leave Hull during the siege of the town to track you down.'

'So, what are you going to do about it?' sneered Franks.

'I also believe you killed my brother on Beverley Westwood Common and hid his body behind that old cottage.'

'He was your brother; I thought he was just Mary's outraged lover; he shouldn't have come round making demands,' said Franks.

'Now... I'm going to kill you,' Mathew's voice became a little high pitched as the tension of the encounter increased. Franks laughed, sending a shiver down Mathew's spine. Mathew instinctively pulled his knife, as did Mortimer.

Franks laughed again, 'amateurs, you're always the same.'

Mathew hesitated a moment before passing his knife to his left hand. Mathew and Mortimer stood shoulder to shoulder as Franks walked towards them.

'I don't care who you are, or who they were. You die tonight,' Franks drew closer, his sword held out in front of him, the tip of his sword pointing alternatively at Mathew and then Mortimer. The two men backed off a little. With his right hand, Mathew pulled the pistol from beneath his coat, cocking it as he brought it in front of him. Franks stopped advancing at the sight of the gun. At such close range his adversary couldn't miss and, though the pistol was small, at this range it was big enough to kill. Mathew levelled it at his opponent. Mortimer followed suit and removed his pistol from his belt pointing it at Franks.

Franks took another step back, 'you haven't got the balls to pull the trigger; you're nowt but a soppy lad,' he hissed at Mathew. Those were the last words that Franks ever spoke. It was as if someone had cast a spell over Mathew, the words burned in his mind, his vision narrowed to tiny pinpricks; totally focused on Franks, the world around Mathew seemed to slow to a snail's pace, all of Franks' movements seemed to become predictable. Mathew squeezed the trigger of his pistol. He watched as the flint struck the frizzen of his firearm and as the flame and ball erupted from the mussel, each action happening in slow motion. As the bullet hit Franks, the world suddenly jumped back to normal speed. The bullet took Franks on the bridge of the nose creating a neat black hole as the lead projectile took nasal bone into his brain, shredding the grey matter inside as though there had been an explosion inside Franks' head. Franks' head tilted back with the force of the bullet, Mortimer fired his pistol a split second after Mathew had fired, the larger ball hitting Franks in the belly. The heavier ball made Franks' upper body jerk forward. Franks rocked backwards slightly at the impact of Mathew's bullet and then came forward as Mortimer's caught in his midriff. Franks slowly tumbled forwards, his hat somehow staying on his head as he crumpled face down in the gutter; the clatter of his sword deadened by the closeness of the trees and bushes in the churchyard behind him. Mathew, shocked by the realisation of what he had done, dropped his pistol and both he and Mortimer fled.

Once again on Fish Street, the people of Shrewsbury took no notice of the two sweating men emerging from the lane. A pieman called out to passers-by, drunks sang out of tune as they staggered down the street, no one seemed to have noticed that a murder had just been committed only yards away down the alley. A cold sweat covered Mathew's back, and his knees felt like jelly. He retched against the wall, wanting to rid his stomach of the brick he felt lay inside it. Mortimer took him by the arm and tried to lead him on but, for Mathew, the world around him was spinning.

'Come on, Mathew,' Mortimer yelled at him, the voice sounding distant and faint.

Mathew staggered forward, 'I need a drink,' he said barely able to get the words out through his dry mouth, 'I need to sit down and have a drink,' he repeated.

Mortimer dragged him through the door of a tavern and wedged him into a booth seat in the back corner.

'A Bottle of brandy-wine, Landlord!' Mortimer yelled across the taproom.

Mathew emptied the cup of fiery liquid, gulping it down as though his life depended on it. Mortimer filled his cup again, then scanned the taproom for the third time wondering when someone would raise the alarm and come looking for them. Mathew took another gulp of the brandy, nearly choked and coughed most of it across the table.

'What have we done, what have I done?' he hissed between clenched teeth.

'You got your revenge; that's what you've done; that's what you wanted wasn't it?' Mortimer snapped at him.

'Yes, yes – but I didn't think I would feel like this afterwards,' said Mathew.

'How the hell did you think you would feel?' said Mortimer. There was silence between them as they both took large gulps of brandy.

'Think of it this way... Franks and his friends killed Elizabeth, her father and your brother and no telling how many other innocent people over the years. Tonight we gave them justice,' said Mortimer.

Mathew sat shakily for a while thinking about what Mortimer was saying. His words didn't help much. He took another drink, thinking back to what he had done.

'It was the justice I'd promised to bring him, and he deserved what happened. So why do I feel so sorry for it?' he asked Mortimer. Mathew emptied his cup and filled it again, his hands shaking as he did so.

'How many people have you seen die while you were training under Surgeon Adams?' asked Mortimer.

'I don't know, lots,' answered Mathew. 'But we were trying to help those people.'

'Did Surgeon Adams ever turn anyone away; someone who he knew he couldn't help? asked Mortimer.

'Yes – some, but they were going to die no matter what Surgeon Adams would have done,' said Mathew.

'Ah, yes – but what if Surgeon Adams had tried harder, examined those patients more thoroughly, maybe he could have saved them instead of condemning them to certain death. Wasn't that a form of murder?' said Mortimer.

'Yes, maybe – no, he may have brought about their deaths sooner had he tried to treat them and be blamed for their deaths instead of trying to save them,' said Mathew.

Mortimer thought for a moment. 'Have you or Surgeon Adams ever had to cut away bad flesh to stop gangrene infecting clean parts of a wound, doing it to save a patient?' asked Mortimer.

'Yes, many times,' answered Mathew.

'Well, we have just done what Surgeon Adams would have done. We have removed a gangrene from the world, only this time we don't know the names of the people we have saved from the likes of Franks and his friends. Think of it that way,' Mortimer emptied his cup. 'Now come on and let's get away from here, we've stayed too long already.'

Chapter Ten

Not far from Shrewsbury Castle the king called a meeting at his residence in the Council House.

'Loyal men continue to stream into Shrewsbury from Lancashire, Chester and Wales, Your Highness. The army is growing so quickly we are struggling to supply the men with arms and armour, there are food shortages, and we are running out of places to billet the new recruits,' Sir William Dugdale informed his King. The king smiled and called for his nephew, Prince Rupert, to draw closer.

'It seems the time has come for us to leave this place and take our fight to the Parliament. Our good nephew here, who I know to be keen to show his metal, shall prepare the way. You will take your horse regiment down to Worcester and make a great show of it. Lord Essex, we have learned, is heading west from Northampton with an army of his own to confront us. He is green in the arts of battle and has much to learn in the art of conducting warfare. Draw him towards

Worcester, but take care, Nephew, none of your rashness now. You are to encourage Lord Essex westward, not try and defeat his army all by yourself. Your purpose is to allow your King a clear passage to Oxford. Once we receive word that Lord Essex has taken the bait, we shall leave this place and meet you again at Banbury, after which we will proceed to Oxford.'

Prince Rupert bowed before the king, 'Sire, I will lead Essex a merry dance until his head spins like a young maiden at her first dance.' A ripple of laughter circled the chamber.

Later that evening as Prince Rupert's men frequented the taverns of Shrewsbury, they made jolly with the news of their departure for Worcester in the morning, and how the king would capture the town with his mighty new army. Mathew, Mortimer and Potter listened intently to the boasting of Prince Rupert's officers.

'We must get word to Major Overton' suggested Mortimer in a hushed voice.

'Then we need to get back to camp, so I can cypher a message to send to the major. Come on, let's go, we don't have much time,' said Mathew. Potter was about to say something but stopped himself and followed his companions to the tavern door. It was as they walked back to camp that Potter voiced what he had been thinking. 'This news doesn't sit right with me.'

'What do you mean?' asked Mathew.

'If the king is planning to make an attack on Worcester, why hasn't the rest of the army been made ready to strike camp?' responded Potter.

'Umm; I hadn't thought of that. But we still have to inform Major Overton of the king's plans,' interrupted Mortimer. 'We can't take the chance the intelligence is wrong.' Mathew stopped walking and looked at his two friends.

'The problem is, either one of you could be right, but something is happening, and it's the major who will have to decide what he does with the news, not us,' Mathew corrected them both.

Back at the camp, the order had been given, and preparations begun for leaving Shrewsbury. As they approached the field, the guards confirmed the orders that Mathew was to prepare to break camp.

'It looks like the rumours are true,' Mortimer said to Potter.

'We'd better hurry,' said Mathew.

'Do you think that Major Overton will be aware of what is going on? asked Potter.

'I can't take the chance that the major is close enough to be aware of what is happening, but I know he will be at the Abbey in the morning, waiting for any news we may have for him,' said Mathew. 'Mortimer can take him a note about what we know for sure.'

It was close to midnight by the time they had everything packed on the wagon.

'Try and get a few hours sleep,' said Mathew, 'we won't be leaving before daybreak. I'm going to cypher the letter, and you can deliver it to Major Overton in the morning before we leave.

It was early morning when Prince Rupert led his men southeast from Shrewsbury. The day was overcast and threatened rain, but the ebullient prince rode ahead of his men with confidence. The day passed uneventfully, they made good time to Kidderminster where they spent the night. They arrived at Worcester late the following morning. With no sign of any organised resistance, Prince Rupert led his men into town. For the most part, the locals welcomed the prince and his men. Prince Maurice, Prince Rupert's younger brother, cautioned him about the risk he was taking in having a regiment of cavalry trapped in the town, where it would be unable to fight effectively if they were attacked, but Rupert was having none of it.

'The town is ripe for the taking, and I shall not deny my men the luxury of a warm bed and wench for the night,' said Rupert. That night, Prince Rupert and his men enjoyed the delights of Worcester, though Prince Maurice did send out patrols to guard against a surprise attack from any enemy forces that might be in the area. It was while Prince Rupert was enjoying the hospitality of the town's taverns and inns that word arrived of a small train of wagons which had got lost en-route from Oxford to Shrewsbury. Prince Maurice had learned that it was carrying silver plate collected from the University of Oxford on behalf of the king. The small

Oxford baggage-train was camped on the southern edge of Worcester, unsure if it was safe to enter the town. On hearing the news, Rupert jumped to his feet deciding he must escort the prized baggage-train into town himself and bring it under his safe keeping. By the time the prince had roused enough men the first hints of daylight were beginning to herald a new day. All was going well with Prince Rupert's plan until his cavalry reached Powick Bridge, where they met a scouting party from the Earl of Essex's army encamped close by and blocking the road to the university baggage-train. Prince Rupert didn't waste a minute; he needed to be across the bridge and reach the baggage train before the Parliamentarians discovered it. With Rhineland Prince at its head, the royalist charged across the bridge and attacked Lord Essex's men before they knew what had hit them. The Parliamentarian's were caught completely unprepared as Prince Rupert's men swept through their camp slashing and cutting with their swords. The prince brought his cavalry to order after their first pass at the enemy, and in less than a minute was ready for a second charge. The Parliamentarian's were still mounting their horses and were in such disarray when the second attack came that they could only manage to put up a feeble defence as the royalist men fell upon them once again. The Parliamentarian scouting party were utterly routed and fled with Prince Rupert and his men chasing after them howling for their blood. Knowing full well that Lord Essex would now march on Worcester, and the importance of the silver laden baggage-train to the king, Prince Rupert cut short his pursuit of the enemy. The triumphant Prince found the university baggage-train safe and sound a few miles further down the road.

At first light, the Shrewsbury baggage-train was ready to leave.

'It's time to say farewell, James. Have you made up your mind yet, are you going home or back to school? asked Mathew.

'I think I will go back to school, Sir. It is what my father would want me to do. Now Mr Clayton has gone, and Mr Potter still has the headmaster's account book, I have nothing to fear. Thank you for helping me, Sir. I'll be going now. James thanked his friends for everything they had done for him, leaving Potter till last. The two spent a few minutes talking until Potter gave James a deck of cards as a parting gift.

'Remember what I taught you,' called Potter as the lad walked away.

Potter climbed aboard the wagon just as a trooper rode up and told them to stand-down and await further orders. They were staying put for the time being.

'This can't be true,' protested Mathew.

'Oh yes it can,' said Potter. 'Either word has arrived telling the king a Parliamentarian army is on its way, or the move to Worcester has all been a big deception.'

'Which do you think it is?' asked Mathew.

'There's no way to know just yet, we'll just have to wait and see,' said Potter.

For two days the Shrewsbury baggage-train was kept waiting. Some of the wagon drivers began to rebuild their camps; others grumbled and complained to the army officers. But all the while more and more soldiers began to appear along the old Roman road outside the Abbey.

After two days Kenneth Clayton and David Seale, kitted out in back and breastplate, and carrying a pike each, were amongst those in one of the first companies to assemble on the old Roman road to London. On that last morning, Mortimer came running out of the Abbey to join Mathew and Potter as their wagon, already on the move, was about to enter the column on the road.

'The major wasn't there this morning,' gasped Mortimer. 'Major Overton must have left for Worcester after I gave him the last message telling him we were about to leave. He doesn't know we have been delayed.'

'I'm sure the major will be able to solve that problem for himself,' tutted Potter. Mortimer glared at him realising he might have overreacted at not finding the major where he had expected to.

'That's enough you two, we don't know how long we are going to be stuck on this wagon so save your fights till later,' interceded Mathew, before a war of words broke out between his companions. Before they had come to the end of the first day's journey from Shrewsbury, Mathew realised they were not heading south towards Worcester, but southeast, which he could only surmise to mean they were heading back into the heart of the English Midlands.

'We're not heading towards Worcester,' he said to Mortimer as he drove the wagon through a shallow stream.

'Are you sure?' asked Mortimer.

'He's right,' confirmed Potter. 'Look here on this map I got from the school. There's another road out of Shrewsbury that would have taken us south if we were going to Worcester. But the villages we have passed through indicate we are heading in a more easterly direction. I think the word that went around yesterday about us all going to Worcester, was a distraction. I can only guess the king is being careful or, may even fear that Parliament has spies within his retinue. But whatever his plans may be, we are not going to Worcester. I think we may be going back to try and capture Coventry again.' Mortimer and Mathew looked at each other.

'No, surely not,' exclaimed Mathew.

'You must admit it's possible,' Potter attested. 'We have a much larger army now.'

'But it means the information I provided the major with was completely wrong; Parliament will be sending their men in the wrong direction. What will happen when Major Overton finds out? He may think I did it deliberately; he'll think that we've changed sides or something,' panicked Mathew.

'No they won't,' said Potter dismissively, 'they know how the games of misinformation and deception are played; that's what politicians spend most of their time doing at Westminster. That is when they are not trying to find ways of feathering their own nests. We won't be the only people spying for Parliament; they will be receiving information from lots of sources. No, so long as we don't make a habit of it, they will just check the evidence of what we say more carefully in the future. That's if they believed what you told them in the first place. As I say, you won't be the only spy they have following the king.'

Mathew relaxed a little, 'I suppose you are right, you've been doing this kind of thing far longer than we have.'

Potter smiled, 'just a little.'

'As soon as we can, we must get word to Major Overton and inform him of our new direction of travel,' said Mathew. 'Each morning before we set off I'd like you to pay a visit to the local church, Charles, and see if the major has caught up with us yet. Judging from your map our next stop will be Bridgenorth. I've had a thought, you're good with cards,' Mathew looked meaningfully at Potter, 'I think you should engage some of the soldiers in a game or two, but I want you to lose. I want you to gain their confidence and find out where we are really heading.'

'You want me to lose,' protested Potter, 'you forget whose money it is, you are being free with.'

'Stop complaining, you've had plenty of free food and beer provided by Mathew,' countered Mortimer. 'And I suspect you'll soon win it all back.'

'Stop it, you two. If we need more money, I'll ask Major Overton to supply us with more. In the meantime you will do as I ask,' said Mathew.

That night the baggage-train stopped outside Bridgenorth and Potter managed to talk his way into a game of cards with a group of soldiers, playing and losing for a couple of hours before giving up. It seemed the soldiers were as mystified about their final destination as Mathew was. It took two more nights of playing cards with the soldiers before Potter was able to get into a game with a few junior officers. It was one of them that let slip that he was looking forward to seeing his family again when they finally arrived in Oxford. For the next few days, the king's slow-moving wagons by-passed Wolverhampton and Birmingham, travelling unmolested by Parliament's troops who were looking in the wrong direction. The king's diversionary tactics seeming to have worked; the baggage-train continued southeast. Sergeants and officers recruiting more men from each town and village they passed through.

'It would seem we have outwitted the Earl of Essex, My Lord Newcastle, we always did consider him a dull fellow,' boasted the king.

'Yes indeed, Your Majesty, your plan to send Prince Rupert to Worcester was a good one,' agreed Newcastle. 'And once we reach Oxford we will be able to formulate a strategy on how to retake London.

'Having a plan is all very well, Newcastle, but no matter how well formed it may be, its success is dependent on all the parts working together as they should. We have put our faith in the Queen and the Dutch. Our plans will work if our foreign allies do their bit.' The king gave Lord Newcastle a questioning stare.

'I am sure they will. Your Majesty has offered the Dutch a great deal in return for their help. I am sure they will see the advantages you have offered to them in return for shipments of arms and blockading the Thames ports. If they are able to prevent food and trade entering London, Parliament will be forced to negotiate with his Majesty. The Dutch have been after greater trade concessions through the English Channel for many years, and the concessions you have offered them are more than generous. Once the citizens of London have felt the bite of hungry bellies for a week or two, they will march on Westminster and demand the return of their King,' said Newcastle enthusiastically. Your Majesty's forces will be able to march to Westminster and force Parliament's surrender while Lord Essex is still blundering around in the Midlands,' continued Newcastle.

'You may be correct, Newcastle, but my navy is loyal to Parliament and will go to the rescue of London. What will happen then?'

'The navy already has a great deal to occupy itself with, and they cannot be in all places at the same time. If they take on the Dutch in the Thames, they must give up their blockades on ports loyal to the crown, thus leaving the way open for Your Majesty to receive support from abroad. If they leave the Dutch to blockade London, it will fall in a matter of weeks. Either way, Your Majesty will win,' said Newcastle.

'One must hope the Queen is as optimistic and persuasive as you are Newcastle.'

'Your Majesty, we will be arriving at Kenilworth shortly. Then, in a couple of days, we will be in Oxford and safe from Lord Essex. Once we arrive at Kenilworth, we must start making preparations to ensure the security of Oxford.'

At Kenilworth Castle, later that night, the king, Lord Newcastle and the generals of The King's Army made plans for their approach to Oxford.

'In two or three days at the most, My Lords, we will be in Oxford, from where we will conduct our business in such a way that we will bring the rebels to our door begging for forgiveness,' said the king. A murmur of approval went around the chamber.

'I propose a ring of steel around Oxford, Your Majesty, in that we fortify all the great houses and towns which surround Oxford, making the country around your new capital impenetrable to parliamentary forces,' suggested Lord Newcastle. 'Each town or house will be able to offer assistance to its neighbour should it come under attack, and Your Majesty will be able to send reinforcements from Oxford should they be needed.'

'An excellent plan, My Lord Newcastle, now that we have that settled, let us enjoy the hospitality of our host, Lord Monmouth. Tomorrow we will make haste to Oxford.

The following morning, the king made a great fanfare of his departure from Kenilworth Castle as he led his lords through the castle gates and out of the town in the direction of Southam.

A lone rider entered Kenilworth from the west, his horse all a lather and panting hard from a long nights tiring ride. He pulled up, slowing to a walk as he drew alongside Colonel Duncombe. The colonel read the note he was handed before passing it on to Lord Newcastle.

'Your Majesty, it seems Lord Essex is no longer at Worcester but is on his way towards Oxford. If he should beat us there, all our plans will be for nothing, and we will be unable to retake London.'

'Then, My Lord Newcastle, we must stop him. We will prevent him from reaching Oxford ahead of our army. It would seem, Newcastle, our new army is to be tested sooner rather than later. We will head south as fast as we can and beat him to the prize,' ordered the king confidently.

'I agree, it is time to act boldly, Your Majesty. We should separate the fast from the slow in our approach to Oxford. With the extra wagons that Prince Rupert brought us, the baggage-train is now so large that it slows down our advance,' advised Lord Newcastle. 'I would suggest, Your Majesty, take his main force south towards Stratford-Upon-Avon, then turn south-east towards Banbury. A smaller force, with the slowest wagons of the baggage-train, should go via a more northerly route towards Southam and Northampton, by-passing Warwick before turning south on the Banbury Road towards Oxford. If we split our force, Lord Brooke will not have enough men to guard both routes. His priority will be to support and join up with Lord Essex as soon as possible; his eyes will be turned south not north. Once we have dealt with Lord Essex, we can reunite with the baggage-train at Banbury and continue on to Oxford.' The king gave the matter some thought.

Other officers around the king overheard Lord Newcastle's advice and disagreed.

'If I may be allowed to say, Your Majesty, I suggest you keep the army together in case of a surprise attack by Lord Essex,' suggested Lord Verney. He received a number of consensual nods of approval from the majority of the attending generals.

'No, no, no, My Lord Verney, Lord Essex will be making as much speed from Worcester as he can. If he has surmised our destination is Oxford, he will do all in his power to beat us there. The man is no great strategist; he will naturally try to cut us off from our destination. We are ahead of him now; we must use that to our advantage. We will go south until we are between Lord Essex and Oxford and find a suitable location on which to stand and force him to confront us. That is where we shall do battle and show these rebels the cost of turning against their King.'

The baggage-train continued its journey from Kenilworth as it had been directed. With it went one regiment of horse and two regiments of foot, all taking the more northerly route around Warwick towards Southam and Northampton. The king, the artillery-train and the rest of the army set off in a southerly direction towards Stratford-upon-Avon, determined to cut off Lord Essex's advance on Oxford. In advance of the king, Prince Rupert went in search of Lord Essex's army. Shortly after leaving Kenilworth the two contingents of The King's Army separated.

The Southam bound detachment had been placed under the command of Sir Nicholas Byron, who sent his horse regiment on ahead to ensure the route to Southam was clear of parliamentarian scouting parties from Warwick Castle. They were followed by two regiments of foot with orders to secure each village through which the baggage-train would pass, leaving only a single company of dragoons to guard the baggage-train as it travelled through the countryside. The route chosen was a well-used drover's road which ran from Kenilworth to Southam.

It wasn't long before the foot regiments outpaced the lumbering slower wagons of the train. By midday, the horse regiment was on the outskirts of Southam where they stopped to rest. They had met no resistance from the Parliamentarians and prepared to enter and capture Southam. The foot regiments had made it to the River Leam near Offchurch by noon, well ahead of the baggage-train which was still struggling along the rutted drover's trail, impeded by heavy loads and by midday had only reached the village of Cubbington, perilously close to Warwick.

Chapter Eleven

The drover's trail to Southam was lined with high, thick hedges to ensure livestock, being driven to a neighbouring town, couldn't escape into the fields either side of the road, and not made for the heavy wagons that now traversed it. The main roads were too dangerous for the baggage-train and small force to use as they ran too close to Lord Brooke's home at Warwick Castle. So it had to be the drover's trail for the king's supplies and its escort.

As the baggage-train crested a gentle hill, common in these parts of the English Midlands, in the distance Mathew spotted riders on an adjacent hilltop, watching the progression of the slow-moving wagons.

'Friendly, or not so friendly?' Mathew asked Mortimer, not sure if he wanted to hear the answer.

'Hard to tell from here,' Mortimer observed.

'We'll know soon enough,' remarked Potter. The three men stared into the distance along with all the other members of the baggage-train. Two troopers galloped past their wagon heading to the front of the column.

'I guess they're wondering the same thing the rest of us are,' added Mathew. He gave the reins a quick flick to encourage the horse to pull a little harder as one wheel dropped into a particularly large pothole. Try as he might to concentrate on avoiding the worst of the potholes, he found it hard to keep his eye on where they were going, his attention drawn continuously to the silhouettes on the hilltop.

'It can only be the king's baggage-train, Sir,' said the trooper to the officer by his side.

'Well done, Sergeant, we will return to Warwick and inform the colonel of what we have found. Leave three troopers behind to keep watch on their progress. Once they stop for the night and have made camp for the night, one of the troopers is to return to the castle to inform us of the royalist's location and direct our return to it in the morning. I have no doubt that Lord Brooke will be pleased with our find.'

The small troop of riders galloped into the courtyard at Warwick Castle, pulling to an abrupt halt outside the castle gatehouse. The young officer jumped down from his horse and marched urgently inside the main building and into the hall. He found Captain John Bridges talking to Lord Brooke, colonel of the Warwick Castle garrison; removing his hat, he strode boldly up to them. 'Sir, I beg you to forgive my intrusion, but I have important intelligence to report.'

The captain and Lord Brooke listened intently to the young officer's report on the movement of the king's wagons.

'Captain, equip two troop of horse for tomorrow morning. I want you to capture and bring that baggage-train back to Warwick. I will be going to search for the main contingent of the king's army; I have had reports that it is making its way towards Stratford-upon-Avon. It is imperative that Lord Essex receives the new intelligence of the king's new direction and possible location,' ordered Lord Brooke. We can't afford for Lord Essex to be miss-informed on the king's whereabouts again.

That evening, a trooper rode through the castle gate of Warwick Castle to report to his sergeant the location at which the royalists had stopped for the night.

All the rest of that day, Mathew's wagon made painfully slow progress from the village of Cubbington towards Southam. The well-used drover's road did its best to hinder the progress of the baggage-train. The wagons became bogged down in the rain-filled potholes, breaking axles and wheels on hidden rocks in muddy ruts, the threat of a surprise attack from the hilltops around them, a constant menace, clawing at the nerves of everyone who was trapped on a road with no turn-offs and nowhere to hide. Fear drove them on but, by nightfall, they found themselves far behind the main body of their escort. Breaking through the hedge that lined the road, the baggage-train pulled into a field near Offchurch and made camp for the night. For

Mathew and his friends, no matter how hard they tried to find other things to talk about, the conversation kept coming back to being attacked by the parliamentarian soldiers from Warwick Castle. Mathew tried to keep Mortimer and Potter cheerful and positive,

'Remember the soldiers ahead of us are making sure the road to Southam and Banbury are safe road us all. Once we reach Southam, it's not much further to Banbury, where we will join up with the rest of the army. Then it's just a short journey to Oxford.'

'I hope you are tight. But I prefer it when we have a nice friendly town near-by,' countered Potter.' They slept fitfully that night, any sudden or unexpected sound making them sit up and listen, staring into the darkness in alarm for enemy soldiers.

Early next morning Mathew and his two friends set off once again. Tonight, Mathew reminded Mortimer and Potter, with luck, they would be safe in Southam. Their expectations for the day rose as the day, though cold, dawned bright and dry. The dragoon escort rallied everyone's spirit with reports that there was no sign of an enemy between them and Southam and that very soon the condition of the road ahead of them improved and they would be able to make better headway.

Long before the sun had risen, Captain Bridges led his troopers and musketeers out of Warwick Castle towards the village of Radford Semele on the main Southam Road.

Sergeant Stephen Baker knew how to motivate his men in the cold, dark early hours before morning as they marched along the country lanes after leaving Warwick. 'Sing up lads; give us a song to cheer our hearts.' Slowly at first, the tired men broke into song as they made their way east towards Radford Semele. Their pace quickened when they were promised food and rest when they reached the village. They had been given orders to get ahead of the wagons, their job to deal with any royalist attack that might come from the direction of Southam.

Captain Bridges and his cavalry followed the trooper guide to the site of the baggage-train night camp at Cubbington, but they had gone.

On reaching the village, Captain Bridges separated his troopers into two squadrons. They would follow the drover's road east towards Southam searching for the baggage-train. One squadron would stay north of the drover's road, the other to the south. When they found the royalist train, they were to attack the royalist troopers escorting it from both north and south at the same time. Their job now was to locate the wagon-train and engage its escort, leaving the wagons defenceless for the foot soldiers to intercept.

The sky had begun to lighten as it turned from an inky black, dotted with stars, to a pale grey, as Lieutenant Troutbridge and the newly promoted Sergeant Baker led their company of musketeers along the country lanes. Just before the orb of the sun rose above the horizon, its rays of golden yellow fanned out across the landscape to welcome the new day. Birds were singing sweetly in the trees and, with the coming of the bright morning, the fear of what lay ahead of them diminished.

Captain Bridges sent two riders ahead to find the baggage-train. The scouting party soon found the tail end of it, deciding to keep their distance, by-passing the wagons to ascertain the whereabouts of the Warwick foot soldiers before galloping back to Captain Bridges.

'We have located the baggage-train, Sir, not much more than a mile ahead and still this side of the Fosse Way. Lieutenant Troutbridge and his men are just ahead of the royalists and should arrive at the Fosse way crossroads before they do.

'Return to your squadron,' ordered Captain Bridges, 'and lead them to the location of the royalists, inform your officer he is to stay on the northern side of the Welsh Road. He is not to let the baggage-train leave the drover's road, I want to trap it when it is at its most vulnerable, on the road to Southam, with no space or opportunity to put up a defence. The corporal sped back to his commanding officer to give him the plan of attack. Captain Bridges led his troopers through the fields on the southern side of the Welsh Road. Hampered by the hedgerows, progress was slower than he had hoped, but the captain was in no rush, he wanted to attack his enemy in broad daylight and not risk his men in the confusion of battle before the sun was well above the horizon.

The sun began to rise above the treetops, the air was still cool as the sun warmed the faces of the troopers while they rode across the fields. Captain Bridges was the first to catch sight of the tail end of the baggage-train and gave the order to his cornet to sound the attack. Giving their horses full rein, the troopers drew their swords and started the charge. Unfortunately for them, the open pasture land which now gave them the ease with which to charge the enemy, also allowed the royalist dragoons escorting the wagons ample time to hear and to see them coming. The royalist troopers wheeled about their horses and made their own charge towards the parliamentarians.

The sun was shining brightly over the trees and from behind the low hills when the attack started in the dazzling clear dawn. On this beautiful September morning, the sun was shining in the faces of the parliamentarian troopers as they charged across the open ground towards their prey. The royalist dragoons had the sun on their backs as they surged forward. As the parliamentarian troopers advanced, their line opened as they raced ahead across the field to engage the enemy. The royalist dragoons, though a much smaller force, drew much closer together forming a wedge. As the two opposing forces met on the open pasture of this sun drench countryside, the royalist dragoons scythed through the parliamentarian troopers, hacking many from their mounts and wounding an unknown number of others. By the time the dragoons slowed their horses and turned to face the enemy once again, the parliamentarian troopers had been split into two groups with lots of stragglers scattered across the open field. Riderless horses bolted in all directions, leaving wounded and dying troopers lying in the mud where the two forces had met in their deadly charge. Rallying his men, the royalist lieutenant urged his dragoons into another charge, heading diagonally across the field at the smaller of the two parliamentarian forces which were still in total disarray after their blooding from the royalist charge. As soon as they spotted the dragoons charging towards them, they bolted towards their only means of escape from the open pasture, a gap in the hedge on the Southam side of the grazing land. The lieutenant of dragoons, embolden by the fleeing Parliamentarians, chased them through the hole in the hedge, but only managed to bring down one trooper at the rear of the fleeing troopers. The dragoon lieutenant gave up the chase and brought his men to a halt, ordering them to dismount and load their carbines. Forming up in two ranks, the dragoons turned to face the larger Parliamentarian force of troopers which was now charging towards them from the Warwick end of the pasture. The royalist dragoons drew back the cocks on their carbines ready to fire.

'Front rank, kneel,' ordered the lieutenant, 'present,' quickly came the second order, the dragoons levelled their carbines, waiting for the order to fire. The parliamentarian troopers came on at full gallop, their swords glinting in the early morning sunlight, the sound of their horse's hooves thundering across the field as they closed more tightly together to focus their revenge on the small group of royalist dragoons blocking their path.

'Fire!' cried the lieutenant, his voice taut with emotion as the parliamentarian charge was almost upon them. All the dragoons fired in unison, each carbine slamming into the shoulder of the man who squeezed the trigger. Ball, fire and smoke erupted from the barrels of the carbines into the face of the oncoming charge. The Parliamentarian horses halted as though they had run into a brick wall, the horses refusing to go further forward into the maelstrom of hot lead, fire and smoke. Parliamentarian riders were flung from their mounts, horses and men fell to die in the mud; their bodies rent open by the heavy lead balls fired by the royalist dragoons. As the smoke began to clear, the royalist lieutenant ordered his men to reload their carbines. They turned to face their first enemy, which had escaped them through the gap the hedge they now defended, only to see the parliamentarian troopers had reformed into a cohesive force and were charging toward the hole in the hedge. There was no time to finish reloading as the Parliamentarians ploughed their horses through the gap and the royalist dragoons defending it. The parliamentarian Troopers took their revenge on the royalists, slashing down hard with their swords to cut through the lightly armoured dragoons, severing arms, cutting through the flesh and bone into the shoulders and necks of the soldiers. After one pass they had wreaked their destruction on the royalist defenders, as all but three men lay dead or wounded. The three survivors throwing down their weapons, kneeling with their heads bowed and their hands behind their heads in a posture of surrender.

Panic broke out amongst the people in the baggage-train. Women screaming, children crying as they all quickly became aware that their progress along the road had come to a halt and that they were under attack. Mathew, Mortimer and Potter stood on the wagon seat trying to get a better view of what was going on around them. Two dragoons rode past ordering them to sit down and be ready to move on as soon as the road was declared clear, just before they disappeared through a small gap in the hedge on the northern side of the road.

To the south of the road, the people of the wagon-train had watched their military escort engage the parliamentarian troopers and cheered as the dragoons split their attackers, causing the Parliamentarians to scatter in disarray across the pasture. But to the north of the road, their vision of the unfolding events on that side was hampered by the thick hedge and trees. They could hear short bursts of gunfire and the occasional clash of steel, but no one could get a clear view of how the battle was unfolding.

Before the people trapped on the road realised what was happening, parliamentarian soldiers came running along the road, one stopping at each wagon and ordering the occupants to climb down. At first, there was confusion and fear amongst the wagoneers as the Parliamentarians ordered men and women off the wagons. While Mathew, Mortimer and Potter stood next to their wagon under threat from a loaded Parliamentarian musket, they could see a knot of men coming down the road, stopping at each wagon and searching through its contents. Time seemed to pass slowly as the parliamentarian soldiers made their way towards them. The soldier guarding them refused to speak to Mathew when he asked what was to become of them, and threatened him into silence. Mathew thought about home and how he wished he had left Shrewsbury after shooting Franks, but it was too late now. He cursed himself for his foolishness. Why had he believed that staying with the army would be of any use in getting closer to home, now it seemed he would never be able to go back to Beverley and his family. He would never be able to question Mary about her knowledge of Franks, Wilkes and Martins? He'd never get to enjoy the king's court again and learn new medical skills. He had made so many mistakes; he should have stayed home and let Major Overton find Franks, Wilkes and Martins.

Eventually, the searchers reached Mathew's wagon. A sergeant asked who it belonged to and Mathew stepped forward. The sergeant ordered Mortimer and Potter to start unloading boxes from the back of the wagon, two soldiers examining their contents. 'I am a surgeon,' Mathew volunteered to the sergeant, 'and these are my assistants,' Mathew waved his arm in the direction of Mortimer and Potter. The sergeant scribbled a note on a scruffy piece of paper before pushing his hat back on his head and staring at Mathew. 'I know you,' said the sergeant,' you're that surgeon that went to Nuneaton to help the people when the town was on fire.'

Mathew recognised the face of the jovial soldier they had met on the road after leaving Coventry, 'Stephen Baker, yes, we met many weeks ago, I'm surprised you remember me.'

'Oh yes. Word of the good work you did that night soon travelled far and wide. The Good Samaritan from the royalist baggage-train is what they calls you in Nuneaton. I'd like to shake you by the hand, My Friend. Mathew duly obliged the sergeant.

'Right you lot, put that stuff back on the wagon and you two', indicating to the two soldiers who had been quite happy ripping open boxes and bags and scattering their contents, 'can help them,' ordered the sergeant. Turning to the soldier guarding the wagon, 'you are to stay here as the officer ordered, but you treat my friends with the utmost respect, or when we get back to Warwick Castle, I'll teach you what the word means, is that understood?' instructed Sergeant Baker. 'I'm sorry for their behaviour, Surgeon. They haven't seen any real fighting yet but, they learn about it soon enough and then most of them will wish they were back home with their mothers.'

While parliamentarian soldiers raided the baggage-train on the road and troopers on the southern side of the Welsh Road finished off or captured the remaining

Royalist Dragoons, Captain Bridges led his northern squadron forward only to be hampered by smaller fields and hedges. To make matters worse, the hedge running alongside the road was thick and impenetrable except for where small gaps had been cut for field access. The royalist dragoons on the road, having seen half their number go off in pursuit of the enemy to the south, turned and engaged Captains Bridges squadron, closing on them from the northern side of the road. But they, too, found it just as difficult to get men through the hedge and off the road to meet the oncoming attack. With the weight of numbers on his side, Captain Bridges was quickly able to make short work of the dragoons who did make it through the narrow gaps in the hedge. The royalist dragoons were unable to form up in large enough numbers to mount an effective attack on the Warwick troopers before they were captured or killed. With little resistance on his side of the road, Captain Bridges made his way across the fields to join up with Lieutenant Troutbridge in charge of the Musketeers holding the road. 'Is everything under control here, Lieutenant?' asked the captain.

'Yes Sir, your plan worked perfectly. I am pleased to report that we have discovered a great quantity of gold and silver plate along with many chests of coin in some of the wagons. It would seem the king has been careless with his valuables, Sir.'

'Show me, Lieutenant; Lord Brooke will be delighted with such a haul. I trust you have it well guarded?' Captain Bridges positively beamed at the news of capturing such riches.

As the day was coming to a close, a triumphant Captain Bridges led the captured royalist wagons over the moat and through the Barbican of Warwick Castle. Mathew looked down into the dry moat. He had expected it to be full of water. To his left, he caught a glimpse of the River Avon at the end of a lane slopping down to the river's edge.

The wagons were parked in the centre of the courtyard and the horses put out to pasture, the arrested members of the baggage-train were separated into two groups: the soldiers were imprisoned in the dungeon of Caesar's Tower, it having been built as a gaol many years before, and the civilian prisoners, who were put in Guy's Tower. The friendly sergeant Mathew had met when the baggage-train was captured was nowhere in sight when Mathew, Mortimer and Potter were pushed up the steps of Guy's Tower to a chamber which was to become their prison. Every chamber on every floor of Guy's Tower was full of people, with barely enough floor space to sit and stretch-out their legs. Men and women shared the same prison with only a single slop bucket in each chamber. The noise was deafening with men squabbling and women and children crying. No food or water had yet been provided, and it wasn't long before the heat from all the people crammed into one small chamber soon made the place hot and stuffy. Though there was one, small, glassed window, it did not open. The once elegant chamber that should have been for visiting guests had been stripped bare to accommodate the unwelcome arrivals.

Captain Bridges ordered the wagons containing the king's treasure to be guarded as it was unloaded. Word of the haul would soon be common knowledge in Warwick and would attract many a ne'er-do-well with hopes and dreams of easy riches to be made. Silver and gold plate, sacks of coins and caskets of jewels were transferred to the cellars below the Great Hall. With the king's riches stored safely below the Great Hall, before the door to the cell was locked, Captain Bridges stood in the open doorway and marvelled at the sight in front of him. He found it hard to imagine that there had been this much amount of gold, silver and jewels in the king's possession. He slowly closed the cell door and locked it, pocketing the key. He left one man on guard at the entrance of the cell with orders that he would be relieved in two hours, that no one was to enter the cell in which the treasure was stored and that he would be the only one to take charge of the key. Very quickly, rumours of the king's treasure spread around the castle garrison and speculation mounted as to its value and what would happen to it.

After two nights locked in the tower room, Mathew was beginning to wonder if they would ever get out or if they would all be incarcerated forever, it already felt like Hell. Water was passed into the cell regularly, but food only once a day. The mad scramble for it on the first day caused the delivery bucket to be dropped and all the liquid from the meagre stew to disappear between the floorboards, leaving everyone some stale bread and a few scraps left on the floor. There was nothing to do all day, people tried to sleep or took it turns looking through the narrow window. The women alternated between bickering with their men, demanding that they do something to get them set free or just sitting and sobbing with despair at being locked into the cramped room. Children constantly cried, with no place to play and the fear of being locked in the strange tower, they were causing more arguments between the prisoners than anything else. In the tower chambers above and below them, they could hear the voices and movement of more prisoners. With the constant noise, it was hard to sleep in the cramped conditions, and the smell from the slop bucket burnt the lining of their nose and throat.

'We have to get out of this stinking hole,' Mathew said irritably to Mortimer.

'Chances are we'll be here for some time. They will be unsure what to do with us. If you want to survive in prison, you say and do as little as possible to upset anyone. I know, this is not my first time in gaol,' confessed Thomas Potter.

'That doesn't come as any surprise,' interjected Mortimer icily.

The third day dragged on like the ones before until Mathew heard something that made him pay attention. He thought he might be dreaming, the voice was so distant. Slowly the sound grew louder: someone was calling out his name.

'Listen,' Mathew gave Mortimer and Potter a nudge. The voice was louder now, 'Fletcher; Master Surgeon Mathew Fletcher!' Mathew sprang to his feet and hammered on the cell door.

'Here, I'm in here,' he cried.

Keys rattled in the lock, and the heavy wooden door creaked open.

'You: Master Surgeon Fletcher?' The guard looked Mathew up and down, 'you're wanted.'

'What about my friends?' asked Mathew.

'No one said nothing about anyone else. Now come on, I ain't got all day.' The guard slammed the door to sounds of protest coming from within the chamber.

'I'll be back for you as soon as I can,' Mathew called out as he was led away.

'Follow me,' instructed the guard, as he strode ahead, leading Mathew down the tower steps. Mathew realised that he wasn't being treated as a prisoner, his hands hadn't been bound. He followed the guard across the courtyard towards the main building. For the first time Mathew was able to see how big the castle really was.

The guard stopped at the front door of the main building, 'Inside, and into the Great Hall, they are waiting for you.'

Not sure what or who to expect, Mathew straightened his jacket and removed his hat. Inside the hall, four men stood talking together. At the sound of his footsteps, two turned to face him. Mathew was suddenly filled with relief, and couldn't help but smile at the faces in front of him.

'I'm sorry I took so long to find you: are you well?' asked Major Robert Overton, his hand outstretched in welcome.

'Very well, thank you, Robert, but in need of a good meal and sleep.' He gave a wary glance towards the other men he didn't recognise. Turning back to the strangers, the major introduced them. 'This is your host, Lord Brooke, and this is Captain Bridges, the man who captured your baggage-train and of course you already know my aide, Captain Maynard. Lord Brooke simply gave Mathew a welcome nod, but Captain Bridges gave him his hand and, in a friendly manner, asked, 'No hard feelings I hope, Mr Fletcher?'

Mathew smiled, 'None at all, Sir, a pleasure to meet you, but...er...my friends are still prisoners in your tower, are they to be released?'

Captain Bridges looked to Lord Brooke for confirmation, Lord Brooke did not respond to Mathew's question, so he turned to Major Overton, who merely nodded. 'I'll see to it,' confirmed Captain Bridges.

'Join me for dinner this evening, Major,' said Lord Brooke after which he immediately turned and left the hall not waiting for an answer.

'We have much to talk about, Mathew,' said Major Overton, looking at Captain Bridges. The captain got the message.

'I will show you to a private office where you can talk, Major, and I will arrange for food and drink to be sent to you, after which I will have your friends released and quarters made available to you all.'

Once they were alone together, Major Overton and Mathew shared a plate of cold mixed meats, cheese, bread, a plate of Knot Biscuits and a jug of beer in a small office used by the senior castle clerk. 'Now tell me everything that happened in Shrewsbury,' requested Overton casually.

'Everything,' queried Mathew.

'You know to what I am referring.' Mathew gave the matter some thought before answering.

'I overheard officers talking about a move to Worcester, I thought...'

'No, no,' interrupted Overton. 'I've heard Franks is dead and I am assuming you had a hand in it. How did you manage it?'

'Oh... that...well, er, it just happened. We set off with a plan to just follow Franks to see where he was going, or if he was meeting anyone. But he must have noticed us following him because he led us up a narrow lane and confronted us. If I hadn't purchased pistols for Mortimer and myself the day before, it would have been us who had died that night not

Franks. Had he known we had the pistols with us, he would no doubt have used his own. But, once he had us cornered, our first instinct was to pull our daggers, so I guess at first, he didn't see us as much of a threat. When we did point our pistols at him, he just insulted us, and that's when I got mad. I don't know what came over me. I was scared to death when he confronted us. I could feel my legs shaking, and I suddenly thought I can't do this. Then he started insulting me, and suddenly the fear was gone. That's when I shot him. Mortimer fired just after I did. Franks fell, and we ran. I didn't know what else to do.'

Major Overton laughed, 'It seems you are proving quite a capable adversary to whoever gets in your way.' Mathew gave an embarrassed smile, not quite sure what to say in response.

'I want to go home, Robert. I believe Mary is or was somehow involved with Franks, Wilkes and Martins. It seems she had dealings with them in Beverley. Not long after we arrived in Shrewsbury, Mary and Ethan left us to go home. Mary had become ill, and Ethan said he was getting too old for all this travelling nonsense. So, now that the murders are dead, I need to return home and question Mary about Franks and his men.'

'I rather hoped you would stay and help me. You seem to have made some influential friends at court which would mean if you completed your training and became a surgeon to the king; the intelligence you could provide me with would be immeasurable in its value. Just think how, in later life, it may influence your career to be able to say you were surgeon to the king. It could bring riches beyond your wildest dreams,' said Overton.

'It could also be the death of me if I made a mistake or got caught spying for you, Mathew retaliated.

'Just give the matter some thought first, before rushing into a decision. I also need to tell you something else. There has been a big battle not far from here, between the king's army and Lord Essex's men. Some of the wounded may be brought here, and Lord Brooke has requested that you lend a hand in dealing with them. That was one of the conditions I had to agree with to get you out of prison.'

'I understand; I will do what I can for the wounded, and I am grateful for your help in getting me released from the tower but, once I am no longer needed, I will be making my way home,' insisted Mathew.

'Yes, yes, all in good time. We'll talk about that again later when you have been able to think things over,' said the major.

Chapter Twelve

Robert Overton left Mathew to go and find Lord Brooke, leaving Mathew feeling frustrated, trapped and used by a person he once respected. As Mathew sat in the small office off the Great Hall, and while the Major was away, he began to think over what he had been told and wondered why it had taken so long for Major Overton to arrive. *It had taken two full days and three nights before Major Overton had got Mathew, Mortimer and Potter released from the tower. Why had it taken him so long to get them set free when Major Overton had followed him wherever he went and was usually within easy reach? Yes, the major had got him and his friends out of that prison.* The more Mathew thought about it, the more he was sure it was only so they would feel obligated to the major and so be willing to do his bidding. *No, I don't owe the Major anything else, it is time to move on and create a new life for myself.* As Mathew sat thinking over his current predicament, the situation he now found himself played over in his mind. Why had he stayed when he could have got away at Shrewsbury? He had to admit there was something about being with the king, and in the army, that appealed to him. An excitement; the opportunity for a new and more prosperous life, he had been to places and done things he would never have experienced had he stayed in Hull. He had met the king and his son, the duke; healed them both. He had used his skills as a surgeon to save more people than he would have done had he stayed safe in Hull. Mathew realised he was changing, had changed, he knew it, he was no longer that naive apprentice rushing to find himself a wife and settle down. The torments he had gone through over Elizabeth's death, leaving his home and family had all forced him to grow as a person. He needed more in his life than Hull and Beverley could offer him. Yes, the major was using him, but he was sure he could also use him to get what he wanted.

His thoughts drifted back to Shrewsbury. Before they had left, no one had raised a Hue and Cry about a dead body being found, even though Franks' body must have been discovered before the baggage-train broke camp. No one had come to the baggage-train camp asking questions about a dead man found outside a church – why? Maybe someone else had been blamed for the death. *He* hadn't robbed Franks after killing him, so, perhaps, when the body had been found by a passer-by, they had picked up Mathew's dropped pistol and then robbed the dead Franks. If that is what had happened, and they had been caught in the act, it would be they who would be accused of murdering the man found in the lane between the churches. The thought of an innocent person being accused of his crime added to his unexpected feelings of guilt. Regardless of how justified he was in killing Franks, it hadn't felt the same as when he had killed the three soldiers to save Ethan, back in Anlaby. Now his only consolation was to repeatedly remind himself that fewer innocent people would die needlessly at the hands of the cruel mercenary. '*Stop blaming yourself this way'*, he told himself, *'I have no way of knowing if an innocent person has been accused of Franks' death, it's just my conscience playing with me. It's in God's hands now, He will decide if I will have to atone for what I have done. What's done is done; it's time to move on.*' As Mathew got up to leave, one more thought occurred to him. Had the major been watching him confront Franks, had the major dealt with Franks' body and that was the reason there had been no Hew and Cry?

As Mathew walked out into the courtyard, the guard, who had shown him the way to the Great Hall, was waiting for him.

'This way,' said the guard. Mathew was led across the courtyard to a small ground floor chamber in the Watergate Tower set in the southwest curtain wall of the castle; Mortimer and Potter were waiting for him. They had been told to stay and not to leave until Mathew arrived.

'You three will have to make do with this. The castle is overcrowded as it is without trying to find room for royalist guests,' the guard sneered.

'We're not royalists, we work for Major Overton,' insisted Mortimer.

'Hmm,' replied the guard as he strode away.

'What about all our belongings, they're still on our wagon?' Mathew called after him, getting no reply. The dirty room looked like it had previously been used by the soldiers for eating their meals, or as a restroom when they were off duty. A table and a couple of benches had been pushed up against the wall; the floor was littered with food waste and the stains from spilt drinks. There was no glass in the slit window, just a wooden shutter to protect them from the worst of the weather. In the wall opposite the window was an old iron sconce.

'We'll have to find and retrieve our personal belongings,' said Mathew. 'I'll go back and find Major Overton. I'll ask him to get the soldiers to release our belongings, the sooner we find and retrieve them the less will have been stolen or lost. You two straighten this place up, I'll be back as soon as I can.'

As Mathew walked back to the Great Hall, he had to pass the captured wagons. They were all neatly lined up in rows in the centre of the castle courtyard, some of the wagons had been emptied, all had been searched. He suspected most had been looted for their most useful and valuable items, even though there were two guards assigned to watch over them. After a quick word with Major Overton, and a note written by one of Lord Brooke's clerks, Mathew went back to fetch Mortimer and Potter, the three of them rescuing all they could find from his wagon.

'I think you need to tell us what is going on,' said Potter as he pushed one of Mathew's medical boxes up against the wall of their tower chamber. 'I'm not complaining about being let out of that prison but, after being crammed in with all those people, it seems strange to suddenly find it's only the three of us sharing this rat hole with the free run of the castle.'

'Loathed as I am to agree with something Potter has said, I have to admit it, I'm curious too' said Mortimer.

'It's all very simple really. Major Overton told me he had been watching and following us after we left Shrewsbury. When we were captured, he came to Warwick and informed Lord Brooke that we are agents working for him and Parliament and that he would like us released. According to the major, Lord Brooke looks on us as contemptible; he doesn't consider spying an honourable occupation. Neither do I truth be told, but that is what we are, for now anyway, so we will just have to put up with what he thinks of us. At least we are free. Major Overton also told me that there's been a big battle between the king's forces and those of the Earl of Essex, somewhere south of here.'

'Which side won the battle?' asked Mortimer.

'I don't know, I didn't ask,' said Mathew. 'I can only guess that if the Parliamentarian forces had won he would have been a bit more forthcoming about the outcome of the battle, so I can only assume it was the king that was triumphant.'

'What do we do now?' asked Potter.

'We enjoy our freedom, what we have of it, explore the castle and behave ourselves until we can find a way of getting out,' said Mathew. 'I suggest we go in search of food first, I'm starving, and they weren't very generous when it came to feeding us when we were locked in with the others.'

'What about all those other people we were locked up with, what will become of them? asked Mortimer.

'I don't know; I expect they will be questioned and released, it's not as though they are any kind of threat to the castle. I should think the soldiers in the other tower will be given the opportunity to change sides; Lord Brooke will have suffered losses during the battle in the south and will need to replace his dead and wounded' responded Mathew.

Having retrieved the last of their stuff from the wagon, they went in search of something to eat.

'What will we do for money; they are not just going to give pies away? The first thing the soldiers took from us was our purses,' said Potter.

'The major gave me two silver shillings for food and drink. There has to be someone in the castle selling food to the soldiers,' said Mathew.

'Two silver shillings won't last long if we have to pay castle trader prices,' complained Potter.

'You seem to forget, that it is me who has the money and I expect the major will find ways to enable us to earn more,' said Mathew.

'Well I don't care who's paying so long as we get something to eat and drink soon,' interjected Mortimer.

It didn't take them long to find what they were looking for, they just had to follow their noses. All along the inside of the castle wall, small shops had been built made from wattle and daub or planks of wood. They housed the traders that serviced the castle – blacksmiths, carpenters, potters and, more importantly for Mathew and his friends, bakers of bread and pies along with brewers of beer.

After satisfying their thirst and hunger, Mathew led the way as they explored the courtyard and the rest of the castle. Within the castle walls was like a town in miniature, every trade you would expect to find in a village or small town. All the significant traders were represented and busily working to supply the needs of the castle and the small army that Lord Brooke had garrisoned there. From early morning till late at night, these artisans provided everything the soldiers needed. A tavern, close to the stables, ensured soldiers spent their money inside the castle instead of in the town, and was the place where most of the noise was coming from. As Mathew and his friends explored the castle grounds, they noted the many towers set in the walls. Apart from the heavily fortified Barbican, there were three tall towers – Caesar's Tower, Guy's Tower and Watergate Tower, where they had been quartered. The Great Hall and the castle's private chambers made up most of the Southeast wall of the castle and overlooked the River Avon. The Barbican was the main entrance to the castle, with a road that led directly into Warwick town. A secondary smaller entrance to the castle was located within the north wall, guarded by Clarence Tower and Bear Tower which together formed part of the keep. But the most prominent part of the castle was the Castle Mound. It was the oldest and highest point of Warwick Castle. It stood impressively above the western side of the castle, a broad, low tower on top of a high mound that dominated the new parts of the castle and overlooked both the town and the river.

'It's nothing like Hull Castle is it?' Mortimer said to Mathew.

'Ha, you're right, Hull's castle is no more than a large tower set into the town walls,' reflected Mathew. But at least the whole town is protected by the wall that surrounds it. Having acquainted themselves with the castle layout, the lure of the castle tavern drew them inside where they spent the rest of the day drinking and talking. Over in one corner, much to his delight, Potter noted a game of cards being played.

'I can see there are opportunities to be had here,' chuckled Potter.

'You've got no money,' said Mortimer.

'Money's easy to come by, if you know how,' said Potter, 'the trick is not to get caught when acquiring it.'

Chapter Thirteen

Mathew rubbed the sleep from his eyes. It was barely light outside, and someone was banging on their tower chamber door demanding for it to be opened.

'Wait a moment,' yelled out Mathew as he forced himself into a sitting position. He could just make out the shadowy shape of Mortimer sat upright on his bed. The banging sounded again. Mathew fumbled on the table for the striker to put a spark to the rushlight. As the tiny flame brought a yellow glow to the chamber, Mathew got a better look at Mortimer, he had his pistol in his hand, cocked and ready to fire. Mathew also noted Potter was missing from his bed.

An urgent voice from the other side of the door demanded that Lord Brooke wanted to see Mathew Fletcher immediately.

'Put that away,' Mathew instructed Mortimer, 'if anyone wanted to kill us they wouldn't knock on the door first and, if Lord Brooke wanted to arrest us, one pistol wouldn't stop him from doing so.'

'I hadn't had time to load it anyway,' said Mortimer, putting the pistol back under his pillow. 'I'd lay odds it's something to do with Potter. He didn't come back last night. It would be just like him to get us all into trouble.'

Mathew, hungry, tired, and irritable, followed the servant, who had awoken him, across the courtyard in the direction of the Great Hall. It was a cold, grey morning, and Mathew wished he could have slept on a little longer. The servant hurried on ahead of him, urging him to get a move on as Mathew shuffled along buttoning his jacket against the morning chill. Once inside the Great Hall, he was taken up to the private apartments of the castle and ushered into a dimly lit bedchamber where he was delivered to Lord Brooke.

Lord Brooke was sat at the bedside of a woman. On hearing the door open and seeing Mathew enter, Lord Brooke looked up and approached him. Lord Brooke stopped Mathew in the centre of the chamber and in a low voice began to explain why he had been summoned.

'She has been prescribed pleuritic pills, but they haven't done any good.' Lord Brooke told him. 'My own physician tells me Lady Brooke will be with our Lord God before the new day is out, which is why I have sent for you. I cannot bear the thought of losing her. Major Overton has told me of the good work you have done curing sick people when others would have given up. I believe even the Duke of York owes you his life, so the major tells me. If you are able to save my wife, I implore you to do so, and I will be forever grateful.' As Mathew pieced together the symptoms Lord Brooke was in such a rush to give him, he suddenly comprehended the enormity of the task with which he had been presented. Mathew didn't relish having to deal with a patient that was about to die with him in attendance. He wanted to walk away, knowing the futility of trying to cure Lady Brooke. He needed time to think of a way out of this dilemma. He looked the usually well dressed Lord Brooke up and down.

From his dishevelled appearance, the master of Warwick Castle looked as though he had been sat by his wife's bedside all night. He couldn't turn his back on Lord Brooke in his hour of need, he had to do something. So Mathew asked permission from his lordship to give Lady Brooke a physical examination with the understanding that, if he thought that there was no hope for her ladyship, Lord Brooke would accept his prognosis. Lord Brooke agreed.

Mathew started his examination of Lady Brooke, her breathing was shallow and rapid, with tenderness in her chest and back; her lips had taken on a greyish hue, and she was hot and sweaty. 'Sir, I am no physician but, I am sorry to say, I too think her Ladyship is in God's hands now.' Mathew hesitated before continuing. 'But... there may be one remedy. I make no promises as to its success. It is a treatment of my own design which, with your permission, I would like to try. I must warn you the treatment involves a surgical procedure, and it is hazardous. I have never had the opportunity to try the procedure before but, as your own physician has already stated, her Ladyship has little time left and is sure to die in the next few hours. I make no promises as to my success, but what have you and Lady Brooke to lose. The decision must be yours to make but, if my procedure works, we will see improvement in her Ladyship's breathing immediately the surgery is over.'

Lord Brooke paced the floor of his wife's bedchamber while he thought through what Mathew had told him. Mathew grew nervous, wondering if he should ever have mentioned to Lord Brooke his theory for a cure. It was only after one of his late night experiments on a corpse, a man who had died of pleurisy, that he had developed the method of draining away the pleuritic fluid. But, before Mathew had a chance to retract his suggestion, Lord Brooke took the decision from him.

'You have given me an impossible choice, Young Surgeon, in setting me this conundrum. Everyone is telling me she will die soon, but now, you say, you may be able to save her. I know if I do nothing, when she dies I will blame myself for not letting you try to save her. But if I say yes, and let you perform your experimental surgery and she still dies, I know I will blame you for killing her, however unfair that may be. If she dies with or without the surgery, I will blame myself for making the wrong decision,' Lord Brooke began to pace back and forth in frustration once more.

'I am sorry, Sir, I cannot make this decision for you. If you wish me to leave, I will return to my own chamber and pray for Lady Brooke. Mathew gave a courteous bow to Lord Brooke and started for the door.

At that moment Lady Brooke coughed a goblet of blood onto her pillow and moaned.

'Wait!' called out Lord Brooke. 'Do what you can for her.' He flopped into a chair, 'and may God forgive me.'

Mathew spun round on the spot; all doubt vanished from his mind. 'I will need my assistant and my instrument chest,' he said as he walked back towards the distraught husband of the patient, 'and the sooner, the better.' Lord Brooke seemed taken aback at Mathew's forthright manner, but agreed.

'I will have them sent for immediately, and two maids to assist Lady Brooke,' said Lord Brooke as he rang a bell on the table by his side. A servant entered, and Lord Brooke gave him his orders.

Mathew's surgical kit soon arrived along with Mortimer.

'Set water to boil over the fire,' Mathew instructed, as he laid out his surgical instruments on a linen covered table, 'and bring me more candles.'

Lord Brooke looked at the array of instruments on the table becoming alarmed at what he saw, 'What are you going to do to her ladyship?'

'I think it better you wait outside, My Lord, this procedure will take some time,' said Mathew as sympathetically as he could.

'I will not,' insisted Lord Brooke taking a step closer to the bed.

'Then I suggest you take a seat, we may be some hours before we know if the procedure has worked well enough to save her,' Mathew directed.

Reluctantly, Lord Brooke retook his seat by the fireplace, repositioning his chair to watch the proceedings unfold. Mathew carefully washed and dried two large suture needles, four cupping glasses and his scalpel. Placing a stool in front of the table holding his instruments for Lady Brooke, Mathew instructed the two maids to seat her Ladyship on the stool facing the table and lower her nightdress to her waist.

'I protest at this outrageous indecency!' objected Lord Brooke, jumping to his feet.

'Leave the chamber or sit quietly!' snapped Mathew, 'I cannot have you interrupting once I start the procedure or Lady Brooke most certainly will die!' Lord Brooke took a step forward and raised his hand as if to strike Mathew, only regaining his self-control at the last minute.

'He must leave,' Lord Brooke pointed at Mortimer, 'Her ladyship's maids will assist you.' Mathew looked at Mortimer and nodded at the compromise, 'I will call for you if you are needed,' he reassured his friend.

Once Mortimer had left the bedchamber, the two maids prepared Lady Brooke as instructed by Mathew. He ran his fingers up Lady Brooke's back, locating and counting her ribs. Happy he had found the correct location, he inserted one of the large suture needles into her back; low down, between the floating ribs, pushing the needle deeper and deeper inside before removing it. Then he applied a hot cupping glass over the puncture wound. Four times Mathew punctured Lady Brooke's back. Over each puncture wound, he applied a hot cupping glass to draw out fluid. There was silence from the chair by the fireplace where Lord Brooke sat. Mathew didn't dare turn to face him. Only the maids, their faces taut with emotion, made any sound as they wept while watching the surgery procedure. Holding their mistress still as instructed, they gave nervous glances in the direction of Lord Brooke. Mathew removed and reapplied the hot cupping glasses to his patient's back and watched as they sucked in Lady Brooke's flesh as the glasses cooled. They raised large blisters with blood seeping from puncture wounds, but Mathew could not see what he was hoping for. Each time he applied a fresh cupping glass Mathew waited as it filled with blood. Nervously he watched for signs of the pleuritic fluid, but it was only blood that was being drawn. Once the vessels were full of blood, he removed them from her ladyship's back and once more inserted the large steel suture needles into her back, pushing deeper into the chest of his patient. His patient, plainly in pain from the procedure, didn't have the strength to resist, her torment reflected in the faces of her two maids. Mathew refused to look at Lord Brooke, it would give away his uncertainty in what he was doing. After heating the cupping glasses again, he applied them to the puncture wounds. As the glasses cooled once again, they began to fill with blood and Mathew began to fear that he had failed. He was getting worried and wondered what he had done wrong. He had no choice but to continue. His hands trembled as he inserted a needle for a third time, pushing it in deeper and harder in a desperate attempt to puncture the pleuritic sack around her lungs. He attached another cupping glass over the hole and prayed. When the change came, it came as a sudden spurt of fluid, first one cupping glass, closely followed by the others, as they filled with a yellow-grey coloured discharge. Mathew quickly emptied the glasses and applied them again, this time there was less blood, but more of the yellow fluid. When Mathew removed the cupping glasses again, Lady Brooke inhaled and let out a whimper. Mathew reapplied the glasses, but this time very little of the yellow fluid came away. He applied another cupping glass for good measure, but it only brought away blood. Cleaning the area around the wounds, Mathew applied an emplaster to Lady Brooke's wounds and directed her two maids to return her to her bed, but to keep her well supported and propped up. Her breathing had improved, and the greyness was slowly disappearing from her lips, but Mathew was unsure as to what he should do next.

'She is in God's hands now, My Lord,' said Mathew, turning for the first time to face the man sat by the fire.

'Will she live?' Lord Brooke asked, rising to his feet.

'In all honesty,' replied Mathew, 'I do not know. I have removed the fluid that was constricting Lady Brooke's lungs. I don't know if the procedure was done in time, or if the fluid will build up again and she will die anyway. But she is breathing more easily for now, and that is a good sign. I will stay with her until I am sure one way or the other.' Lord Brooke went to his wife's side and held her hand, talking to her softly. Mathew ordered food and wine to be brought up for the two of them and, while the maids tended to the patient, Mathew and Lord Brooke settled to a breakfast of dried fruits, cold meat, cheeses, and bread and butter. The two men ate greedily for a few minutes, slating the hunger that had descended on them. As the urgency of their hunger eased, Lord Brooke took a long drink of wine before turning to Mathew.

'Major Overton tells me you have achieved a great deal in your short time while working for him,' Lord Brooke stated casually.

Mathew took a large gulp of wine, felt its effects go straight to his head and remembered the consequences that drinking wine had on him.

'Working for the major is not how I would have quite described it. I would have said working with the major was a more accurate way of describing our relationship, My Lord. My reason for aiding Major Overton was to gain his help in tracking down the three murderers we were both looking for: this I have done: so you see the assistance I gave to the major was to our mutual benefit,' answered Mathew.

'I take it then, that you consider your obligations to Major Overton fulfilled,' probed Lord Brooke.

'My mission, as I see it, is complete. But I have a decision to make. Do I return home and deal with an unfinished private matter, then set up my own surgical practice in Hull or Beverley. I am not a soldier, and I have no desire to continue spying for the major, which is a job I do not feel equipped for,' Mathew took another sip of the sweet wine. 'Or, do I continue to work for Major Overton and return to the king to take advantage of the opportunities that would present to me? I am not a spy, I am a surgeon with a passion for learning, and bettering myself. With civil war breaking out in the country, returning home would seem to me to be the safest choice to make.'

'Nonsense,' said Lord Brooke, 'the information you have passed on regarding the movements of The King's Army have proved most beneficial in allowing Parliament to prepare our forces for his arrival. Had I not received intelligence that the king was at Coventry and been able to get there in time to save the city, the king may have captured the city and have a new capital in the heart of the Midlands by now.'

'But I got it wrong when I said the king was planning to move on Worcester,' confessed Mathew.

'Ha,' Lord Brooke laughed, 'that is all part of the game of disassembling. You do not understand, My Young Surgeon, it is the very fact you are not a military man, but a surgeon, that disarms the people around you, if you will pardon the pun. You gain a man's trust without even having to try. When a man is hurt or dying, he feels the need to unburden his conscience and, when there is no preacher to hand, it is his physician or surgeon who must take their place.'

Mathew listened to Lord Brooke and had to confess that many of his patients did confide in him, be that about family troubles or matters of a more personal nature. He took another sip of wine and waited for Lord Brooke to get to the point he knew was coming. A moan from the bed distracted both men from their dialogue. Mathew went to his patient, 'Her Ladyship's colour is returning, and her heartbeat and breathing are continuing to improve,' said Mathew, pleased at how Lady Brooke was responding to his treatment. The two men returned to their seats. Mathew took another drink of wine, 'she is not out of danger yet but, with your permission, I will leave you with some medicine to help ease her pain and cool her fever. I will return after some sleep to check on her progress. Major Overton has informed me that your wounded troopers from the battle will be brought back to the castle for me to attend to.'

'Yes,' said Lord Brooke, 'have you any objections?'

'No, My Lord, only I had hoped to convince you to allow my friends and I to leave Warwick.'

'The wounded that are being brought here are my officers and friends. I would like you to tend their wounds,' said Lord Brooke firmly. Before Mathew could respond, Lady Brooke let out another moan. Pleased with the interruptions his patient was creating, Mathew quickly went to check on her.

'Lady Brooke continues to show signs of improvement,' said Mathew. He sat on the bed feeling her pulse, reluctant to return to Lord Brooke and his conversation. There was a knock on the door, and a servant entered requesting that Lord Brooke deal with a matter of urgency in the Great Hall. Mathew bowed to Lord Brooke as he left the bedchamber, hoping that having saved Lady Brooke's life her husband would feel obliged to release him and his friends.

It was gone midday before Mathew returned to Lady Brooke. Her condition was continuing to improve though she was not out of danger yet. As Mathew left the Great Hall, Mortimer was waiting for him by the door and fell into step with him as they crossed the courtyard, heading for their chamber.

'You took your time. I guess Lady Brooke still lives or you would have been finished sooner. *Have* you managed to save her?' asked Mortimer.

'I don't know, it's too early to say just yet, but I am hopeful, her condition continues to improve. I get the feeling that Lord Brooke wants me to stay here. He is having wounded brought into the castle for me to attend to. Lord Brooke and Major Overton may be planning on keeping me here for some time.'

'What about me and Potter?' asked Mortimer.

Mathew stopped and turned to Mortimer, 'I don't know, he never actually got round to telling me I had to stay, but I will ask him about you when the time comes. You have to remember, *you* belong to the major, you owe him a debt. It's not that I want to stay with Lord Brooke; in fact, I can't really make up my mind what I want to do next. What I might do is play one against the other and see what happens.'

'I don't want to stay here either,' said Mortimer. 'I preferred working for the major as his steward. My family are employed on the Overton estates; if I could go home, I would be able to see them again. I was happy working for Major Overton until Mayor Hotham ruined my reputation with him.'

'Whatever we do, I don't want things to stay as they are, it's time for me to think of my future, not my past.' Just as Mathew finished speaking there was a kafuffle behind them. Turning to see what all the fuss was about, they saw Potter being tossed out of a side door in the main building and landing in a heap on the courtyard cobbles. Mathew and Mortimer glanced at each other, wondering what their nefarious friend had been up to. Potter dusted himself down and joined his friends.

'Well, are you going to tell us what that was all about?' asked Mortimer. Potter looked from one to the other and shrugged his shoulders and straightened his hat.

'I, er, was just exploring the cellars. You know, looking around,' Potter answered hesitantly.

'Oh yes, and what else were you doing in the cellars?' asked Mathew.

'You don't trust me, do you? You always think I'm up to something I shouldn't,' said Potter looking hurt at the insinuation.

'Well,' said Mathew.

Potter smiled. 'Well, if you insist; you remember when the baggage-train was stopped, and they found all that treasure belonging to the king in some of the wagons. As you know, it's down there in that cellar, under lock and key as you would expect with the door guarded. When I was exploring the castle, the fellow guarding it took exception to the questions I was asking him, and to the reason I was down there, so I was asked to leave.'

'Asked you to leave nicely did he?' interjected Mortimer. All three laughed out loud.

'Er, no,' confessed Potter, 'which means I could do with a drink. Shall we go find somewhere to sit, and I'll tell you what I have been up to?

Finding a bench outside the tavern, Mathew, Mortimer and Potter sat cups in hand and a large jug of beer to share.

'Come on then,' said Mortimer, impatient to hear what Potter had been doing all last night and this morning.

'It's a little difficult to know where to start,' said Potter.

'You'd better tell us the real reason why you were in the cellar to start with,' demanded Mathew.

'Um, er, let me see, it started last night. I was playing a friendly game of cards with some of the soldiers,' recounted Potter.

'I'd bet you've never played a friendly game of cards in your life,' sneered Mortimer. Potter ignored the jibe and was about to continue with recounting what had happened the night before when Mathew interrupted.

'Where did you get the money from? We only had two shillings, and most of that has gone.'

'Er, I think you will find that it has all gone now,' confessed Potter. 'But, don't worry, I can pay it back,' he patted his jacket where an inside pocket was located. While Mathew examined his now empty purse, wondering how Potter had managed to empty it with him noticing, Potter continued his story.

'The game was proceeding well, nice and friendly you might say. I was beginning to win when one of the players drops a bright shiny florin into the pot. Well, the sight of it stopped the game. Everyone wanted to know how he'd come by that amount of money. I mean, with stoppages for this and that, a soldier would be lucky to get a shilling a week to call his own and, up to that point, we'd only been playing for pennies. It's not often you see a new, shiny, silver florin. But, bold as you like, he just told everyone that he'd won it in another card game. So I matched his bet with copper from my purse, and we continued the game. When it came round to his turn to bet again, he dropped another florin into the pot. Now that was too much for any of us to take. I mean, I had the winning hand,' said Potter proudly.

'How did you know you had the winning hand if everyone was still betting and the game was still in play? asked Mortimer.

'I'm....er... a better player than most people,' Potter's explanation sounded feeble, but Mathew urged him to continue with his tale.

'Two players dropped out, saying the stakes had become too high. I managed to match his bet and went on to win the hand. I was expecting the soldier to be a sore loser, but he just shrugged his shoulders and left the table. I excused myself from the game and went to join him. I bought the soldier a few drinks, well, more than a few, he was a big man, and we talked. Eventually, I got the soldier drunk enough to ask him where the money had come from, but all I could get from him was that he had a wealthy friend. I was getting nowhere with him and had just about given up on the soldier. He was almost unconscious by that time anyway, when a sergeant came into the tavern to find him. The sergeant was furious; he was shouting at this fellow, saying that it was his turn to be on watch in the castle cellar and that he was going to have him flogged for being drunk on duty. The sergeant dragged him out of the tavern and led him away. That was when I got to thinking, what or who is so important, that it needs to be guarded during the night when it is locked in the castle cellar?' Potter paused to take a drink. 'It had to be the king's treasure.'

'Come on,' urged Mathew. 'What did you do next?'

Potter put down his cup and turned his eyes to the sky shaking his head, 'The king's treasure. I suspected that the soldier had found a way of helping himself to a few coins and I was curious to find out how he was doing it. So I thought why not go and see for myself.'

'And that's when you got kicked out of the cellar,' quizzed Mortimer.

'Nooooo,' said Potter. 'The sergeant had the soldier arrested for being unfit for duty. I figured the sergeant would find someone else to do the guard duty, so I followed him. He went to the guardroom at the castle gate and, moments later, came out with the new guard. I tagged along discreetly. I saw which door they used to go into the cellar and, after the sergeant had gone, I went inside. It didn't take long to find the guard sitting on a stool outside one of the doors. I told him I'd come down to get a leg of pork for the kitchen and took the opportunity to search the cellar. I found the leg of pork and, for good measure, took a couple of apples. I gave the apples to the guard and took the pork to the kitchen and picked up a tankard and a jug of wine. I returned to the cellar and gave the tankard and wine to the guard. We had a little talk. After drinking most of the wine, the guard soon fell asleep. That's when I went to find a hiding place from where I could watch the door but, not long after I'd got settled, I fell asleep and woke up this morning. I managed to stay hidden until just before midday watching for someone to open the guarded door. But I was finally found by one of the cooks who played merry hell with me, accusing me of stealing food, and that's when I was thrown out.

'All that, and you found out nothing,' exclaimed Mortimer.

'Spying on people is what I do well: it takes time and patience to bag a prize. I think the reason that no one turned up last night was, that whoever it is who is stealing from the cellar, saw the wrong guard on duty and decided it would be better to try again later when their friendly guard had returned. So, that is why tonight I'm going back to the cellar in the hope that our card playing friend is on duty again,' said Potter triumphant in his reasoning. 'I will go better prepared this time. I will take a jug of ale with me. If it is my card playing friend on duty tonight, I will sit and talk to him and try to learn more about where his sudden wealth comes from. If it's a different guard, I'll leave the ale and find somewhere to hide and watch. That way I will able to see who is stealing the money and know for sure how they are going about it. Mathew and Mortimer sat in awe at the devious antics of their partner.

'Maybe we can turn the information that Potter gets to our advantage,' said Mathew.

'What!' said Potter. 'If there is any advantage to be taken, I'm taking it.'

'You can't,' said Mathew. 'For one, I won't let you and two; you don't yet know who the thief is. If it turns out to be someone of importance, it would be your word against his, and you don't have the best reputation anyone could wish for. Find out who you think it is and report back to me tomorrow morning, then we can decide what to do next.'

That night, Potter descended the stone stairs from the kitchen to the cellar and crept along the passageway to his hiding place from where he would watch the guard on the treasure store. Setting aside the jug of beer and two cups, he climbed on top of the sacks of beans to wait for the next change of guard. In the dim light and with nothing to do, it wasn't long before Potter began to feel Morpheus drawing on his eyelids beckoning him to the world of dreams. Potter tried shaking his head and rubbing his face to stimulate his mind, but his eyelids soon began to droop. He pulled out a deck of cards from the inside of his jacket but, in the dimly lit cellar, it was too dark to read them. Having no means to measure the time as he waited in the dimly lit basement, time seemed to drag on endlessly. When someone from the kitchen came looking for a round of cheese, the fear of discovery startled him into full alertness, making his heart beat rapidly as he crouched behind the sacks. Once the person was gone, and his heart settled to its steady rhythm again, the need for sleep once again began to creep over him. More than once he nearly succumbed to the temptation to nap for a short while, only to awaken moments later with a jolt as though someone had poked him with a stick. After what seemed like a night of torture, he heard booted footsteps coming along the passage, and his fat friend appeared in the dimly lit space outside the treasure store door. It was the, now sober soldier from whom he had won the money that unknowingly waited for him. The two guards exchanged greetings before the first one got to his feet and left. Potter waited until his card playing friend settled himself on the stool by the door. With his jug of ale in hand, he went to greet his new best friend.

‘I was just bringing this down for the new guard,’ said Potter. ‘I didn’t expect to see you here. Did you get into much trouble with the sergeant last night?’ he asked cordially, handing over the jug.

‘No, not really, the sergeant had me thrown into a cell to sleep it off, he was all for having me flogged for being drunk when I should have been on duty. But, when they woke me up, I was told not to do it again and that I could leave. The only thing the sergeant said was that I had to get some sleep because I was on duty again tonight and that I better stay sober this time.'

'You were fortunate,' said Potter.

'Ah,' said the guard, touching his finger to the side of his nose. 'I've got a friend.'

'That's a good and powerful friend you've got if he can make a sergeant change his mind about punishing you for being drunk when he should be on duty,' quizzed Potter. 'Is he coming down here to see you tonight?'

'No, not tonight,' the guard took a long draft from the ale jug. 'He doesn't want to bump into the sergeant when he comes down to check I'm still awake.'

'I'd better leave you to your guard duty. I don't want to get you into trouble with the sergeant again. By the way, what's your name; I'm Thom, Thomas Potter?

'William Flowers, my friends call me Bill.'

'Right then, Bill, I look forward to playing another hand of cards with you. I'll leave you to your duty,' after a friendly handshake, Potter left the cellar.

Chapter Fourteen

A rider galloped over the barbican of Warwick Castle. With a brief stop to talk to the guard, for the stranger to ask directions, he continued on into the courtyard, stopping outside the Great Hall. The rider stepped down from his horse, brushed the dust from his clothes and retrieved a satchel from his saddle. A soldier ran up and took charge of his horse.

'Is there anything I can help you with, Sir?' asked the soldier.

'Where can I find Lord Brooke?' asked the rider.

'I suggest you ask in the Great Hall, Sir. You will find someone there who will know the whereabouts of the colonel.' The stockily built officer strode confidently off in the direction he'd been shown. Inside, he found the hall busy, clerks sat working at tables spaced around the walls of the hall. He wasted no time in marching over to the nearest clerk: 'I'm here to see Lord Brooke; I've come directly from the Earl of Essex. Where is your commanding officer?'

The clerk stood up, dropping his pen on the page to which he had been making notes, 'I'm sorry, Sir, he is indisposed, may I take your name and I will ascertain if his Lordship will be available to see you later today.'

'It is Captain Broadwaters, and I will see the colonel now.' The captain thrust a document under the nose of the clerk, who read it briefly before looking back up into the captain's hard set expression, the captain's grave face left the clerk in no doubt that this officer was used to being obeyed. The clerk dithered a moment, trying to decide who's wrath would be the worst to face, then gave up, 'excuse me a moment, Captain.' He stepped away from his table and went in search of Lord Brooke.

Captain Broadwaters surveyed the Great Hall for the first time since arriving. Its walls were festooned with hunting trophies, suits of armour, swords and shields, each item telling its own story of wars or hunting parties long ago. The clerk took a backward glance over his shoulder before disappearing through a Lancet Arched doorway in the far wall. Two more clerks, writing at tables in the hall, slipped him sideways glances wondering what could be so urgent that a captain could demand to see the lord of the castle. The missing clerk returned and begged Captain Broadwaters forgiveness for keeping him waiting and informed him Lord Brooke was ready to meet him.

Lord Brooke greeted the captain, somewhat irked at the intrusion by the stranger, 'Good day to you, Captain, my clerk showed me your warrant from the

Earl of Essex. I can assure the Earl and John Pym that the captured treasure is stored safely in the vaults of this castle and is available to Parliament as soon as they can provide wagons and escort for it to be taken to London.'

'Thank you, Sir,' said the captain, 'But what happened to the wagons that brought the treasure here?'

'Many of them were damaged and are unserviceable, some I have used for other purposes, but a few still remain.'

'Then my next duty is to make an inventory of the king's treasure so its true value can be ascertained for Parliament,' said Captain Broadwaters.

'I have already had a tally made of the haul; my clerk will provide you with an inventory of what is stored below in the cellar.'

'Forgive me, Sir, you miss-understand. My instructions come directly from Lord Essex, *I* am to make a count of the captured treasure myself, and *I* am to ensure its safe delivery to London as quickly as possible, but I will accept the offer of a copy of the inventory *you* have already taken.' declared Captain Broadwaters.

Lord Brooke stiffened noticeably at the insult to his integrity but refrained from defending himself. If the captain really had the ear of Lord Essex, he didn't want ill spoken of him when the captain returned to his master, or any word of his unhelpfulness getting back to John Pym and Parliament.

'May I suggest you start your count first thing in the morning, Captain? You must be hungry and thirsty after your journey. Let me have someone show you to a chamber where you can rest before joining me for dinner tonight. I can assure you, Captain, the treasure hoard is quite safe where it is.'

The captain thanked Lord Brooke for his hospitality and conceded that rest and a change of clothes would be welcome, so he agreed to Lord Brookes' suggestion in letting the count wait until the following day.

Bright and early the next morning, Captain Broadwaters commandeered six soldiers and a clerk. While two of the soldiers emptied the cellar store of each chest of captured treasure, a clerk made an itemised inventory of what was brought out, with Captain Broadwaters making a second list of his own. The remaining soldiers guarded the entrances and passageways of the cellars. Captain Bridges kept an eye on the proceedings, unhappy at having to surrender control of the key to the treasure store. The meticulous stock-take took all day, Captain Bridges insisting that every coin was counted, but was finally completed late in the evening. With the door to the cellar store locked and Captain Broadwaters now in possession of the key, he took all three inventories back to his bedchamber.

In the privacy of his surroundings, Captain Broadwaters first compared his inventory with that of the clerks taken at the same time as his. Apart from some very minor differences they were the same. When he compared his list to the one Lord Brooke had made when the treasure first arrived at Warwick Castle, there was a marked difference, too big a difference for it to be put down to counting errors. He made a note of the differences, sat back in his chair and thought about the significance of what he had discovered. The obvious questions were, who had taken the missing treasure or was the difference in totals down to incompetence on the part of the original counting clerk who made the inventory. At this stage, it was too early to accuse Lord Brooke of stealing the treasure. The logical place to start to look for proof of a possible theft is with the clerk who wrote the original inventory.

The next morning Captain Broadwaters allowed Lord Brooke to compare the two inventories, the original take at the time the treasure was captured and the one he had taken the day before.

'This is outrageous,' exclaimed Lord Brooke. 'Someone here? Stealing the king's treasure from under my own nose. I will have the castle searched immediately. I will have everyone searched, Captain Bridges!' he yelled at the top of his voice.

'No, no, you will be wasting your time and give away the fact the missing gold and silver have been noticed. If someone is stealing from you, he is doing it a little at a time or else the losses would have been noticed sooner. They won't keep what they have within the castle in case it is found but, when the thieves have spent the money they have taken, they *will* come back for more. They will have grown more and more confident and careless each time they returned. Patience is our ally; it is patience that will catch our thief, but I cannot do the investigation alone, I need someone not connected with the castle to help me do the investigation. Do you have any suggestions?'

Lord Brooke thought about it a moment, 'I may have the person you need, Major Overton is a highly trusted officer who has three...how would I describe them...useful associates to assist him. I believe they will suit your purposes very well.'

'Thank you, Colonel, in the meantime I will question the clerk who took the original inventory,' said Captain Broadwaters.

Within the hour, Major Overton had been summoned and informed of the situation.

'This is not the work I'd had in mind for my men,' insisted Major Overton. 'But I understand the urgency to discover the thief. I will speak to Mathew, and we will work out a plan. I will get them to ask around and find out what they can from the soldiers within the garrison. If the thief is from within these walls, they will find it hard to keep their thieving a secret. I will set my men to work straight away.'

Under a lean-to outside the washhouse, Mathew had set up a make-shift medical post. He'd found that the castle surgeon was often drunk and his work sloppy and unprofessional. Soldiers, who had fallen sick or become injured, avoided going to the castle and many of them now complained of infected wounds and ineffective medicines. When Mathew offered to treat the soldiers in his stead, they were happy to agree.

Major Overton found Mathew and Mortimer at their new post, treating a soldier for a neglected skin sore which had become infected.

'Good day, Mathew, are you busy? I need to have a word with you in private,' said the major.

'Oh, not feeling well, Major, I'll be right with you. Mortimer can finish binding this man's arm. How can I assist you?'

'It's not a medical matter. Let's go to your quarters where we can speak more freely,' insisted Major Overton, indicating the direction of Mathew's chamber in the tower.

The two men made small talk until they reached the tower and the chamber door was firmly closed behind them. Major Overton informed Mathew about the missing treasure.

'I don't want to get involved. I'm a surgeon not some kind of money clerk. What do I know about stolen gold and silver? I've had enough of spying for you; I've done what you have asked of me until now, but no more. God forgive me, and I am grateful for your help, but I have repaid the debt I owed you, and now it's time for me to move on,' declared Mathew stubbornly.

'I know, I know, and I am grateful for what you have done for me, but I still haven't managed to convince Lord Brooke that you are not really a royalist — yet. He needs to be sure he can trust you before he will let you go. I've tried to reassure him about you and the others, but he's not so sure. Helping me to discover who the thief is, will prove that to him,' dissembled the major.

Mathew was speechless, enraged by the blatant lie he had just been told, knowing he was being manipulated by Major Overton again and being powerless to do anything about it. His frustration erupted. 'Why the hell didn't I leave with Ethan and Mary?' he yelled at the top of his voice. 'Why didn't I just go when we left Shrewsbury? Why?' angry and frustrated with his own indecision back then, as much as with the major's manipulation of him now.

Major Overton waited, asking Mathew to sit down again, but he wouldn't; he stayed on his feet, pacing to and fro.

'Ambition,' said the major casually. 'You want to be better than who you are right now. You have tasted success, favour, and the gratitude of others more privileged than yourself. You have a keen skill as a surgeon and medical man, and you have a thirst for knowledge that you will not satisfy in Beverley or Hull.'

Mathew spun round to face the major, 'You bastard,' he said in a low, even, menacing manner, loaded with all the venom and bite of a cobra.

'You know it to be true,' continued the major, 'even if you have spent all this time trying to avoid the reality of it. I know you better than you do yourself. If you stay with me, you have the chance of advancement; gaining greater medical knowledge and prestige; once that is, I find a way of returning you to the king. You know if you leave and return home, the chances are you will remain a simple town or village surgeon, dealing with cuts, and sores and other boring day to day ailments and then, occasionally, if you are lucky, someone will need a stone removed. If they survive the operation, you will become noteworthy for a short while. If they die, chances are your reputation as a surgeon will be ruined. You will make a little money, have a family and, for the rest of your life, you will wonder what you could have made of yourself had you stayed with me. The choice is yours,' said Major Overton smugly.

Mathew continued to pace back and forth in the chamber, thinking, seething with rage. Eventually, his pace eased, 'what do you want me to do?'

'All I want you and Mortimer to do is the same as you have always done; mix with the soldiers, and keep your eyes and ears open. Talk to the men when they come to see you, drop the occasional hint about the treasure in the cellar, but under no circumstances say anything about any of it going missing.'

'What about Potter? asked Mathew.

'Potter; I plan to put his talents to a different use. Where is the little weasel anyway?'

'Probably playing cards somewhere!' Mathew deliberately declined from telling the major that Potter was already looking for a means to get his hands on some of the gold and silver.

'I'd better go find him.' The major stood up to leave, 'you are doing the right thing in staying with me, Mathew, our stay in Warwick won't last forever, and then you will be free to rebuild your own life in any way you see fit.'

Mathew returned to Mortimer, arriving as he was putting a couple of stitches in a cook's sliced thumb. Mathew ignored him and sat on a stool still, seething after his encounter with Major Overton. Once the cook had left, Mathew informed Mortimer of the major's instructions and how he felt about being manipulated by the man. As Mathew tried to talk to Mortimer, a steady stream of patients kept interrupting him, but, having to deal with honest minor wounds instead of dwelling on his own situation with the major, the work eased his mood. After they had finished for the day, they collected food and beer from the castle kitchen and took it back to their chamber. Working for Major Overton again had some advantages. The major had agreed that they could draw their food from the castle kitchen and not have to pay for it. By the time they got back to their lodgings, Potter was waiting for them.

'Guess who came to see me today,' said Potter with a smile.

'Major Overton!' said Mathew and Mortimer in unison.

'Ah, you're not happy about something,' said Potter.

'I'm still waiting to find out what he and Mathew were talking about myself,' said Mortimer. 'Mathew's been like a bear with a sore head all afternoon after speaking with Major Overton.' Mathew didn't answer.

'Come on, now we have some time to ourselves, tell us what he spoke to you about?' Mathew asked Potter.

'He wants me to get down into the cellar and see if I can find out who is helping themselves to the king's gold and silver plate. I thought about telling him that I had already started but decided that it might not be wise. He might have started to ask questions I don't want to answer just yet,' confessed Potter. 'But, he did say that anything I do discover, I have to report to you, and not go directly to him with it. He said people are used to seeing you come and go freely from the private chambers within the castle. The times when you give Lady Brooke her medicines and speak to Lord Brooke, so your comings and goings wouldn't raise anyone's suspicions.'

'Are you going down there tonight?' asked Mortimer.

'Yes, that's why I'm here now. I want to get a few hours sleep before I slip down into the cellar. I will be going through the kitchen entrance again now I know where to hide. The major has arranged for me to help out in the kitchen, so people get used to seeing me there.

Later that night, while servants brought down the remains of Lord Brooke' dinner from his private chambers above the hall, Potter slipped into the kitchen and down the stairs into the cellar. Finding his previous hiding place, he settled in for the night and a long wait. As time passed, the noise from the kitchen diminished, and the music from the Great Hall subsided. Potter lay silently and patiently on the sacks of beans into which he had devised himself a comfortable hiding place. The guard on the treasure store door changed, and Potter caught sight of Bill's familiar features. For about half an hour Bill stood next to the store door, halberd in hand, then he tired and sat on the stool which had been left for him. Time passed painfully slowly until the sound of footsteps made Potter pay attention.

Chapter Fifteen

By the time Mathew and Mortimer were ready for their breakfast, Potter still hadn't returned from his night in the cellar. 'Should we go look for him?' asked Mathew.

'No, he'll be alright, and besides if we go searching for him we'll give away that he's been hiding down there,' said Mortimer.

'Yes, you're right. You go get us some breakfast, and I'll set up the medical stall. I wonder how many customers we'll get today.

Shouts came from the Barbican as a young woman drove her cart into Warwick Castle and brought it to a halt close to the washhouse door. On the back of the cart were three wounded men. She had taken it upon herself to collect wounded soldiers found on the battlefield near the village of Kineton, and treat their wounds as best she could. Those beyond her skill she had decided to bring to Warwick Castle in the hope that they would receive the treatment they needed.

'Who is this lot and why have you brought them here?' Cried an agitated sergeant of the guard, who came running over to ask why the woman had refused to stop at the castle entrance. The young woman, with long wavy red hair that fell past her shoulders, was in no mood to listen to the sergeant.

'They are here because they are your soldiers and your responsibility,' she told him.

'These are not Warwick soldiers,' protested the sergeant, 'take them away.'

'Well, if they're not from Warwick, then it is your men who have caused their injuries, so it is still your responsibility to care for them,' she yelled at him.

'I told you to take them away, we don't have room for them here,' demanded the sergeant, trying to turn the horse and cart back towards the castle gate as the woman struggled with him for control of the reins.

Mathew and Mortimer watched the argument play out, between the two equally matched antagonists, as they crossed the courtyard to get a better look at the affray. As the sergeant tried to drag the horse and cart towards the castle gate, the young woman was just as adamant that it should stay where it was as she tried to prevent the sergeant from leading away the horse and cart. Mathew and Mortimer joined the growing crowd gathering to watch the entertainment. Seeing the wounded men on the cart, Mathew got closer and began to examine their injuries as the wooden vehicle was jostled back and forth. The young woman and the sergeant of the guard stopped arguing and stared at Mathew.

'Leave those men alone,' protested the young woman.

'Sergeant, wait! Have these men put in the washhouse, I will tend to them,' said Mathew.

The sergeant glared at Mathew, 'who the hell do you think you are giving me orders?'

The woman spun around, 'leave those men alone.'

'I am surgeon to Lady Brooke. If you don't believe me and want me to drag the colonel from his sick wife's side, to order you to do as I ask, I am perfectly willing to do so,' retorted Mathew angrily.

The sergeant faltered, wanted to protest a little more, but then thought better of it.

'Put them in the washhouse yourself,' releasing the horses halter he stormed off towards the guard house.

'Thank you, Sir,' said the young woman. 'May I inquire who it is that has saved these men?'

'My name is Mathew Fletcher, as I said, I'm a surgeon. I'm here as a guest of Lord Brooke you might say.'

'Well, Surgeon Mathew Fletcher, I am grateful for your intervention. My name is Susannah Moyses of Kineton. Two days ago, a great battle took place close to the village. There are lots of wounded and dying soldiers who have just been left behind by your army.

They have been left in the fields where they fell, or have been lodged with the people of my village, who are expected to accommodate, feed and care for them. Our men are digging pits to bury the dead, but we cannot cope with all the wounded. So I borrowed this cart from the miller and brought some of the wounded here.'

'Are there really that many dead and wounded soldiers?' asked Mathew.

'More than anyone has been able to count. Many of the wounded have been robbed and then murdered where they lay. News of the battle has travelled far and wide, and now strangers have come looking for rich picking's. The wounded lucky enough to be found by more compassionate souls from our village have been rescued from the fields.

'How many more do you plan to bring here?' asked Mortimer.

'As many as I can. Some of the not so badly wounded have left the village already. The villagers tell me the wounded have had enough and that those that can are going home and don't want to fight anymore,' said Susannah.

'You're a brave woman bringing these men here on your own. I will speak to Lord Brooke for you and ask him if he will take in some more of the wounded, but I don't think it will be many, the castle is overcrowded as it is. We were captured with the king's baggage-train, three days passed,' said Mathew.

'You mean you are one of the king's men; how is it the lord of the castle lets you walk free?' asked Susannah.

'It's complicated, but the simplest answer is, I don't take sides. As a surgeon I heal the sick and wounded no matter which side they were fighting on,' said Mathew.

'What's so complicated about that?' asked a puzzled Susannah.

'War; what it makes people do and why they do it,' said a reflective Mathew. 'Look at you for instance, why aren't you at home with your husband and children, won't they be worrying about you, or is your husband one of the wounded?'

'If you must know,' said Susannah, 'I'm not married, and I don't have any children, unless that is, you count my four brothers and one sister. Our parents died a few years ago, and I just seem to have taken over the running of the family. I'm the oldest; then there is Oliver, Amos and Walter who are of working age. They earn enough for us all to live on. Roger does odd jobs when he can, and little Grace helps me around the house.'

A groan of pain from a man lying in the cart brought their attention back to the wounded soldiers.

'Let's get the men inside so I can examine them,' said Mathew. As Mathew and Mortimer lifted the first wounded man from the cart, Susannah entered the long single story building set against the castle wall which was used as the laundry. The air inside was warm and thick with moisture. She could smell and taste the lye soap infused with lavender emanating from three large wooden vats, around which a group of women were washing clothes. One of the women stopped work and came over to Susannah, drying her red swollen hands and arms on her grubby apron.

'You the new girl they've sent to help,' she barked at Susannah.

'No,' responded Susannah, her hands going to her hips in a stance of defiance. 'I have brought wounded soldiers to the castle to be treated by the surgeon. He said they had to be brought in here until more permanent quarters can be found for them. I need a dry, clean corner out of the way to lay them down.'

'You're not bringing no men in here. We've got enough work to do. This ain't no sick room,' said the woman squaring up to Susannah. At that moment Mortimer and Mathew staggered into the washroom carrying a wounded soldier.

'Where are we putting him,' demanded Mathew. Susannah looked around and pointed to an open door.

'You can't go in there,' protested the washerwoman. Susannah pushed past her and went to inspect the second room of the wash house. As she had suspected, it was a drying room with a fire at one end and ropes strung from one wall to the opposite wall on which washing was hung to dry.

'Lay the men here, in the corner where they will be out of the way,' instructed Susannah.

'I've told you, I don't want these men in here. This is no place for men, sick or not. You wait till Lady Brooke gets to hear about this, she'll have you and your friends chucked in the gaol, you just wait and see,' scolded the washerwoman.

Mathew laid the wounded man on the cobbled floor and turned to the washerwoman.

'My Good Woman, I am Lady Brooke's surgeon. These men will stay here, where my assistants and I will tend to their wounds. Susannah here, with help from yourself and the other women, will nurse them until they are well enough to leave, or I will speak to Lady Brooke and have you all replaced,' Mathew didn't wait for a response, he and Mortimer went to fetch the next soldier from the cart.

'Well, really,' huffed the washerwoman, giving Susannah a look that would curdle milk, before returning to the other washerwomen still working in the next room.

When the last man had been brought inside, Mathew sent Mortimer to find three palliasses and blankets for the men to sleep on. Susannah stayed with the men as Mathew went to make peace with the washerwoman. The promise of extra pay, for the inconvenience of tending to the men, seemed to do the trick.

A few hours later, Mathew, Mortimer and Susannah stood outside the wash house. It felt cold to be outside and away from the stuffy, damp warmth of the washroom.

'Those men will recover quickly enough, their wounds look worse than they really are. None of their wounds are life-threatening so long as they are kept clean,' Mathew informed Susannah.

'You mean I've wasted my time and your time bringing them here because they would have recovered anyway,' snapped Susannah.

'No, not at all, those men can count themselves very lucky that you brought them here. They will receive good care while they are here and will recover all the quicker. Had they been left to the mercy of the villagers in Kineton, their wounds may not have been treated correctly, and they would have become ill and died of disease or an infection. No, no you have probably saved those men's lives by bringing them here,' responded Mathew in a conciliatory manner. 'Come and join us while we eat. You must be hungry; it has been a long day for all of us.'

'Thank you, I would like to, but it's getting late. I want to get home before it gets dark,' said Susannah.

'Too late for that,' said Mortimer, 'it'll be dark in an hour or so. You don't want to be on the road on your own at night.'

'He's right,' said Mathew. 'I would suggest you stay with us, but three men and one woman spending the night in one chamber wouldn't be seemly.'

'You could spend the night in the washhouse,' suggested Mortimer. 'If anyone were to ask what you are doing there you could tell them you are nursing the sick men. They're in no fit state to bother you and, if it would make you feel better, Mathew could give you a sleeping draft to put in their drink that would make them sleep all night.'

'Very well, I'll do that. Now, if I'm to be your guest, you can buy me my supper like good gentlemen should. But tomorrow, I'll have some explaining to do when I get home, my brothers will be wondering what has happened to me,' confessed Susannah.

Later that night, after Susannah had left them, Mathew and Mortimer returned to their chamber for the night to find Potter waiting for them. As they walked through the door, Potter jumped to his feet.

'Where have you been?' demanded Potter.

Mathew and Mortimer looked at each other confused as to why Potter was so agitated.

'We went for something to eat and drink. What's wrong?' asked Mathew.

'Last night, I was watching the guard in the cellar, the one I told you about with the florins. While he was on duty he got a visitor and, judging from the way he was dressed, it's an officer from the castle,' said Potter.

'Who?' asked Mathew.

'I don't know. The man had his back to me, the light was not good for me to see clearly, and I was too far away to hear what the two were saying,' said Potter.

'You fool, it could just have been an officer checking on the guard,' said Mortimer.

'No it wasn't,' insisted Potter. 'Officers delegate that job to sergeants and, if the officer had been checking on the guard, he was very casual about it. They were talking in low voices, and the officer stayed with the guard far too long for it to simply be a routine check to see if the guard was awake or not. I wanted to stay longer after the officer left, but I was getting tired. I couldn't afford to fall asleep and start snoring, so I went to the tavern for a drink and a game of cards. By the time I came back here, you were gone. I'll go back to the cellar again tonight and prepare somewhere to hide from where I might be able to hear what the officer says if he comes back. If the officer had just turned around, I would have seen his face.'

The air in the washhouse felt colder and damper than it did earlier in the day when it had been a hive of activity, and the smell of lye soap and lavender burned the back of her throat. A fire was still burning in the hearth, though it was only a token of the one she had seen earlier as it heated cauldrons of water to wash the castle linen and soldiers clothes. In the roomy interior of the laundry, she could hear the sound of snoring coming from the drying chamber. Susannah went to see her patients one last time before she settled for the night. As she stood in the doorway to the drying chamber, she could see that two of the men were asleep, but one lay on his straw-filled bed scratching at his arms and chest. She knelt down beside him and asked what was wrong with him.

'Lice, Miss, they're eating me alive.' He pulled up the sleeve of his shirt and, even in the gloomy half-light offered by the fire in the back wall, she could see the raised spots on his skin.

'Give me your clothes' demanded Susannah.

'What?' exclaimed the soldier.

'Just do it,' demanded Susannah, 'you have a blanket to cover your modesty. She looked at the two sleeping soldier's, they too showed signs of lice on their bare arms and necks. She woke them up demanding that they too gave her their clothes. For the next couple of hours, Susannah washed the soldier's clothes in the tepid water left in the wash tubs. Setting the clothes to dry in front of the fire in the drying chamber, she added more wood to the dying fire and brought it back to life. As the warmth in the chamber increased, the wet clothes began to steam. She returned to the men with a bucket of water and a block of soap, 'now it's your turn,' she said emphatically. The soldiers began to protest. Finally, they came to a compromise; they would let her wash what was not covered by their blanket, and the soldiers would clean the private parts of their bodies. All went well until she arrived at the last of the three; he threw back his blanket to reveal an erection pointing at the rafters.

'What do think of that?' he grinned proudly.

Susannah dropped a cold, sopping wet cloth onto his private parts, 'I've got a twelve-year-old brother at home who can boast a better manhood than that. If I were you I would keep that hidden from the ladies, you wouldn't want to put them off before you had a chance to bed them.'

The other two men howled with laughter as Susannah walked away to fetch the sleeping draft that Mathew had prepared for her. Back in the washing chamber, she began to scratch at her clothing, '*ooh. No, I've picked up lice as well'*. Susannah wanted to strip off her clothes there and then, but hesitated, remembering the men in the next chamber and how they no longer seemed as sick as she had once feared. She added some small beer to the sleeping draft and returned to the men, telling them it would ease their itching. Happy the men in the next room would soon be asleep, Susannah went in search of something clean to wear. She found a basket of linen in which a pile of men's shirt had been folded ready for returning to their owners. Standing in the darkest corner of the laundry, Susannah stripped off her own clothes and put on the shirt, it only came down to her knees. '*It will have to do,'* she thought, as she set about washing her own lice-infested clothing.

She built up the fire in the washroom and put her own wet clothes to dry in front of it. With no bed of her own, she used the remaining linen in the basket for a pillow to lay down on a low wooden table used to keep the clean laundry off the floor. As her own clothes steamed in front of the fire and the irritating sound of snoring came from the soldiers, she drifted away into a fitful sleep in front of the fire.

Chapter Sixteen

As the new day brought life to the castle, and more and more people filled the courtyard to begin their daily business, Susannah woke with a pain in her hips and shoulders from sleeping on the table. She stretched her aching limbs. The washerwomen would be arriving soon, so she dressed in her own clothes and rekindled the fire, easing her aching muscles in the warmth of its glow.

A yell of pain and alarm from outside brought her to the door of the laundry to see what had happened. Outside, the terrifying scream had made everyone who heard it stop what they were doing and look in the direction the noise was coming from. Confused moments passed as the disturbance continued, and then women began to scream and run, all calling out the words that no one ever wanted to hear, words that could send shivers down the spines of even the strongest man.

'Mad Dog! A mad dog has got him' cried the terrified voices.

As Mathew and Mortimer made their way to visit Susannah and the sick men in the laundry, they too stopped and watched in horror as a large dog with massive jaws tore at the arm of an elderly man. The dog had him on the ground, pulling on his arm, dragging the old man after it towards the castle wall. The dog's jaws were covered in blood-stained foam, its wild eyes filled with pain and terror. As the old man tried to pull away from the animal, it only made the dog more determined to drag him away as it shook his arm and snarled. Spectators watched from a distance, too afraid to go near the dog less it turn on them as well.

From a door in the base of a tower emerged a soldier. Pushing through the onlookers he marched up to the dog, confidently stepped astride its back, and crooked his arm under its neck and drawing its head up and back with his right hand he drew a long broad-bladed knife from his belt and slit the dog's throat. With a brief whimper, the dog went limp releasing the old man's arm. The dog dropped to the ground, blood still oozing from the deep cut which had almost removed its head, its blood soaking into the dirt between the cobbles of the courtyard. The old man pulled away nursing his arm as an old woman ran to his side.

Mathew and Mortimer rushed across to the old man. With his own knife, Mathew cut away the old man's sleeve to examine the wound. The crowd drew closer as the old man lay on the ground shaking and crying. Mortimer knelt at his head and raised it up slightly to rest his head and shoulders on his lap.

'How bad is it?' asked Mortimer.

Mathew took a moment before answering, 'His arm is badly torn, and both the Ulna and Radius are broken. The wound and the bones will heal in time, but if he has contracted rabies from the dog, he'll not live long enough to regain the use of it. The sooner I clean and set his arm the better; we'll just have to hope the dog was not diseased. Mortimer lifted the old man from the ground and carried him towards the stall outside the laundry which Mathew used for treating the sick.

'No, bring him into the guardroom,' said the soldier.

Mortimer laid the old man on the guardroom table.

'I know this man,' said the soldier,' in his younger days he was a sergeant here and treated me well when I was new to soldiering. I must get back to my work, I'm on duty up yon tower if you need me, but make sure you treat my old sergeant well, or you will have me to answer to.' The soldier lumbered outside.

'If Lord Brooke had a garrison of soldiers the size of that man he'd be able to defeat the royalist army and make himself king,' suggested Mortimer in a low voice.

'Yes,' agreed Mathew, 'he doesn't look like the kind of person you would want to make an enemy of.'

The old woman held onto the former sergeant's good arm, tears in her eyes as she fretted over her husband.

'I can't pay you,' she confessed, 'we've got no money, except what we can beg. The soldiers here see we don't starve, but we've got nothing to give you.'

'Don't worry about it,' said Mathew, 'I can pass the cost onto some who can afford it. I would like to bleed him and draw away any poison from his injured arm,' he informed Mortimer, 'but he is too old, and I suspect he has lost too much blood already. The loss of more blood would only make him weaker, and he's going to need all the strength he can muster to recover from these injuries. Stay with him and keep him as calm as you can, I'll be back as soon as I can, with my surgeon's box, to treat the wound,' instructed Mathew.

By the time Mathew returned to the guardroom, Mortimer had cleared another table of cups, jugs of beer, bowls and scraps of waste food on which to place Mathew's surgeon's chest. Setting some flasks and jars to one side, he removed his surgical instruments.

'Mix me up these ingredients will you, Charles, *four ounces of Spirit of wine, one ounce of treacle of Andromache.'*

Mortimer busied himself with Mathew's request and smiled inwardly at Mathew's use of his Christian name. The old man began to shiver, the blood draining from his face, Mathew could see the pulse beating rapidly in his scrawny neck.

'Pass me the *laudanum*, he's going into shock,' said Mathew.

After a few sips of the sticky brown liquid, the old man began to relax a little. Mathew examined his torn arm, cleaning away bits of cloth and loose tissue, the broken ends of the Ulna and Radius easily visible as they protruded from the old man's flesh. Mathew surveyed the wound, gave the old man a few more sips of *laudanum* and went to see how Mortimer was getting on.

'Had he been younger, I would have amputated the arm,' said Mathew, 'But I don't think he would survive the operation.'

'What are you going to do then?' asked Mortimer.

Mathew thought about his reply before answering, then in a low voice so the old woman wouldn't hear him. 'The kindest thing I can think of. I'm going to clean the wound and set the arm in a splint, then dose him up with *laudanum* and hope for the best. After forty days, if we see the signs of melancholy followed by a fever, thirst, the fear of water and extreme convulsions, he has mad dog disease and will die. That is to say, if he doesn't die of infection, shock or heart failure first brought on by these wounds.'

Mortimer turned to look at the old man lying on the table, 'Poor old bugger. Have you told his wife?'

'No, she looks a bit confused about what's happened to her husband already, there's no point in giving her more bad news,' said Mathew.

Mathew picked up a thick bandage, and the mixture Mortimer had made for him. 'After I've repaired as much of the arm as I can, I'm going to spread some of that mixture you've made on his arm and make a clout to cover the wound. Then we'll take him and his wife home. I'll come back and check on him every day and hope for the best.

As Mathew and Mortimer carried the old man from the guardroom, Susanna Moyses drove up with her cart.

'Word has gone round that you are treating the man attacked by the dog, I've come to see if I can help, but you seem to have finished. You can put him in the back if you like: where does he live?' she asked.

'We have a place outside the castle in one of the cottages near the river,' said the old woman.

'Who's looking after the men in the laundry?' asked Mathew.

'The washerwomen are looking after them. The extra pay you told them about has encouraged them to become nurses.'

Moments later, Mathew had the old sergeant on the back of the cart with the old woman, and while Mortimer walked alongside the cart, Mathew sat next to Susannah on the driver's seat. They were soon outside a dilapidated old shack which the elderly couple called home.

'Jeremiah, we are home,' said the old woman as the cart pulled to a halt. The old man seemed to perk up a little at the sound of his name and home.

'We need to put him to bed,' said Mathew as he jumped down from the cart. The old woman ignored him, shuffling off the back of the wooden wheeled vehicle to go and open the door of their shack. When she returned, she looked at the old man on the cart.

'You daft bugger,' she wailed at him, 'What have you gone and done now?' Wiping tears from her cheek and nose with her apron using one hand, she gave her husband a poke in the side with her stick using the other.

'Be careful!' said Mortimer, 'you know what happened to him; you saw it.'

'Yes,' said Mathew, 'don't you remember, he was attacked by a dog and badly mauled?'

'What dog, where?' asked the old woman.

'In the castle, you saw it happen, we have just brought you both home,' insisted Mortimer, confused at why the old woman was acting as though she had just met them for the first time.

'It doesn't matter now,' said Mathew. 'It's as I suspected. We'd better get him inside where he can rest.'

The old woman stepped aside as Mathew and Mortimer lifted Jeremiah from the cart.

'Humour her,' Mathew said to Susannah, 'she is suffering from confusion of the mind, it sometimes happens to old people.'

Susannah took the old woman by the arm, and they both followed the men into the shack.

'On there,' the woman pointed to a pile of rags heaped on a sagging rope bed in the corner of the dirt floor room. A feeble fire struggled for life in the hearth with a pot of something simmering on a trivet that Mathew assumed to be soup. A single rush light sat on the table waiting to be lit. The only other light venturing into the shack came through the open door and a small glassless shuttered window in the front wall. Susannah sat the old woman on a rickety stool which in better days had once been a chair.

'Can I get you anything?' Susannah asked.

'Stop fussing girl,' said the old woman. 'There's nothing wrong with me, it's that silly fool lying there that needs a woman's hand.'

'I'll come and check on him tomorrow,' Mathew told the old woman. 'So I can change his bandages.'

'We've no money if that's what you're after,' said the old woman shaking her head and pointing her stick at Jeremiah. 'He does what little he can to earn a crust and begs from the rest. I'm surprised we've lasted this long, what with winter coming. Mark my words, this'll be the last winter we see before God takes us to a better place.'

The old woman got up and made her way over to Jeremiah. 'I've got some soup left from last night's supper, do you want some?'

'Just a drop, is there any bread left?' he asked.

'No, you had the last this morning, you'll have to do without,' she told him. 'What have you done to that arm of yours, have you been fighting again? I've told you about fighting, but you never listen.'

Mathew indicated the door to Mortimer, Susannah also got the message.

'I'll get some bread and cheese for them tomorrow,' said Susannah, 'shall I meet you here?' She smiled at Mathew. He blushed, she smiled all the more.

'I'll take that as a yes then,' as she spun on her heel and climbed back on her cart. But, before she drove away, she gave Mathew another big smile and a wave that told him she would be back for more reasons than bringing bread and cheese for the old couple.

'I think she likes you,' said Mortimer trying to hold back a snigger.

'She was just being polite,' said Mathew as he marched off towards the Barbican gate, leaving Mortimer behind laughing.

The big soldier, who had killed the mad dog, climbed the steps to Caesar's Tower, an officer of the castle waiting for him at the top. As the giant soldier came onto the turret top, the officer dismissed the guard that was on duty.

'You took your time getting here,' snapped the officer.

'I got delayed. What do you want?' asked the soldier.

'That Captain Broadwaters who came from Lord Essex is asking too many questions about the gold in the cellar. He had it all checked again and has noticed some has gone missing. Now he's started an investigation to try and find out who has taken it.'

'How's he going to find that out, there's only you and me knows what's happening to it, and where we are storing it,' said the soldier.

'Yes, I know, but when he reports back to Lord Essex that a portion of its gone missing, more people will be sent to investigate the loss, and I want to ensure I get my fair share of it before that happens. I intend to get rich out of this war, and I see that gold as part of the spoils of war for the taking.'

'You'd better not forget my share,' said the soldier stepping menacingly close to the officer.

'No, no, I'll see that you get your share, then we go our separate ways as agreed,' said the officer. 'But first I want more gold and jewels; I intend to live well after this war is over and done. Tonight that idiot will be on guard at the door again so we will help ourselves to another box or two of the treasure. But first I have a little job for you to do. Captain Broadwaters has confided in me, so I have arranged to have a private talk with him, but it will be you who is waiting for him. Once you have dealt with him, I want you to put this note in his purse.'

Chapter Seventeen

Captain Broadwaters climbed the steps of Caesar's Tower. He was deep in thought as he made his way up the steep, narrow, spiral, stone steps. The lantern in his hand gave just enough light to see a few paces ahead of him. It was a strange time and place to have a rendezvous, but the note the soldier had given him implied its writer had vital intelligence to impart about the theft of treasure from the cellar. The note specified the time and place to ensure the anonymity of the informer from the rest of the garrison officers who at that time, were dining with the colonel in the Great Hall. As Captain Broadwaters stepped out onto the turret top, the wind blowing across the top of the tower almost relieved him of his broad-brimmed felt hat; he clutched at the brim instinctively to hold it in place. He wished he'd worn a cloak, the wind had a bite to it as it blew across the top of the castle walls. He would have to discuss this latest intelligence with Captain Bridges after the colonel's dinner. Captain Bridges had promised Captain Broadwaters his full support in tracking down the thief, and the two men had agreed to keep each other up to date with their investigations. Now it seemed Captain Broadwaters was on the verge of a breakthrough.

He greeted the soldier on guard duty and went to look out over the edge of the tower at the river which ran close to the castle. For a brief moment, the clouds broke and a large moon reflected off the water below before the image was washed away when clouds dashed across the heavens blocking the silver orb from view.

Captain Bridges had been a loyal officer serving with Lord Brooke for many years, so if anyone would have an idea of how this crime was being committed, he would. Captain Broadwaters, sensitive to the fact that he had already insulted Lord Brooke once by insisting on checking the treasure store for himself, didn't want to give His Lordship the news that the treasure was being stolen from under his nose. So, by asking for Captain Bridges help, he hoped the captain would act as an intermediary and smooth the waters between himself and Lord Brooke, and that Captain Bridges and himself could present the colonel with the thief.

If the inventory taken when the treasure had been captured was accurate, someone in the castle had already helped themselves to a small fortune. Captain Broadwaters' superiors had given him a list of the silver plate removed from Oxford and which Prince Rupert had secured at Worcester, but now half of that silver plate was missing, along with caskets of coins.

He wished he hadn't been given this job. He should be back in command of his company; it had been his job as a lawyer in private life that had marked him out for the task he now undertook. Truth be told, he needed to know if Lord Brooke had been taking the treasure or if it had been stolen by scavenging soldiers. He'd been told Captain Bridges had insisted, that as soon as the treasure wagons had been discovered, they remain well guarded until they could be unloaded into the castle cellar store. He felt reasonably sure that whoever the thief was it was someone in a position of authority within the castle. Captain Broadwaters felt his stomach grumble with hunger and hoped that Captain Bridges wouldn't keep him waiting too long. He had been looking forward to dinner with the colonel. The moon broke from behind a cloud again distracting his thoughts as he stared at the white orb in the dark sky before it was once again blocked from his view by clouds skidding across the stars, plunging the world around the castle into darkness.

Inside the Great Hall, Lord Brooke sat at the head of the table with Major Overton and Captain Bridges sitting either side of him. Other officers from his command also sat waiting for the colonel to signal the start of the dinner. Two empty seats were conspicuous by their occupant's absence. Captain Broadwaters and Captain Jeffries were missing from the dinner table.

'Blast those men, if they haven't the manners to turn up on time or send an apology for their tardiness then we shall start without them,' Lord Brooke slapped his hand on the table. The servants sprang into action bringing through the evening meal. Part way through their dinner, a young officer arrived in the Great Hall and begged Lord Brooke' pardon for being late.

'Take your seat, Captain Jeffries, you can explain to me first thing in the morning why you insult my guests by being late to the table,' said Lord Brooke.

Captain Broadwaters caught the sound of a footstep behind him and ignored the guard as he paced the tower top. He continued to look out across the landscape waiting for the clouds to break and the vista before him to become flooded with silver light once again. By the time he realised the footsteps had stopped behind him a hand was across his mouth, pulling his head back taking him by surprise. He reached up and grabbed the large wrist that held him in an iron grip, at the same time trying to wriggle free and face his attacker. A sharp stab of pain just below his left ear and then across his throat made his body stiffen for a moment. He tried to call out, but the giant's hand across his mouth prevented it. For a brief time his lungs expanded sucking in a mixture of blood and air; then very quickly, his eyes began to feel heavy, and his knees becoming weak and buckling beneath him. The moon broke briefly from behind the clouds, then was gone, it left its imprint on his mind as his vision fogged; there was no more strength left in his arms to fight the hand across his mouth. He felt cold, and then he felt nothing, the world around him had turned black.

If anyone had looked up at the edge of the tower a moment later, they would have seen a massive shadowy figure discarding Captain Broadwaters stout frame between the crenulations of the turret top, allowing it to fall head first to the ground below.

Later that night a finely dressed man spoke to a large and powerful soldier.

'You have done well. Here take this and leave the castle tonight. Do not go home, if anyone suspects you were involved in the captain's murder that is the first place they will look for you,' instructed the finely dressed figure.

The soldier weighed the purse of coin in his hand and smiled.

'I've nothing to go back home for anyway,' said the soldier.

'When you feel safe, send word to me about where you are, I may have need of you again.'

The two men left the shadow of the tower wall in different directions, one to the main gate the other towards the Great Hall.

At Lord Brooke's dinner table a young officer entered the Great Hall, bowed to Lord Brooke, 'With your leave Sir, I have a message for Captain Bridges.'

The junior officer approached Captain Bridges and whispered in his ear, then left.

Captain Bridges apologised to Lord Brooke, 'Please forgive the intrusion, Sir, it is a trivial matter that could have waited until later. I will reprimand the officer later, but I think it best I deal with it myself.'

As the first light of day began to break across the River Avon and over the town of Warwick, it bathed the walls of Warwick Castle in a warm, amber glow. Cocks crowed, and dogs barked as the town's folk began their new day. Boatmen at the river's edge prepared their craft to take on new cargos. New arrivals, bringing sugar and tobacco from Bristol, queued to take their turn at the quayside. The owner of a riverside store-house, set against the base of the castle walls, opened the double doors to his store ready to remove the empty wine casks which needed to be loaded onto the waiting boats moored at the quayside and receive fresh supplies for the castle and town of Warwick. The sailors quickly set about the business of loading their boat, while the store-man, happy that the day's work had begun, left his son to keep an eye on how the work progressed. He went behind the store-house to relieve his bladder. As he rounded the back of the building, he found a body curled up against the back wall of his store. At first, he thought it was a drunk sleeping off the drink from the night before, it wouldn't have been the first one he'd found, but this one looked different. As he drew closer the blood down the front of the man's clothing told him all he needed to know. The storeman stared in horror at the corps, not wanting to believe what he was seeing.

Regaining his wits, he ran into town calling for the constable.

By the time the store-man returned with the constable, they were leading a crowd of curious town's people, all wanting to see the body of the well-dressed man at the base of the castle wall. As they arrived at the riverside store, there was already a group of sailors gathered around the body.

Chapter Eighteen

Mathew awoke from a dream about Suzanna Moyses. He shifted position, he was uncomfortable laying face down, and the smell of mouldy straw from his palliasse was giving him a headache. On his bed, up against the other wall, Mortimer snored loudly, which Potter somehow managed to sleep through in blissful ignorance. Perhaps it was because he seemed to have the largest and thickest palliasse of the three of them even though he was the smallest of the three. Dawn was bringing the castle to life, Mathew could hear voices from outside. The window into their chamber was too small and set in the wrong wall to let in much of the morning light just yet. Mathew looked around the chamber, only able to make out the shadowy shapes about him. Looking toward the unglazed window and at the grey sky outside, he shivered. Lying on his bed with the sound of nailed footsteps on cobbles outside reminded him of being locked in the tower. The urgent sound of marching feet grew louder, finally passing outside the chamber window. He waited for the banging on his door to start as he pulled his thick woollen blanket up to his chin and rolled onto his side. As he thought they would, the footsteps entered the tower passage and stopped outside his door, but instead of someone banging on his door, the door flew open, and a gruff-voiced called his name.

'Surgeon Fletcher, you are needed urgently: come with me.' A determined looking soldier in a helmet and wearing back and breast armour filled the doorway, his frame illuminated with yellow light by the lantern in his hand.

'What's the Matter; is the castle under attack?' asked Mathew flippantly.

'No, just come with me, you're wanted,' barked the soldier. Mathew looked at his companions who were now wide awake and propped up on their elbows watching the soldier in the doorway, curious as to why Mathew had been summoned so early in the morning.

'Do you want me to come with you?' asked Mortimer.

'No, I'll be fine. If I were under arrest, the soldier wouldn't be asking me to go with him. Just save me some breakfast for when I get back.'

Mathew threw his blanket aside and grabbed his shoes. The tower chamber was cold as he buttoned his waistcoat. He pulled his jacket on and rescued his hat from the stool at the foot of his bed.

'Where are we going?' He asked as he followed the soldier out of the door. The soldier didn't answer and marched on ahead. To Mathew's surprise, he was lead towards the Barbican and out into the fringes of the town, then down the lane that ran to the river. There, below Caesar's Tower and behind a small house and goods store was a body. Major Overton and Lord Brooke conversed with another man a short distance from the store-house. Captain Bridges stood over the body with two soldiers looking at the grizzly remains. On spotting Mathew, Major Overton came to meet him, 'a body has been found at the foot of the wall,' he informed Mathew leading him over to see the corpse.

'I suggested to Lord Brooke that you should see the body before it was removed,' said the major.

Mathew looked confused, 'If he's dead what can I do for him?'

'I don't know, something,' said Major Overton, 'when word of this gets back to London, John Pym and the Committee of Safety will want to know why their representative was murdered. I just want you to look at the body and tell me if there is anything about it that might indicate who the murderer could be.'

Mathew scratched his head, 'I don't know what to look for. I haven't got any of my instruments with me, but if it pleases you, I'll look him over.' Mathew knelt by the body, rolling Captain Broadwaters corps onto its back, the gaping wound in his neck all too apparent. He spent a few minutes turning the body one way and then the other. The limbs had begun to stiffen as Rigor Mortis set in, so he was unable to fully unfurl the body from its foetal like position. After a quick examination of Captain Broadwaters, Mathew searched up the bank from the back of the store-house where the body had been found.

'He wasn't killed here,' said Mathew. 'There's not enough blood on the ground. If he had been killed here, there would be blood everywhere. Look at the front of his jacket, it's soaked in blood. Both his arms and one of his legs are broken. He was either badly beaten and killed before he was dumped here, or more likely, killed up there (pointing at the tower top) and pushed over the edge. The body then rolled to a stop at the base of the bank and up against the store-house.'

'Are there any clues as to who the killer may have been?' ask the major.

'Not that I can tell while he lies here, and I'm not really sure what it is I would be looking for to find out, but if I can be allowed time to examine the body somewhere undisturbed, I may learn more,' said Mathew.

'Very well, I will speak to Lord Brooke and ask him to provide somewhere for you to perform your examination of the captain and we'll see what you can find out,' said Major Overton.

In a small hut built up against the inside of the northern wall of the castle, Captain Broadwaters body was laid out on a table in the centre of the single-roomed dwelling. On the other side of the castle, Mathew, Major Overton, Lord Brooke and Captain Bridges climbed to the top of Caesar's Tower. It didn't take long for Mathew to find the spot where Captain

Broadwaters had been murdered. The stone blocks at the base of the crenulations and across the walkway, though having been flushed with water, still bore the dark stains of the captain's blood.

'I will find out who was on guard duty last night,' said Captain Bridges as he left the tower top. Lord Brooke eyed the location suspiciously and stepped around the darkened blood stains to look over the edge of the wall. Mathew and Major Overton joined him as though to confirm this was the place that Captain Broadwaters fell from. The height made Mathew's vision blur and his head spin, he was about to tumble forward when Major Overton grabbed him by the belt and dragged him back.

'Mathew! – Careful, heights can do strange things to a man's mind.' Mathew leaned against the wall and took a deep breath, letting it out slowly. He could feel his heart trying to beat its way out of his chest, and every nerve in his body seemed to be tingling; slowly the dizziness and the urge to fall forward passed.

'Thank you, Robert, I don't know what came over me – I've never been so high up before,' said Mathew. 'I think I would like to go down now and examine Captain Broadwaters' body.' He could feel a cold sweat running down his back, he shivered and entered the doorway at the turret top. The touch of the stone walls and being enclosed once more easing his tense muscles.

When Mathew entered the makeshift mortuary, Mortimer was waiting for him, Captain Broadwaters was on a table in the centre of the room, and a smaller table had been put to one side to hold Mathew's surgical instruments. Though Mortimer had placed a number of lanterns around the interior of the hut, there was still less light than Mathew would have wished.

'Open the door please, Charles, I need more light and, once I start to examine the body, the smell in here is going to get worse than it already is,' requested Mathew.

The earth floor was damp and smelt of urine, and cobwebs hung like dirty, shredded tapestries off the walls and roof beams. Mathew shivered again; he couldn't decide if it was this hut or the memory of looking over the edge of the tower that bothered him. The intrigue of examining the dead captain focused his mind on the task at hand; the thought of having permission to do his first autopsy on a dead body was something he never thought would happen. This kind of undertaking was usually reserved for senior physicians in London, and then only on rare occasions. The Major had been correct about one thing, something like this would never have happened to him in Hull or Beverley.

'Help me undress him, then you can leave if you don't want to watch, but stay by the door, I don't want to be interrupted,' Mathew instructed Mortimer.

'Er – no, it's fine. If I want to be your assistant, I will have to accustom myself to such sights. Just tell me what it is you plan to do to him?' asked Mortimer.

'The first thing I want to know is; was the captain beaten before he was killed, so I'm going to look for signs of contusions and injuries on his body that might have happened before he died. After that I shall examine the wound to his throat, to see if I can learn what sort of weapon was used to cut him. Oh, before I start, run and get a pen, paper and ink, you can make notations of what I find during the examination,' Mathew requested.

'I'll do that for you,' came a voice from behind the two men.

Mathew and Mortimer turned as one to see Susannah Moyses standing in the doorway.

'I saw the body brought in here earlier, so I waited to see who would turn up to take charge of it. When I saw a surgeon's chest taken into the hut, and later you two turn up, I just had to come and find out what was going on,' said Susannah.

While Mathew and Mortimer stood agog at the sight of Susannah, she drew closer to the table to look upon the naked captain.

'You can't stay here, this is an official examination which is about to take place and no place for a woman,' protested Mathew.

'Don't be silly. I can help you. I can write better than your friend Mortimer. So if I record what you find, he can assist you in your examination of the captain. This is not the first or the only dead body I've seen. It is not just the wounded I've been bringing off the battlefield at Kineton. There have been plenty of bodies to remove and bury; many of them defiled beyond recognition by shot and sword. I am also the eldest of six children, four brothers and the youngest child a sister. When I was ten years of age, I helped my mother when she gave birth to my sister. Three days later I sat by my mother's bed and held her hand as she died. A year later I held my father's hand as he died of consumption. Death no longer frightens me. I carried those wounded men off the battlefield because I've seen too much death. So I decided that if I can save the life of just one of them, then some wife, mother, father, brother or sister will get their man back. *So,* Mathew Fletcher, I am going to help you regardless of whether you want me to or not.' Susannah marched out of the hut.

Mathew and Mortimer stood rooted to the spot, speechless, before Mortimer spoke up, 'now I know for sure that she likes you.'

Minutes later Susannah returned with pen, ink, paper and a stool to sit on.

'Well, as you seem determined to stay, look in the captain's purse, and make a note of what you find. Was this a robbery?' Mathew instructed Susannah.

Susannah quickly found the captain's purse and emptied the contents out, 'there is money here, not a great deal, five silver shillings, a silver Groat, two silver pennies and a note.' Susannah read the note, 'This note asked for Captain Broadwaters to meet a Captain Jeffries at the top of Caesar's Tower at eight of the clock last night, something to do with thefts from the cellar.'

Mathew and Mortimer looked at each other, but they didn't voice their thoughts; Susannah wasn't privy to what was happening in the cellar.

You had better let me have the note,' requested Mathew, 'the major will want to see it. Write down that you found it in the captain's purse before we start the physical examination of the captain's body.'

Slowly and carefully with Mortimer's help, Mathew examined the body as they rolled the captain first one way and then the other.

'There appear to be no outward signs that the captain was subject to maltreatment before he was killed,' said Mathew speaking slowly so Susannah could keep up with him as she made her notes.

'The wound to his neck is deepest just below the left ear. I suspect that this is where the blade struck first and then see how it passes through the left Jugular vein and Carotid Artery and into the Sternomastoid muscle before it carries on into the larynx and then out the other side before severing the right Carotid Artery and Jugular. Um, stand in front of me, Charles.'

Mortimer stood facing Mathew wondering what he was about to do. Mathew raised his arm as though he was holding a knife and passed it in front of Mortimer's throat.

'Um, now turn around.'

Mathew came up behind Mortimer and put his left arm over Mortimer's left shoulder. Then, grasping him below the chin, pulled his head backwards. Using the thumb of his right hand as an imaginary knife, he traced it across Mortimer's exposed throat in the way he thought most similar to that of how the real killer's blade could have been struck into his victim's neck and drawn across his throat.

'Yes,' said Mathew, 'that seems to be the most likely way the killer struck the captain: he came upon him from behind without being seen and not giving the captain time to defend himself, grabbed him and slit his throat in this fashion.'

Susannah made a careful note of Mathew's experiment with Mortimer. Mortimer, on the other hand, shuddered, the blood draining from his face, 'funny to think I've just been murdered,' he jested, trying to make light of his feelings of uneasiness at how Captain Broadwaters had been killed.

Mathew picked up a scalpel, 'now I want to know why he had two broken arms and a broken leg.' Mortimer watched as Mathew sliced through the flesh of the captain's upper arm exposing the broken Humerus bone. Slicing further up the arm to the shoulder He found the Humerus dislocated from the Scapular. It didn't take him long to realise the Humerus, having been driven into the Scapular Acromion bone, had snapped it away from the rest of the Scapular.'

'Look at how these bones have been broken,' said Mathew to no one in particular; absorbed entirely in his work and fascination with the human body.

'I wonder if the other arm suffered the same kind of damage?' continued Mathew, talking out loud.

Mathew moved around the table to change places with Mortimer wanting to examine the captain's other arm. This time it was the Ulna and Radius bones in the forearm that were broken. Slicing through the flesh with his scalpel, Mathew soon found the shattered bones and exposed them. 'Both bones are broken at the same point, midway along their length.' Mortimer followed Mathew's directions as he pointed out the different parts of Captain Broadwaters' forearm. Mathew felt the shoulder joint: it was still intact, so he didn't bother to investigate it. Next, he moved down to the captain's leg. The lower part of the left Fibula was protruding through the skin, with a deep cut running up the captain's leg from the exposed broken bone. Mathew relayed his findings to Susannah. It looks like the Fibula broke, punctured the skin and as the leg buckled the protruding bone ripped along the lower leg where the flesh is thinnest.

'There is no bruising around the open fracture; therefore I think this injury occurred as a result of the fall from the tower or when the captain's body hit the store-house.'

Mathew stepped away from the table and studied the man lying before him.

'In my opinion, Captain Broadwaters died at the top of the tower when his throat was cut; death would have been quick to follow. The rest of his injuries were caused by the fall from the tower. All I can say about how he died is obvious; he died from loss of blood when his throat was cut. But looking at the neck wound – I would say it was caused by a wide bladed knife. Look here,' Mathew indicated for Mortimer to look as he pointed at the neck wound.

'See the difference between the cut to the neck that killed him and the cuts I have made with my scalpel. The neck was cut with one slice of the blade; to me, that indicates a long wide blade was used. Whereas, when you look at my incisions with the smaller blade of the scalpel, which has caused ridges in the tissue because I have used many small incisions to get deeper into the captain's muscle tissue.'

Mortimer reluctantly looked closer. Susannah, fascinated by what Mathew had been describing, decided to take a look for herself.

'Umm, yes, I see what you mean, the neck wound is similar to the wounds I have seen in dead men on the battlefield at Kineton; those that died by the sword had even deeper wounds, but still similar to the shape of the cut in the captain's throat. It would seem to me, Captain Broadwaters was killed by a soldier's blade,' said Susannah.

'I suspect you are correct,' agreed Mathew as he covered the captain with a blanket. 'It's clear Captain Broadwaters was murdered. Susannah, will you make two copies of your notes? I would like to keep a copy of them for myself; Lord Brooke will want the other copy. The problem is, in a castle full of soldiers, having a strong suspicion that a soldier killed the captain is of very little help.'

'After watching you dissect the captain like that, I'm in need of a drink. In fact, I should think we could all probably do with one,' said Mortimer.

'Yes, its thirsty work, but first I have to report what I have discovered to Major Overton, and while I'm with him, I will ask him to get the captain's body removed from here and arrange for his burial.'

They were just leaving the hut when an old woman came hobbling across the courtyard to find them.

'Sir, Sir, begging your pardon, Sir, it's my husband.'

It took Mathew a moment or two to recollect who the old woman was, 'Ah, yes, how is your husband?'

'Oh, he's taken to his bed and can't get up. He is suffering real bad,' said the woman.

'It's too soon for any signs of madness to show up after being bitten by the dog. What has happened to your husband? enquired Mathew.

'He's taken bad, he's awful pale, and he says his chest hurts, he says he can't breathe properly,' said the fidgeting old woman.

'You must help the woman,' said Susannah insistently.

Mathew, Susannah and Mortimer followed the old woman out of the castle to her shack at the edge of River Avon. Inside on the rope bed, which consisted of nothing more than a heap of rags, lay the old man. The little earth floor shelter stank of damp and rot, with the window fastened shut, the single roomed dwelling was gloomy and smoky. At this visit, Mathew noticed daylight through the bottom of the wooden walls of the shack where the rats had eaten their way through.

Susannah coughed as she entered, she tried to hold back the instinct to retch at the smell, stepping outside again for a moment. Mathew knelt on the damp floor next to the man; he took the old man's wrist and felt for his pulse, then listened to his chest after which he examined his eyes. Getting to his feet, Mathew led the old woman outside, 'it grieves me to tell you, but your husband is dying; his heart is failing. The strain of being attacked by the dog has been too much for him to bear. I'm sorry, but I don't think he will last until tomorrow, you need to make preparations for his passing.' Mathew informed the old woman as sympathetically as he could, but she collapsed to her knees wailing in grief. Susannah sprang to her side and put her arms around the old woman's shoulders, helping her to her feet, she took her back inside the hovel to her husband.

'Isn't there anything you can do for the old man?' asked Mortimer.

Mathew sighed and shook his head, 'What would be the point. It is better that he dies this way, rather than from the madness he probably picked up from that rabid dog which bit him. At least this will be quicker, and he will suffer less.'

Susannah joined them. It was a sombre trio that returned to their chamber in the Watergate Tower. I must go tell Major Overton about the captain, wait here I'll be back as soon as I can.

The major was grateful for Mathew's report of the autopsy. 'You are very welcome, Major; I have often longed for the opportunity to do such an examination, there is so much that we don't know about the human body. That knowledge will only come when medical men are allowed to study the human form in greater detail and discover its secrets.'

'It's not an occupation that appeals to me, though having benefitted from your skill as a surgeon, I will always be grateful it was you who treated my wounds and not one of the usual army surgeons. I want you to remind your friends that they must not speak of what you have discovered today or speak of Captain Broadwaters to anyone. I want to find the murderer, and I don't want anyone alerted to what you have discovered. In the meantime, I will have Captain Jeffries arrested and questioned as to why he was missing from Lord Brooke's dinner table last night around the time the murder was committed,' said the major.

When Mathew left to return to Susannah and Mortimer, Major Overton went in search of Captain Jeffries.

The Captain was in his quarters, Major Overton, Captain Bridges and Lord Brooke sat at his table while soldiers stood either side of the captain as he faced his superior officers.

'Why did you murder Captain Broadwaters?' demanded Captain Bridges.

'Wait a moment, Captain, we don't yet know that it was Captain Jeffries who killed him. The note simply stated they were to meet, it didn't say what night that was to be, the note could have been an old one,' intervened Major Overton.

'Why were you late for dinner last night, Captain?' asked Lord Brooke.

'I'm sorry, Sir, I didn't kill Captain Broadwaters. I was here in my quarters, I had fallen asleep,' Captain Jeffries hung his head in shame.

'You expect us to believe a feeble excuse like that when a note from you was found on the murdered captain,' sneered Captain Bridges.

'Now, now, Bridges, allow Captain Jeffries to answer the question in his own way,' said Lord Brooke.

'Why should we believe you?' asked Major Overton, 'Can you prove you fell asleep here and were not at the top of Caesar's tower murdering Captain Broadwaters?'

'I came off duty late yesterday afternoon and returned here to put on a clean shirt to attend the dinner. I had changed and had a little time to spare, so I sat in front of the fire with a cup of wine. I drank one cup and took another. The next thing I remember, I was waking up feeling groggy and realising I was late for the colonel's dinner. Look, you can see the stain on the floor where I dropped the cup of wine when I fell asleep.'

Everyone looked at the boards in front of the fire where a dark stain stood out from the dusty wooden floorboards.

‘That’s not proof of anything except your clumsiness,’ insisted Captain Bridges.

‘Do you still have any of the wine from last night?’ asked Major Overton.

‘Yes, Sir, on the board over there.’

Major Overton brought over the wine jug and took a little sip of the wine, it tasted bitter, ‘This wine tastes as though it is going sour; do you normally drink wine like this?’

‘I don’t often get wine at all, Sir, I can’t afford it. The wine was on this table here when I arrived yesterday, I thought someone had made me a gift of it,’ said Captain Jeffries.

‘Hmm, I want to take this and show it to my surgeon, this wine has a familiar aftertaste, I think Mathew’s findings may be relevant to your testimony,’ said the major.

‘What about the note with his name on it?’ asked Captain Bridges.

‘Do you have other examples of your handwriting available, Captain Jeffries?’ asked the major.

‘Yes, Sir, I have a letter I am writing to my parents, telling of my part in the battle with the king,’ Captain Jeffries retrieved the half-written letter from a box on the board next to where the wine jug had stood, and passed it to Major Overton. He compared the handwriting from both documents, then showed them to the colonel, both examples of writing were utterly different.

'Take him outside,' Lord Brooke instructed the two guards.

Once Captain Jeffries was out of earshot, Major Overton explained to Lord Brooke that he suspected the wine was drugged and that Captain Jeffries was being made to look like a scapegoat. Captain Bridges agreed with the major.

'Once the wine has been tested we will know for sure,' said Major Overton.

'Very good, Major; as soon as you are sure, let me know immediately,' said Lord Brooke.

Major Overton took the wine jug to Mathew, who tasted it and confirmed it had been drugged.

Yes, Major, the wine tastes like it has been laced with *laudanum*, and a lot of it, that's why it tastes so bitter. Whoever put the *laudanum* in the wine had no idea how much to use. It wasn't someone with medical training,' Mathew assured the major.

'Thank you, you have probably saved an innocent man from the gallows. I will go and give Captain Jeffries the good news. All we have to do now is find the real murderer,' said Major Overton.

Chapter Nineteen

'I have to go home; will you come with me?' asked Susannah.

Mathew stopped and looked at her, taken aback by the sudden request.

'I can't leave here, Lord Brooke and Major Overton, have told me I can't go.

'Why..... why can't you leave; they don't own you, you're not a prisoner are you? You're not a royalist sympathiser. What hold do they have over you?' demanded Susannah.

'I can't tell you. All I can say is... I am beholden to Major Overton. I wish I weren't, but there is nothing I can do about it. I wish I were free of all this, but I'm not,' said Mathew.

Susannah stared at him, her long hair hanging loose on her shoulders, framing a face livid with indignation.

'Ask them if you can come with me to Kineton to help the wounded that are too sick to travel. Promise them you will return in a couple of days, anything. Those soldiers that have been abandoned by both sides need your professional help. The people of Kineton need your help. Isn't that what you are supposed to do, help sick people,' pleaded Susannah.

Mathew looked helplessly into her face, his thoughts confused by what he was feeling towards her. Susannah waited for an answer. For some reason, Elizabeth's image came into Mathew's mind. His body and soul had missed her and longed for her so much over the past months, but that feeling of terrible emptiness was now gone. Her image evaporated. Was it because he had finally been able to take his revenge on the man responsible for Elizabeth's death, only for it to feel hollow and fill him with guilt, or had his feelings for Elizabeth changed? The image of Franks' face and the shock of acceptance it expressed when he had realised he was going to die replaced the image of Elizabeth. Mathew took a deep breath; Franks vanished as he focused on Susannah.

'I....I,' stuttered Mathew.

For the first time since meeting her, Mathew looked closely at Susannah's face and saw a beautiful young woman. With her green almond shaped eyes, her pale skin with just a faint hint of freckles which ran over her nose from cheek to cheek, her pink lips and slender neck, all framed by her auburn hair, he felt his heart racing as she held his gaze, waiting for an answer.

'Well!' said Susannah.

'Very well,' Mathew heard himself say, 'I will ask the major.' He suddenly felt as though a weight had been lifted from his shoulders. Susannah gave him a big hug.

'Come on them, no time like the present,' said Susannah.

Now, somehow, he felt free of a burden which he had carried for months and which had clouded his world. Susannah was nothing like Elizabeth and yet.....he couldn't quite work it out.....she was more than Elizabeth had been. She was not the apothecaries' daughter who got excited when Princes came to town or wanted beautiful clothes and status. Susannah's priorities were helping those in need, the same that he had vowed to do when he became a surgeon and had wanted to do since the day his mother had died. Susannah took him by the arm and led him towards the Great Hall. He didn't resist her; he knew he wanted to go with her. Before they entered the hall, Mathew insisted she wait for him outside. He would find Major Overton first and explain what they wanted to do and ask him to speak to Lord Brooke on their behalf.

Major Overton returned after a few minutes. As the major walked towards him, Mathew became nervous, what if Lord Brooke has said no? Susannah's request for him to go with her had become very important to him, for some reason he felt he needed to win her trust and return the friendship she had shown him.

'I was able to convince his lordship that letting you go could be useful. But, there are conditions to him releasing you. Mortimer and Potter must remain here, and you will return in three days. Also, while you are in Kineton, you must speak to the wounded and gather whatever intelligence you can on what the king's next move might be. But, whatever happens, I want you back here in three days, is that understood?' said Major Overton.

At first, Mathew was lost for words, he was so angry with the major putting conditions on his departure from the castle. He was being treated like a prisoner on parole. Mathew bit his tongue; it was his only way to get out of the castle with Susannah and without having the major or Captain Bridges escorting him. Later, he decided, he would deal with the major, but for now, he would go back to Susannah and give her the good news.

'Thank you, Robert. I will make preparations to leave,' said Mathew.

'By the time you are ready to go, I will have a pass made up for you to leave the castle,' said Major Overton.

Mathew left Major Overton without acknowledging his last remark, just wanting to get back to Susannah and give her the good news.

Mathew sighed with relief as he drove Susannah's cart away from Warwick Castle. Mortimer had helped him load his bulky surgeon's chest on the back along with a few personal belongings. Now Mortimer waved them both farewell as they left, saying he wished he could have gone with them. Potter was missing, so Mortimer promised he would tell him of Mathew's departure when he turned up again.

It didn't take long for Mathew and Susannah to get away from Warwick and head south on the Banbury Road towards Susannah's home village. This time it felt good to be sitting on a cart with the reins in his hands.

'Did you actually see the battle?' asked Mathew.

'Some of it; we watched from a distance. Many of the king's soldiers passed close by the village, so we followed them for a while until they stopped at Edgehill. The battle was confusing once the fighting started. Before the battle begun, both sides took up positions facing each other. The king's men were along the ridge at Edgehill and the Parliamentarians in the fields below. I thought the fighting would start during the morning, but nothing happened for hours, then in the afternoon, the battle started. I don't know who won. It looked like the Parliamentarians left the battlefield first, though from what I've seen from the numbers of dead and wounded, it seems that both sides suffered about the same number of dead and wounded. I didn't want to get involved at first, but I kept hearing stories of villagers going out to the battlefield and robbing the dead, then killing the wounded and robbing them as well. There was so much talk about the suffering of those left behind on the battlefield that I went out to the fields to see for myself. I found a soldier still alive, so I put him on my cart planning to take him home and care for him. Then I found another one, and then another. I couldn't take them all home with me, so I decided to take them to Warwick when one of them told me he was from Warwick Castle. Officers had come to our village with some wounded and said we had to take care of them and Parliament would refund our expenses, but there were so many of them we couldn't cope with them all. How did you get involved?'

Mathew wasn't sure how to answer the question and gave the matter a few moments thought before replying.

'Well... I ... just sort of fell into it. I helped Major Overton when he was wounded in a skirmish outside Hull and, once he recovered, he asked me to stay and help him,' answered Mathew not wanting to go into detail.

'But I thought you were captured with the king's baggage-train,' queried Susannah.

'Ah, well, yes....and er...well it's complicated,' stuttered Mathew.

'Were you captured by the royalist army and forced to work for them?' asked Susannah.

'No, not quite,' said Mathew.

'You mean you changed sides and went to work in the king's army because you wanted to,' continued Susannah.

'No, not that either,' said Mathew.

'Well, what were you doing with the royalists......spying on them?' said Susannah.

Mathew's face turned bright red, his mouth opening and closing with no words coming out.

'Ha; no wonder Major Overton doesn't like the idea of you leaving the castle, you've been spying on the royalists for him,' laughed Susannah.

'Shush,' said Mathew.

Susannah laughed all the more at Mathew's embarrassment. 'Some spy you must make if you look as guilty as that when anyone asks you a question or mentions the word spy around you.'

'It's not like that. As a surgeon I help people, and sometimes they tell me things or I overhear conversations that I can pass on to the major, that's all I do,' said Mathew.

'I expect the major thinks you may hear something useful from one of the wounded in Kineton and that's the reason why he let you leave. You said you had to be back in three days,' said Susannah. 'Is that to tell the major all the secrets that you are going to coax out of your patients? Do you tell him about me as well?'

'Nooo,' said Mathew. 'I only tell him what he needs to know. I've told him you have helped me and that is all. Why, do you disapprove of what I do? Are you going to turn me in once we arrive at Kineton?'

'I don't know,' said Susannah. 'It all depends.'

'On what?' asked Mathew.

'On how good a surgeon you are and if you are going to be nice to me,' smiled Susannah.

Mathew returned Susannah's smile, 'I'm the best surgeon you'll ever meet, and as far as being nice to you, well, I'm only nice to people who are nice to me.'

The rest of the journey to Kineton seemed to pass by in the blink of an eye as they enjoyed each other's company. Then as evening brought a chill breeze in from the east, they entered the village of Kineton.

'I live in a cottage on Manor Lane, it's up there past the church,' said Susannah.

As the cart came to a stop outside the front door, two children came out to greet them. Susannah hugged them both.

'Grace, Roger, this is my new friend, Mathew. He is a surgeon and has come to help heal the soldiers we have been bringing off the battlefield.'

Grace gave a little bob of a curtsey and Roger a nod of the head.

'You have taught them well considering they have no parents to show them how to behave,' said Mathew.

'The other three will be home later. We are a very close-knit village, so when it came time for the boys to start work, tradesmen in the village were very kind and took them on as apprentices. Oliver is the eldest; he is apprenticed to the blacksmith, Amos is training to be a baker and Walter wants to be a carpenter.

'You must be a popular family in the village,' commented Mathew.

Susannah blushed, 'we do what we can for each other.'

As the children led Mathew into the cottage, he was confronted by a simple, but clean room with little furniture. Two men lay on palliasses up against the back wall. An open stair led up to the attic. In the wall opposite the stairs was the hearth, with a pot simmering over the fire.

The soldiers lay unmoving on their beds, Grace beckoned Susannah over to them, 'they have a fever, I didn't know what to do, so I went to see Mrs Monday. She said I had to wait for the fever to break and to just keep giving them sips of water.'

Susannah pulled her sister close, 'you did the right thing; I'm sorry I was so long, but now Mathew is here he will know what to do.'

Mathew began to examine the patients, 'I assume you don't have a surgeon in the village: is there an apothecary?'

'There's no surgeon, and the apothecary is old and does not have the wit to dispense herbs anymore,' said Grace.

'I see,' said Mathew smiling at her. 'Come on Roger, you can help me bring my surgeon's chest inside. I have brought lots of special medicines with me that we can use to heal these men.'

It wasn't long before the cart was unloaded. Roger took the mule and cart around the back of the cottage, feeding and settling the animal in for the night. While Mathew made preparations for his new patients with Grace intently watching everything he did, Susannah busied herself with the pot over the fire. Amos was the first of the brothers to arrive home, carrying a large loaf of bread under his arm. Oliver and Walter came in an hour or so later. After introductions had been made, the family squeezed around the small family table, gave thanks for their food and tucked into a dish of Gravysoop, made from chopped ox tongue, onion, celery, and spinach, mopping up what was left with the bread Amos had brought home.

Mathew became the main topic of conversation as each, and every one of Susannah's family wanted to know everything about him, the tales of his travels after leaving Hull, and for the older ones, news of any other battles that he had been involved in. It was late into the night when Grace and Roger began to fall asleep where they sat, so Susannah called time for bed. She explained how Oliver and Walter had divided the attic into two so Susannah and Grace could have some privacy in one half and the boys the other. Mathew would have to make do with a palliasse downstairs near the fire with the two patients.

After an uncomfortable night, not helped by the snoring of the two injured soldiers and Amos getting up and needing to be out well before there was any sign of daylight, Mathew added some sticks to the fire and warmed away the chills of a cold night. As the flames grew higher, giving off the first hint of warmth in the cold room, Mathew stretched and wondered if he would ever feel the comfort of a real bed again. He checked on the patients. Their fevers still ran high, it would be another day or so before the fever broke and their fate decided. Oliver was the one to get up next. He greeted Mathew and went out back to a small storeroom returning with a large jug of beer, before disappearing again to wash in the trough out back. Susannah came next and stood by Mathew at the fire as the flames grew in size. She warmed herself briefly before pouring a cup of beer for Mathew and setting about slicing up what was left of the bread from yesterday, then fetching a plate of cheese from a cupboard attached to the wall in the corner of the room.

'Come on eat up,' said Susannah, 'or there will be nothing left once this lot set about it.'

Mathew took the smallest piece of bread and cheese and went to sit by the fire again wondering how the family managed to stay so cheerful when they had so little. Once Oliver and Walter had left the cottage, Mathew administered to his patients with their morning dose of medicine made from *Black Cherry Water, Plague Water and sixteen drops of laudanum*, followed by a Clyster made from *cow's milk, sugar, and syrup of violets*. After his patients had been made comfortable, he asked Susannah to take him to visit the others being cared for by villagers. All that day Mathew and Susannah worked together, moving from house to house doing their best to heal the wounded. By dusk, they were both exhausted.

'I'm starving,' said Mathew.

'Don't worry,' smiled Susannah, 'Grace has become an excellent cook, and Amos will bring home two loaves of bread tonight.'

She quickly started to gather up the instruments that Mathew had been using on his last patient.

'I'll wash these for you when we get home.'

Mathew wondered where she got her energy from as she scurried for the door leaving him to give instructions to the householder on how to care for the soldier they had taken in. As they drove home on Susannah's cart, she quizzed him on his medicines and where he had got them from. Mathew explained that Mary had made most of them, but that she had left him to return home after being brought low by the melancholy. He told her about Mary being his sister-in-law and how, when they first set out, she had insisted on travelling with him, but the journey had become arduous and had got too much for her. In return, Susannah told him that she worked around the village, getting what jobs she could or helping neighbours in return for some task they could perform for her. She confessed to Mathew how she would love to travel further afield, but Grace and Roger still needed her. Before they reached home, Mathew stopped at the baker's and bought the biggest meat pie they had. The baker told him it was made from lean beef steak, lamb, orange juice, raisins, thyme and parsley. Susannah protested, but Mathew said they had worked hard that day and deserved a treat. It didn't take them long to return to the cottage, where Grace had made a simple stew from vegetables and some salted pork.

Grace and Roger rushed out to greet Susannah, 'guess what has happened,' squealed Grace with delight.

'Grace and I have work at the Manor House,' interrupted Roger. 'Grace is going to work as a kitchen maid, and I get to work in the stables.'

Susannah stared into their happy faces, but she was shocked by the idea of them working away from home at such a young age. For Susannah, the thought that Grace and Roger were growing up and would soon no longer need her care and help wounded her profoundly. She wondered if this was how all parents thought as they watched their children grow into adults. Putting on a brave face, she smiled in delight at their news.

‘Look what Mathew has brought us,’ she showed them the pie.

‘Wow,’ said Roger, we’ll be having a feast tonight.

Grace and Roger scurried indoors, leaving Mathew and Susannah alone.

‘You look shocked by the news,’ said Mathew.

‘Yes, I am a little. I knew it would happen one day, I just didn’t think it would come so soon. Mrs Baxter at the manor had mentioned it to me a couple of weeks ago, but in all the confusion since the battle, it had gone completely out of my mind.’

Over their evening meal, Grace and Roger talked excitedly about going to work at the manor. Susannah tried to sound enthusiastic for their sake, but Mathew could see the sadness in her eyes.

Amos, who was sat opposite Susannah, noticed it too, ‘think of it this way sister: with Grace and Roger at the manor, you are now free to pursue new interests.’

He gave a sly sideways glance towards Mathew. Susannah's face reddened as she scowled at her brother.

'When does Mrs Baxter want you to start work?' Susannah asked her younger siblings.

'Mrs Baxter said you were to take us up to the manor as soon as was convenient, but not to leave it too long because they are short-handed. She said the master has taken in ten wounded soldiers and they are taking a lot of looking after, and Mrs Baxter and Mr Hollis are complaining about all the extra work.'

Susannah sat back on her chair and sighed, not feeling as hungry as she had done earlier.

'We can take them together, tomorrow,' said Mathew, 'and while we are there, I can take a look at the soldiers at the same time. It will give you an excuse to stay with the children for a while longer, get them settled in, just in case they decide they don't like it there after all and want to come home again,' suggested Mathew.

Susannah smiled at him, 'yes, we'll do that; thank you, Mathew.' Reassured, Susannah returned to her meal.

Apart from Amos, who had set off for work very early, everyone else was up at the same time. Oliver and Walter wanted to say farewell to Grace and Roger and, though the children didn't have much in the way of clothes and personal things to pack, the excitement of leaving home had given them a disturbed night, and both looked bleary eyed and tired. On arriving at the manor house, Mrs Baxter was waiting for them in the stable yard.

'I saw you coming, so I thought I'd come to meet you,' said Mrs Baxter. 'How are you, My Dear?'

'We are very well, thank you, Mrs Baxter,' said Susannah. 'Grace and Roger are eager to come and work here, though I must say I will miss them.'

'Oh, think nothing of it,' said Mrs Baxter. 'Now Master William and his two boys have gone off to join Lord Essex on some mad crusade, the mistress and her father are all a flummox not knowing if they are dead or alive after the battle over yonder. The house is in a real mess now there are wounded soldiers to care for. They create too much work for Mr Hollis and me. The mistress let most of the house-staff go when Master William and the boys left for the army, and now we find we need more help than ever before.

Your young Grace has such a lovely way about her, she will fit in here very nicely, and you and your family have done so much for people in this village over the years, it's only right that we help you in return.'

Susannah blushed and turned away fumbling with Grace and Roger's possessions still on the cart.

'Who's this nice looking young man, then?' asked Mrs Baxter.

'Oh, I'm sorry, I've also brought Surgeon Fletcher from Warwick Castle, Lord Brooke said he could come and help with the wounded for a couple of days.'

'See what I mean, no one else in the village thought to go fetch a surgeon to help these poor men. It's time you started to think about yourself Young Lady: get yourself a man before it's too late, and they all get killed in this here fighting that's started,' said Mrs Baxter.

'I think you'd better show me where the wounded men are,' said Mathew, 'before you embarrass Susannah anymore.'

Mrs Baxter chuckled and led the way to the barn. 'The mistress said to put the wounded men in here, she didn't want blood in the house, and they also stink quite a bit.'

Susannah kissed Grace and Roger farewell, 'go with Mrs Baxter and make sure you always do as you are told, and remember, I will come to see you from time to time and make sure you are all right.' As Mrs Baxter led the children away, Susannah went inside the barn to join Mathew, who was already checking over his patients. Most were suffering from incised wounds caused by swords or other blades, one had lost his right leg below the knee, and another was severely burned along the right side of his body and face.

'There is a lot of work to be done, these men should have been seen by a surgeon days ago. I'll start with the man with the missing leg. The stump needs cleaning and closing correctly. I'm surprised he hasn't bled to death already. It may already be too late for him if the gangrene has set in. Go ask Mrs Baxter for plenty of hot water while I get this old table ready to perform the surgery,' ordered Mathew. He dragged the old table to the barn doorway where the light was at its best and found a box on which to lay out the instruments he was going to need. Susannah returned with a cauldron of hot water and began to wash the table. Mathew carried the one-legged man to the table. He didn't complain, he couldn't, he was taken by fever and oblivious to what was about to happen to him. While Susannah washed the remains of the wounded leg, Mathew prepared sixteen drops of *laudanum* in a small cup of brandy, forcing the liquid down the man's throat a little at a time.

'We will need help to hold this man down when I start to cut, is there anyone in the house who can help us?' Mathew asked Susannah.

'I'll speak to Mrs Baxter,' she replied.

She returned minutes later with Mrs Baxter and the steward of the house, Mr Hollis.

'I've tied his good leg and his body to the table which will help hold him down. I would be grateful if Mr Hollis would help me by holding his injured leg in position as I operate, and Mrs Baxter would you give him more sips of *laudanum* if he needs them. Susannah can help me with the instruments and surgery.'

All three assistants looked woebegone about what was about to happen but complied with Mathew's wishes.

Mr Hollis lifted the leg stump off the table as instructed while Mathew trimmed away black and putrid flesh from the stump. The soldier moaned but moved very little. As fresh blood began to flow from the stump, Mathew instructed Susannah to tie a cord around the stump, just below the knee. Having cleaned the dead flesh away, Mathew exposed what was left of the Tibia and Fibula, sawing away the fractured ends of the bones. With his Crows Bill forceps, he withdrew the ends of the more significant veins and arteries so Susannah could tie off the ends with silk thread. Having cleaned and prepared the stump as best he could, he got Mr Hollis to squeeze the flesh of the open wound together. Mathew sutured the two sides of the stump together, leaving a small opening at each end for the ends of the silk thread to trail out and downwards for the pus to drain along them and away from the wound. Mathew wiped the blood from his hands and the sweat from his face.

'Will he live?' asked Mr Hollis.

'I don't know,' said Mathew. 'I shall bandage the leg, so long as the wound is kept clean and his bandages changed every day, he stands a chance, but it will be God who decides his fate now, I have done all I can for him. Thank you both for your help, I know it is not what you expected to have to do. I think Susannah and I can manage the others on our own.'

Mrs Baxter stepped away from the table, staggered and fainted. Susannah rushed to her side, cradling her head in her lap while Mathew searched for his smelling salts. After a sniff of the smelling salts and a sip of brandy-wine, Mrs Baxter was back on her feet telling everyone not to make such a fuss. Mr Hollis escorted her back to the kitchen and the children. Mathew indicated the soldier with the burns was the next patient to be operated on. After dosing him with *laudanum*, he soaked the soldier's shirt with rose water.

'Susannah, would you go to the kitchen and ask for two onions and a cup full of salt. I'd like you to chop and crush them, and then mix them with the salt into a paste?' asked Mathew. 'While you are doing that, I'm going to cut away as much of this man's shirt as I can, but parts of it are stuck to his flesh. When you return, I'll need you to help me pluck away what has stuck to his flesh. The next thing we will have to do is remove the un-burnt gunpowder grains from his skin, and then spread the onion paste on the burns.'

When Susannah returned, the soldier was on the table with much of his shirt cut away. Susannah could clearly see the extent of the gunpowder burn up the side of his body, neck and the right side of his face. His skin was a patchwork of black, red and orange raw flesh. The worst burnt parts of his flesh oozed a clear orangey coloured liquid; other parts were spotted with fresh blood from where his shirt had been pulled away taking skin and burnt tissue with it. The unconscious soldier lay trembling on the table.

'Is he awake?' asked Susannah.

'No.... not really,' replied Mathew. 'I've given him a large dose of *laudanum*, but his body is in shock. He is in a lot of pain, though the *laudanum* will help. With deep burns, the body loses so much fluid the patient's body trembles like this. If he recovers, over time his mind will block out the memory of the worst pain. At the moment I can only hope he is not aware of it. The first thing we have to do is remove the remains of his shirt. It's become embedded in his skin as scabs have formed. Then we have to remove as many of the unburnt gunpowder grains as you can find, they will look like bits of grit. They are poisonous and will corrupt his blood. Once we have done all that, I shall cover the burns with the *onion and salt paste.* He will then need to be covered with a mixture of *turpentine, plantain, egg yolk and linseed oil* to help the skin heal. It will take many weeks for him to recover so I will have to leave instructions with Mrs Baxter because the dressing will need changing every day and I have to return to Warwick. I just don't have enough time to do all I need to for these people. It was the same with the wounded soldiers in Beverley; I did all I could do for them, but the army decamped and moved on, leaving the wounded behind.'

'Will he live?' asked Susannah.

'He may, but he will be horribly scarred. He will be in a great deal of pain, and his skin will take a long time to heal so he will run the risk of infection setting in and killing him. It may be kinder if he just slipped away in his sleep.'

Mathew and Susannah worked on until they had dressed the wounds of every soldier in the barn. Before they left the manor, Mathew gave Mrs Baxter instructions on how to care for each of the wounded and Susannah said a tearful farewell to Grace and Roger.

On the ride back to Susannah's home she was reluctant to talk; it was only when they had reached their destination with the front door shut behind them that Susannah burst into tears.

'What in heaven's name is wrong?' asked Mathew.

Susannah turned and threw her arms around Mathew's neck, sobbing into his chest, 'How can you stand it? All those mutilated men, the pain, the suffering they go through, and you ignore it as though it is not happening.'

Mathew held her close, his arm around her shoulder, his right hand gently wiping away the tears from her cheek, 'I feel for them just as much as you do or anyone else, but I have to block out their suffering. I console myself by thinking about how much I am helping them. Without me, most of them would die a long lingering death in awful pain. I give them a chance of life and a future; that's what I tell myself and how I manage to do this job every day. I have had to learn to ignore their suffering. It was hard at first, but later, when the sick and injured start to recover and thank me for making them well again, it gives me a feeling of fulfilment. In time my patients forget the pain they were in; that is their real reward to me, not the money they pay me. The money is what I need to buy food and, one day, a home of my own. Sometimes, when treating someone who can't afford to pay me, I pass the charge onto those who can, to compensate for the loss. In some ways I'm selfish, I love what I do so much it becomes the only thing that matters to me. I am so fascinated with how the human body works, and why it stops working, that everything else that is happening around me is of little importance. I wish I could devote all my time to delving into the body's mysteries and learn all its secrets, but that is for wiser men than me, I think,' Mathew confessed to her.

Susannah looked up, her eyes full of tears. She stared into his face for a moment, closed her eyes, then lifted her chin and presented him with two perfectly formed pink lips. Mathew hesitated a moment, then lowered his lips to hers and held her tight. He felt her body relax as her arms reached up and around his neck. It was Susannah who broke their embrace, taking a step back, 'I need you to show me love; I need to hold you closer.'

Stepping away from Mathew, but keeping a hold on his fingertips, she drew him towards the stairs that led to her bedchamber, leaving the sleeping patients on their beds. Alone together in Susannah's chamber, they enjoyed the intimacy and shyness that all first-time lovers share. Wrapped in each other's arms, the wounded soldiers, the battle, Warwick Castle and Major Overton were all forgotten, as they gave themselves to each other in a world without time and worries.

It was only when Amos returned home and slammed the door that Susannah and Mathew awoke. They looked at each other with guilt-ridden faces.

'Susannah!' called Amos. 'I know you are up there, I came home earlier and heard you. It is getting late;

Oliver and Walter will be home soon, so you and Mathew better hurry.'

Susannah appeared at the top of the stair dressed only in her chemise, 'I'll be down momentarily.'

Mathew pushed passed her fastening the buttons on his breeches, giving a guilty look at Amos as he crossed the kitchen and went to fix the fire which had gone out.

'There's no dinner ready,' complained Amos, enjoying the torture he was inflicting.

'I'm sorry,' came the voice from upstairs, 'I've been busy.'

'I noticed,' said Amos with a titter.

'Amos!' yelled Susannah.

Mathew turned to look at her brother; the two couldn't help but smirk at each other like young boys caught seeing something they shouldn't. Susannah, with her dress finally in order, came down from her bedchamber, 'we will just have to have a cold supper tonight,' she said in as dignified a manner as she could muster.

'Don't worry,' said Mathew, 'We will go to the tavern and get a hot meal. I will pay; it will give us time to talk and get to know each other as we eat.'

Mathew had no sooner stopped speaking when Oliver and Walter came home.

'Turn around lads, we are eating at the Half Way House tonight,' said Amos.

'What?' said Oliver.

'Why?' said Walter, 'where is our dinner?'

'It wouldn't be seemly to ask,' said Amos, indicating with his head in Susannah's direction. Susannah's hair was still a mess and uncovered.

It took a second or two before Oliver and Walter caught on, but when they did, they about turned and scurried out into the street. Susannah could hear them laughing outside as Amos, obviously relishing the telling of his tale, was probably embellishing all the more to entertain them.

Chapter Twenty

After his three days in Kineton with Susannah, when Mathew arrived back at Warwick Castle, he went to see Major Overton to report on the soldiers he had treated in Susannahs village.

'No, the only men I found were ordinary soldiers. There were no officers amongst them, most of the soldiers had no idea where they were, even when they were given the name of the village it meant nothing to them. So I'm sorry, I have no intelligence to report,' said Mathew.

'That's disappointing; I was hoping you would have come back with at least some news to give me. How did you get on with Susannah?'

'Very well, because of the help they give to others, she and her family are much respected in the village,' said Mathew, reddening slightly. 'If I'd been allowed to spend more time to stay in the village, I would have been able to attend to more patients and maybe even find a royalist officer for you.'

'As you say, if you'd had more time, but I need you here. Once I know what the king plans to do next I want to be able to send you back to him with a suitable excuse for your absence,' countered Major Overton. 'You can go now, I will send for you when I need you.'

Mathew smiled as he walked away from Major Overton; he hadn't even tried to find out anything from the king's men he had treated. It was his little bit of defiance against being used and taken for granted. Mathew was pretty sure he would have spotted an officer had he come across one, but he certainly wasn't going to go out of his way to find one just to please the major.

Mathew thought about the time he had spent with Susannah. It was with a longing to be back to Kineton that he went in search of Mortimer and Potter. He found Mortimer in the tent the soldiers used as a tavern.

'Ah, the wanderer returns,' called out Mortimer when Mathew stuck his head inside the door. Mathew settled himself down next to his friend.

'As bad as that was it?' asked Mortimer.

'No, not at all: I've just come from speaking with the Major. He's unhappy that I didn't bring him back lots of intelligence from the survivors of the battle. He also reminded me he is making plans for my future and that I have to stay here until he decides the time is right for me to leave, which means you and Potter stay as well,' said Mathew.

'You sound like you need a jug or two of beer,' said Mortimer, 'it may lift your spirits.'

'Where's Potter?' asked Mathew.

'Oh, he's over there. He's playing cards with the soldiers,' Mortimer indicated a table in the back corner of the tent. 'I've been watching him. He wins a few hands and then loses a few and so on through the evening, but each night when he returns to our chamber, he counts his winnings. I don't know if he cheats or if he's just a good card player.'

'Probably a bit of both knowing him,' said Mathew.

'Aye, you may be right. Did you find many sick soldiers?' asked Mortimer.

'Quite a lot, there wasn't time to get around and treat all of them, I wasn't there long enough. But I think I saved the lives of one or two and eased the suffering of a few more. From what I did see I can only assume the battles we saw around Hull and Beverley were tiny compared to the number of dead and wounded from the battle near Kineton. The villagers are digging mass graves for the dead, and every home has at least one wounded man lodging there. Susannah proved very helpful, she is well liked by the villager's, and I've sort of grown fond of her as well,' confessed Mathew.

'Yes, I can see you've taken a liking to her,' smirked Mortimer. 'You seem happier than you have done for a long time. He wanted to add, so you're over Elizabeth then but thought better of it. He just wanted to hear Mathew's response.

'She's. . . .different. She's sensible like Mary and more mature than Elizabeth was, but there is something about her that makes me feel . . . . .I don't know, I like her.'

'Will she be coming back to Warwick?' asked Mortimer.

'I hope so, I really hope so,' confided Mathew.

Late the following day, Susannah arrived at the castle and went straight to the chamber in the tower which Mathew and the others now called home. Not finding him there, she went in search of her surgeon friend.

'Oh, here you are. I might have guessed you would be eating at this time of day.' Susannah found Mathew and Mortimer sitting against a wall close to the castle kitchen sharing a large pie and a jug of beer.

'I've just spent the entire morning treating soldiers for drunkenness, minor wounds, bad backs and one case of French Pox,' protested Mathew. 'I have earned my dinner.'

'Yes, yes of that I have no doubt, but I have more interesting things to talk about. Look at this.' Susannah waved a document in front of Mathew. 'It was given to me by a woman in Kineton. She found it on the body of an officer she found in some bushes. He must have fallen from his horse and lay hidden until she discovered him. I've no doubt she took all his money and anything else of value, but this paper meant nothing to her, so she brought it to me wondering if you might be interested in it. When I read it, I thought of you. As you can see, it's addressed to Lieutenant

General Robert Bertie, Earl of Lindsey. It states that the king plans to take up residence in the town of Oxford and that all preparations should be made to conduct the war on Parliament from the new temporary capital of England,' said Susannah excitably. She unfolded the paper and pointed to the part she had mentioned. Mathew jumped to his feet and shushed her, telling her to keep her voice down.

'You can't wave things like that about telling anyone in hearing distance it was found on the body of an officer. There are people here who would kill without a seconds thought for something like this,' said Mathew pulling Susannah closer to the wall. 'Now tell me again where did it come from?'

Mathew took the document from her and looked at it for himself as Susannah repeated her story. 'I will have to give this to Major Overton, this is just the type of intelligence he is looking for.'

'Why else do you think I brought it with me? I didn't come all this way just to see you,' said Susannah, sarcastically, but when she looked up at him, it was her eyes that gave away her true feelings. Mathew looked hurt for a moment and then smiled when he saw she was mocking him.

'Wait here, I'll be back soon,' said Mathew.

Major Overton read the letter, 'This is exactly the kind of intelligence we have needed. We have had our suspicions that the king was planning to make use of Oxford, but this is the first real evidence confirming what we thought. This means we can concentrate all our efforts keeping him penned within the town and wear down his resources. This may be the biggest mistake he has made since starting this war. Well done, Mathew, and well done to Susannah, please thank her for me.'

Mathew rushed back to Susannah and Mortimer to tell them how pleased Major Overton had been with the letter.

'I think we are ready for the rest of that beer you were drinking,' said Susannah. 'I will have one cup with you. I can't stay too long I need to get home before it gets dark.'

'Why not stay the night, it's a long way back to Kineton, you could set off early tomorrow morning,' suggested Mathew.

'And where would I sleep, I'm not staying in that laundry again, and you can't expect me to share a small chamber with three men?' said Susannah indignantly.

'No one here knows who you are and I could rig a curtain around your bed. I would sleep on the floor,' said Mathew.

'You wouldn't want to risk it getting dark before you got home; you know how soon the sun goes down this time of year. You would be out on the road, in the dark, on your own,' said Mortimer.

'Yes, and I would be worried sick about you getting home safe,' agreed Mathew.

'I'll think about it,' said Susannah cautiously.

By the time the jug of beer was finished, Mathew and Mortimer had assured Susannah that she couldn't reach Kineton before it became dark and it would be safer for her to stay overnight in the castle. She agreed to stay but would decide where she would sleep, later. Susannah spent the rest of the day helping Mathew with his patients. For the rest of the afternoon, Mathew and Mortimer speculated on where she was going to stay the night. The subject of her sleeping arrangements was avoided for most of the evening. It was when Susannah began to fall asleep in her seat while they sat talking and drinking, that Mathew suggested that they retire for the night. The moment Susannah had been avoiding to think about was suddenly upon her. Where she would sleep, had to be faced. As they left the tavern and crossed the courtyard, Susannah lagged behind, walking more slowly than Mathew and Mortimer, having second thoughts about going back with them for the night.

'Don't worry,' said Mathew, 'I'll make sure you have some privacy,' doing his best to sound reassuring.

'No, I think I should go. I'm sure I will be safe enough if I stay off the main road,' said Susannah apprehensively.

'You can't do that, it's not safe; you'll be out all night. It's safer for you to stay here. I promise,' Mathew reassured her.

As they passed the stable Mathew snatched a length of rope hanging from the wall. Distinctly doubtful, Susannah followed him to the Watergate Tower. As Mathew and Mortimer entered their chamber, Susannah hung back in the passage, reluctant to join them.

'Let me show you what I mean,' said Mathew, tying one end of the rope to the iron sconce on the wall. He attached the other end to the hinge of the window shutter then, threw a blanket over the line.

'There you are, see, all proper. You can have my bed, and I'll sleep on Potter's bed as it looks like he won't be using it. More reassured about her surroundings, Susannah entered the chamber to inspect her new sleeping arrangements.

'Don't worry, Miss Susannah, I'll make sure he behaves himself. I'm a real light sleeper and, if he decides to start exploring the chamber, I've still got my gun. I'll shoot him where it hurts,' said Mortimer, pulling his pistol from below his pillow. Susannah looked startled at the sight of the gun until Mathew pointed out that Mortimer didn't have any shot or powder for it.

'Thank goodness for that, I wouldn't want you to shoot him somewhere I might need later on,' said Susannah. For a moment there was silence in the chamber as Mathew's face reddened, then laughter broke out as the tension broke and all three settled into a more relaxed acceptance of their situation. They quickly settled down with Mathew taking advantage of Potter's empty bed, though he'd had to give up his blanket to act as a curtain for Susannah. After some brief chatter about their day and plans for the next, Mathew blew out the rushlight, and it wasn't long before they were all asleep.

The door to the chamber opened slowly and quietly, and then closed as a dark figure stepped silently across the floor. The figure paused, standing over Mathew in the darkness, and with outstretched arms, lent forward towards the sleeping surgeon. Mathew awoke with a start and a yell as cold hands touched his face. The dark figure jumped back in alarm. Susannah awoke and screamed at the sound of Mathew's cry. The mysterious figure spun around bumping into the blanket curtain, not expecting to find it there. Susannah screamed again. The shadowy figure recoiled away from the high pitched female and stumbled against Mortimer who, with his pistol in his hand, struck out at the stranger, making the intruder stagger back and forth in the centre of the chamber. The intruder yelled in pain as the handgrip of the gun struck him in the thigh twice more.

'Stop it, stop it. It's me, Thomas Potter. What the Hell's going on. Why is there a woman in here?' The commotion in the room stopped at once, with only the sound of somebody fumbling for something on the table. Seconds later there came the sound of a flint being struck and then a small flame illuminated the table as it was put to the rushlight. The small yellow flame lit enough of the chamber to show Potter rubbing his thigh and looking around in confusion as Mathew got up from his bed.

'What's she doing here?' demanded Potter.

'Why are you sneaking in here in the middle of the night?' countered Mortimer.

'Where have you been, why were you touching my face?' asked Mathew.

'Who is he?' yelled Susannah.

'I was trying to go to bed without waking anyone up. I didn't expect to find someone else in my bed,' said Potter indignantly.

There was silence as everyone looked from one to another waiting for someone to start explaining, then everyone started talking at the same time.

'Stop,' shouted Mathew.

In the silence that followed, Mathew explained why Susannah was in the chamber. 'Why were you sneaking in so late at night?' asked Mathew.

Potter looked at Susannah, 'I have been making some discrete enquiries on behalf of the major. And now, I want my bed back, I'm tired and hurt,' he nursed his thigh as though to prove the point, 'and I need to get some sleep.'

Everyone looked at each other again, wondering who was going to speak first.

'Very well,' said Mathew,' getting up from Potter's bed, 'I'll sit here and sleep in the chair.'

Potter snatched his blanket from the rope and made himself comfortable on his bed. Susannah pulled her blanket up tight under her chin and lay down. Mortimer looked from Potter to Susannah to Mathew, shrugged his shoulders and laid down.

'Someone put the light out please,' said Susannah.

Mathew looked around the chamber and blew the light out before retiring to the chair for the night.

Chapter Twenty-One

At the manor, Mrs Baxter rushed down to the kitchen to prepare the old master's breakfast. The new mistress always liked to lay abed till late with her husband and sons being away, but the former master, her father-in-law, would soon want to be up and about. He wasn't a big eater these days, but he did like his bread, butter, and cheese with sweet stewed apples in the morning, all washed down with a glass or two of sweet red wine. Mrs Baxter had become very fond of the old master over her years of service to the family. She had joined the household as a young girl when the 'Old Queen' was still on the throne, and from the start, the old master had always been kind to her. Now they had both grown older, the old master's son had taken over the running of the farm, and Mrs Baxter had risen from kitchen maid to become housekeeper. Though the old master's son now owned the estate, she still looked on the former employer as being the real head of the family, even though these days he spent most of his time reading or tending his plants in the garden. Mrs

Baxter loaded his breakfast salver ready to take it up to him, still wondering what was keeping Grace. Knocking on the old master's bedchamber door, but not waiting for an answer, she entered, setting down the salver on a small table near the bed and drawing back the heavy drapes which covered the windows. 'Good morning, Sir. A fine day today, did you sleep well?' She pulled back the bed hangings. She hated this part of her duties, she never knew if she would find the old master cold and lifeless in his bed, now that the years were catching up with the squire. The old man awoke slowly, his watery eyes adjusting to the sunlight from the windows.

'Good day to you, Mrs Baxter, are you well this morning?' he asked cordially.

'As well as can be expected, Sir. There's a bit of a nip in the air today, Sir; would you like me to set a fire for you before you rise?' asked the housekeeper.

'If you wouldn't mind, My Dear, I don't have the meat on my bones to keep me warm like I once did. It seems harder than ever to stay warm these days, or is it that the winters are coming early do you think?' asked the old man.

'I have to admit the winters do seem to be getting earlier and colder, I don't think it will be long before the first frosts start to arrive, Sir,' she responded. 'I do hope we'll soon hear from Master James and the boys, it isn't like them not to send a word or two about what they are doing.'

After setting light to the fire to warm the chamber for the old squire before he rose, Mrs Baxter emptied his piss pot out of the window; *he was bound to need it again before he came downstairs.* After ensuring the salver of food was within easy reach of her master, she asked him if there was anything else he required before she returned to the kitchen.

Mrs Baxter cleared her kitchen table ready to make some more bread. *Where is Grace, that girl should have been up and cleaning out the hearth by now,* she thought. *That girl has been getting slower and slower this past couple of days; I hope I haven't made a mistake by taking her on, she seemed to have made such a good start.* Going to the bottom of the back stairs Mrs Baxter called up to Grace, 'come on girl, the days wasting away and you're still in your bed. When I see Susannah, I'll be telling her I'm having second thoughts about you staying on.'

Mrs Baxter went back to the kitchen table and measured out the flour she would need and set the flour, salt and sugar to one side. No sound of movement came from the servant's quarters upstairs. Leaving the water, yeast, milk, butter and sugar to warm in a bowl near the fire, she cleaned her hands on her apron. *I don't believe that girl, I'll teach her to ignore me when I've got all this work to do.* Mrs Baxter climbed the stairs grumbling as she did so about how this would never have been allowed when she was a lass.

'Grace, if you are not out of that bed and dressed by the time I get to your chamber I'll send you back to Susannah, My Girl,' Mrs Baxter pushed open the door to Grace's bedchamber. 'What did I tell you? You should have been up a long time ago.'

The girl stirred in her bed, muttering incoherently.

'Whatever is the matter, Child?' Mrs Baxter was at Grace's side in an instant, placing her hand on the girl's forehead, 'why, you're burning up.' Pulling back the blankets, Mrs Baxter inspected Grace's arms, back and chest; she was covered in small scabs and was hot and sweaty with fever. Re-covering the girl, she went back downstairs to find the steward of the house. He was in the yard talking to a couple of stablemen when Mrs Baxter flung open the kitchen door and called to him.

'You had better go fetch Susannah from Warwick,' she instructed the steward.

'Aye, right you are. How did you know young Roger's looking right poorly? He's got a fever and covered in scabs.'

'So is Grace,' cried Mrs Baxter.

'Is that what's making 'em sickly?' asked Mr Hollis.

'Possibly,' said Mrs Baxter, not wanting to alarm Mr Hollis more than needed. 'Now get yourself off to Warwick as fast as you can and tell Susannah to bring that surgeon friend of 'ers back here as well, just in case it's something serious.' Even though she secretly suspected what the sickness was that was ailing Grace and Roger, she didn't want to alarm the other staff. If she were correct, they would find out soon enough, and there would be more sickness to come for the people in the house and also the people of the village.

Chapter Twenty-Two

Oliver finished work early at the smithy, it had been a slow day, and his master was feeling a little unwell, so had decided he would rest and start fresh again tomorrow after a good night's sleep. So Oliver went to meet Amos at the bakery, they could walk home together. Amos was a little surprised but pleased to see his brother call at the bakery. With two loaves of warm fresh bread ready to take back for their supper, Oliver and Amos set off for home talking about their day. They had not long left the bakery and passed the flour mill at the end of the street, when coming in the opposite direction they saw a company of pikemen led by an officer dressed in fine clothes, thigh length boots and a large hat sporting ostrich feathers. The people of Kineton stepped to the side of the road, as did Oliver and Amos, to let the column of soldier's pass-by. Just before the column of soldiers reached Oliver and Amos, a cry was heard from someone in the crowd, 'God and Parliament, No Bishops, No Popish Lords.' The officer leading the column stopped his men and spoke to his sergeant, both men giving sideways glances towards Oliver and Amos.

'I think we need to leave,' said Oliver to his younger brother.

'Why?' asked Amos.

'I just think it would be the right thing to do,' Oliver took his brothers arm and turned him in the direction of a lane which would allow them to circle around the soldiers. They had no sooner turned the corner when they both heard the shout.

'Hey, you two, stop!'

Oliver and Amos kept going. Seconds later they heard the sound of running feet coming from behind them, getting closer. Instantly, both Oliver and Amos broke into a run. They made it around the corner into Mill Lane. The lane was clear of soldiers.

'Let's hide in the mill,' shouted Amos.

'No, that's the first place they will look when they can't see us. If we can make it onto Mill Street, we can go through one of the taverns and out the back. That should lose them,' said Oliver.

The sound of running feet behind them began to sound fainter as Oliver and Amos pulled ahead of their pursuers. As the brothers turned the corner onto Mill Street, they found the officer and about a dozen of his men standing in the middle of the road waiting for them, with swords drawn. Skidding to a halt, there was nowhere else for the brothers to run as the sound of running feet behind them once again grew louder. Four soldiers sprang forward and seized Oliver and Amos. The brothers gave in without a struggle.

'Caught you, though you thought you could get away with it, you rebel supporters of Parliament. My men fought and died to protect your village,' sneered the officer. 'And, what makes it worse - you have bread, while my men go hungry.'

Amos looked down in bewilderment at the two loaves of bread he was still carrying, was this really all they were after. He held out the bread loaves to the officer.

'Here, take them. It wasn't us who made that call for Parliament; we were just, waiting, watching you as you passed by. I work at the bakery. I get a loaf each day as part of my wages,' pleaded Amos holding out the bread loaves.

'You may not be the ones who called out, but you ran, which leads me to the conclusion that you are Parliamentarian sympathisers, a crime that needs to be punished. You have bread, while my men go without; that is the same as stealing food from the mouths of my men when they can barely find enough to eat,' said the captain scornfully. 'Take them to the village square, we will show these peasants what happens to those who side with Parliament and steal from the king's men.'

With the bread taken from them, Oliver and Amos were dragged to the marketplace on Banbury Street. A crowd began to gather and followed behind the soldiers to learn the fate of the two young men. On

Banbury Street, the officer stopped and gave his orders.

'Remove their coats and shirts then tie them to the hitching posts.'

There was no market today, but the small marketplace soon filled with a crush of villagers.

'Keep them back,' shouted the officer. The sergeants organised their men to form a large circle around the two prisoners to keep the spectators at bay.

'These men have been caught proclaiming the rights of Parliament over your king and stealing bread from my soldiers,' announced the officer to the gathering villagers. 'The soldier's who protected your village, not three days ago, from a delinquent Parliamentarian horde, who defy your king's right to rule this land as he sees fit and proper. Each of these men will receive one hundred lashes as a punishment for his crime and as a lesson to all those who think siding with the Parliament rebels or stealing food from my men will go unpunished.'

A murmur of disapproval rippled through the crowd.

'Commence the punishment,' ordered the officer.

Two soldiers came forward holding leather straps and began to lay into the bare backs of the brothers. After five strokes the younger brother, Amos, was on his knees, his back bloody and torn. Shouts of disapproval were heard from the rear of the watching crowd. After ten strokes of the strap Oliver was also on his knees, but by now Amos was unconscious. The jeers from the crowd grew louder. The onlookers pushed forward trying to get through the soldier's cordon around the punishment area. The officer stopped the punishment, fearful he would have to use his men to subdue the whole village. That would be an action his superiors wouldn't countenance. Equally, he couldn't be seen to lose face in front of his own men. He ordered water to be thrown over the prisoners, reassured they were both conscious again, the officer declared in a loud voice, 'I give each of you a choice to which both of you must agree. You can join my men and become soldiers of the king, or the punishment will recommence to its conclusion.'

Oliver looked at his younger brother, he could see he was struggling to stay cognizant and knew he wouldn't survive the one hundred lashes.

'I will join the army,' shouted Oliver.

Amos lifted his chin to look at his brother. Oliver smiled back at him, 'do it, say it,' he urged his sibling. Amos' mouth moved, and he whispered the words, 'I agree to join.' Oliver repeated what his brother had said so all could hear.

'Cut them down,' ordered the officer. 'Let it be known to all that Captain Harrison is a merciful man,' he announced to the multitude triumphantly, and thankful that his diversionary ploy had worked. He reformed his company of soldiers with Oliver and Amos at their centre and marched them away from the Kineton marketplace.

Walter was on the point of going to look for his brothers when there was a loud and frantic banging on the door, it burst open, and two men burst in.

'Oliver and Amos have been taken,' bellowed the first man.

'One of the army officers had them both flogged in the marketplace, and then took them away,' barked the second man.

'What; what are you talking about? You're not making sense. Why would an army officer have Oliver and Amos flogged and taken away, they are my brothers, they haven't done anything wrong,' said a bewildered Walter. 'Show me where it happened; take me to my brothers,' demanded Walter becoming confused and panicky.

He grabbed his coat and hat and hurried after the two men who'd brought him the distressing news. As they rushed through the streets to the marketplace, people stepped aside to let them pass, some pointing at Walter and shaking their heads. Walter's anxiety for his brothers grew with every step as they got closer and closer to the marketplace. He hoped to see his brothers coming towards him as he turned each corner, hoping that somehow this was some kind of horrible prank his brothers were playing on him, but they didn't come. When he arrived at the marketplace most of the crowd had drifted away, only pockets of people remained to discuss the ordeal and injustice the brothers had undergone.

'That's where it happened,' said the first man pointing to the hitching post. A woman came over to talk to Walter.

'They're gone; gone off with the soldiers,' she said in a sympathetic voice.

'I can see that,' snapped Walter, 'Where have they gone?' he demanded more sternly than he had intended.

'Don't ask me,' snapped the woman. 'I just came to tell you what I saw. Don't blame me, I didn't drag them off,' she wittered on about Walter's rudeness, as she turned her back on him and walked away. 'Some people; you try to help them, you get no thanks for it at all.' Water heard her say as she left him.

The preacher from St Peters came to speak to Walter. 'I saw what happened. Oliver and Amos did nothing wrong except run when they should have stayed. As the soldiers came through the village, there were anti-royalist calls from someone in the crowd. The officer must have thought it was Oliver and Amos who were calling out because he stopped the column and sent a sergeant and four soldiers to get them. But your brothers made matters worse when they started to run away, the officer must have thought he was right in his assumptions, so he deployed his men through the village streets to cut off their escape and so capture Oliver and Amos to make an example of them.'

'What do I do now?' asked Walter?

'Your brothers were taken up the Banbury Road. You could try following them and plead their innocence to the officer in charge,' suggested the preacher.

Walter looked confused, unsure of what he should do.

'Come on lad, I will go with you if you wish, I can tell them what I saw and heard, maybe the officer in charge will listen to me' said the preacher.

Walter gave a sigh of relief that someone was going to help him. So Walter set off toward Banbury. They both walked until darkness fell and, though they caught up with the tail end of the king's army, no one they spoke to claimed to know anything about Oliver or Amos, or an officer by the name of Harrison.

Chapter Twenty-Three

Walter returned home to an empty house for the first time in his life. Without his brothers and sisters there filling it with noise, it didn't feel like the home he had once known and loved, it had become a silent empty shell. Walter sat at the table wishing his parent or Susannah were there to advise him on what he should do next. He had walked for hours and travelled miles of road in the vain search for his brothers. He was hungry, thirsty and tired. On the table in front of him sat a small piece of stale bread left over from breakfast. He smothered it in butter and bit into the hard crust. Within a few bites, it was gone, and his stomach was begging for more. He felt very alone and just a little frightened. He had worked hard all day; his head was buzzing, he felt weak, he needed to eat to stop his stomach grumbling for more food. He remembered that in a pot on a shelf in the corner, was a large wedge of cheese and next to it a jar of plum preserve. A little of each would sustain him until he could work out what to do next. As he bit through the creamy white cheese and sweet plum preserve he thought about how to get word about Oliver and Amos to Susannah. He was sure she would know what to do, and maybe her friend the surgeon could help as well.

During his time at Warwick Castle, Mathew had given little thought to the rest of the people who had been captured with him on the baggage-train, assuming that they would be released soon after he had been. His time in Warwick Castle had been taken up by the work he was doing for Lord Brooke and Major Overton, but also by his feelings for Susannah. Every day she was always at the forefront of his mind, distracting him from his work, hoping he would catch a glimpse of her. So it came as a shock when he was on his way to the latrines before going to find breakfast with his companions when he saw a body being carried from Guys Tower, and he remembered the prisoners incarcerated there. Two gaolers, wearing kerchiefs tied over their nose and mouth struggled with the body of a man as they carried him towards a cart. Keeping his distance, Mathew asked what had happened.

The gaolers paused a moment to speak to Mathew, 'the prisoners are falling sick and dying, we've been told to bury this un outside of the town.'

'You're telling me that all those people are still locked in the tower. What about the children?' asked Mathew.

'They were the first to start dying, 'said the first gaoler.

'All the young ones are sick now,' said the second gaoler.

Mathew looked at the gaolers in disbelief, 'I must go to Lord Brooke and get those people set free, but first I want to visit them and try to discover what it is that is making them sick.'

'You'll have to ask him first,' said the first gaoler pointing to table at the base of the tower. Two more gaolers were sat at the table outside the tower even though the weather was not what he would have thought to be warm enough to do so. As Mathew drew closer to the tower, he noticed the stink coming from the open door.

'I want to see the prisoners,' Mathew demanded.

'You're not allowed in there,' one of the gaolers responded lazily.

'The prisoners are sick. I demand you let me see them,' said Mathew becoming more forceful.

'No one goes in there without my say so, now piss off,' intervened the gaoler at the end of the table, slamming down his wooden cup.

Mathew straightened his back and lowered his voice, 'you can let me in now, or I will go and return with the captain of the castle, and you can explain to him why you will not let me in to see the prisoners.'

The gaoler at the end of the table looked into Mathew's eyes weighing him up and if he was bluffing or not. 'You won't like what you find in there; they're all rotten with fever, that's why we stay outside. Hey,

Jonathan, take this fellow to see the prisoners, there's a good lad.'

The younger gaoler stepped away from the table, his hair lip giving his face the permanent expression of a sneer, and his clubfoot making his body roll from side to side as he walked. As Mathew entered the tower the full force of the stink hit him, causing him to choke and rush outside to vomit. The gaoler at the table laughed and howled as Mathew emptied his stomach against the wall.

'Not got the stomach for it then,' shouted the head gaoler before roaring with laughter again.

Mathew spat the last remnants of bile from his mouth, wiped his lips on his sleeve, and re-entered the tower. The stone slabs, leading to the steps up to the first floor where the prisoners were kept, were splashed with human waste, As Mathew climbed the stairs the mess became worse, making the stone more slippery with each step they took. The higher they went, the worse the smell became. When they arrived at the first floor, they could hear the moans from the sick inside the cell and with it the sound of a low hum. Mathew ordered the cell door to be opened. He pushed it open a little and looked inside; a black undulating cloud hovered over the bodies lying on the floor. It was the source of the humming sound as it moved about the cell and changed shape. Mathew pushed the door fully open to go inside, he could feel the heat generated by all the people crammed into the tiny space. As soon as the door was pushed further open, the cloud of black flies drew tightly together, before darting past Mathew and the gaoler onto the first-floor landing. Mathew leaned against the wall of the chamber retching even though his stomach was empty. Steeling himself for what he would find, he moved about the cell examining the people lying in the filth on the floor. No one looked up as he walked amongst them, everyone was filthy, their clothes in rags and the slop bucket on its side in the corner; its contents spread across the floor. Mathew retreated to the landing and retched again, the pain in his empty stomach making him double over in pain. These were the worst scenes of filth and degradation he had ever seen.

'Are the people in the chamber above in the same condition?' Mathew gasped to Jonathan.

'More or less,' shrugged the young gaoler, who didn't seem to be affected by the scenes inside the chamber or the smell emitting from it.

Mathew made his way down to the ground floor and outside, sucking in lungs full of clean air, before turning to the head gaoler sitting at the table.

'I'm going to report what I have found to Lord Brooke. While I am doing that you will get all those people out of the tower and clean the filth from the walls and floors. You will get clean clothing for all those people and burn the rotten rags they are wearing. You had better have a good reason for allowing them to fall into such a poor and foul state,' demanded Mathew. Without giving the gaolers time to protest Mathew set off in the direction of the Great Hall.

'Best do as he says, lads, I smells trouble coming with this fellow,' said the head gaoler as he heaved his great carcass away from the table.

Mathew stormed into the Great Hall in search of Major Overton and Lord Brooke. He found them both in discussion in the centre of the hall and, without waiting, he broke into the conversation the two men were having.

'I need you to release the prisoners in Guy's Tower immediately,' interrupted Mathew.

Lord Brooke turned on Mathew immediately, raising his hand, about to strike the interloper. Pushing Mathew aside, Major Overton intervened; begging Lord Brooke's pardon and insisting that he would deal with Mathew and punish him for his rudeness. The major continued to push Mathew further away from the outraged Lord Brooke.

'What are you trying to do, get yourself locked-up or killed?' demanded the major.

'The prisoners from the baggage-train are dying in the tower. They're all sick with fever; why have they just been left there to rot?' demanded Mathew.

'Which prisoners, which tower?' said the major.

'The people, the civilians from the baggage-train I was with when we were captured after leaving Stoneleigh Castle. They've been kept locked in the tower, and now they are dying. They have to be set free, now,' demanded Mathew.

'Let me see; take me to them and show me what has happened,' said Major Overton.

Once outside both men could see the gaolers carrying the prisoners out of the tower and sitting or laying them against the tower walls. Passers-by began to gather to stare at the sight of men, women and children being brought from the tower, stripped of their clothes and the naked bodies left on the cobbles as their clothes were burnt, the spectators ensuring they kept a safe distance from the filthy, smelly prisoners and what ailed them.

Mathew noticed that as the sick were brought out of the tower that the conscious ones would shield their eyes from the weak sun. It was another clue to the disease from which they were suffering. The major soon grasped why Mathew had been so insistent that the prisoners were released.

'Is it *the* plague?' he whispered to Mathew.

'Of a type, though I don't know what else to call it apart from it is some kind of severe flux of the stomach,' responded Mathew.

'Will it spread throughout the castle?' asked the major, placing his kerchief over his mouth and nose.

'It will unless I can do something to stop it. The best ways of doing that, is to get those people who can be made well enough to travel, out of the castle as soon as possible, and keep the rest of them isolated from the castle garrison to recover before they infect everyone else in the castle and the town,' insisted Mathew.

'Do whatever you need to do. I will explain what I have seen to Lord Brooke and ask him to give orders that you are to be put in charge of dealing with these people. We cannot let this flux or plague spreads to the rest of the castle garrison and contaminate the town as well. You must do everything you can to prevent it from spreading,' instructed Major Overton.

'Do you know the whereabouts of Potter?' Mathew asked, 'I will need all the help I can get with so many patients to attend to.'

'Potter is helping me in regards to who killed Captain Broadwaters; you will have to manage without him. Lord Brooke is keen to have the murder and the issue of the missing treasure resolved as soon as possible,' responded the major before leaving Mathew to get on with his latest task.

Mathew watched the major leave; pleased he had gained the prisoner's their freedom and had authority to do what he thought was best for his patients. Even after the tower had been cleaned, he wasn't going to have the sick returned to their old prison. Mathew had to find somewhere to put the sick before they froze to death on the cobbles. The only place left to house so many sick people in one place was the laundry; so that is where he instructed the jailers to put the ill prisoners.

Inside the laundry, Mathew confronted the women who worked there. 'Stop what you are doing. I will be bringing a lot of sick people from the tower in here. I need you to provide them with blankets, beds and clean shirts. First, they will need to be washed, the clothes they were wearing, are being burned outside. With the authority of Lord Brooke, I am turning this place into a hospital, and you will become my nurses,' demanded Mathew.

The woman in charge of the laundry, a burly woman with a dry red face, hands and arms to match, waddled towards him, 'Hey, Mr High and Mighty, I give the orders in my laundry? Three sick men in the corner is bad enough, but if you think you can fill my laundry with sick prisoners and make demands of my good ladies you can think again and so can Lord Brooke.'

'You will find, Madam, I have the full support of Lord Brooke. The lives of everyone in the castle and the town of Warwick are in jeopardy if I cannot stop this sickness from spreading. There has been an outbreak of the Stomach Flux, and I need this place to house the sick. You have the only space large enough with the means to cope with that number of sick people. They have been kept locked in that tower, and now they have become sick, some are already dead. If I cannot keep them away from the rest of the castle garrison, there is every possibility everyone with fall ill and many more will die. There are men, women and children lying naked on the cobbles outside, so I need you to find all the blankets and spare shirts you can. Have plenty of hot water ready. The only way I know how to help these people is to keep them clean and feed them little and often.' Mathew tried to stay polite while speaking to the woman, but he could see from the expression on her face and her stance that she was going to rail against his intrusion into her domain. He didn't give her the chance to respond; he turned on his heel and walked out of the door, heading towards Guy's Tower. The washerwoman followed behind complaining loudly, struggling to keep up with Mathew, her large frame impeding her progress to follow him. Mathew arrived at the base of the tower just as some children were being brought out and laid on the bare ground. The fat washerwoman huffed and puffed to a stop beside Mathew, 'Lord protect and preserve us,' she exclaimed loudly as a small girl began to whimper.

'Why didn't you tell me there were children amongst the sick, you great useless lump. Get them brought inside at once, I'll have my women clean them up like they were back home in their own beds,' the washerwoman heaved her great weight back to the laundry.

Mathew went to instruct the gaolers.

'You!' said Mathew indicating to Jonathan the gaoler, who had shown him up to the fetid cell earlier on. 'Help me carry these people into the laundry!'

As the sick were taken into the laundry, those that still had clothes were stripped of their rags, and their bodies washed. Once clean, Mathew began to examine his patients as they were laid out on blankets. He could see now, that all the sick had a rose-spot rash on their bodies. Those patients who were semi-conscious twisted to lie on their side in the foetal position, to ease the pain in their bellies. All that could turn away from the light coming through the open door and window of the laundry did so, shielding their eyes, even though the sunlight wasn't bright.

Turning to one of the washerwomen, Mathew told her he would return soon and that he was going to fetch his assistant. Mathew and Mortimer returned carrying Mathew's medical chest between them. Susannah followed on behind carrying Mathew's recipe book of herbal remedies. Mathew found a suitable corner to put his large, cumbersome medical chest before issuing orders.

'I am going to prepare a mixture of *Wine, egg yolk, broth, and Guttae Vitae.* As soon as it is ready, I want Charles to start feeding it in small amounts to the men. For the women and children, I'm going to make up a mixture of *Euphorbia Esula, fresh milk, sugar and wine.* Susannah will feed the women and children. If we can dry up the flux and stop them all vomiting we have a chance of saving these poor wretches.'

For the rest of the day, the two men and Susannah went from patient to patient feeding them the medicine they hoped would cure the disease which was ravaging the survivors from the tower prison. But only minutes after taking a mouthful of the medication, each one cried out in pain and voided it from their bodies, either up or downward. The washerwomen scurried back and forth with buckets of water, cleaning up the mess and redressing the patients in fresh shirts. Rows of wet linen hung close to the fire drying as the women tried to wash and dry the shirts as quickly as they could. Mathew began to despair as his patients showed little or no sign of improvement. Susannah comforted the patients as best she could, especially the children, but nothing seemed to be working.

As the day came to an end and darkness began to fall over the castle, two of the youngest children died, Mathew watched helpless and dejected as the washerwomen wrapped the little ones in sheets and carried them outside. Susannah wept, inconsolable for a time, before picking up a bowl of medicine, wiping the sweat from her brow and began to dose the patient's once again.

'I'm going to lose them all; they are not showing any sign of improvement,' Mathew confessed to Mortimer as he sipped a cup of beer.

'Can't you give them twice the amount of medicine?' asked Mortimer.

'Not really, they would just expel twice as much from their already weak bodies,' shrugged Mathew. 'I will have to try something different; I can't just let them all die.'

The two men looked around the laundry at the patients lying on blankets on the hard stone floor, feeling at a loss as what to do next.

'Why don't you try mixing both medicines together?' suggested Susannah, 'you've got nothing else to give them.'

'Because my medical book states there is one medicine for men and a different one for women and children,' said Mathew.

'Are your books always right?' demanded Susannah.

Mathew and Mortimer looked at each other for a moment before turning to the table and pouring both medicines into one bowl and then dividing it between them.

'Let's start again.' said Mathew. 'Just give each patient a tiny spoonful, only one spoon per person so they can ingest it slowly.' They began their rounds of the sick, and an hour later they had finished feeding the last of the patients, none of whom had voided any of the mixtures.

'Again,' said Mathew, 'we will keep this up all night until they are all dead or showing signs of improvement.'

Mathew, Susannah and Mortimer made round after round, feeding each patient a tiny spoonful of medicine, only stopping to make more of the mixture. The washerwomen fed the fire or replaced burnt-out candles, waiting for more soiled clothes to wash. One by one the washerwomen stopped working and found a seat, falling asleep slumped where they sat, while Mathew, Susannah and Mortimer pressed on relentlessly. Just as they were coming to the end of their third round of feeding, Mathew noticed that none of the patients had fouled their beds or nightshirts any longer, some even seemed to be sleeping peacefully instead of restlessly.

'We may be making progress,' Mathew told Mortimer and Susannah, directing his two assistant's to stop and take a rest. As Mathew stretched, the pain of his tight, tired muscles made him wince.

'I need to eat, I can't keep this up,' declared Mortimer.

'I'm past eating,' declared Susannah, 'I just need to sleep.'

'You're right,' agreed Mathew, 'it wouldn't do if we became ill as well. There is nothing more we can do here so we'll go to the kitchen and get something to eat and drink. Susannah was reluctant to leave the patients, but hunger, tiredness and Mathew's reasoning convinced her to go with them.

By the time they returned to the laundry the washerwomen had begun to stir. Mathew made a fresh batch of the medicine and gave the washerwomen instruction on how to administer it.

'We just want to get a little sleep then we'll carry on,' said Mathew.

It was gone noon when Susannah awoke Mathew and gave Mortimer a shove. The large washerwoman stood in front of them, 'that one there,' she said, pointing off to the back of the laundry, 'says he's hungry. Do we feed them or not?'

Mathew jumped to his feet to stare in the direction the woman was pointing. Mathew stumbled over to the patient, 'How do you feel?'

'Like death warmed up,' replied the patient, 'and I'm awful hungry and thirsty.'

'Yes, yes,' responded Mathew, unable to hide the smile on his face, 'I'll get you something to eat and drink.' Mathew excitedly returned to Susannah and Mortimer to give them the good news that one of the patients was awake and hungry.

Over the remainder of the morning, more of the patients began to show real signs of recovery. For Mathew, Susannah and Mortimer, their tiredness faded as they rushed about feeding their patients on small amounts of thin broth and small beer.

'I think we've done it,' exclaimed Mathew, 'They are all beginning to show signs of recovery.' By the time it began to get dark again, Mathew felt confident enough to leave the sleeping patients in the care of the laundry women for a few hours while they went to get some more food and well-deserved sleep.

'I will meet you back at our chamber, said Mathew, 'I need to report the good news to Major Overton.' Mortimer asked Susannah if she wanted anything to eat as he was going to the kitchen.

'No thank you, I'm too tired to eat, I just want to sleep first,' said Susannah as she headed off towards the Watergate Tower and a place to rest.

He was the last person she expected to see at Warwick Castle. Mr Hollis stood in the centre of the castle courtyard looking around bewildered, wondering where to start looking for Susannah. She called to him, trying to be heard above the multitude of interlacing noises coming from horses, soldiers, traders and the day to day hubbub of castle life. As Susannah drew closer to him, he eventually spotted her. The look of dread on his face sent a cold shiver down her spine; her tiredness evaporated, she just *knew* something was wrong with Grace or Roger.

'What's wrong; what's happened?' pleaded Susannah, tears beginning to prick the corners of her eyes.

'Mrs Baxter sent me to fetch you, It's them young ones of yours, they've been taken sick,' said Mr Hollis, scrunching his hat in his hands.

'What's the matter with them,' implored Susannah, the tears now flowing freely down her cheeks.

'They be covered in scabs and sweating with fever, little Grace looks awful sad and keeps asking when Susannah is coming home' Mr Hollis looked at his feet dolefully. 'Mrs Baxter said you should bring that surgeon fellow with you.'

'I can't, he's needed here. I'll come with you now. With a bit of luck, it might just be one of the sicknesses all children get when they are young. If we need Mathew, I will come back to get him, and besides, we have an apothecary in the village who knows how to treat sick children, I can get medicines from him.' Without waiting to tell Mathew where she was going, she got Mr Hollis to drive her home through the darkness and cold of the night.

Chapter Twenty-Four

As Susannah burst through the kitchen door at the Manor, she expected to see a sorrowful looking Grace and Roger sitting at the table with a dutiful Mrs Baxter feeding them sympathy and honey cakes, but she was sadly disappointed. At the sound of the kitchen door opening, Mrs Baxter came rushing downstairs, her first words to Susannah, 'where is Mathew?'

'He couldn't come, he's needed at the castle; where are Grace and Roger?' asked Susannah breathlessly.

'They are up here; I really think you should have brought Mathew with you,' said a clearly distressed Mrs Baxter.

Susannah followed her up the stairs to where Grace and Roger lay. Kneeling next to Grace, Susannah brushed the hair from the girl's sweat covered face.

'Grace, Grace, it's Susannah, I'm here now.' The little girl failed to open her eyes but managed a slight smile at the sound of her sister's voice. Susannah kissed her on the forehead before turning to Roger.

'How is my little man?' she asked him, her voice beginning to tremble.

Roger opened his eyes and smiled at his big sister holding up his hand for her to take. As she took his hand in her own, his eyes closed as he fell asleep once again.

'Why didn't you bring Mathew with you, I told Mr Hollis to tell you to fetch him here?' said Mrs Baxter.

'There's been an outbreak of fever and sickness at the castle, I was helping him with his patients. I am so tired, I can't think properly. I just hoped there was nothing seriously wrong with Roger and Grace,' wept Susannah. 'But I've made a stupid mistake.'

It was too late in the day to return to Warwick Castle. Susannah was too exhausted to make the journey so, sharing Mrs Baxter's chamber, she stayed the night and prayed that Grace and Roger would live long enough for her to return to Warwick the next day, and fetch Mathew back to The Manor.

Susannah was on the road before it was light and arrived at Warwick Castle by midday, rushing to find Mathew and give him the distressing news about Roger and Grace.

'You must come and help them,' cried Susannah.

'Yes, yes, of course, I will, but first I must inform Major Overton and get permission to leave Warwick. Is it the Stomach Flux and fever? You left yesterday without saying you where you were going. I was worried about you. I didn't know where you had gone. I asked a guard at the gate who said you left with an elderly man. From the guard's description of him, I took it to be Mr Hollis.'

'Yes, yes,' said Susannah, 'just go tell the major you are needed; tell him the children are sick; tell him I need you to come straight away. Hurry, we don't have time to waste, go speak to the major, Mortimer and I will load your surgeon's box and medicines onto the cart. Mr Hollis is waiting to take us back,' declared Susannah, almost shoving Mathew out of the door of the laundry.

'Yes, you can go, but don't be any longer than you need to be, just do what you can for the children and hurry back. I need you here,' instructed Major Overton.

As they drove up to the manor house, Mrs Baxter had seen them coming and was in the yard to greet them. Before the cart had stopped, Susannah was out of her seat ready to climb down and rush to the side of her youngest siblings.

'Oh, thank goodness you are here at last. I have put the two young ones in my own bedchamber, so I can care for them more easily. God help them,' cried Mrs Baxter. 'They are in a poor state.

'Take me to them, quickly,' insisted Mathew.

Mathew retrieved his small surgeon's box from the back of the cart and followed the women into the rear of the house. Susannah and Mrs Baxter led Mathew up the back stairs from the kitchen to the servant's chambers in the attic. Grace was on a cot in the corner, while Roger lay on a palliasse on the floor, the faces of both children were covered in scabs. Susannah knelt beside Grace's cot and felt her forehead, she was hotter than yesterday when Susannah left her.

'They have both been very thirsty and coughing,' Mrs Baxter informed Mathew, 'but they sleep most of the time now. They've both had terrible diarrhoea, but they seem to pass very little water and, when they do, it is very dark and smelly. They sweat a great deal, so I have been giving them small beer to drink, though they tend to bring it back up.'

'Let me examine them,' said Mathew firmly. Mrs Baxter stepped aside, but Susannah refused to move from Grace's side. So he examined Roger first; he soon found what he feared the most. The lad's face was thick with scabs, including the inside of his nostrils and the lining of his mouth. They were so thickly covered with scabs the boy was struggling to breathe.

'Let me see Grace,' demanded Mathew, pushing Susannah aside. He found Grace infected in the same way as Roger. Mathew stood up slowly as Susannah returned to hold Grace's hand. Mathew looked at Mrs Baxter who was standing in the doorway and gave a little shake of the head. Mrs Baxter grabbed her apron and covered her face bursting out into tears and wailing loudly. Mr Hollis, who had come to join her, led her away to the kitchen.

'What have you told her?' demanded Susannah. 'Tell me, tell me!'

'It is the Small Pox, it's common in children, most of them get it, but they have it worst than most. I promise you, I am going to do everything I can for them, my very best, but you must be brave and prepare yourself in case of the worst,' said Mathew as softly as he could.

'Noooo,' cried Susannah as she stood up to face Mathew. 'You can save them, I know you can. You can do anything. Save them please,' Susannah grabbed at Mathew's jacket shaking him as she became inconsolable and wept in his arms.

'It's my fault. I should never have let Grace and Roger come here. They should have stayed at home. I should have brought you here sooner. Mathew do something, anything, but save them, please.

'I promise I will do everything in my power to help them,' said Mathew with as much confidence as he could muster. Mrs Baxter returned her face still red and tearstained.

'Come downstairs my love and let Mathew do his work in peace,' Mrs Baxter put her arm around Susannah's shoulder and led her away.

In the kitchen Mrs Baxter produced a book, 'this is the only book I own. It was given to me by the old master many years ago. There is a passage in it which I think is right for a time like this, and I think we should read together.'

O Holy Jesu, thou art a merciful High-priest, and touched with the sense of our infirmities; thou though knowest of the sickness that ails Grace and Roger thy children, the clouds are gathered about them. Lord let thy mercy support them and guide them and lead them safely through the valley of their death, that they may praise thee for your mercy in days to come.

Susannah faltered over the words as she read the passage in the book. The act of reciting the words reminding her of the frailty of life, but at the same time giving her hope, that by some miracle, and the skill of Mathew, Grace and Roger would recover.

Mathew appeared at the bottom of the stairs, his sudden appearance startling both women.

'Mrs Baxter, I would like you to make me a Bread Panada, sweetened with *loaf sugar*, would you also add to it some *sack*, and *whey*, if you please. Susannah, I would like you to make me a posset from *roasted apples* and *small beer*,' instructed Mathew before returning to the children.

'How are they,' Susannah quizzed him before he had time to disappear upstairs again.

'I'm doing what I can for them, be reassured. Now, as quick as you can, do as I have asked,' implored Mathew before returning to the sickroom.

While the two women busied themselves making the medicines Mathew had requested, there was a knocking on the kitchen door. Mr Hollis stepped through with Walter all covered in sweat and dust. Mrs Baxter and Susannah looked around startled at the sight of the lad in the doorway.

'Oh, you've heard about Roger and Grace,' said Susannah, 'but where are Oliver and Amos?'

Walter remained at the entrance, his face a mass of confusion, his mouth opening and closing but with no words coming out.

'Come, sit a moment,' instructed Mrs Baxter. 'Drink this and get your breath back.'

'Why haven't Oliver and Amos come with you?' Susannah asked again.

Walter looked from one to the other, unable to speak.

'I've just told him about Grace and Roger,' said Mr Hollis, 'He has more bad news to tell I'm afraid.'

Mathew heard the scream of anguish and ran downstairs to the kitchen to discover what had happened. Susannah was sobbing uncontrollably, slumped across the table. Walter explained to Mathew why he had come to find Roger and Grace and to break the news to them about Oliver and Amos. He hadn't known they had been taken ill and that Mr Hollis had brought Susannah back from Warwick. As Mathew looked at the people in the kitchen; Susannah had stopped crying, and everyone was staring up at him. After a moment's hesitation, he began to give orders.

'Susannah, you go with Walter and find the preacher. Learn all you can about this Captain Harrison and where he might have taken Oliver and Amos.

'But what about Grace and Roger?' she protested.

'Leave them to me,' insisted Mathew, 'go with Walter, now, the sooner we know more about what's happened to Oliver and Amos the better. Mrs Baxter, go speak to the master of the house, explain what has happened and ask for permission for me to stay with the children. Then ask him if he knows anyone in authority in the county who could help us get Oliver and Amos released once Susannah has found them. Then, I would like you to come back and finish making the medicines I've asked for. Mr Hollis, find me a cot or something to sleep on in the kitchen or, better still, a bedchamber close to the children. They are going to need a lot of attention over the next day or two.'

Very quickly the kitchen emptied of people as they went about their assigned tasks. It was Mrs Baxter who returned first to Mathew, finding him with the children applying a salve to their scabs to ease their dryness.

'The master is happy for you to stay and care for the children. He will speak with you later, only he has guests with him at the moment. He has instructed me to give you all the assistance I can,' said Mrs Baxter.

'I will thank him when we speak. He also needs to know about the Small Pox and that it is likely spread through the people of the village. I must warn you this is one of the worst cases of the Small Pox I have ever seen, and I am not confident of a happy outcome for the children. I need you to make me up a gargle to ease the swelling in their throats, it's made from *Columbine leaves, water, wine and red port.* I didn't want to speak so frankly in front of Susannah and frighten her. I will break the news to her more gently later, but I will try everything I know to save Roger and Grace, but they are in God's hands now as much as mine,' Mathew confessed to the elderly housekeeper.

With tears on her cheeks she nodded her head, 'I know you will do your best for them. I've seen many a child taken by the Small Pox, even a couple of my own, though that was many years past,' Mrs Baxter confided to Mathew. A noise from downstairs drew Mrs Baxter's attention.

'That'll be Mr Hollis, I'd better see what he's up to before he wrecks my kitchen,' She left Mathew with the children. She was soon back again leading Mr Hollis. 'This way,' he heard her giving him instructions. The banging noises changed to one of scrapping as Mrs Baxter appeared in the bedchamber doorway.

'I'm getting Mr Hollis to put me a cot in the bedchamber next to this one. It used to belong to the last cook, but that was when the master had a bigger family, and more servants were needed, You can sleep in here with the children, in case they need you during the night, and I will be next door if you want any help' said Mrs Baxter.

Susannah and Walter found the preacher in St Peter's Church, sweeping the floor. The preacher looked up as they entered, 'any news on the whereabouts of Oliver and Amos? he asked laying his broom aside.

'No,' declared Susannah, 'that is why we have come back to see you. What can you tell us about this Captain Harrison?

'Not a lot, I'm afraid, only what people have said in passing. They say he is the youngest son of a noble from somewhere south of here and that he came to join the king to try and make a good impression on him in the hope of gaining favour at the king's court. I'm told he fought bravely on the day of the battle and that he volunteered to stay behind with his men, to act as a rearguard while the king moved his army on to Banbury. I can only guess that it was in that direction he was marching his men when he came across Oliver and Amos. I suggest you look towards Banbury to find your brothers,' advised the preacher.

'Thank you, Preacher.' Susannah took Walter by the arm and rushed him outside. 'We must follow them and try pleading with this Captain Harrison to let them go.'

'How?' We will never be able to catch up with them before it gets dark. We know the army is heading for Banbury, we should return to the manor and ask if we can borrow Mr Hollis's horse and cart, then set off first thing in the morning,' suggested Walter.

Susannah wanted to protest, she wanted to go now, but she could see the wisdom in Walter's words. As she realised that there was nothing more she or they could do that day to help Oliver and Amos, the last of her reserves of energy gave way to exhaustion, as she crumpled to the ground outside the church. Passers-by stopped to stare at her as Walter wiped her face with a kerchief moistened from a water trough.

'Let's go back home, you need to rest,' suggested Walter.

'No, we need to go back to the manor. At least there I can be with Grace and Roger,' said a dejected Susannah.

As Susannah and Walter walked back to the Manor House in the failing light, the two-storey Tudor framed building with its thick thatched roof looked foreboding at the end of the day. The owner of the house, Mr Benjamin Spencer, hadn't managed his financial affairs well, and the farm, along with the manor had become neglected. The only servants left were Mrs Baxter and Mr Hollis and few labourers who were hired when needed. It was only because Mrs Baxter and Mr Hollis are advancing in years that Roger and Grace had been employed. Now the sight of the manor had taken on a sombre air. Susannah wished that she had never agreed to let her two youngest siblings start work there. As they entered the yard, light in the stables indicated that Mr Hollis was still at work, probably bedding down the horse that had brought Susannah and Mathew back from Warwick. The kitchen door was open, and the smell of cooking food wafted to her on the breeze, she was hungry. Walter smelt it too, reminding him of his hunger. They looked at each other, both of the same thought.

‘Maybe it’s a good sign,’ said Walter forcing a smile for Susannah’s benefit. Their pace quickened with Susannah entering the kitchen first.

‘Are they any better yet?’ asked Susannah hopefully. Mrs Baxter turned away from the pot she was stirring.

‘Mathew hasn’t come down since you left. Why don’t you go up and see how he is getting on,’ said Mrs Baxter as she wiped her hands on her apron. ‘I’ll have something hot and tasty for you when you come back down. Come on Walter, its ready now, sit yourself down and cut some bread.’

As Susannah entered the bedchamber, Mathew was just administering the next dose of throat gargle through a syringe into Grace's mouth. The little girl coughed and spluttered as the liquid trickled into her throat. The girl struggled to accept the few drops of liquid, so much so she began to expel it through her nose as well as her mouth. Susannah gasped at the distressing sight and burst into tears, ‘stop it, Mathew, you’re choking her,’ she called out in panic.

Mathew laid the syringe aside and went to comfort her, ‘I know that it looks distressing, but it is a common event in cases like this. Come, let me take you down to the kitchen, some food will help you.’

‘I don’t feel like eating,’ snapped Susannah, shrugging off his hand from her arm.

‘Well I do and, if I can’t think properly because I’m hungry, I won’t be able to do my best for Grace and

Roger, and the same goes for you,' said Mathew sternly. Susannah relented and allowed herself to be led downstairs. In the kitchen, Mrs Baxter quickly laid out two bowls. As Susannah and Mathew sat at the table, Mrs Baxter's questioning eyes met Mathew's, all he could think to do was shrug his shoulders, or else alarm Susannah more than she needed to be right now.

To her own surprise, Susannah ate all the mutton stew she had been given plus two thick slices of bread.

Mathew stood up from the table, 'I'd better get back to my patients,' he said as he headed for the stairs. 'Mrs Baxter, may I stay the night as well?' asked Susannah.

From behind Susannah's back, Mathew shook his head.

'I'm sorry, My Dear, I've nowhere to put you. I already have the children and Mathew staying. Let Walter take you home so you can get a good night's rest, then come back in the morning when you'll be fresh to help Mathew,' insisted Mrs Baxter.

'I could sleep in the kitchen, I don't mind,' begged Susannah.

'Maybe not, but I do. If the old master came into the kitchen during the night, what would he think? No, you go home, get some rest and let Mathew do his work. Walter, take your sister home,' instructed the housekeeper.

It was late, very late. The moonlight shone through the window, its silvery glow illuminating the bedchamber in an eerie cold light. Mathew awoke with a jolt; something had woken him as he lay on the bed. He felt cold, despite the thick blanket around his shoulders. It took his addled mind a moment or two to clear. He looked around the chamber before he remembered where he was. It was then he spotted the little form writhing on the bed, suddenly he was wide awake and on his feet. He dropped to his knees at Grace' bedside, she was struggling to breathe. He fumbled for the tinder and flint next to the candle on the table and, after two attempts, managed to get the candle lit. As he looked into Grace's mouth, he could see her swollen tongue and throat with its mass of scabs, frustrating her breathing. Her only chance now was to remove her uvula and open her blocked Trachea, to allow her to breathe more freely. As he stood to go downstairs to retrieve his surgical instruments, he noticed Roger too, had started to convulse like his sister. Mathew ran down the stairs to the kitchen where his large surgeon's chest sat on a side table, throwing open the lid he searched for the instruments he had used so rarely, but now needed in earnest. In a small narrow bag, Mathew found the constrictor ring, noose and cauterising rod. It was then that he realised he needed hot coals for the cauterising iron to be of any use. Turning to the fireplace, Mathew urged the failing embers back to life with a few small sticks adding larger ones to create a good flame. All the while he was aware of the need for haste, but his planned surgery would be for nothing if he could not cauterise the wound after the surgery to remove the children's uvulas. *Why had he allowed himself to fall asleep, he should have been better prepared. He should have had the foresight to bank up the fire for just this kind of situation.*

Mrs Baxter appeared at the bottom of the stairs.

'What can I do to help?'

'I need a pan to put hot coals in so I can heat a cauterising iron. Lots of clean linen, and honey and lemon juice,' instructed Mathew. 'And please hurry.'

After a little rummaging about, Mrs Baxter produced an old metal pot with a handle.

'Excellent,' said Mathew taking the metal pot into which he scooped hot ashes topped with more small pieces of coal. He grabbed his instruments and with the flaming metal pot headed for the stairs.

'Bring up the linen, the honey and lemon mixture can come later,' said Mathew.

As soon as he was in the bedchamber, he placed the metal pot on the floor and dropped the small cauterising iron into the flames. Taking up the constrictor ring, he threaded it with a single long horse hair in preparation for slipping it over Grace' uvula. The tough horse's hair from the tail of the animal would tighten around the uvula to sever and remove it. He opened Grace' mouth, it moved freely and stayed open, the little girl was no longer gasping for breath. Taking her by the shoulders he shook her, calling her name, but there was no response her eyes remained closed, her fragile body lifeless. Laying her head on the pillow he turned to Roger, fearing what he might find. He too lay still and silent, his life choked from him by the disease that had raged within him. It had taken too long to prepare what he needed. Mathew sat on the bed, feeling dejected. He had failed again to save someone he cared for.' With his head in his hands, Mathew wondered if he was cursed. His mother had died while he held her hand, he had failed to save the life of Elizabeth and Hazel had died while in his care. This time he had been unable to cure the children because he had fallen asleep. A desperate feeling of inadequacy enveloped him, crushing him with guilt. He heard Mrs Baxter coming hurriedly up the stairs. When she arrived at the bedchamber door the sight before her eyes needed no explaining.

'Oh, my Lord, have mercy on them,' she exclaimed, 'May God in heaven keep them safe at his side.'

'Keeping them safe was supposed to be my job,' muttered Mathew.

Chapter Twenty-Five

The sun was only just above the horizon, and the cockerels were crowing in the yard when Susannah rushed into the kitchen. She found Mrs Baxter sat in her nightdress with a blanket over her shoulders and Mathew asleep at the table, his head resting on his arms. The expression on Mrs Baxter's face confirmed Susannah's worst fears.

'It can't be true,' screamed Susannah. 'Which one, please tell me it wasn't Grace.' Mathew woke with a start at Susannah's sudden outburst. Spinning around in his seat, he quickly got to his feet and took Susannah's hands in his.

'I'm sorry, Susannah, I did everything I could for both of them, but the disease took them both.' The lump in his stomach and the guilt he felt over the children's deaths made the words seem hollow to his ears, and he felt ashamed by his failure. But what good would it do Susannah to know that he had allowed himself to fall asleep, and forget to prepare the vital equipment that may have saved the children? He silently vowed that he would never let it happen again, no matter what it would take to do so. Susannah sank to her knees sobbing loudly. Mrs Baxter dropped to her side, wrapping Susannah in her arms to console her.

'I'm so sorry, My Dear, but Mathew is right, he did everything he could and more. When I saw how quickly the little ones took sick and how they were covered in the pox, I knew that they had it bad and that there might be little hope. I just didn't have the heart to tell you. In my many years, I've seen too many children taken in this cruel way.'

Mathew felt lost. He had seen death so many times, adults as well as children. He looked at Susannah, not knowing what to do or say.

'Go break the news to Walter,' Mrs Baxter instructed Mathew,' he'll be working at the Jameson farm on the far side of Kineton. Mr Jameson is having a new barn built. You can leave the little ones to us now, this is woman's work. I know what needs to be done.'

Mathew paused in the kitchen doorway and with one final look over his shoulder, said 'I'm sorry Susannah, I truly am,' then he closed the door behind him.

After breaking the sad news to Walter, Mathew couldn't face going back to Susannah. It was many hours later before Mathew returned to the manor house; where he had been, he couldn't say, he had just walked, lost in the desolation of his failure. Mathew stopped at the stable yard entrance and looked across at the kitchen door. It may as well have been the entrance to Warwick Castle with the drawbridge up and the portcullis down and he the only invader, outside an impregnable fortress, he didn't dare to try to gain entry. A noise from the stable drew his attention away from the kitchen door. In the stable he found Mr Hollis cleaning out a stall. Mr Hollis stopped work and looked at Mathew, neither man saying anything. The silence was just understood. Mr Hollis went back to work while Mathew watched him. After a moment or two, Mathew picked up a broom and began to sweep while Mr Hollis held the shovel as they mucked out the stalls. Before long all three stalls were clean and refreshed with clean straw.

‘I would like to return to Warwick, may I borrow a horse and cart?’ asked Mathew. Mr Hollis placed his pitch folk in the corner, ‘Aye lad, that’ll be fine. I’ll come with you so as I can bring the cart back. I’m done for the day now. You’ll be wanting your stuff from the house I imagine?’

‘Yes, please. Would you mind getting it for me, I don’t think Susannah will want to see me just yet,’ conceded Mathew.

‘Hmm, you might be right. Help me hitch up the horse then I’ll go over and load your surgeon’s chest and anything else you’ve left in there,’ said Mr Hollis.

Three hours later Mathew waved Mr Hollis farewell from Warwick Castle, thanking him profusely for his help. Mortimer helped Mathew carry his surgeon's chest inside.

'You look like you need a drink, my friend, maybe lots of drinks and then you can tell me everything that has happened.'

It was gone noon before Mathew awoke the following day, the pain in his head and his churning stomach making him vomit. The pain of vomiting made him collapse on the floor, but with his eyes closed the world spun out of control, he retched again, but this time only yellow bile came up. Mathew opened his eyes, but the light coming through the window just made his headache even worse. The only position he could maintain without feeling that he wanted to die was on his hands and knees, in the corner of the chamber, facing away from the light. Mathew stayed in that position until the pain in his knees equalled the pain in his head. He eased himself onto his side, wanting to die and feeling like he deserved to. The door opened, but Mathew didn't bother to look at who had entered.

'Do you want a small beer or willow bark tea?' asked Mortimer.

'Both,' Mathew grunted. Mortimer placed both on the floor within easy reach of his friend, before sitting on the edge of his cot. Mathew's hand slowly reached for the steaming bowl of tea, he sipped at it, tasting the sweetness of the honey before spilling a bit of the hot liquid over his chin. He eased himself into a sitting position with his back against the wall and continued to sip the sweet tea. After about half an hour Mathew had drunk the tea and the large cup of small beer. The pain in his head had eased just enough for him to ask Mortimer to help him to his bed. And there he stayed, suffering from guilt and self-doubt as much as the effects of a hangover, until the following morning. He awoke to the sound of movement in the chamber, 'feel any better today?' asked Mortimer.

'I don't know yet, I'm not sure it's safe to get off this bed,' said Mathew.

Mortimer laughed, 'You sound and look better than you did yesterday.'

Mathew had just finished washing his hands and face when the door opened, and in walked Major Overton, he looked around the chamber, 'Where is Potter?' he demanded.

'I sent him to fetch us something to eat and drink for Mathew, he'll be back soon,' declared Mortimer.

'Good, I'll wait,' said the major, sitting at the small table below the window. Mathew and Mortimer looked at each other puzzled by the major's intrusion.

'Well, are you going to tell us why you are here?' asked Mathew.

'I'm not going to repeat myself, you can wait until Potter arrives,' said the major irritably. An uneasy silence fell on the chamber. The major tapped impatiently on the table, Mathew finished dressing, and Mortimer tidied up a little.

Potter kicked open the door, a jug of beer in one hand, a pan of stew with a pie sitting on top of it in the other hand, and a loaf of bread sticking out the front of his half fastened jacket.

'Bloody hell, I nearly dropped this lot, twice, coming back from the kitchen,' he announced as he delivered it all to the table to relieve his aching arms.

'Good day, to you, Major, it's a good job I brought plenty. I didn't know you would be joining us,' Potter continued.

'Sit down, shut up and listen,' said the major. 'I don't have a lot of time. As you are aware, some of the king's treasure has gone missing from the cellar; well a lot more than we at first realised has been stolen, so we need to find it and who took it, urgently. Tonight you three are going to help me catch the culprit!'

'Why us?' asked Mortimer.

'Because we four have no connection to the castle or the people who live and work here, so we are the only ones that Lord Brooke can trust. Whoever is stealing the treasure knows this castle very well and is able to remove the treasure without being seen, as Potter can testify. I've had him watching the cellar night after night, and he hasn't seen anyone enter or leave the store, but treasure is still going missing. So the person who has been stealing the treasure has to be someone who has been here for some length of time and knows the castle inside and out. Lord Brooke has his suspicions but cannot prove anything as yet. So, he has asked for our help.'

Later that night, Potter lay in wait in his usual hiding place amongst the grain sacks. Mortimer had been given a job as cook's assistant in the kitchen and had been told to watch the kitchen staff. Mathew hid in the doorway to the washhouse to watch and see if anyone tried to enter the cellar from outside. Major Overton waited in the Great Hall, to watch for anyone entering the kitchen from the official parts of the castle. Later that night, as with previous nights, Bill Flowers came on duty at midnight as usual, stood for a while at the storeroom door before slumping down onto a stool with a jug of beer which had been left for him. He drank the beer, lent back against the wall and was soon asleep and snoring. The night passed slowly, and uneventfully. That morning, after returning to their chamber in the tower with Major Overton, they ate a breakfast of bread and honey washed down with cider.

'What happens now?' asked Mathew.

'As soon as we have finished this we go back to the store with Lord Brooke and Captain Bridges, check the storeroom and discover if anything was taken last night.

An hour later, Lord Brooke, Captain Bridges, Major Overton, Mathew, Mortimer and Potter stood outside the storeroom door. Captain Bridges inserted the key, turned the lock and swung the door open.

'Right Gentlemen, let us begin the count and discover if our thief helped himself again last night,' directed Lord Brooke.

'But my men haven't slept, My Lord,' protested Major Overton.

'Then the sooner we get this job done, the sooner they will be able to go to their beds,' declared Lord Brooke.

By midday, the count was completed, and Lord Brooke compared the inventory with the last one taken. Some minutes passed as he ticked off items and rechecked parts of the treasure. From the centre of the storeroom, he made his announcement.

'There are three chests of gold and silver coin missing.'

'There can't be, no one entered or left the cellar apart from the guard,' insisted Mathew.

'And *he* spent most of the night asleep outside the door,' added Potter.

'No one entered through the kitchen,' said Mortimer timidly as everyone turned to look at him.

'I didn't see anyone either,' stated Major Overton.

'Well the treasure didn't walk out on its own, and I don't think it's the mice,' said Captain Bridges sarcastically. 'I'm sorry to have to say this, Major, but it looks like it has to be one of your men, they were the only ones in or close to the cellar all night.'

A roar of protest came from Mathew, Mortimer and Potter.

'That's not a fair judgement of my men; I can personally vouch for the integrity of each of them. Allow me time to speak to them, there is more going on here than we know. Allow us time to come up with a new plan to catch the thief,' insisted Major Overton.

Back in their tower chamber, Major Overton paced the floor while Mathew, Mortimer and Potter waited for him to speak.

'We need to stand guard again tonight but, if we didn't see the chests removed last night, we probably wouldn't see anything removed again tonight, so we have to change the way we work this problem through. If we can't find out who is stealing the treasure, Lord Brooke is likely to charge one or all of us with the offence to ensure his name is not tainted with the thefts. What is it we aren't seeing?' said Major Overton.

'The treasure,' answered Potter flippantly.

'That's it,' declared Mathew triumphantly, getting to his feet. 'One of us should be locked in the storeroom with the treasure tonight, that way they can't fail to see who is stealing it.'

'It will have to be done without anyone other than ourselves knowing about it,' Mortimer included.

'That's a good idea,' said the major, 'but Lord Brooke is the only one with a key to that door, and I can't very well just ask him for it or we risk word of our plan getting back to the thief. Then if more treasure goes missing without us catching the thief, he will definitely blame the one in the cellar, if not all of us.'

A cough from Potter brought him everyone's attention. 'Who needs a key? If the guard on the door can be distracted for a few minutes sometime today, I might, if I've still got the touch, be able to open the door to let someone slip inside.' Smiles lit up the faces of Mathew, Mortimer and the major.

'I could put a few drops of *laudanum* in some beer and take it to the guard,' suggested Mathew.

'Better still,' said Mortimer. 'I take him some salted ham from the kitchen. It's bound to make him thirsty which will encourage him to drink the beer all in one go.'

'Then that's what we will do,' declared Major Overton. 'Mortimer will take the ham and the beer to the guard. Once Potter gives us the signal that the guard is asleep, we can all slip down to the cellar, and Potter can open the door, then Mathew . . . Er, no it's too dangerous; Mortimer can go inside the treasure store to be locked in by Potter. The rest of us return later tonight. Mathew and Potter can hide until they hear Mortimer banging on the door to signal he knows who the thief is. I'll stay in the Great Hall in case Lord Brooke or Captain Bridges decides to make a late night inspection. Thank you, Gentlemen, now we have a plan of action, we will get a few hours sleep. Everything must be in place before the change of the guard at midnight.'

Later that night everything had gone to plan, Mortimer was locked in the cellar store and made himself comfortable in the corner with a candle and a deck of Potter's playing cards to while away the time. Potter and Mathew hid amongst the grain sacks and the major feigned writing reports in the Great Hall. At midnight Bill Flowers came on duty and once again seated himself on the stool to drink his beer, and before long he was asleep.

'Someone else probably puts a few drops of *laudanum* in his beer as well,' Mathew whispered to Potter.

Inside the treasure store, Mortimer heard the guards talking as they came and went off duty. He'd got bored with playing games of patience with the cards and was rummaging through the treasure thinking about what he would do if he owned this amount of wealth. He thought of his mother, brothers and sisters working on Major Overton's family estate in East Yorkshire. With just one of these chests of gold or jewels, they would never have to work for anyone again. He closed the lid on the chest and went back to sit in the corner. He'd no sooner picked up the deck of cards when he heard a faint scraping sound. Mortimer picked up the steel, flint and tinder he'd prepared to relight his candle after he had blown it out. His ears alert to every sound in the darkness, he heard the rumble of Bill Flowers' snoring outside the door. Then he listened to the faint scraping sound again, only this time it was a little louder and closer. The next sound Mortimer heard was stone scraping against stone; his heart beat wildly, and his hands began to shake as a light appeared out of the floor. It came as a faint glow at first with just enough light for him to see the layout of the storeroom. A hand emerged from the hole holding a lantern, bathing the cellar store in bright light. The hand placed the lamp next to the stone slab which had been lifted from the floor. The treasure in the store glittered in the light as the flame in the lantern settled and burned brighter. The head and shoulders of a man came up cautiously out of the hole. Mortimer froze, there was nowhere to hide, if the figure turned around, in a second or two he would be seen. The figure emerging from the hole didn't look around, but climbed out and stretched his arms and legs. Mortimer couldn't wait to be spotted first. Springing from his hiding place at the back of the treasure store, Mortimer threw himself at the figure silhouetted by the lantern, at the same time he screamed for help.

Outside the storeroom, on top of the grain sacks, Mathew and Potter listened to Bill Flowers snoring contentedly.

'He sounds like a pig with a sore throat,' said Potter.

'You should listen to the sounds you make when you come back after a night of playing cards and drinking. If I didn't know how good you were with those pasteboards, and you weren't here with me now,

I'd have suspected you of having a hand in all this,' said Mathew sarcastically.

'Huh, insults, that's all I ever get, and after all I've done for you,' sneered Potter light-heartedly.

'Like what?' Mathew reposted.

'Er, I don't know, just give me time to think . . . .I opened that storeroom door, didn't I?' sniggered Potter.

Their bit of banter was interrupted by the sound of a loud thud, followed by the sound of falling boxes coming from within the treasure store. Mortimer's voice calling for help followed. Bill Flowers didn't respond but slept on. Mathew and Potter jumped down from atop the grain sacks, stumbling towards the door.

'Quick as you can, get the door open,' demanded Mathew unnecessarily as Potter knelt before the door with his lock-pick in his hand.

The sounds of a struggle continued from behind the door as Potter fumbled with the lock. Their hearts missed a beat when they heard the sound of a gunshot from within the storeroom.

'Hurry, hurry!' demanded Mathew.

Major Overton heard the gunshot and sat bolt upright in his chair, he hadn't given out any guns: the gun could only have been fired by the person attempting to steal the treasure. Dropping his pen to the paper on the table, he jumped to his feet, running towards the kitchen and the stairs down to the cellar.

Mortimer caught the intruder off guard, forcing the thief to crash into the treasure stacked against the wall. Boxes toppled, tipping their contents across the floor. The lantern was knocked over on its side, but the candle inside stayed lit. As the lantern rolled away, it cast strange, eerie shadows across the ceiling and walls, before coming to a stop against the wall. Mortimer's fists pummelled the intruder mercilessly as fear took over from reasoned thought. His opponent lay face down, trying to shield his face and head from the tirade of blows being metered out to him.

'Help, Help,' yelled Mortimer in panic.

All of a sudden the storeroom was filled with a burning bright light and the sound of thunder. Mortimer was hurled from the thief's back and slammed against the door.

'Come on, we need to get out of here. How badly are you hurt?' yelled the head and shoulders of a man sticking out of the hole in the floor.

'Just winded,' said the first thief. They heard the sound of someone working the lock on the door. The first thief scrambled to his knees and headed back to the hole in the floor.

'Get out of my way, there's someone about to come through the door.' The head and shoulders of the second thief bobbed down out of sight, followed by the first thief as he scrambled down the hole. He stopped to replace the missing stone slab.

'Leave that, you fool,' came the voice of thief two from further down the tunnel, 'they'll find it anyway.' The two thieves scrambled along the tunnel and into the night.

Mortimer lay on top of a heap of treasure that had been disgorged across the floor by the falling boxes during his tussle with the first thief. His right ear was missing, and blood poured from a large gash in the back of his scalp.

The door burst open. In Mathew's haste to get into the room first, he tripped over Potter and stumbled into the storeroom before Potter could get to his feet. Major Overton pushed Potter aside to join Mathew inside the treasure store. Major Overton spotted the hole in the floor and cautiously peered inside using the lantern left behind by the thieves to illuminate the interior of the shaft. He could see the glint of water reflecting the candlelight back at him and hear the sound of water running along a tunnel. A cool breeze stirred the gunpowder smoke in the storeroom as it pushed the black cloud out through the open door and into the rest of the cellar. The pungent smell of the river came wafting up out of the hole. As Major Overton shone the light around the store, it illuminated wet footprints on the floor.

Mathew pulled Mortimer clear of the door. A large pool of blood gave evidence of his injury. Mathew examined the wound. Mortimer's right ear was gone, and there was thick gouge running from along his skull from the Mastoid Process across to the External Acoustic Meatus. Mathew checked Mortimer's breathing, he was still alive. Potter stood in the doorway looking down at Mortimer and Mathew and then at the treasure which littered the floor.

'Run up to the kitchen,' Mathew instructed Potter, and find me some muslin, they must have some for wrapping puddings in.' Potter was gone in an instant.

Major Overton looked around the storeroom and then back down the hole and let out a sigh, *if I'd had more men I could have sent them after the thief.* Looking back at Mortimer, 'I'm sorry, Mathew, I should have thought to have at least given him a pistol,' said Major Overton.

'He is still alive; thank God. Help me get him out of here so I can treat his wounds,' demanded Mathew.

'I can't, I have to stay here and guard this lot,' Major Overton responded. 'Potter will help you. Take Mortimer into the kitchen and dress his wound in there.'

More people, alerted by the gunshot started to arrive in the cellar. Major Overton ordered two of the onlookers to help Mathew take Mortimer up to the kitchen while he closed and guarded the storeroom door. After struggling to get Mortimer into the kitchen and, sending Potter for his portable surgeon's box,

Mathew set about cleaning and closing the wound in the back of Mortimer's head.

The following morning, Lord Brooke, Captain Bridges and Major Overton waited on the banks of the River Avon at the entrance to a natural outflow below the castle walls.

'You can't see this entrance from the quayside, said Captain Bridges. 'So it's gone unnoticed by the castle guards. The thieves must have used a boat to transport the stolen treasure away, and that's why none of the treasure was found in the castle or was seen being taken away.'

A soldier crawled out of the tunnel covered in mud. 'The tunnel passes right under the castle, Sir. I think water that collects in the moat on the far side of the castle has found a way through and washed away the soil, creating this outflow to the river. Parts of the roof of the tunnel have dropped away, so there's enough room to stand up. It was pure bad luck that one of those spots was right under that storeroom. It must have been like this for years, Sir.'

'So that proves it then, the thief or thieves are from right here in the castle, My Lord,' added Major Overton.

'So it would seem,' said Lord Brooke angrily as he turned and marched away. 'Captain Bridges,' bellowed Lord Brooke. The captain duly followed his master.

Back in their tower chamber, the unconscious body of Mortimer lay on his cot.

'I need to redress and clean Mortimer's wounds, you are going to have to help me,' Mathew told Potter.

'But I don't know anything about doing things like that,' said Potter.

'You don't have to, I'll just tell you what I want, and you do it, that's all,' said Mathew, snapping at the little man.

There was a little knock on the door, 'Go away,' shouted Mathew. 'I'm busy.'

The knock came again only this time the door opened, and Susannah sheepishly stepped inside. She took one look at Mortimer, dropped her cloak where she stood and went to kneel next to Mathew.

'Let me help, *please*? She asked.

'I'll go get lots of hot water, at least I know how to do that,' said Potter.

Chapter Twenty-Six

In a private office above the Great Hall, Major Overton summoned Mathew and Potter to a meeting.

'Now *Lord Brooke* has discovered that the thief stealing the king's treasure is someone within Warwick Castle, he has set about making his own enquiries as to who the thief or thieves might be. He will also be sending a report to John Pym about how he uncovered the thefts,' Major Overton informed Mathew and Potter.

'What, we get no credit at all,' exclaimed Potter indignantly.

'No, none at all and that is how I want it to stay. I don't want your names connected with this matter in any way,' said Major Overton. 'Except, that is, in one way, and that is for it to be known that you stole the treasure or at least some of it.'

'What! Why?' exclaimed Mathew.

'Because he has a plan and we are going to be mixed up in the middle of it,' interrupted Potter.

Major Overton glared at Potter. 'I have been given permission by John Pym to give you one wagon load of treasure, on the understanding that you deliver it to the king. You are to convince him that you have escaped from Warwick Castle, having stolen the wagon load of treasure. Your intention, to return it to the king and resume your duties as his surgeon at the royal court,' explained the major.

'What happens if I say no?' quizzed Mathew.

'You stay here, a semi-prisoner, until Lord Brooke or I can find no further use for you.'

'But that is not fair,' protested Mathew.

'The choice is yours.'

'I need time to think about it,' said Mathew, affronted by someone he once thought of as a friend. He stormed off followed by Potter who had to almost run to keep up with him.

As Mathew marched across the castle courtyard, Susannah came to meet him. 'What did the major want?'

'Nothing,' said Mathew angrily.

Susannah fell into step with Potter as they followed Mathew back to the chamber in the tower. Mathew threw open the door and stormed inside to sit on the only chair the chamber possessed. Mortimer lay on his bed, his head wrapped in bandages, his face blackened, bruised and swollen, he didn't attempt to get up and struggled to hear what was being said. He looked at Susannah questioningly, but all she could do was shrug her shoulders. Though Mathew was keeping him heavily dosed with *laudanum* to subdue the pain, Mortimer still wanted to know what had been said at the meeting.

'Thomas, would you fetch us all something to drink, please?' Susannah asked Potter.

The little man was about to protest, but Susannah smiled sweetly at him, and his resistance crumbled.

'Will you tell me what the major said that has made you so angry?' asked Susannah. With her left hand she reached across and took his hand in hers, and with her right hand, she cupped it around the side of his face, caressing his cheek gently, trying to ease the tension he so openly expressed.

'He has a job for Potter and me. He wants to send us back to the king. We either help him, or we stay here indefinitely as prisoners,' said Mathew.

'That wouldn't be so bad, would it? I'd get to see you any time I wished, you'd be here, safe in this castle and away from the fighting,' said Susannah softly.

'Susannah, you are the only truly good thing that has happened to me since I left home,' said Mathew endearingly. 'But, I will have to do as the Major asks if I am to stand any chance of not being trapped here. He said he is going to make it known that Potter and I have had a hand in stealing some of the king's treasure, which means he has complete control over us. He would even stop me from seeing you if he thought it would be an advantage to him.'

'Would he really do that to you?' questioned Susannah.

'Oh yes. The Major wants us to go to Oxford and rejoin the king and spy on him and his army,' said Mathew indignantly. 'He is obsessed with defeating the king.

'Then I am going with you,' said Susannah defiantly.

'You can't, you are needed at home,' said Mathew, then, regretted what he had said. 'I'm sorry, I didn't think.'

'I'm going with you,' said Susannah determinedly. 'You are right; I'm not needed at home like I once was now there is only Walter left. I have good reasons for going to Oxford. While I'm there, I can search for news about what's happened to Oliver and Amos, and I won't live in a house that continually reminds me of Grace and Roger . . . But most of all......being in Oxford will mean I will be with you.

'What about me?' mumbled Mortimer from his bed.

'You, My Friend, stay here with the major. Your injuries will take a long time to heal, and you will probably always be deaf in your right ear. You have given enough; the major said he wants you to be his steward again. You have finally earned his trust once more,' Mathew said loud enough for Mortimer to hear him.

Potter returned, 'are we celebrating or drowning our sorrows?' he asked as he slammed down the jug of beer on the table.

'Both,' said Susannah, 'and we'll need more beer than that.'

From his newly established capital in Oxford, the king, with the aid of his senior nobles was already making plans for his campaign against his Parliament.

'Your Majesty, we should strike at the army of the Earl of Essex while it still licks its wounds. Very soon they will be in Northampton and out of reach,' argued Prince Rupert.

'No, Nephew. We must consolidate our hold on Oxford and, what's more, the battle at Kineton was not a won easily. It was very costly in both men and equipment. It would not be wise to get caught in a protracted confrontation away from our new capital with winter soon to be upon us. It is far better that we stay here to gather and train more loyal men and make them ready for the coming year.'

The council of war was interrupted when a messenger arrived and gave a note to the Earl of Newcastle. 'Your Majesty, dreadful news has arrived from Ireland.'

'Well, what is it?' demanded the king.

'News of Parliament's revolt against Your Majesty is spreading amongst the Irish people. The Catholic peasants have started a revolt against their English masters.'

The king sank thoughtfully into a chair, pounded his fist onto its upholstered arm.

'Fate is a wicked master, Lord Newcastle. Do you think the Irish will collude with Parliament and turn against us?'

'No one can say for certain, Your Majesty. We barely have enough men and materials to bring this parliament to book as it is and now those wretched Irish peasants look likely to take advantage of the situation and take over Ireland. With no army to spare to put down this uprising, we will have to hope they don't have the wit to cross the sea and become a thorn in our side,' said Lord Newcastle.

'Is there nothing we can do to save our loyal subjects over there?' asked the king 'The English in Ireland will just have to deal with the uprising themselves, it would be unwise for us to try and fight a war in two countries simultaneously,' advised the earl.

The king gave the matter some thought. 'Yes, My Lord, once this rebel parliament has been subdued, we will be able put our mind to Ireland once again.'

'As you wish, Your Majesty,' pleased the king didn't want to send troops to fight a second war. Lord Newcastle helped himself to a glass of Madeira, sipping at the warming liquid as the king sat thoughtfully staring into the flames of a roaring fire in the hearth.

'My Lord Newcastle,' exclaimed the king, 'this Irish problem may work to our advantage. If we let the Irish bog trotters reclaim their filthy land unopposed, and if we were to allow them to practice their popish religion freely in Ireland, we could let it be known that we are not unsympathetic to their grievances. With Ireland at peace with itself, they may be induced into helping their King in England. We will start by repatriating our ministers of the English faith back to England as a sign of our goodwill. Send a message to the leaders of the Irish mobs that their King is willing to hear their requests for religious tolerance in Ireland.'

'Very good, Your Majesty.'

Mathew, Susannah and Potter watched their wagon being loaded with the king's treasure as it stood in the courtyard outside the Great Hall at Warwick Castle. Musketeers armed with Doglock muskets surrounded the wagon and its passengers.

'How do we explain how we managed to smuggle the treasure out undetected?' asked Mathew.

'You tell the king the truth or a variation of it. You tell the king that, when you were captured, you told an officer that you are a surgeon. Lord Brooke got to hear of it and asked you to treat his wife's sickness; and in return, if you gave your word not to try and escape, he would give you your parole, so long as you stayed within the confines of the castle. Potter learned the whereabouts of the treasure in the cellar, and you found the tunnel by accident when you were asked to investigate the death of Captain Broadwaters. You thought to use the tunnel as a means of escape; it was only when you discovered the tunnel led to the treasure chamber that you got the idea to steal as much treasure as you could before returning to the king with it. You say that over a number of days you and Potter stole the treasure and hid it away until you could escape from the castle. Tell him you met Susannah here in the castle and convinced her to help you. It was she who acquired the wagon, and she was the one that helped you escape from Warwick,' explained Major Overton.

Chapter Twenty-Seven

Ethan's Goodman's wagon passed under the Beverley Bar, Mary was almost home. She'd only been away for three months, but it had felt more like three years. Over the two weeks, they had spent travelling from Shrewsbury to Beverley, Mary's melancholy had eased to a point where she felt more in control of her own emotions. The distance she had put between herself and Mathew had helped her come to terms with the fact that she would never command his love in the way she had hoped. The memories of what she had done to Hazel during their stop at Nottingham still haunted her at night, and she knew one fateful day she would have to answer to God for what she had done. But now she was home, although it was a home with no husband to welcome her, she would attempt to make the best of it.

As they drew closer to Cuckstool Pit Lane, the fear that someone might have discovered her involvement in her husband's death suddenly felt very real, and she almost asked Ethan to continue on to York and not to leave her here, but how would she be able to explain her change of mind to him? The panicky moment passed as she consoled herself with the knowledge that the only people who knew the truth about what had happened on Beverley Westwood Common four months earlier, were either dead or many miles away. Returning back to the only place she could call home would have to suffice until she could make alternative plans and make a new life for herself.

Ethan had remained cheerful throughout the journey and not bothered her with questions, and slowly, as the days passed, she had opened up to him about her feelings for Mathew. Much to her relief, he had listened nonjudgmentally, and she had learned to trust his gentle words of advice. As Ethan's wagon drew to a halt, she looked down at her clothes which had once again become ragged and worn through lack of care. Wearing the dress that Mathew had bought for her, she found it difficult to put the loss of him out of her mind. With the few possessions remaining to her, she climbed down from the wagon at the end of the Cuckstool Pit Lane. Just a few yards further down was the Fletcher wheelwright's yard, her dead husband's family and her home. She found the idea of meeting them after all this time and looking so dishevelled, terrifying.

'Thank you, Ethan, and safe journey.'

At the top of the lane, she looked towards Beverley Market. There were only a few traders out today, but Beverley didn't seem to have changed in her absence, though it seemed a lifetime since she had last walked these streets. Picking up her bundle of belongings, she walked down the lane to the yard, her heart thumping like a hammer in her chest, trepidation in her heart, wondering what kind of reception she would receive. The yard looked the same as it always had only there was no one at work fixing or making wagon wheels, just a black and white dog sniffing in the corner near the stables. It looked up at her as she entered the yard. The dog began to growl and bark at the stranger, then sniffing the air, its tail began to wag as it approached cautiously until Mary called its name.

'Bess!'

The dog bounded over jumping up in wild excitement, whining and barking; its tail wagging furiously in greeting to a long lost friend, before running back and forth between the house door and Mary.

'Bess, you've grown up. I've missed you so much,' said Mary. She bent down to allow Bess to lick her hands, and so she could pet the dog that welcomed her so warmly.

At that moment the door to the house opened, and a young girl paused in the doorway. Mary and the girl looked at each other in silence for a moment, the girl smiled, she called to Bess. The dog scampered to her side sitting obediently at her feet, the girl petted the dog's head and neck. Turning to face towards the house the girl called to Mr Fletcher, but when the girl looked back, Mary was gone.

****

Seeing Bess sat at the girl's feet, Mary left the yard with tears in her eyes. She realised time had moved on, changes had been made, this was no longer her home and Bess had found a new friend. There was no longer a place for her in the Fletcher home. Gathering up the hem of her dress, she hurried up the lane, and into the marketplace. She wandered through the crowds and stalls; it all felt so familiar and yet so different. A few spots of rain made her look up at the sky, '*where will I sleep tonight*?' The cloud was thickening, threatening more rain to come. Looking for shelter Mary entered the Push Inn situated at the corner of the market and took a seat. She ordered a cup of beer from a serving girl and counted out the pennies in her purse. Nine pennies wouldn't last long. She sipped at her beer and looked around the taproom desperately searching for a familiar face. One of the serving girls came towards her, 'want another cup of beer, dearie?'

Mary looked at her a little startled by the question; she hadn't the money to waste on more drink. 'No thank you, I'm finished now; I must get home before it rains.' Mary gathered up her bundle and headed for the door. The rain was getting heavier, and she hesitated in the doorway not knowing which way to turn when she caught sight of a woman with a baby in her arms. *Margaret, Margaret would take me in. After all, I did help her when she went into early labour. She and her mother are always on the lookout for an extra penny or two. If I stay with them for a bit, I may find some work to enable me to pay my way, and then I could watch for Mathew in case he comes home.'*

****

'What's the matter, Ruth,' William Fletcher looked past the girl into the yard as Bess ran to the gate.

'There was a woman here. I think she was trying to steal Bess,' said Ruth.

William ran to the gate calling to Bess as the dog went in search of Mary up the lane, but the lane was empty.

'Here Bess, good dog, come on inside,' said William Fletcher. The dog came running back, giving one last look up the lane and sniffing the air before it entered the wheelwright's yard.

'Thank you, Ruth, you can go home now. Tell your mother you worked well today, the house is nice and tidy. You can come back next week, but remember this is only a temporary arrangement; one day Mary and Mathew will return.'

'Thank you, Mr Fletcher. My mother needs the money you pay me, so I hope they don't come back too soon,' said Ruth.

William smiled and waved the girl farewell, but her words had hurt him with her innocent wish.

Mathew drove his wagon along the broad thoroughfare of St Giles as it passed by the church of the same name. They were close to their destination; St Magdalene's Church was just up ahead and beyond it the Northgate entrance to Oxford. At the Northgate, they were stopped by the city militia, but before the militia sergeant had time to begin questioning him, Mathew demanded to be taken to the king.

'And who the hell do you think you are making demands to see His Majesty,' scoffed the guard, signalling more soldiers to his side in case of trouble. Mathew withdrew the letter he had been given weeks before stating he was to train as a surgeon to the king and showed it to the guard.

'I am Master Surgeon Mathew Fletcher, Surgeon in Ordinary to the king of England, and these are my assistants. We have escaped from Lord Brooke at Warwick Castle and have returned to give service to His Majesty. Furthermore, we have managed to rescue some of the king's treasure which had been captured with the baggage-train after it had left Kenilworth Castle. So, Sergeant, you will provide us with an escort and safe conduct through the city until we can return the gold and silver to His Majesty.'

To emphasise the point, Potter rashly held up a jewel-encrusted golden goblet. The guard stepped back with his mouth agape at the sight of the gold. Passers-by, also noticing the glittering cup, began taking an interest in what was happening at the gate. Mathew frantically indicated for Potter to return the goblet back to its box.

'Come on man,' demanded Mathew, 'we haven't got all day.'

With the guard's attention back on Mathew instead of the gold cup, the sergeant went to get help, 'I'd better speak to an officer first; you wait here,' he said.

Even though the sergeant had placed some armed men around the wagon, word soon spread up and down the street of the gold carried by the newcomers. The guards drew more attention to the wagon, its contents and the people onboard it. Susannah shuffled closer to Mathew on the seat, for reassurance. It wasn't long before the sergeant returned with the officer, followed by the rest of the gate guard.

'My name is Lieutenant Chadwick; what's all this talk about gold and the king?' he demanded.

Mathew showed his letter, and Potter retrieved the gold goblet and opened the lid on a casket full of jewellery. The young officer's stared in amazement at the sight of the jewelled cup. There was an 'Ooh,' from the guards and the crowd as greedy eyes coveted the precious object.

'Sergeant, keep two men and stay on duty at the gate, the rest of the guards will come with me to escort Master Surgeon Fletcher safely to the king.

Lieutenant Chadwick led the way, and with halberds on their shoulders, the militia guard escorted Mathew's wagon along North Street towards the Corn Market. It was as though the cart was full of Lodestone, the magnetism of gold and riches drawing a crowd which noisily followed the wagon. As the wagon passed St Peter's in the East heading towards South Street, more and more people became attracted to the train, trying to discover what everyone else's fascination with the wagon could be. The nervousness of the occupants of the wagon was apparent as the crowd grew more significant and more vocal. Calls from the people following the wagon, demanding to see the treasure it carried, became more frequent. Lieutenant Chadwick drew his sword; the guards brought their halberds to the thrusting position, ready to strike at anyone who got too close. Horses and carts blocking the street ahead of Mathew slowed their progress to the college but did not entirely bring them to a halt. All the while the crowd grew larger, noisier and pressed closer. As they entered South Street, a youth leapt from the crowd onto the rear of the wagon, much to the amusement and delight of the spectators, only to be struck by the butt end of a halberd and sent rolling into the gutter. The crowd jeered and began to throw vegetables at the guards and wagon. Susannah was hit by an onion causing her to cry out in pain. Mathew gave the reins a flick, encouraging the horses to pick-up the pace, the lieutenant, forced to jump aside to avoid being trampled and run over, recovered his balance and called after them.

'Go,' cried the officer, 'my men and I will slow the crowd.'

Mathew whipped on the horses causing people ahead of him to scatter.

The officer deployed his men across the street in a vain attempt to stop the crowd chasing the wagon. With the wicked points of the halberds aimed at the chests of the angry mob, silence momentarily fell over the street. A turnip, thrown from the back of the crowd, bounced off the chest plate of one of the guard's armour.

Instinctively he thrust forward with his halberd opening up the belly of the man closest to him. The man fell to the street clutching the wound, screaming in pain. The crowd surged forward grappling to take hold of the guards. The guards managed to hold their ground for no more than a few seconds before the multitude of angry citizens disarmed them and beat them to the ground.

Mathew made it to the gate of Christchurch College without further incident. But, the clamour down South Street had brought the king's guards to the alert, and Mathew's wagon was met by a reinforced gate guard.

'Leave the bloody goblet in the box this time,' Susannah snapped at Potter. Mathew handed the sergeant of the guard his letter, hoping he wouldn't need to give further explanation as to his presence in Oxford. The sergeant took his time reading the letter; his lips moving silently as he formed the words to make sense of what he was reading. The remainder of the gate guard kept looking up South Street towards the town centre wondering what all the commotion was about. The crowd began to surge along the street towards the wagon. The sergeant handed the letter back to Mathew, 'take your wagon through the gate and wait until someone comes to tell you what to do next.'

Once inside the grounds of Christ Church College, the guards closed and locked the gates. Mathew and his passengers breathed a sigh of relief, finally feeling safe after their long journey and the drama in the street.

Susannah released Mathew's arm, onto which she had been desperately clinging, and burst into tears. 'I've never been so frightened in all my life.'

'The sight of gold can make people do strange things,' said Potter. They both looked at him. He shrugged his shoulders, 'sorry, how was I to know that would happen, I just wanted that guard to understand we were telling the truth.'

A man came towards them from the main building, his clothes were plain in style but well made and clean. He stopped and inspected the wagon and its occupants from a distance before coming closer.

'If you are delivering goods you have come to the wrong door, you want to be over there,' said the man pointing to his left.

'I am the new surgeon to the king, I have escaped from Warwick Castle, and I am carrying things that will be of great interest to His Majesty,' declared Mathew, unable to keep the stress he was feeling out of his voice.

'What kind of things?' asked the man.

Mathew's temper snapped, 'Find Lord Newcastle and tell him Master Surgeon Mathew Fletcher is here from Warwick Castle!'

The man hesitated a moment, Mathew jumped down from the wagon and took a step towards the dumbstruck servant. Before Mathew could take a second step, the man had turned and was running back to the building from where he had come. Susannah and Potter joined Mathew. Mary had stopped crying. She looped her arm through his unsure what would happen next, but pleased to be able to stretch her legs after spending so long on the slow-moving wagon. The quiet of the square gave them the chance to inspect the buildings surrounding it, while they waited for the servant to return. Having come through a gate, they were now in a courtyard surrounded by buildings on all sides. In one corner of the quad stood a church, rising higher and more prominent than the rest of the sandstone buildings. The rest of the buildings were all of two stories in height with clay tile roofs. The roofline, on each of the buildings that formed the square, was edged with small crenulations. From the first floors, small windows overlooked the courtyard, at ground level the windows were fewer in number but interspaced with doors. It was warm in the quad, even this late in the year, protected as they were from the wind on all four sides. The sound of a door closing and feet walking over cobbles drew their attention. The man had returned accompanied by another servant more finely dress than the first, who Mathew recognised from his dress to be one of the king's stewards.

'This man tells me you are Master Surgeon Mathew Fletcher and that you are demanding to see Lord Newcastle. He says you told him that you have something of interest for the king,' questioned the steward.

Mathew handed him his letter, which the steward quickly read, 'and what have you of interest to the king, Sir?'

Mathew noted the change in the steward's tone, 'I have this.' Mathew reached into the wagon and brought down a small casket. He opened it to show the contents. 'We escaped from Warwick Castle and managed to steal this wagon load of gold and silver plate, along with a few other things from Lord Brooke before we left. As their rightful owner, I thought the king would like to have them returned to him. The steward stared at the casket of jewels for a moment before sending the plainly dressed man back to the building. He returned moments later with two guards. The steward instructed the guards to protect the wagon until an officer gave them further instructions.

'Would you like to follow me, I will escort you to somewhere comfortable where you can rest, I'm sure Lord Newcastle would like to question you himself,' directed the steward.

Inside they were taken to a chamber used as a refectory and given food and drink before Mathew was summoned to an audience with Lord Newcastle. Even though Lord Newcastle recognised Mathew from past meetings, he questioned him over and over, testing the detail of how he had managed to steal the treasure and make his escape from Lord Brooke. Finally, convinced Mathew was telling the truth, Lord Newcastle had Mathew, Susannah and Potter shown to private chambers in the college.

They were situated in one side of the quod overlooking the courtyard where their wagon still stood. Mathew and Susannah had been given two rooms on the first floor.

'I will inform Dr Harvey of your arrival, but as for the rest of the day, I suggest you rest and make these chambers as comfortable as you can,' said the steward who had escorted them to their lodgings. 'Mr Potter will be a little further down. I will show you the way and then leave you to settle in.'

'What do we do now?' asked Susannah.

'Exactly as the steward suggested,' said Mathew. 'We'll retrieve our personal belongings from the wagon and make ourselves at home.'

'Oh no,' not me, where do I sleep, there is only one bedchamber and one bed. Now we are guests of the king, I have my reputation to think of,' insisted Susannah.

'But what about when I stayed with you in Kineton?' pleaded Mathew, 'and, we aren't exactly guests of the king, we work for him. And as far as the bed goes,' Mathew looked at Potter. 'Don't you have your own chambers to go to?'

'I'm going, I'm going. I'll leave you to work out your own sleeping arrangements. But if you are sharing the same chambers, you may as well share the same bed. And now, with my advice freely given, I will be on my way. Once I've sorted out my stuff I think I will pay a visit to a tavern or two in town and treat myself to the best meal and wine I can find.'

'How are you going to do that with no money?' asked Mathew.

Potter held up a purse and jingled it about, 'no one counted or made an inventory of what we brought from Warwick, so no one knows I've got this,' smiled Potter.

'We do,' said Susannah.

'That's why I took the liberty of filling three purses, so we could all have one each,' Potter laughed again and threw Mathew and Susannah a purse each.

'You've forgotten one thing,' said Mathew, 'If you leave the college now, how will you get back in without a pass? No one here but us knows who you are. There's something else you haven't thought of either, throwing your money around in Oxford is bound to draw attention to yourself; it won't take people long to work out where your gold coins might have come from. So I think we had better wait a while before we find out what fate has in store for us in Oxford,' suggested Mathew.

'Mmm, you may have a point. I still plan to go into town though. There will be plenty of places to discover, for someone with my talents.'

As Mathew and Susannah made themselves at home in their chambers, he wondered what would become of them. He'd always thought he would go home after dealing with Martins, Wilkes and Franks, but Major Overton had changed his expectations. Mathew had been shown a world beyond Hull and Beverley. New opportunities had been opened up to him, and he met Susannah. As the new woman in his life, she was intelligent and beautiful; filled with confidence, and kindness. She had restored his optimism and his dreams for the future. Then another thought occurred to him, *Major Overton will find it hard to reach me here in the heart of Oxford. The major can wait until I'm of a mind to contact him.* The king, Oxford and Susannah were going to be his future now.

'Susannah, I think you are being a bit unreasonable about not sharing the bed with me. I can't very well go and ask for an apartment of my own, everyone knows we are together. They will be expecting us to sleep together.'

'No! When we were in Kineton it was different, you caught me at a vulnerable time. Now that we live in a city and you are a member of the king's court we have to be respectable. People will soon start to talk when they learn we are living together and they see that I'm not wearing a wedding ring. I'm not going to risk a full belly as well.'

'But I'm a surgeon; I know ways of preventing you from becoming pregnant.'

'Yes, so do I, and the surest way is for you to sleep in here and, I will sleep in the bedchamber.'

The following morning, Mathew awoke to the sun shining on his face as it came through the frosted mullioned window. Susannah had refused to allow him to sleep in the bedchamber with her, but now he was awake on what looked to be a cold frosty morning. His back ached because of the thin palliasse, on which he had been forced to sleep, as it needed more straw stuffing. The sun was shining in his eyes on a cold November morning preventing him from sleeping, so as Mathew lay wondering if he should rise from his bed, he was surprised to hear a faint scratting at the door. No sooner had he turned his head to look at what the noise could be when he saw a folded piece of paper shoved underneath it. Mathew looked at the fireplace for any hint of a warming flame, but there was none. The note lay on the floor, tormenting him with its hidden message. There was no alternative, he would have to brave the cold and leave his bed with its multitude of blankets keeping him tolerably warm and snug. The soles of his feet slapped against bare boards as he darted to retrieve the note and return to his bed before it became cold. Unfolding the slip of paper, he read the contents.

The king is to meet parliamentary commissioners with a petition at Colnbrook on the 9th October. Find out what you can and give the information to Potter.

Overton

Mathew read the note over and over, not believing that Major Overton had managed to track him down so quickly, and also wondered why Potter hadn't told him he knew the Major was in Oxford?

'*No, not this time, my friend, it is too soon. You will have to get someone else to help you with this one, Robert. I'm going to establish my surgical reputation at court before I risk all, running errands for you. I now have Susannah to consider; I want to help her find Oliver and Amos before I set off on one of your adventures.'*

Mathew took the note over to the fireplace and dropped it into the hearth, before adding some kindling and lighting it, to warm his room.

Captain Bridges locked the door in the cellar of his grandparent's house, stacked barrels in front of it and pocketed the key.

'I have restacked the wine barrels for you, grandfather. I must go now, duty calls, but I will call again soon, to look in on you and see if you need anything.' The captain checked his heavy purse was safely attached to his belt and wished his grandparent's farewell.

Bibliography

Atlas of the English Civil War
By P R Newman

Edgehill and Beyond
By Philip Tennant

The English Civil War Day by Day
By Wilfred Emberton

Pharmacopoeia Extemporanea
By Thomas Fuller M.D. 1714 edition.

Enchiridion Medicum, Manual of Physick
By Prof Robert Johnson MD, London.
original1684edition

The Shakespeare Cookbook
By Andrew and Maureen Dalby

Dr Sydenham's Compleat Method of Curing almost all Diseases.
By Thomas Sydenham, original 1695 Edition

Pepys at Table
Christopher Driver and Michelle Berriedale-Johnson

Mechanical Essays of the Animal Oeconomy
By James Hadley, Surgeon, 1721 edition.

A Compendium of the Theory and Practice of Chirurgery in Seven books
By William Salmon M.D. original 1698 edition.

Select physical and chyrugical observations.
By William Salmon Professor of physick, 1687 edition.

The Rule and Exercises of Holy Living
By Jeremy Taylor, Chaplain to Charles I

Three and Fifty Instruments of Chirurgery, London 1631.
By Ambrose Pare. reprinted in 1975 by Theatrum Orbis Terrarum Ltd

The Real Historical People

Major Robert Overton 1609-1678
Educated at St John's College Cambridge and served in the East Yorkshire Trained Bands at the start of the English Civil War. Given the rank of Colonel with the New Model Army by Sir Thomas Fairfax in the 1645, he rose to the rank of Major General.

Earl of Newcastle 1592-1676
William Cavendish, polymath, swordsman, politician, diplomat and soldier. A loyal supporter of the King, but after defeat at Marston Moor, he and his family left England for Europe. He was made a Duke by Charles II for the support he gave to Charles's father during the war.

Lt Col Sir Edward Duncombe
Royalist officer in the regiment of The Kings Guard of Dragoons, Duncombe changed sides in 1644 when the Scots entered Yorkshire.

Sir John Meldrum d.1645
A soldier of Scottish origin who spent 36 years in the service of the Stuart kings of Scotland and England. In 1642, he found himself opposed to the policies of Charles' government and supported the Parliamentarian cause in the Civil War. A captain in the

Hull Trained Bands, he was killed at the siege of Scarborough Castle.

Lt Col Sir Edward Duncombe
Royalist officer in the regiment of The Kings Guard of Dragoons, Duncombe changed sides in 1644 when the Scots entered Yorkshire.

Captain William Legge **1608-1670**
On 7 August 1638 Legge was commissioned to inspect the fortifications of Newcastle and Hull and to put both in a state of defence. Appointed master of the armoury and lieutenant of the ordinance for the first Bishops' War.

John Bellasyse **1615-1689**
MP for Thirsk. King's Charles' intelligence officer in the North of England. Member of the Sealed Knot.

Thomas Bellasyse **1627-1700**
Military commander, he rose to the rank of Major General in the Kings army.

William Harvey **1578-1657**
Personal Physician to Charles I. Discovered the blood circulation system, in that blood flowed from the arteries into the veins and back to the heart.

Lord Brooke, **1607-1643**
Robert Greville
Killed by sniper Litchfield Cathedral

Captain John Bridges **b1610**

Information was laid against him on 22 August 1649 that said he had captured and concealed 25 wagons, many laden with plate and other treasure, belonging to the late King.

John Pym **1584 – 1643**

Pym became involved in solving the financial problems of the Parliamentary side, heading the Committee of Safety from 4 July 1642. He was a key organiser of the loans and taxes that Parliament needed to fund its army.

Robert Bertie **1582 – 1642**
1st Earl of Lindsey

Royalist officer; died of his wounds at the Battle of Edgehill.

Patrick Ruthven **1573 – 1651**
1st Earl of Forth

Scottish Nobleman, general and diplomat. Joined the king at Shrewsbury with 29 other Scottish veteran officers. Commanded the Royalist forces at the battle of Edgehill. Following the battle, he was appointed general-in-chief of the Royalist army.

Sir Edward Fitton **1603 – 1643**

Royalist commander of a foot regiment; died of consumption at the siege of Bristol.

Now you can buy any of these books direct from the publisher.

Friends and Enemies
The Enemy Within
Farewell to a friend

To order simply call this number

07564640442

OR
Facebook: Steven Turner-Bone

OR
Email: steventurnerbone@aol.com

Prices and availability subject to change without notice.

35891954R00233

Printed in Poland
by Amazon Fulfillment
Poland Sp. z o.o., Wrocław